CANADIAN BOYFRIEND

JENNY HOLIDAY

FOREVER

New York Bo

ALSO BY JENNY HOLIDAY

THE MATCHMAKER BAY SERIES

Mermaid Inn

Paradise Cove

Sandcastle Beach

THE BRIDESMAIDS BEHAVING BADLY SERIES

One and Only

It Takes Two

Three Little Words

Copyright © 2024 by Jenny Holiday
Reading group guide copyright © 2024 by Jenny Holiday and Hachette Book Group, Inc.

Cover illustration by Leni Kauffman
Cover lettering by Caitlin Sacks
Cover copyright © 2024 by Hachette Book Group, Inc.

Forever
Hachette Book Group
1290 Avenue of the Americas, New York, NY 10104
read-forever.com

First Edition: January 2024

Forever is an imprint of Grand Central Publishing. The Forever name and logo are trademarks of Hachette Book Group, Inc.

The publisher is not responsible for websites (or their content) that are not owned by the publisher.

The Hachette Speakers Bureau provides a wide range of authors for speaking events. To find out more, go to hachettespeakersbureau.com or email HachetteSpeakers@hbgusa.com.

Forever books may be purchased in bulk for business, educational, or promotional use. For information, please contact your local bookseller or the Hachette Book Group Special Markets Department at special.markets@hbgusa.com.

Library of Congress Cataloging-in-Publication Data
Names: Holiday, Jenny (Romance author) author.
Title: Canadian boyfriend / Jenny Holiday.
Description: First edition. | New York : Forever, 2024.
Identifiers: LCCN 2023036409 | ISBN 9781538724927 (trade paperback) | ISBN 9781538724941 (ebook)
Subjects: LCGFT: Romance fiction. | Novels.
Classification: LCC PS3608.O484324 C36 2024 | DDC 813/.6—dc23/eng/20230908
LC record available at https://lccn.loc.gov/2023036409

ISBN: 9781538724927 (trade paperback), 9781538724941 (ebook)

Printed in the United States of America

LSC

Printing 1, 2023

For ZT, the OG CB

CONTENT WARNING

This book contains references to disordered eating and to the death of a spouse that occurred prior to the events of the story.

PROLOGUE
ONCE UPON A TIME

I was sixteen years old when I invented my Canadian Boyfriend. I was twenty-nine years old when I manifested him in the flesh.

We "met" at the Mall of America, and I don't know why I'm putting that in quotation marks, because we really did meet.

Well, I know why. Let me start over.

I was sixteen years old when I met a boy at the Mall of America.

He was in town from Winnipeg for a hockey tournament, and I was working at Caribou Coffee.

"Did you want the whipped cream"—I tilted the cup to read the name off it—"Erik?" I was in the habit of asking specifically about the whipped cream even when there were no instructions written on the cup suggesting it was unwanted. Whipped cream was a more controversial topic back in those pre-keto days, and you'd be surprised how many people would order something like a large turtle mocha, a drink that contained 980 calories and 105 grams of sugar, but consider whipped cream a bridge too far.

When my Canadian Boyfriend answered, I assumed he was Erik. He seemed like he was really exerting ownership over that mocha.

"Erik definitely wants the whipped cream. The more the better, eh?"

"Does Erik always speak of himself in the third person?" I was wittier, and more outgoing, at the mall than at school. At the mall, I didn't have anyone's preconceived notions about me holding me back. I could be a normal girl. A girl who spent her lunch hours laughing with her friends in the cafeteria. A girl who spent her lunch hours *actually eating lunch* while laughing with her friends in the cafeteria. "Is Erik using the royal *we*?"

I hadn't made eye contact with my Canadian Boyfriend. We were slammed—I had cups lined up on the bar as long as my ballet frenemy Emma's perfect arabesque—and even though I was talking to him, I had registered him as a presence rather than an actual and specific human being.

But when he said, "Sorry, what?" I looked up and we locked eyes. His were deep green and topped by a brow furrowed in bewilderment. His straw-colored hair was flirting with mullethood, and he had a full dirty-blond beard a few shades darker. He was holding a cup with a teabag tag sticking out of it.

I'm not saying it was love at first sight, but I'm not saying it wasn't.

"I just meant," I said, trying to explain away those forehead lines, "you said, 'Erik,' like you were talking about yourself in the third...You know what? Forget it." I guess I *wasn't* wittier at the mall. For that to work, people had to get your jokes. As usual, something about me wasn't quite hitting.

At that moment, Erik—the real Erik—clattered up to the bar, enormous and galumphy. Later, when I learned a bit about hockey—just enough to suit my purposes, thank you, *Hockey for Dummies*—I decided it was probably because Erik was an enforcer.

"Can you shake some shit on that whipped cream?" Erik asked.

"You must be Erik. And Erik, you'd like some *shit* on your drink?" I widened my eyes in what I hoped was a comic fashion, because if at first you don't succeed and all that. "A turtle mocha comes with turtle pieces and caramel sauce. I also have chocolate chips, brownie pieces, and chocolate mints, but I'm fresh out of shit."

My Canadian Boyfriend chuckled, which thrilled me almost as much as being praised in class yesterday for my grand battement had.

"Give me everything," Erik said. "You know, like when you go to McDonald's and you put a little of every flavor of pop in your cup?" I did not know, at least not from experience, as I consumed neither pop nor McDonald's, but I was familiar with the concept.

My Canadian Boyfriend raised his eyebrows at me in what seemed half solidarity, half dare, so I got out my toppings and went to town. When I passed the drink over, my Canadian Boyfriend wrinkled his nose. "I don't think I'm a fan of candy in coffee."

"Me neither," I said, because it was true. Or I thought it was true. Or at the very least, if it wasn't true, it was my excuse. If I had any hope of making it to New York—and *in* New York—it certainly didn't involve large turtle mochas with extra "shit," and I didn't even need my mother to tell me that.

He smiled at me then, my Canadian Boyfriend, and his pine-tree eyes went all twinkly. It was sudden and blinding, that smile of his. So blinding it took me a second to register that he was missing a tooth, which was startling, but, oddly, didn't detract from his rugged beauty. Or maybe it made him seem a little dangerous, danger being another thing that was not part of my life, unless you counted the ever-present fear that I would refracture my fifth metatarsal.

He and Erik were back the next day. I was working the cash register when they appeared. "Hi," Erik said. "Can I get a double-double, please?"

"Can you get a what?"

My Canadian Boyfriend intervened. "You're speaking Canadian, dude. They give it to you plain here, and you add what you want." He pointed at the station with the cream and sugar, and to me he said, "A large coffee and a large black tea, please." He dipped his head like he was embarrassed. "Sorry."

"No problem. So you guys are from Canada?"

"Yep," Erik said. "A town near Winnipeg."

I set their drinks on the counter. "No coffee with candy today?"

"Nope," Erik said. "I save that for later in the day. Right now, I just need to wake the fuck up."

"*Erik*," my Canadian Boyfriend said. "Language." He winced in my direction. "Sorry."

That was his second *sorry* in the space of fifteen seconds. "You Canadians really *do* apologize a lot."

His green eyes did the twinkly thing, but this time I noticed there were gold flecks in the green. "We're up early for an emergency dental appointment." He flashed me his broken smile, and my stomach flipped.

"Hmm. Canadian, missing tooth. Let me guess. You're in town for hockey." A lot of hockey teams came through the mall because they stayed at the attached hotels.

My Canadian Boyfriend looked momentarily surprised, then shot me yet another of those lethal smiles, a dart straight into my squishy, vulnerable insides. "We are." He stuck out his hand. "I'm Mike."

"Rory." I gave him my hand, and he did this thing where he kind of held it without shaking it. He pressed his thumb against the web of skin between my thumb and index finger and stood there and smiled at me, all guileless and gap toothed, and in that moment I knew. I knew who he would become. I might as well have birthed him directly from my head, like Zeus spawning Athena. Except not, because he wasn't my child; he was my boyfriend. My boyfriend who lived in Canada, which was close enough to Minnesota to be creditable but far enough away that he wasn't ever going to have to make an appearance.

A woman behind him in line cleared her throat. It broke the spell between us, and he tugged, trying to get his hand back. I let go, painfully aware that the fact that he'd *had* to tug meant I'd been holding on too long. Trying too hard. I was reverting to my real persona, the one I didn't want to use at the mall, the one that felt comfortable but confining, like a straitjacket made of fleece.

He rubbed his newly freed hand across his jawline. I wondered how old he was. He'd referenced a hockey tournament, so that had to be high school, but that beard seemed lush for a teenager. Eighteen, I decided, and I had that power because he had now splintered into two people. There was Mike, corporeal entity standing in front of me, and there was my Canadian Boyfriend.

I thought about this past Friday's biology class. Frog dissection. I'd had no idea what I was doing because *Nutcracker* dress rehearsals had kept me out of class the previous few days. So Mr. Sherman had told me to sit with a pair of girls who *did* know what they were doing when it came to frog innards.

The talk turned to the upcoming homecoming dance. Each girl said who she was going with, and there was this moment when they both looked at me. There was a pause, and then they went back to their discussion as if it were a foregone conclusion that I wouldn't be going. I *wasn't* going, but for once not because of ballet getting in the way, but because I did not have a date. I didn't even have any girlfriends I could go with en masse.

"It was nice to meet you. I gotta go get my teeth fixed."

I hoped he'd come back. I hung around after my shift, but he never reappeared. All I got for my trouble was a call from my mother. "Where are you?"

"I had to cover for someone who's sick." I never lied to my mother. I was a little surprised at how easy it was. "I left you a message."

She made a noncommittal noise. Mom fancied herself a modern single mother/career woman who was Doing It All with No Help from a Man, and she didn't like it when she was caught dropping a ball. "I thought you were going to work on your en dedans this evening."

"I did that for an hour in class yesterday."

"But did you hit eighteen?"

I didn't answer. Because the answer was that my mother had converted the basement of our house into a studio for me. Therefore I would be spending the evening pirouetting.

"Do you have homework?"

"Just trig."

"You didn't finish it on your lunch break?"

"No." At lunch I'd been doing laps of the mall, hoping to catch a glimpse of my Canadian Boyfriend.

"Well, I guess you have a long night ahead of you, then. I have an open house in Plymouth, so I'll be late."

I should have done my homework at lunch. But I couldn't regret those laps. Because as I'd been on the lookout for Mike, I'd solidified my theory that when you are a person who has a Canadian Boyfriend, you are somebody. If your Canadian Boyfriend cannot make it to homecoming because he knocked out a tooth? Totally understandable.

And if you are lonely at school, where you have no friends, in part because of your ballet schedule and in part because of… you, your Canadian Boyfriend makes it matter less. If someone sees you sitting alone at lunch, it can be because you need some time to write your Canadian Boyfriend a letter.

And if you 100 percent made up your Canadian Boyfriend? If he is perfect but also super-duper not real?

Who cared? It wasn't like it hurt anyone.

Until it did.

1—OVER THE TOP

RORY

The first time Olivia Kowalski came back to class at Miss Miller's of Minnetonka after her mom died was the night everything changed. Nobody but Miss Miller, aka my best friend Gretchen, and I knew that Olivia was returning.

"Let's keep it between us," Gretchen said before my Tap 3 class. "She doesn't need everyone primed to gawk at her."

By *everyone*, Gretchen meant the Minnetonka Dance Moms™. And would they ever gawk, if their performative grief when Olivia's mom, Sarah, had been killed in a car crash seven months ago was anything to go by. They wanted to know how Olivia was doing. They wanted to know if Gretchen would pass along Olivia's address so they could drop off a Tater Tot hotdish. (Gretchen would not.) They wanted to know what was going to happen to Olivia.

Well, really, they wanted to know what was going to happen to Olivia's *dad*, who was allegedly an extremely good-looking player for the Minnesota Lumberjacks. I, not having followed hockey since high school, didn't know anything about Olivia's dad. I didn't even realize he played hockey until the chatter about Sarah's death started. I had no memory of ever having met him. If I had met him, it would have been in passing at recitals, since Sarah was the one who'd brought Olivia to class. Even though recitals no longer gave me literal panic attacks, I was still more focused on getting through them than I was on any hot dads who might be in attendance.

Olivia's dad had taken the rest of last season off after the accident. He'd pulled Olivia out of dance, and out of school, too, according to some of the girls who'd been her classmates. We hadn't seen Olivia since last January.

Gretchen's understanding of the habits of the Minnetonka Dance Moms™ was such that she'd suggested Olivia show up late that August afternoon, so there would be less fuss made over her return. I had always liked Olivia. She wasn't the best dancer, but she had heart. She used to arrive every week with a big smile on her face and shuffle off to Buffalo with great enthusiasm, if not great aptitude. She *liked* dancing, and you'd be surprised how often that didn't seem to be the case with these girls. I wasn't, but you would be.

So I was looking forward to seeing Olivia again, but also, per Gretchen's instructions, primed to play it low-key.

When she arrived, we were working on over-the-top jumps. "Cross left over right, point right, plié, and…jump! And again, right over left! Good!" I smiled at my herd of little elephants, metallic *thunk*s heralding their landings. "Try not to let the left foot touch the ground. Let's do five more in unison without me talking you through it. We'll start again, and—one!"

We got into a rhythm, all of us leaping and landing in time. This was what I liked about dancing. What I had salvaged from it. That sense of your body as part of a larger machine, a dedication to precision allowing, paradoxically, a kind of freedom. It didn't matter if you were doing the "Waltz of the Flowers" in the corps de ballet of a professional company or over-the-top jumps with a roomful of tweens in suburban Minneapolis.

I was in the zone.

Until Sansa's mom, who was watching as she always did, stage-whispered, "Oh my God! Here comes Mike Martin."

I was supposed to be playing it cool, but apparently I was no better than the Minnetonka Moms™. I swiveled my head just as he appeared in the doorway between the studio and the viewing area, which was separated from the dance floor by a half wall and was where the parents who wanted to watch sat. The parents sitting there were not watching the class at that moment though; they were watching him.

As was I. He had straw-colored hair, and he was holding a cup with a teabag tag sticking out of it.

No. My brain had randomly conjured a phantom from my past.

But then Sansa's mom said something, and he opened his mouth to answer her.

He was missing a tooth.

Holy shit with a grand plié.

I tripped over my own feet, not quite making it over the top of over-the-top jump number four. I stumbled toward the parents, fell, and landed on my butt—at the feet of Olivia Kow-alski's dad, who might or might not have been the corporeal manifestation of my imaginary high school boyfriend.

"She's the one who was a ballet dancer in New York?" he said.

Creases appeared on his forehead. I was pretty sure those creases signaled skepticism, which, given that I was sprawled in an inglorious heap at his feet after the world's least graceful over-the-top jump, was fair.

"Yes!" Olivia said. "Miss Rory went to the Newberg Ballet School!"

One corner of his mouth turned up. After a beat, the other side turned up, too, and OK, calm down: he had a *dimple*. That settled it. There had been no dimples in evidence with Mall Mike. This was a strange coincidence.

He extended a hand to help me up. "Maybe you should look into getting a refund."

I tried to smile. Even though I didn't know him, I could tell his teasing was not mean-spirited. I was an expert at distinguishing among subtle shades of mockery. But I was still reeling from this freaky encounter, and I couldn't quite get my mouth to work the way I wanted it to.

The skin of his palm was rough, rougher than would seem attributable to hockey. He pulled me up, but he didn't let go once I was upright. He kind of…stroked my hand with his thumb?

No. I must have made that up. Been so lulled by his magnetic good looks that I forgot where I was. Forgot *when* I was.

I reminded myself that *this* man had a dimple.

It did, however, occur to me that a person could have a dimple but if that person *also* had a beard, as Mall Mike had, that dimple might be hidden.

Olivia's dad turned holding my hand after helping me up into shaking my hand. "I'm Mike Martin." He pulled off his sunglasses with his other hand. He pulled them off slowly, though, like he was starring in a slo-mo montage from *Top Gun*. I watched, transfixed, as he revealed a pair of gold-flecked green eyes.

Well. Holy shit with two grand pliés.

I'm not saying it was love at first sight, but I'm not saying it wasn't.

Earlier, when he'd been joking about my (lack of) grace, his smile had come in two parts, like the clicking up of a Chap-Stick. One click—one side of his mouth. Another click—the other side. This time, there was a third click, and both sides inched up a little more.

"Miss Rory!" Olivia exclaimed. "Your knee is bleeding!"

"It's that nail on the edge of the dance floor that keeps coming up," I said calmly, like my heart *wasn't* about to beat out of my chest.

Gretchen appeared with a hammer and pounded the nail down. "I'll take over. After you clean yourself up, can you get Olivia's registration squared away? I've prorated it for the weeks she missed, and the forms are on the desk."

"Sure." I nodded and, realizing I hadn't properly greeted Olivia, said, "I'm so glad you're back. I missed you." She startled me by coming at me with a tackle-hug. She held on hard enough, and for long enough—and her dad watched us intently enough—that I started to feel awkward. I could feel the parents watching us. "Go join the class so I don't bleed on you. That wasn't how I was imagining welcoming you back."

I gestured for Olivia's dad to follow me as I clacked into the lobby, though what I really wanted to do was riff-walk my way right out the front door. *Jazz hands! Nice to meet you! Hope to see you again never!* But I ordered myself to get it together and said to him, this ghost of malls past, "Have a seat. I'll be right back."

While bandaging myself in the bathroom, I did my tapping routine—ha ha, not that kind of tapping, though I was still wearing the shoes. I made a couple of rounds, letting the pad of my middle finger ping off the bones around each eye, and soon I had control. Thankfully, this one hadn't gotten very far—panic attack lite, anyone? Before I left, I rehearsed several questions:

What happened to your tooth?
When was the last time you visited the Mall of America?
When was the first *time you visited the Mall of America?*

And, because I am not a monster: *How are you and your daughter doing?*

Back in the lobby, Mike Martin was sitting with Kylie's mom on one side of him and Sansa's mom, having abandoned her spectating, on the other. They were asking him questions, but none of the ones I had.

"Will you be coming to the holiday recital?" (It's August, Jan. Calm down.)

"Did you know that for Tap 3, the requirement is a blue leotard and pink tights?" (It's a suggestion, not a requirement, Darla.)

"Would you like some help shopping for the correct leotard?" (Stand down, Jan.)

"How is poor Olivia?" (Oh, for God's sake.)

Mike Martin was looking at his hands and murmuring vague "Not sure yet" and "We're fine, thanks" responses. I pitched my voice to cut through the women's gooey, mercenary concern. "I have the registration forms for you, Mr. Martin."

He popped up and jogged over to the desk. "You never told me your name. You're the famous Miss Rory, I think?"

I rewound the tape, and yep, he told me his name after he helped me up, but I'd been too busy being agog and, you know, bleeding, to reciprocate. "I feel like in some cultures, me collapsing into a heap at your feet would count as an introduction.

We even sealed it with blood." I kicked my leg up so it cleared the reception desk and showed him my Dora the Explorer Band-Aid—Gretchen had been out of the regular ones, so I'd raided the stash she kept for the little kids.

He laughed, a single bark that was equal parts surprise and amusement. To make such a man laugh sent a thrill through me.

"But yes, I'm Aurora Evans. People call me Rory."

"Aurora Evans," he said, stretching my full name out over his tongue, like he was trying it on. "Rory."

Oh my God. Would he *remember*?

Was there anything to remember? I'd started out sure this guy was my Mall Mike, but there was still the dimple to account for.

There was also the fact that the odds of that *same guy* showing up in this studio all these years later were *impossible*.

I wished Mall Mike had told me his last name.

Click-click-click: this Mike, whoever he was, deployed the three-stage, ChapStick-tube smile again. "That is a great name," he said breezily. "It sounds like the alter ego of a superhero."

OK, so he didn't remember. Which was probably because it wasn't him, because there was nothing *to* remember.

And/or because normal people did not remember mundane retail interactions from thirteen years ago, much less build up entire fantasy worlds based on them.

I attempted to click my own lips up into something approximating a smile. "Ha. Right. Klutzy dance teacher by day, but by night…" I had nothing. I could think of no magical abilities to assign myself. "What's my superpower?"

"I don't know yet."

I'd asked the question glibly, trying to match his tone, but he'd pivoted and answered it earnestly, his easy smile replaced by a quizzical expression. There was something about that *yet*, about the way he studied me as if *he* had superpowers, as if he had the ability to see *inside* me, that felt...well, kind of ominous. As if letting him hang around long enough to figure out my superpower would cause more damage than a scraped knee.

I turned my attention to the forms. "I need you to sign this registration." I handed him the paper and picked up another that was lying on my side of the desk. "It also looks like Gretchen printed a copy of Olivia's emergency contact form, if you want to..." *Cross off your dead wife's name.* "Update it. You can write over it, and we'll make the changes in the computer." I set it in front of him with a pen.

Mike Martin had had such an expressive face, up until this point in the proceedings. Those gold-flecked green eyes had danced with laughter and crackled with...something when he'd pondered the question of my superpowers. But that emergency contact form hollowed them out. They turned flat, like cartoon eyes, except you know how in cartoons, there's often a little bit of white on the colored part? Light being reflected, to indicate life or something? There wasn't any life in Mike Martin's eyes. They turned into the green version of black holes. He picked up the pen and contemplated the form. He stood there for longer than it should have taken to read it, and I was suddenly aware, in a way I hadn't been earlier, of the steady attention of Sansa's and Kylie's moms. Of course they'd been watching this whole time, but as I had learned, Mike Martin, when he had life in his eyes, was capable of shrinking the world down so it was only you and him and his X-ray vision.

The air was heavy but silent, and when Mike Martin clicked open the ballpoint pen, it echoed against my eardrums like a door slamming. He still didn't write, though, just stood there staring at the form with his flat eyes.

I wondered if he'd felt the door-slamming sensation, too. I wondered how many doors had shut on him lately, and whether he sometimes encountered those doors in places he didn't expect, in places that seemed benign, like his daughter's dance studio.

"Jan! Darla!" I came out from behind the desk, trying to make myself big in order to shield Mike Martin. Even though my ballet career had been rife with instances when I'd been deemed "too big," my rational mind, the mind that had never been in the vicinity when costume mistresses had been tutting at me, knew that I was, in a normal, civilian sense, a smaller-than-average person. Mike Martin, by contrast, was a larger-than-average person. So to puff up my chest and put my hands on my hips as if I could *actually* shield him from anything was absurd. I did it anyway.

It wasn't until I was standing directly in front of them that Jan and Darla reluctantly pulled their gazes from Mike Martin. I had to give them something big enough to distract them long enough so he could update the form in peace. I lowered my voice conspiratorially. "Gretchen has the holiday recital costumes in, and she thinks the skirts are too short." This was a lie. "She values your opinion." Also a lie. "She asked me to show them to you on the down-low."

There was nothing like perceived insider status to perk up those two, so when I gestured for them to follow me downstairs, they didn't hesitate. I led them into the storage room, having no idea what I'd find.

"Hmm," I said after making a show of looking through a few boxes, "Maybe she sent them back already." I hoped enough time had elapsed that when we went back to reception, Mike Martin's eyes would be back to normal.

Upstairs, he was nowhere to be seen. The moms looked around not subtly, and I went back around the desk.

Our emergency contact forms had space for three people. Olivia's original had her mom listed as number one, a person named Renata Kowalski second, and Mike Martin third.

Mike Martin had crossed off his late wife's name and that of Renata Kowalski. He'd used a single pen stroke for his wife's but had almost completely obscured Renata's with a series of dark Xs. Next to his own name, he'd drawn an arrow indicating it should move to the top spot, and he'd added a Lauren Zadorov as number two. There was no number three.

There was, however, a Post-it—he must have snagged one from behind the desk—stuck to the form.

Can you tell Olivia I'm waiting for her in the car? Thanks. —MM.

I should have taken my class back; instead I returned to the bathroom and opened Wikipedia.

Michael McKenna Martin. Canadian professional ice-hockey player currently playing for the Minnesota Lumber-jacks NHL franchise. Thirty-four years old.

I did the math. It couldn't have been him, all those years ago. Because *that* guy had been in town for a high school hockey tournament. *This* guy, Olivia's dad, was thirty-four, which would have made him twenty-one at the mall—too old for high school. So in addition to the dimple in the "It's Not Him" column, the ages didn't line up.

On the other hand: The eyes. The handshake-caress.

And of course the entire "hockey player named Mike from Canada" thing.

On the other *other* hand: there must be literally thousands of hockey players named Mike from Canada.

I skipped to the "Personal Life" section.

Martin was born to Ed and Diane Martin in Portage la Prairie, Manitoba.

I clicked over to Google Maps and learned that Portage la Prairie, Manitoba, was an hour's drive west of Winnipeg.

Holy shit with three grand pliés.

He has an older brother, Christopher Martin, who is a goaltending coach with Pittsburgh. Martin grew up idolizing his brother and credits him with sparking his interest in hockey.

He is close with fellow Lumberjacks defenseman Ivan Zadorov, the pair having appeared in a *Sports Illustrated* spread on bromances in sport.

Martin was married to Sarah Kowalski, whom he met while playing for Chicago in the American Hockey League. They married at the Art Institute of Chicago and served pie, which was a favorite of both, at their wedding instead of cake.

There was a citation on that last bit that looked like it referenced a *Chicago Tribune* article about the wedding. I made a mental note to read it later.

Kowalski died in a car accident in Montreal while in town to attend a Minnesota versus Montreal game.

Someone knocked on the door. I fumbled my phone away. "Just a sec!" I called in a voice that sounded like it was coming from someone who was not me.

Maybe that person could go finish teaching Tap 3, too. But no. Whatever else was happening, Olivia Kowalski was back after a long absence, and it was time to tap my way into class and welcome her back.

2 — DEPRESSION CAR

RORY

After class, I was standing at the bus stop reading that *Chicago Tribune* story about Mike Martin's wedding when the man himself pulled up in a convertible the same color as his eyes. Olivia was in the back seat eating an ice-cream cone.

"Aurora!" Mike Martin called over the car's noisy engine. "Can we give you a lift?"

It was a simple yes/no question, and the answer was no, but instead of saying that, I blurted, "Your car matches your eyes."

Click-click-click. Out came the dimple, and how could a grin that was a tooth shy of a full set be so powerful?

"It's our depression car," Olivia piped up from the back.

Huh? I forced myself to stop pondering the paradox that was Mike Martin's broken yet inexplicably alluring dental situation.

The car behind him beeped. Yeah, there was no way I was letting Mike Martin drive me home. For many reasons, not the least of which was that accepting a ride from him would force me to postpone the urgent task that was currently using all my brain cells: reading everything Google served up on him so I could match him up—or not—with the boy from the mall.

"I'm fine, thanks." That was true. "The bus will be here soon." That was a lie. Buses were few and far between in this fancy suburb, with the exception of the express buses that took the Minnetonka Men™ to their jobs in downtown Minneapolis in the mornings and home at night. My car had died a few weeks ago, and since I hadn't gotten my finances organized yet to get a new one, I was stuck on the bus.

Another honk sounded from the car behind Mike Martin, this one longer and decidedly less polite. "That guy sounds pissed. You'd better get in," Mike Martin said.

I got in.

"Where to?" he yelled over the vroom of the engine as we pulled away.

"I live north of Cedar Lake Road, east of the Hopkins Crossroad." Did he need directions beyond that? Apparently not—he hit the gas without another word.

"Miss Rory, your hair is so long!" Olivia called from the back seat.

The kids didn't generally see me with my hair loose. I'd taken it down on my walk to the bus stop because I'd done a poor job with my bun today and the bobby pins had been digging into my scalp.

"And your hair is so amazing!" I called back. Sometime in the past seven months, Olivia had dyed hers lime green.

"I was inspired by Miss Miller!"

Gretchen was known for her seasonally rotating brightly colored hair; it was one of the things that made the kids adore her.

We tried to keep talking, but when Mike Martin got on the highway, it was hard to make ourselves heard over the rush of the wind and the noise of the engine.

"This is the part where you sit back and enjoy the drive!" Olivia shouted.

I glanced at Mike Martin. He was wearing the mirrored sunglasses and steering the car with his right hand while his left arm rested on top of the door. He was the picture of freedom, the poster boy for a carefree summer, cruising along on a still-sunny evening, which just went to show you how easily pictures could lie. I had seen his green-hole eyes.

I had a picture of me, an actual physical picture my mother had had printed and framed, dancing the part of Aurora, my namesake, in the Minnesota Ballet Center's production of *The Sleeping Beauty* twelve years ago. It was a still photo they'd used for PR, a shot of me dancing the wedding pas de deux with my prince, en pointe, dressed in a white confection of a costume that made me look like a music-box ballerina. And—this is the lie part—I was smiling widely for the camera, as if I were happy. I kept the picture hidden in my dresser except for when my mother came over.

I had so many questions for Mike Martin. The same ones from before but also new ones. What was a depression car? Did it have anything to do with him waiting in it for Olivia's lesson to finish, or had he merely been fleeing the Minnetonka Moms™ because he was a rational human being?

Also: *How* was he here?

Was it even *him*?

I directed him into the parking lot at my place. I probably should have been embarrassed. Home sweet home was a big, nondescript apartment complex made of three-story beige stucco buildings.

I thought of the face my mother had made the first time

she'd visited, the lemon-drop face, I used to call it—in my head—when I was little. I told myself what I'd never had the guts to tell my mother, that there was nothing wrong with this place. It was modest, but that was not a crime.

"Is there a pool here?" Olivia asked as Mike Martin cut the engine.

I twisted around to look at Olivia, whose eyes were wide with excitement in a way that made her look younger than her years, which in turn caused something in my heart to twinge. I had a thoroughly middling mother, but at least I had one. "There is."

"You are so *lucky*."

"You can swim at home anytime, Liv," Mike Martin said with fond amusement in his voice.

"Yeah, but a pool doesn't have *fish* in it. It doesn't have *seaweed* in it." There was an edge in her rebuke, and she held Mike Martin's gaze with what seemed like defiance. I wondered if I'd imagined that, though, because when she turned back to me, she was rocking some serious puppy-dog eyes.

"Do you…want to come for a swim sometime?" Was it a conflict of interest to invite a student to swim at my apartment? Was it a conflict of interest to invite the daughter of the man who might or might not be my imaginary Canadian Boyfriend made flesh to swim at my apartment?

"Yes!" Olivia said, with an urgency that made me worry she thought I meant *right now*.

"Olivia," Mike Martin said. "You can't just invite yourself over to someone's house."

"I *didn't*," she said indignantly. "She invited me."

"Yes, but—"

"She. Invited. Me." Indignation had crystalized into something closer to anger. This was not a version of Olivia I saw in class. Mike Martin put his hands on the steering wheel. He closed his eyes. I wondered if, when he opened them, they'd be flat.

"The pool is closed for cleaning right now," I lied, trying to steer us out of this logjam. "So you're out of luck, but maybe another time?" When I looked back at Mike Martin, he was no longer gripping the steering wheel, and his eyes were open—and not flat. I turned back to Olivia. "I'm glad you're back in class."

"Do you think I'm going to be behind?" she asked, her tone shifting with whiplash-inducing speed from peevish to tentative.

"I do not."

"I kept messing up today."

"You'll get your groove back."

"But the session is almost over."

"Summer sessions are short and informal, and we're going to roll right over to fall, and that always brings with it a few new faces, so everyone will be playing catch-up to some extent." She looked only slightly placated. "Remember 'Miss Miller's Morals'?" I said, citing Gretchen's famous studio rules. "Dancing is supposed to be fun, right? Not stressful. You have nothing to worry about. I mean that sincerely."

"OK, thanks, Miss Rory."

I turned to Mike Martin, who'd been silently watching our exchange. "Thanks for the ride. I hope it wasn't too far out of your way."

"Well," Mike Martin said, "what else were we going to do?"

———

The next Tuesday, Mike Martin offered me a ride home again. He cornered me after class right there in front of Gretchen and the Minnetonka Moms™ and said, "Aurora, can we give you a lift again?"

He smiled, and he had all his teeth. What? Had I hallucinated the missing one last week?

"'Again'?" Gretchen, who was standing next to me behind the desk, said under her breath—sufficiently under, I hoped, that no one else heard. I avoided her gaze. I had not told Gretchen about the ride home last week, which was weird because I told Gretchen everything.

"But we're getting ice cream first, remember?" Olivia said to Mike Martin. There was an ice-cream place in the same strip mall as the studio, and the kids were always lobbying their parents to visit it after class. I would have thought Olivia's request a run-of-the-mill one. But after witnessing her tense exchange with Mike Martin last week in the parking lot at my building, I thought I detected a note of that same pique in her tone.

"Right." He looked at me. "You want to join us, then we'll run you home?"

The place went silent. I kept my attention on him, but I could *feel* Gretchen—and everyone else—looking at me. My heart started beating rapidly.

Damn it.

The thing to know about me was that while I looked fine, I was not actually fine—or at least not all-the-way fine. I had my life mostly under control. I did the same things over and over, and I had become adept at doing them without incident. Job number one, job number two, hang out with Gretchen. I was still getting used to life without Ian, my ex-boyfriend, and to life alone in a too-big apartment empty of the furniture he had taken with him when he'd left a month ago, but I had mostly recalibrated. I mean, I needed a sofa, not to mention a new apartment—the rent was too much for me on my own—but I was basically fine.

My mother could throw a wrench in things, but we were good Midwestern citizens who had mastered the twin arts of emotional sublimation and Minnesota Nice.

My point is, I wasn't unhappy. I loved job number one. I didn't mind job number two. I loved Gretchen. I didn't miss Ian as much as I'd thought I would and was even starting to enjoy the peace of singledom. I had a good life.

I just…ran into trouble sometimes. That trouble was often heralded by a spike in my heart rate and a floppy feeling in my stomach.

But OK. Concentrate. *Your brain does not have to follow your body.* That's what my old therapist used to say. She'd taught me a lot of useful stuff I still relied on. I let my left hand float up to my temple. I couldn't do my full EFT tapping routine in public without looking like a freak, but sometimes I could do a quick tap-rub at my favorite points.

It worked. Not completely, but enough that I could tune back into the thick silence in the room.

I contemplated the question that had set me off. Did I want a ride home from Mike Martin? I did. Not only would it get me home faster than the bus, but I also wanted to ride in the green convertible and feel the wind in my hair.

"Why don't you guys get your ice cream," I said to Mike Martin, "and I'll meet you outside Suz's in a few minutes. I have some wrap-up to do here."

"No you don't." Gretchen physically edged me away from the computer where I had been entering attendance. "I've got everything under control. You go." She swiveled so she was facing me and mouthed, "Again."

Gretchen was always trying to get me to do two things. One was go on dates. She had never been Team Ian, and when Ian finally pulled the plug on our wheezing-along-on-life-support relationship, she'd said "Good riddance," wrested my phone from me, and downloaded Tinder. The other was take a vacation. I resisted on both fronts. I had no money for a vacation and no desire for dating.

She made a shooing motion. I was going to pay for this later in the form of an interrogation.

At Suz's, Olivia ordered a double scoop of watermelon and birthday cake on a waffle cone, and after some hesitation Mike Martin ordered a single scoop of coconut on a regular cone. "I'm going back to hockey this season," he explained. "It's been hell getting into shape, and ice cream won't help." I knew the feeling.

When it was my turn to order, I tried to pass. "I'm not really an ice-cream person." I had not had ice cream for years. Eleven, to be precise.

"How can you not be an ice-cream person?" Olivia exclaimed.

I wasn't convinced that my body wouldn't reject ice cream if I tried to eat it, my white blood cells mustering like a line of good little soldiers going, "Nope!" Conversely, it was possible that once the first bite crossed my lips, my brain stem would embark on a campaign to fill whatever was empty inside me with ice cream and not stop until I was frozen and alone, like Princess Elsa in her icy prison-palace.

Either way, ice cream was risky.

"Come on," Mike Martin said. "Treat yourself." But then, seeming to backpedal, he added, "If you want."

I should be able to do this. These days, I ate pizza with (almost) no trouble. Gretchen and I had sleepovers during which we split a bag of her favorite, Flamin' Hot Cheetos. One scoop of ice cream wasn't going to kill me. Probably.

"I will have a single scoop of…" What? I didn't want any of the wild flavors on offer, but if I was actually going to eat ice cream, plain chocolate or vanilla seemed too boring. I settled on the first boring-but-not-too-boring option my gaze landed on. "Mint chocolate chip. In a cup."

The teenager behind the counter plopped a truly enormous, dubiously "single" scoop into a cup, and I dug in my purse for my wallet while keeping my eye on that ice cream like it was a drink I had set down at a crowded bar full of sketchy dudes.

"I got it." Mike Martin passed the teenager some cash.

"No, no." I did not want him to pay for my ice cream, but he was already pocketing his change. "Thanks," I said weakly, telling myself not to stress over three dollars.

There were picnic tables outside, but Mike Martin and Olivia made straight for the car. I thought about how my mother would never have let me eat ice cream in the car. Well, my mother wouldn't have allowed ice cream to begin with, so the prospect of eating ice cream in the car was hypothetical. But she never let me eat *anything* in the car, even in those years when we'd had to race from school to ballet classes downtown that would run into the evening. "I have to drive clients around in this car," she'd say. "I can't have crumbs from your garbage granola bars everywhere. You might as well eat an actual candy bar."

Mike Martin opened the passenger-side door for me, and I got in. I thought he was going to open Olivia's door next, but instead he wordlessly took her cone from her and watched while she did a little run, leaped over the closed door *Dukes of Hazzard* style, and landed in the back seat with a thud.

"Good one." Mike Martin handed her cone back, and they both raised their free hands and high-fived.

Mike Martin jogged around, got in the driver's side, and took a big bite out of his ice cream, like with his teeth, rather than licking, like you'd think was more...normal.

But how did I know what was normal? I hadn't had ice cream for eleven years.

I watched as he finished the ice-cream part and hit the cone. In a few big crunches and a matter of seconds, it was gone.

He started the car, glanced over at me, then down at my untouched ice cream. It was starting to get melty, and I was starting to get sweaty. Here went nothing. I scooped up a blob with my spoon and shoved it into my mouth, and—

Oh!

It was as if all my senses had, unbeknownst to me, been muted, and someone had suddenly cranked them up to eleven. No. Not some*one*, some*thing*: mint chocolate chip ice cream. Cold, sweet, mentholy, *perfect*. Goose bumps rose all over my skin even as a wave of warmth that felt like relief radiated through my body. The world looked brighter as my vision sharpened. I felt like a superhero. I still didn't know what my superpowers were, but I was pretty sure they were rumbling to life, conjured by mint chocolate chip.

"What's wrong?" Mike Martin asked urgently.

I forced myself back to earth. "Why do you call this a depression car?" This car was cool. It was fun to ride in, and, I assumed, fun to drive. Mike Martin and Olivia seemed to have a whole schtick around her getting into it. They ate ice cream in it. It seemed like the *opposite* of a depression car.

Mike Martin blinked a few times. I opened my mouth to clarify that I wasn't trying to pry. To explain that I was merely complimenting his car because I was enjoying eating ice cream in it so thoroughly.

"When my mom died, we decided to get a convertible to cheer us up," Olivia said.

Ah. "So really, this is an antidepression car? An antidepressant with a retractable roof?" I took another bite of ice cream and tried to keep my freak-out over its amazingness internal.

Mike Martin chuckled. "We decided to get a convertible because we like going on long drives, and Olivia wanted a green one, which turned out to be surprisingly hard to find."

"Well, there was that Porsche, and it was *bright* green. Like, *lime* green. I loved it. It's why I dyed my hair this color."

"I vetoed lime green." Mike Martin smirked. "And also the price tag."

Hmm. If I had thought about the automobile-buying habits of professional athletes, which I had not until that moment, I would have thought they picked up cars on a whim, like adding a scratch-off lottery ticket to your otherwise sensible grocery purchase.

"He said he's not a Porsche guy." I could hear the eye roll in Olivia's tone, but it sounded like normal tween annoyance. It was less venomous than the way she'd spoken last week. "But then we found out the newest Mustangs also come in really bright green, so I still don't know why we couldn't get one of those."

Mike Martin twisted in his seat to look at Olivia. "You picked the color family; I picked the specific hue." Then he turned to me. "We went with a Mustang, but vintage since the new ones don't come in dark green. If we were getting a green car, I wanted it to be dark green."

"Why?" I asked, thinking that if you were going for an

uplifting color, lime would be a more logical choice than this forest shade.

Click-click-click went the smile, and I knew I was in trouble before he even opened his mouth. "I wanted my car to match my eyes."

———

Inside my apartment, I made a beeline for the closet in my bedroom. I studied my reflection in the mirrored door. My hair was ridiculous, thanks to the convertible ride. I looked like I'd stuck my finger into an electrical socket.

I moved things around until I could reach the box at the very back of the closet, the box full of old programs and dried flowers and other remnants of a life I'd left behind, and got out my old red three-ring binder. I hadn't opened this binder since I'd written the last letter in it. I'd made a decisive break from my past when I quit ballet. The only thing from my old life that remained in my new life was my mother. Or, as Gretchen called her, the Wicked Witch of Wayzata. But other than Heather Evans and her flying monkeys, the past was in the past.

Or at least it had been until recently.

Dear Mike,

I think I might have to quit the mall. Now that I'm in Level VI at ballet, I have class every day after school until seven. Between that, actual school, and homework, I'm about to fall over by Friday night. But I don't <u>want</u> to quit. I like my weekends at the mall. It's peaceful there, which I realize makes no sense because it's crawling with people. In a weird way, I'm more at home behind the counter at Caribou, joking with my coworkers, than anywhere else. Mom said it's up to me whether to quit, which is a new one. Like, what? Heather Evans does not have an opinion on something?

I'm going to try to hold out through the holidays. Even if I get ~~a big part~~ any part in The Nutcracker, *I'll still be able to work over winter break. It's school that gets in the way. I <u>have</u> thought about the fact that if I started doing B work instead of A work, it would take a lot of the pressure off. But as Mom points out, B work is not going to cut it. Which is rich, because she's the one who wants me to put off college and audition for companies right away.*

Anyway, blah, blah, how are you? Please do not feel bad for not being able to make it to prom. It's not your fault your hockey finals conflict with prom. That's much more important than a school dance!

Love you to the moon and back,
Rory

P.S. Say hi to Erik for me!

3 — BRIGHT THINGS

MIKE

Sarah told me once, when I asked her how she'd gotten through the hard times in her life—and she'd had some hard times—that the trick was to "look for the bright things and hold on to those."

Aurora Evans was a bright thing.

I could see why Olivia liked her so much.

Mind you, I wasn't sure I should trust a single God damn thing Sarah had ever said to me, but as my shrink was always pointing out, that wasn't fair. And since getting back into our normal routines was what Liv and I were supposed to be doing this fall, I was making it a point to put us in Aurora's path.

As my mom had said when she'd left after spending six months with us—as she'd said nearly every day of those six months—the only way out is through.

Olivia hadn't wanted to go back to school this fall. I'd pulled her out after the crash last January and filed a homeschool plan and let her finish grade five with a tutor. But Liv had to go back. Things needed to return to normal. On the surface, anyway.

Maybe the insides would follow.

In preparation for this fall, Dr. Mursal—the shrink—had asked Olivia to write down two things that made her happy, which made me laugh because nothing made Olivia happy anymore, especially not since my mom left. Which I could understand— my mom was great—but could I catch a break for one single second? Anyway, Dr. Mursal had suggested we figure out a way to make sure Olivia's two happy things did not fall by the wayside as the school year and the hockey season started. Those things turned out to be Olivia's dance classes at Miss Miller's— "tap with Miss Rory especially"—and driving around the lake.

The driving part had been a surprise but easy to keep doing. It had started a couple days after the funeral. When we were out, in those early days, I'd find myself resisting going home. I didn't want to see Sarah's shoes in the entryway or her pile of magazines on the nightstand. I didn't want to face the shape of our house, of our lives, without her in it. So I'd told Olivia I wanted to drive for a while, expecting her to object.

I was surprised when she hadn't, and even more surprised when she'd suggested, the next day, on our way home from a session with Dr. Mursal, whom we'd started seeing together and were now seeing separately, that we do it again.

We kept doing it. When spring grew heavy in the air and started serving up the odd day that reminded you that the deep, sharp cold of a Minnesota winter had not, in fact, been a permanent state of affairs as you'd been beginning to fear, we started cracking the windows. The cold air smelled like thawing, and thawing seemed like a good smell. As summer arrived, we rolled the windows all the way down and stuck our arms out. I wouldn't let Olivia stick her head and torso out the window like she wanted to, but I understood the impulse. So I came up with the idea of a convertible. It was maybe a little weird that driving was our "thing" when Sarah had died in a car, but if Olivia was cool with it, so was I.

Driving aimlessly reminded me of summer in Manitoba. Summer, when there was no hockey, had always seemed so long, and my buddies and I would drive around in my crappy old Kia, going too fast down country roads, the corn whizzing by like background static. At our destination, be it a fast-food place or the shores of Crescent Lake, we'd shoot the breeze about hockey. Didn't matter what kind. NHL, NCAA, my own experiences in the WHL, my old high school team where my buddy John played. We loved it all. I missed those days.

But Olivia turned out to be a pretty good driving companion, too, even if we didn't talk hockey. We didn't talk about anything, which honestly was part of the appeal. If we weren't talking, she couldn't be mad at me.

There was one day, before Christmas last winter, when Lauren and Ivan had walked across the frozen lake to our house. I'd built a bonfire. Sarah had made a batch of some kind of spicy hot wine in a Crock-Pot, which you'd think would be too fancy for my basic, Labatt-loving self but somehow was not.

As I looked around that day at my family and friends zipping around on skates on a patch of lake I'd cleared, the whole thing lit by these old-timey lights Sarah'd bought and had me string up on poles, I thought to myself, *Damn, I have it made.* Ivan had told me that night that he and Lauren were trying for a baby, or, as he put it in his terse, Ivan way, "No longer trying to prevent one, anyway." They were starting to think about postretirement life, as were Sarah and I—or so I'd thought.

After my last few laps on the ice, taken solo—everyone else had gotten too cold and gone inside—I turned off the lights and looked at the stars and entertained a fantasy of a future in which Lauren and Sarah were pregnant at the same time. Our kids would be the same age, and once they got a little older, Olivia would be old enough that we'd have a built-in babysitter.

That future had seemed so close, like a perfect, crystalline snowflake about to land.

And now it was gone, and I was focused on putting one foot in front of the other, doing what Dr. Mursal told me to, including working on Olivia's two things.

Olivia had ballet on Saturdays and tap on Tuesdays after school. She liked tap better than ballet, and I could see why. It was partly the format. Tap seemed less finicky than ballet, and the noise those shoes made was oddly satisfying. It reminded me of snapping bubble wrap. But mostly it was Miss Rory. I'd been watching Liv's classes, and Aurora was funnier and less strict than Miss Riley, the ballet teacher, yet she seemed to get better results. She was a natural coach.

I liked Aurora. She had a lot of emotional intelligence. Dr. Mursal said I did, too, and from the beginning she'd said that was how Olivia and I were going to get through. I didn't see it, even when she explained that emotional intelligence was different from the regular kind. Aurora, though, I could *see* doing things like distracting those nosy moms that time I was having a freak-out about the emergency contact forms. Or shutting down problematic behavior in class without making a big thing of it. Plus she was a bit weird, but in an endearing way. Like how she seemed to view eating ice cream as a life-changing event and how she wore this clanky bracelet with a bunch of charms on it, including a Snoopy one.

So when we got into the habit of driving Aurora home on Tuesdays after class, it was the perfect mixture of Olivia's two priorities: dance with Miss Rory and driving. And it suited my desire to postpone going home and looking at Sarah's shoes, which I still hadn't cleared out of the entryway. I didn't want to get rid of them, but I also didn't want to look at them, which made no sense, but there it was.

Aurora always thanked me profusely when we dropped her off. I didn't know how to tell her she was doing us a bigger favor than we were doing her.

"Ice cream?" Olivia said when we left the studio the Tuesday of the second week of September. She'd been back to dance for a month, my mom had been gone for a month, and my first away game was in a month. It was possible that we were in the eye of the storm. It was possible that things were about to get really bad.

"I was thinking maybe we'd eat dinner first?" I said. Suz's had an ice-cream counter up front, but it was also a full-service, old-school restaurant where you could get a table and order a Juicy Lucy and fries along with your root beer float.

I thought the idea of eating out would be welcome, but as Olivia so often informed me, I didn't know much. She wasn't wrong, in general but also as it related to my ability to predict when the rage that always seemed to be simmering inside her would boil over.

"Yes! Dinner!" Olivia said, and, relieved, I turned my attention to Aurora. I didn't want her to think I was making a move or anything. Well, I was going to make a move, but not that kind. Aurora had frozen in the middle of taking her long, auburn hair down from the bun it had been in for class. Most people with long hair put it up to ride in a convertible, but Aurora did the reverse. Like the Snoopy bracelet, it was another quirky thing about her.

Now, though, she was getting that deer-in-headlights look

she sometimes had. She'd gotten that look the first time we went for ice cream. Maybe she didn't like Suz's.

Aurora unfroze and said, "Dinner sounds great. I'm finally getting a new car—a new old car—next week, so it can be our farewell. It's been fun hanging out with you guys."

Hmm. Her getting a car might mess with my plans, but all I could do was try. After we ordered, I pulled out a twenty-dollar bill. "Liv, you want to hit the arcade until the food comes?"

Her mouth fell open. It wasn't normal for me to hand over so much money for her to blow on games. In the before times, we used to talk a lot about not spoiling Olivia. But one thing I had learned in the post-Sarah era was that sometimes you had to sacrifice one thing in order to concentrate on another, more important thing. Olivia snatched the cash out of my hand and ran off as if afraid I'd change my mind.

Aurora laughed. She had a high, melodious laugh that erupted out of her in little bursts that sounded the way light looked. Part of her bright-thing appeal, I guess.

I laughed, too, but mostly at what a rule follower I was. Here I was combining Sarah's advice about bright things, my mom's adage about muddling through, and Dr. Mursal's recent instruction that I start asking for help beyond Lauren and Ivan. What can I say? I'm good at following directions. In the hockey world, people always said I was very coachable. And this was a logical solution to the one problem about my return to work I had not solved to my satisfaction.

I fiddled with my napkin—I was good at following directions, but that didn't mean it was easy to do. When your skating coach tells you your edge control is sloppy, she might not be wrong, but that's hard to hear. "I have a proposal for you."

"OK." Aurora was looking at me kind of funny with her big

brown eyes that were the same color as the mud pit our backyard at home used to become in the spring after our homemade
rink melted. She was skeptical, which was fair. I was probably
giving off nervous vibes. I was more accustomed to distrusting
people than to trusting them. It came with the territory of my
job, my life. I had no interest in people whose only interest in
me was the fact that I was overpaid to play hockey.

It was hard to find the other kind of people.

"Oh my God, are you Mike Martin?"

See? I huffed a sigh, even though what I wanted to do was
scream, and turned to the woman approaching our table. Mid-
forties, Minnesota-blond hair. She looked like a hockey mom.

"Any chance you'd sign this for me?"

This turned out to be her forearm.

"Sure," I said flatly. She handed me a Sharpie, and I scrawled
my name on her skin. It was the path of least resistance.

"I was *so sorry* to hear about your wife." The woman made
what I called the fake-sorry face: head tilted, forehead wrinkled, but nothing in the eyes.

"Thanks," I said, again opting for the answer that was going
to get rid of her the fastest.

"Training camp's about to start, though!" she trilled. "That'll
be a good distraction! And we're so—"

"Excuse me," Aurora cut in. "I'm sorry, but we're kind of in
the middle of something." She made the fake-sorry face, too, a
perfect imitation of the woman's from a few seconds ago, except
it was exaggerated, obviously yet subtly mocking. It startled a
laugh out of me. Which was rude, but so was interrupting a
man's dinner and acting like you cared about his dead wife
you'd never met.

"Yes, of course," the woman said, but I didn't miss her little sniff. I watched her walk back to her table, and when she'd sat and resumed talking to her companion—probably saying something snarky about me—I returned my attention to my mission. To Aurora.

She rolled her eyes sympathetically, as if we were in league together. It was buoying. "I have to go back to work in a few weeks," I said. "Well, I'm already back, but I have to start traveling for work."

"Right. I understand you're some kind of hockey star?" Her eyes danced.

"Not a star. Just a reliable stay-at-home defenseman." I'd never been one of the giants of the league, even when I was younger and faster, and for that I was thankful. I would freely admit that I had a complicated relationship with the low-level fame that came with my job. Well, no, it was actually pretty simple: I hated it. Happily, I wasn't recognized very much. Most of the media attention I'd had over the years had been about other people—my romance with Sarah, which because of her rich parents had captured the interest of the Chicago society pages, and my so-called bromance with Ivan. I tended to make the news only as half of a b/romance, and that was more than enough for me.

But I also probably owed my ability to keep a low profile to the fact that I was, let's face it, a third-pairing player in the twilight of my career. These days, it was only serious fans, like the woman who'd approached our table, who knew me by sight. Or people in my hometown, where I was a bit of a "star," as much as I loathed that word.

"'A reliable stay-at-home defenseman.'" Aurora nodded sagely. "I have no idea what that means."

With most people, even if they hadn't initially known my

name or face, the fact that I was in the NHL became...a thing. They were hockey fans, like the latest Ms. Fake Sorry. Or they weren't, but they were attuned to the stuff that came with being a pro athlete—the fame, the money, whatever. So my first reaction when people went all starry-eyed over me was to bristle.

I just wanted to play hockey, and I hated all the other shit that came with it.

Aurora, though, seemed ignorant about both hockey and my role in it. "It means I hang back while the other defenseman roams around more. I'm the guy you send out when you're trying to protect a lead."

"It sounds like being in the corps de ballet."

"Sorry?" I'd done a bit of poking around, and I knew that Aurora had attended the school at the Newberg Ballet, which I'd learned was a famous New York company. But I didn't know ballet.

"There's a hierarchy of roles in a ballet company. Principal dancers are the stars. At the bottom is the corps de ballet—supporting players."

"Mm, I think maybe the hockey analogy is a grinder." She looked at me blankly. This woman did not give a crap about hockey, and I *loved* it. If she said yes to my proposal, it would be because she cared about Olivia, not me and my "status." "It's not important. The point is I'm going back to work, which is a bit of a surprise."

"How so?"

"I'm old and decrepit—" She started to object. "I'm old and decrepit for hockey; it's a fact. Last season was the last on my previous contract. So when I took the last chunk of it off in unpaid leave, I assumed that would be it for me. It's not normal to take that much time off, even for a death. But I was..."

Not handling things well. But she didn't need to know that. "Anyway, to my surprise, I've been offered another two-year contract." I paused and considered whether I should explain why I was going back when the easiest, most obvious move would be to retire, but I remembered Dr. Mursal telling me I didn't have to defend my choices.

"When the season starts, I'll have to be on the road a lot. Olivia is going to stay with my friend Ivan's wife, Lauren, while the team is traveling. Ivan's on the team, and they live near us. Lauren will make sure Olivia gets to school and back when I'm not in town, and she can do Olivia's Saturday ballet class run. The problem is your class on Tuesdays. Lauren has a yoga class at the same time. She's offering to quit it, but I'm trying to find another solution. Olivia loves your class, and I've promised her she won't have to give it up." Aurora made an aw-shucks face. I probably should have led with how much of a fan Olivia was.

I was starting to sweat. Why was this so hard? Why couldn't I find my stride like I could on the ice? A game could throw anything at me, impossible odds and power plays, and I was cool, but I couldn't ask for a favor? "Since that four o'clock class is the last one you teach on Tuesdays, I'm wondering how you would feel about driving Olivia home afterward—well, driving her home and hanging out with her until Lauren can pick her up after yoga. I'd been planning to get you a car if you agreed."

There. It was out.

"You can't just give a car to a person you barely know."

"I wouldn't be. It'd be a long-term loan."

"You can't long-term lend a car to a person you barely know," she parried without missing a beat.

I smiled. In another context, in another *life*, I would have enjoyed bantering with her. "I can, though."

She looked at me like I was a few sprinkles short of a sundae. This wasn't working out the way I'd hoped. I leaned forward, contemplating going with the truth. Why not?

"Look, Olivia is struggling. More than you see—she loves your class, so she's nice to you. I'm struggling, too. I'm racked with guilt about going back to work. I'm racked with guilt over how much I'm leaning on Lauren. Basically, I'm racked with guilt, period. If you can't do it, or don't want to, that's fine. I don't mean to sound like a jerk, but I can easily afford to lend you a car. Or you can use your own—I didn't realize when I hatched this plan that you were going to be buying one. And you can name your price."

"My price for what?"

"Well, obviously, I'd be paying you."

She looked at me for a long time, and I could not read her expression. "Can I ask you a question?"

"Shoot."

"Did you go to college?"

That *was* random. And possibly a little insulting? Was she trying to say I wasn't smart enough for her? I was well aware of my shortcomings. If I hadn't made it in the NHL, I would probably be pouring coffee at Tim Hortons with my dad.

"Did you play hockey in college, I mean," she clarified. "NCAA hockey?"

"No. I didn't go to college. I played in the WHL." She looked confused, so I added, "Western Hockey League— a junior league in Canada."

"You wouldn't do both?"

"'Both' meaning go to college and play in the WHL?" She nodded. Wow, she *really* didn't know hockey. I continued to appreciate that fact, even as I was confused by this line of questioning. "No. The NCAA considers the WHL a pro league, so if you play in it, you're ineligible to play NCAA hockey at US schools."

It occurred to me that maybe Aurora's questions weren't laden with hidden meaning. She didn't know me, not really, and I was asking her to take responsibility for my kid. Maybe this was her way of doing a background check. I had done a version of the same, via Google and Gretchen Miller. If that was what Aurora was doing, I was, uncharacteristically, happy to talk about myself. "I played major junior hockey in Canada—that's hockey for guys aged sixteen to twenty. I moved to a town in northern Manitoba for it. They put you up with local families, kind of like being an exchange student, and you play hockey and finish high school at the same time."

She was looking at me intently, like she was trying to solve a math problem. "So you didn't play normal high school hockey?"

OK, she was definitely checking me out, which actually reflected well on her as a babysitter. I relaxed. "For my original high school at home? I did for one year, but not after I started in the WHL. After that I spent a few years in the AHL—that's the American Hockey League, which is the development league for the NHL. I played in Chicago, which is where I met Ivan, Lauren's husband." Also where I'd met Sarah. I paused, eyeing Aurora. Did she want more? "When I got called up, we moved to Raleigh. From there I went to Tampa. I was traded here five years ago, which I was happy about, as the South is not for me."

"OK," Aurora said decisively. "I'll do it. But I don't want you to pay me. I'll take the loaner car in lieu of payment."

"I can't not pay you."

"Here's the thing. I recently got dumped."

I sat back, surprised, though I didn't know why. People got dumped. It was a thing that happened. It was just hard to imagine it happening to Aurora. But I liked the plainspoken way she said it. *I got dumped* instead of *I went through a breakup* or something vague.

"So I'm paying more rent than I have been historically—he left, but I'm still in the apartment. Then my piece-of-crap car died."

"I'm sorry about the breakup," I said, because it was what I was supposed to say.

"It's OK." She cocked her head and looked into space, like she was surprised by the revelation. "It's really OK."

"Yeah?" I pressed, though I had no idea why. It was none of my business.

"I have a history of bending myself to please other people, and sometimes, when you stop doing that, it's an unexpected relief." She shook her head while I was absorbing that simple yet deep observation and said, "My point is, this stretch without a car has been a big pain. I can walk to my other job, but getting to and from the studio has sucked."

Other job. I hadn't known about that.

"I'm also trying to pay off a bunch of student debt," she went on. "So what do you say you lend me a car and I get to use it all the time, not just for taking Olivia home on Tuesdays? Then I don't have to get a car loan. That's worth more to me than whatever you'd pay me."

I started to say that by all means she should use the car whenever she wanted. I had assumed as much and had planned to pay her on top of that. But something held me back. Aurora didn't care that I was a hockey player. She had two jobs and student debt. I put all these things together to paint a picture of a woman who needed to feel like she was entering into a fair arrangement. Her saving my bacon was worth any amount of money to me, but just because I could afford to throw a lot of cash at her didn't mean she wanted me to. I understood having pride. I respected it.

I stuck my hand out, intending to revisit the issue of payment later but content to start our arrangement on Aurora's terms. "Deal."

We shook on it, and I noticed, as I had before when I'd been helping her up from the floor at Miss Miller's, that the skin on her hands was freakishly soft. Which was followed immediately by my noticing that noticing such a thing was inappropriate. Anyway, we weren't done yet. "I'm going to have to tell you some stuff about Olivia's and my...situation." I eyed the arcade area.

"I admit I have wondered about the different last names." She winced. "But not in, like, a gross way."

I knew what she meant by "gross way." That was the usual way people were interested in me, at least since Sarah's death. There was a luridness to their inquiries that made me bristle. But if Aurora was curious about Liv and me, I knew it wasn't in that way.

"I was thinking next week we could go to our place after class," I said. "We can have dinner and get you oriented."

"Sure."

"The short version is that—" We both must have sensed Olivia's impending return, because we turned at the same time, and sure enough, there was my girl, on her way back looking sulky. I truncated what I'd been going to say, distilling the truth to its essence. "Olivia is *mine*."

Liv slid into the booth next to me a few seconds later, so I didn't have time to be sheepish about my little outburst. I wanted to sling my arm around her shoulders, but she would probably shrug it off, and I was already feeling a bit raw from the whole asking-for-help thing. I wasn't up for adding public humiliation at the hands of a tween to the mix.

Dinner was uneventful, and while the server was clearing the table, I asked, "Who wants dessert?" I turned to Olivia. "Well, I know you do. What about you, Aurora?"

She looked at me kind of intently and answered my question with one of her own. "Did you have a missing tooth when I first met you?"

"Yes!" I laughed and realized that answering a question with another, unrelated question was another quirk of Aurora's.

"Hockey players knock their teeth out a lot, right?"

"Well, I don't know about a lot, but it is an occupational hazard. That one wasn't hockey related, though. Leave it to me to knock a tooth out chopping wood."

"You knocked your tooth out chopping wood? How does that work?"

"I lost my balance as I was swinging the ax back and fell on my face on the chopping block. Anyway, I'm used to it. I lost the tooth next to it years ago, so now I've got two fake ones"— I shot her a wide-lipped smile and pointed at the veneers.

She pressed her hands down flat on the table as if steadying herself.

"There was so much blood," Olivia said matter-of-factly.

"It's OK, though," I assured Aurora, who had gone pale— which made me notice she had a faint sprinkling of freckles across the bridge of her nose. "Got it fixed. Good as new."

If only everything were that easy.

———

On the way home, Olivia and I did the loop around the lake even though it was late. Soon we'd have to put the convertible away for the winter. Hell, soon I wouldn't even be here a good chunk of the time. Lauren wasn't going to do loops around the lake. I mean, she would if I asked her to, but I'd asked for so much already. Anyway, loops around the lake were a Liv-and-me thing.

Olivia seemed to like me a whole lot better in the car than at home. Probably because in the car, with its loud engine, I couldn't ask things like: *You have homework?* I cut the engine in front of the house and spoke quietly, as if the volume of my question would have an impact on the tone of her answer. "Reading responses?"

"Yeah, I have to finish today's." The happiness drained from Olivia's face. As much as I didn't want her to be sad, I would take it. Sad was better than angry.

"The reading or the response?"

"Both."

"You want to shower, then I'll sit with you while you do it?" Would my luck hold? More often than not, at the end of a long day, Olivia lashed out, and it had gotten worse since school had started. Dr. Mursal said it was because there was a lot happening. She said Liv was yelling at me because I was safe, and that that was a good thing. I tried to remember that.

"I *know* how to read, *Mike*."

Nope, my luck was not gonna hold.

"I know you do," I said, ignoring the *Mike*. Olivia had been a year old when I met her. Later, after she and Sarah moved in with me, she'd started calling me Dud, which was how her toddler self had pronounced it. Nothing before or since had made me that giddy. Dud had become Dad, and that had endured until after the crash. Dr. Mursal said we weren't going to care about Olivia's calling me Mike. She said it exactly like that: *We're not going to care.* "It makes her feel like she has some control, and it doesn't do any harm." I wanted to say it did do harm, to me, but I got what she meant, so I kept my mouth shut. I'm known for my coachability, right?

"I thought some company might make the task less painful," I said as I followed Olivia into the house. The task was to read—whatever she wanted—for twenty minutes and write a one-to-two-paragraph response. Olivia's school had a no-homework policy through grade six unless you didn't finish your reading response during reading time at school, which Olivia never did. Which punted it to home, where it had been a nightly battle. I didn't remember this being a problem in past years, but as I was learning, I didn't know everything about how my own household operated. I'd tried buying her magazines, books about dance, you name it, but it was like pulling teeth. "Or I can leave you alone with it, but you're going to have to do it one way or another."

"*Fine*," she huffed. The dog vroomed over to greet her, but she ignored him. Wow, she was *really* mad. He was usually exempt from her crustiness. She stomped off.

I shook off her disdain more easily than usual, because I had a mission. I waited until I heard the shower come on to contemplate the shoes.

One of the startling things about Sarah, early in our dating relationship, had been her love of shoes. In the initial months of my acquaintance with her, she'd been working, so she'd worn runners—I'd spent a lot of time watching her as she paced the diner in pink Skechers, taking orders and shuttling plates to and from the kitchen. I went on to learn that she loved and collected all kinds of shoes—fancy pumps, boots that went over her knees, fashion runners in crazy candy colors.

We had a shoe shelf in the mudroom off the garage. When the shoes would get out of control and end up strewn about willy-nilly, someone, usually me, would get fed up and put them back. I still did that, but now it was only Olivia's and my shoes. The pairs Sarah had in rotation when she died occupied the bottom of the three-row shelf, but they never moved: lavender-and-white checkerboard Vans, canary-yellow Keds, Birkenstocks, and the New Balance runners she wore for actual running. Shoes were such a signature Sarah thing, it had been hard to face getting rid of these remnants of her. So I hadn't.

In the beginning I'd cried a lot, which I guess should be embarrassing, but it had felt like a mechanical, almost automated response. It was an *easy* response, as odd as that sounds. As if it wasn't even being initiated or controlled by me. Your wife dies; you cry.

The hard part was after the crying phase. *What comes next?* That was the scary shit. I imagined it as looking into a black hole, or standing next to an abyss.

Worse even than the idea of teetering at the edge of the abyss was the idea that *I* might be made of the same stuff. Of that same nothingness. Like there were these holes in me I had never noticed before, little pinprick-size voids made of black-hole material. If I stood long enough next to the abyss, I feared those pinpricks would somehow recognize the larger void as the same kind of entity and they'd sort of...ooze together.

And when you discover that you thought you were a regular person but no, you're actually half-missing? You're just a scaffolding where a whole person should be? That is some terrifying shit.

Then I found the pills.

The blister pack of tiny pills labeled with days of the week. A box with the prescription info on it. Reclipsen. Sarah's name, our local pharmacy. "Refills: 6."

At which point I stopped cleaning out Sarah's stuff. I stopped letting Mom do any culling, either. I was afraid of what we might find, of what might be lurking beneath the surface of the life I thought I'd been living. Though I didn't tell my mother that. I let her think my sudden reluctance was about not wanting to let go.

Which wasn't a lie. I *didn't* want to let go. I'd had a vision of my life, my marriage, my future. Those pills, and the sleuthing I'd done later, told me that my vision had been a mirage.

I heard Olivia's footsteps coming down the stairs—for a dancer, she did not tread lightly—which meant I had been standing in the mudroom for longer than I'd realized. Looking at Sarah's shoes made me feel wobbly, like when you're so hungry you get shaky. But there was no amount of food that could fill the voids I had inside me. Pinpricks sound small, but if there are a lot of them, they add up to an alarming amount of empty space.

All right, enough. I looked at the dog, and he gave me a sympathetic woof. I gathered the shoes and took them upstairs and dumped them in a box in my closet. Stowing the shoes in that box and closing the door to the closet made my chest feel like someone was stomping on it, and not in brightly colored canvas shoes but in something closer to the steel-toed boots I wore when chopping wood.

It was necessary, though. Aurora Evans was going to need a place to put her shoes.

4—VOCABULARY LESSONS

RORY

The next Tuesday, I got to the studio earlier than I needed to, because I wanted to talk to Gretchen about my new gig. On weekdays, there was a break between when the little-kid classes ended and when the after-school crews started rolling in.

"I probably should have talked to you first," I said in conclusion. "It's belatedly occurring to me that this might be a conflict of interest."

Gretchen had seemed unfazed as she listened and Swiffered the floor. "How so?"

"Maybe I shouldn't be getting into a side hustle with a student. Is that favoritism? Or perceived favoritism?"

"Hello, this is a suburban strip mall dance studio that was almost a pet groomer's, not a presidential campaign."

"I know, but what will the dance moms think?"

"Once again, I remind you that this is a suburban strip mall dance studio that was almost a pet groomer's." She used the handle of her Swiffer to point at "Miss Miller's Morals," a document the kids called "The Rules" that hung in an ornate gilt frame on the far wall of the studio.

I went over and perused it fondly. All these years later, I still loved looking at it.

Miss Miller's Morals
Everybody is welcome at Miss Miller's.
Everybody can dance.
Dancing is supposed to be fun.
The end.

"Miss Miller's Morals" epitomized why I had taken this job. I had never imagined, after flaming out in New York, that I would set foot in a dance studio again. Dance had beaten me. I had conceded defeat, flown the white flag, total knockout.

But having struck up a friendly acquaintanceship with Gretchen at the Starbucks where I worked, which was near a high school where she'd been doing choreography for a student musical, I allowed myself to be wooed into her employ. I still worked at Starbucks, but I loved teaching—and I loved Gretchen. Like, *loved* her. The night of our job interview, she lured me to her studio and showed me "Miss Miller's Morals." I looked at Gretchen in that moment, her impossibly blue Minnesota-Scandinavian eyes glinting with both passion and kindness, and I'm not saying it was love at (almost) first sight, but I'm not saying it wasn't.

I used to try so hard with Emma, who had gone to the Newberg school with me. We'd roomed together—you know that saying about the devil you know? All those years of classes together in Minnesota, then in New York, and it was so much *effort*, like walking a high wire. With Gretchen, it was just…easy.

"I'm really glad you decided not to go the pet grooming route." Gretchen shared my philosophy on dance. Well, no, I *learned* my philosophy of dance from Gretchen. She danced because she loved it, and she rejected a lot of what she called the culture of dance. I hadn't realized a person could do that. But she also loved cats. To hear her tell it, she'd wanted to be her own boss, and she'd thought, *What can I stand to do all day long?* She'd narrowed it down to cats or dance and ultimately decided that clipping feline toenails was less appealing than wrangling roomfuls of waifs, though she sometimes said, usually when up to her eyeballs in recital tutus, "Maybe I made the wrong choice."

"The only downside I see in your arrangement with our local star athlete is that I wish Ian was around to witness it. He was a hockey fan, wasn't he?" Gretchen wrinkled her nose.

"It's not like that. At *all.*"

"If you say so."

Gretchen, surprisingly, hadn't given me a hard time about my new habit of leaving on Tuesdays with Mike Martin and Olivia, and I wanted to keep it that way. "His wife just died!"

She stopped Swiffering and sobered. "I know, I know." Her serious expression was soon replaced by a mischievous one. "His wife died nine months ago, though. That's almost a year."

"*So,*" I said loudly, derailing the train of thought she'd gotten on, "if you don't see any problem with this gig, I'm going to take it. I like Olivia, they need the help, and not having to buy and insure a car is really going to help with my finances."

"You know you can always pick up Riley's classes, right? Say the word, and I will actually get around to firing her."

Riley was a college student who taught several classes at the studio—when she could be bothered. She was unreliable, and when she did show up, she was often quite obviously hungover. Gretchen had been stressing about whether and how to fire her.

"No, thanks." The answer came as a reflex.

"Still postballet?"

Maybe it was stupid, but when I left ballet, I *left* it. I didn't even want to teach it to kids in a strip mall dance studio. I had settled into teaching tap and jazz, but ballet was a no-go. "Sorry."

"Don't be sorry. Just be you. And don't ever change. 'Cause you're great."

It was on the tip of my tongue to tell her that I might have met Mike Martin before, thirteen years ago in passing at a mall. That I'd manufactured a whole imaginary boyfriend based on that meeting. That I'd used that imaginary boyfriend as an excuse to get out of all sorts of social events at which I was not wanted anyway.

But I was an adult now. I didn't need imaginary people. The fact that I once had was embarrassing.

Imaginary people do have one perk, though: you can abandon them at will, leave them in the past where they belong, with zero consequences.

Or so I had always thought.

———

I started writing my Canadian Boyfriend when I was in high school. I sat in the cafeteria and wrote him letters, and in so doing, I felt less alone. He became a diary. Well, sort of; those letters were half diary, half fiction. Half what was happening, half what I wished were happening.

I stopped writing when I quit ballet. By the end of my time in New York, I was starting to get a little worried about how much I needed him, this fake person I'd created when I was a teenager. About how I was pouring out my heart to him—my fears and humiliations—even as I was making him into the lifeline I so needed. Since ballet had been the source of my problems, I reasoned, quitting ballet should also mean quitting writing. Quitting lying. So when I came home to Minnesota and had it out with my mom, I put the red binder of letters in a box in my closet. Cold turkey.

All of which meant I had never imagined my Canadian Boyfriend, who when I stopped writing to him had still been at the University of Denver—one of the top hockey schools according to my research but also far enough from New York that he was never going to be able to visit—going on to have a pro career. He had *certainly* never grown into an actual adult who might do things like get married and have a kid and live in a fancy house on a lake.

Gretchen's was not the kind of spot that drew people from far away, which was exactly why I was there. So most of the kids at Miss Miller's of Minnetonka lived in or near the well-to-do suburb the studio was named for. And thanks to Wikipedia, I already knew Mike Martin lived on Lake Minnetonka. Still, I went a little wide-eyed when we started passing actual mansions on our way to their house on the lake—or on Crystal Bay, as Olivia informed me from the back seat of the Depression Car. "Lake Minnetonka is actually not one lake, but a collection of kettle lakes, did you know that? Do you know what kettle lakes are?"

I had the vague notion that Lake Minnetonka had a lot of squiggles in it, but I'd never really looked that closely on a map. "I don't, but I bet you can tell me." Spending time outside of class with Olivia had shown me an outgoing side of her I hadn't seen in the studio.

"They're lakes inside depressions left by retreating glaciers," she informed me. "We're doing a geology unit at school."

Mike Martin smirked as he turned up a graveled driveway.

The house was more modest than I'd expected. Made of gray-painted wood accented with white trim, it looked vaguely Cape Cod–ish. "I'll leave the car here since we're driving you home, but let me show you the garage," Mike Martin said.

We went around the side of the house. He fiddled with a keypad, and one of three doors rose. "I'll give you the code, and an opener and all that."

Olivia went inside, leaving us in a garage bigger than my entire apartment. It had bikes mounted on one wall and a truly astonishing amount of firewood stacked against another. There was a home gym in one corner and a ginormous black SUV in another.

"Oh, I don't think I can drive that thing." My parking spot at home was at the end of a row, flush with an exterior wall of one of the buildings, and I was not at all confident about my ability to maneuver that beast into what had already been a snug fit for my old Hyundai Accent, may she rest in peace.

"Oh, no, that's my car. It's for hauling hockey gear around."

"I'm not borrowing the Depression Car!" A loaner was one thing; a loaner vintage Mustang was another.

"I have another car," he said quickly. "It's a . . . normal sedan."

Had he hesitated because he thought I was going to be offended by a "normal sedan"? He had no idea what a step up in the world that would be for me, assuming "normal" meant it didn't have plastic sheeting instead of glass in one of its rear windows, or an honest-to-God cassette deck.

"It's . . . off-site at the moment." He nodded kind of weirdly—as if agreeing with himself?—and added, "I'm getting it tuned up."

I wondered if he was hesitant in talking about this "normal sedan" because it had been his dead wife's car. Sarah Kowalski's car. I was desperately curious about her in a way I hadn't been when she'd been hanging around the studio. I had not found much about her on the internet beyond the fact that she was from Chicago and had been thirty-two when she died. There was some coverage of her wedding with Mike Martin in the Chicago media, but other than that, just obituaries. I remembered Sarah as a pretty, dark-haired, quiet woman. She'd never been in our faces like some of the other moms. I wished I'd paid more attention.

Inside, Olivia was in the mudroom loving on a dog who paused in enjoying its belly rubs to happy-bark at Mike Martin. It started wiggling its torso, and Olivia turned it over, which was when I noticed this wasn't your average dog. "Is that...a bulldog on wheels?"

"It sure is. Aurora, meet Earl 9." Earl 9's legs were strapped into a small wheelchair-type contraption, and once he was upright, he zoomed away after Olivia, front legs pumping and wheels rolling. "When I played in the WHL, my team was the Thompson Bulldogs," Mike Martin said. "They had an elderly mascot who was ready to retire, and I took him." He chuckled. "That Earl and I had bonded."

"*That* Earl?"

"Yeah, that was Earl 7. This is Earl 9. The team mascot is always named Earl. I guess because it's always an English bulldog? They call the dog the Earl of Thompson. Earl 9's career was cut short when he was a puppy—he got hit by a car and was paralyzed. They couldn't find anyone locally to take him, so they called a certain alum known to be a sucker." He smirked self-deprecatingly. "But don't worry about him. He goes where Olivia goes. So he'll be at Lauren and Ivan's when I'm traveling."

Well, if that wasn't the cutest story. "You actually call him Earl 9?"

"Yep." He shrugged.

Inside, the house was stunning. The main area, which was an airy, open-concept kitchen-dining-living situation, was full of warm wooden finishes. A windowed sunroom where Mike Martin installed Olivia with an iPad overlooked the lake. "What can I get you to drink?" he asked as he pulled a tray of bratwurst out of the fridge. "Wine? Beer?"

I hesitated. A cold glass of white wine sounded good, but I didn't want him to think I'd be drinking when I was here, given that my job was to drive his kid around.

"Say yes if you're at all inclined. I made a deal with myself when my wife died that I was only ever going to drink socially. I don't drink on the road, and here it's usually just me and Olivia. So I rarely get to have a beer."

"So I'm your excuse to drink beer."

He shrugged and did the eye-twinkling thing, zapping me with those green kryptonite lasers. And ugh, the *dimple*.

"I'd love a glass of white wine, thanks." I should probably have opted for beer because how wasteful would it be for him to open a bottle of wine so I could have one glass? I was conditioned to be sensitive to people making outlays on my behalf—thanks, Mom. But I had noticed an undercounter wine fridge, and honestly, after visiting the garage, I didn't think I needed to worry about this guy's finances.

"Any preference as to kind? I know nothing about wine. You want to come have a look?"

"Surprise me."

He poured a glass and handed it to me, picked up his beer and the tray, and hitched his head for me to follow him. "Olivia!"

he called as we crossed the living room toward a back door. "Aurora and I are going outside." He paused and listened to the silence. "Acknowledge me. Where will I be if you need me?"

"Outside!" she shouted, and the edge was back in her voice.

He rolled his eyes as we stepped out onto a deck. We were on the top tier of an impressive, multilayered structure that climbed down the house. There were little seating areas on various tiers. "Wow. Cool deck."

"Thanks. I built it myself."

Of course. I almost rolled my eyes.

"Barbecue's down there." He nodded for me to descend to a ground-floor patio. "Or I guess I should say *grill*. In Canada we call it a barbecue, and the act of cooking on it is barbecuing, whereas when I say that here, people think I'm talking about a style of food—you know, like southern barbecue? I had a lot of funny "Who's on First?" conversations when I first went to North Carolina."

I wondered if I'd ever had my Mike use the wrong terminology when I'd been talking about him at school.

"If you sit on the chesterfield, you'll have the best view of the lake. Sorry, sofa. Or I guess couch, as Minnesotans seem to say?"

"Are we having a United Nations vocabulary moment? Allow me to sit on the chesterfield and watch you barbecue our dinner. Who knew Canada was so different?" Apparently not I, who had done actual research on the subject. *Canadian History for Dummies* had sat on my bookshelf next to *Hockey for Dummies*.

I should tell him. Or at least probe a bit. Ask if he'd ever been to Minnesota before he joined the Lumberjacks. If it wasn't for the fact that he was too old to have been the guy at the mall that day, I would have sworn it was him. But it *couldn't* have been. He'd told me he'd only played the one year of high school hockey, and Mall Mike had definitely been too old to be a freshman.

But...how many hockey players from Manitoba named Mike with missing teeth and crazy green eyes were there in the world?

Round and round I went. I told myself to cut it out. I had something else to tell Mike Martin tonight. One bombshell at a time.

Mike Martin lit the grill/barbecue and started loading it with way more brats than three humans could possibly eat, even accounting for one of them being a hulking professional athlete. I took the opportunity to study the house, which had looked modest from the front only because it was oriented toward the lake. It was built into the land such that it was both taller and wider here than on the road side. The whole house had two stories, and about half of it had a third, lower level.

I swiveled to look at the lake, which was calm and dark blue against a lighter-blue sky. The sound of waves lapping the shore was pleasantly lulling. Or maybe that was the wine. I wasn't much of a drinker, so I was a lightweight. I didn't like to drink calories. Not that I was counting them anymore. In theory. But the cold, yellow wine was going down easily, which was just as well, because I was worked up about what was going to come next.

Since it couldn't be avoided, I blurted it out: "I need to tell you something that might make you change your mind about this arrangement, and I need you to know that it's OK to change your mind."

Startled, Mike Martin transferred his attention from the grill to me. "OK."

"I have panic attacks."

"OK," he said again.

I hadn't thought about this aspect of things when he'd asked me to be Olivia's chauffeur. It had only occurred to me later, which was probably a good sign, given that there had been a time when my entire life was ruled by the prospect of having a panic attack.

"Not a lot," I elaborated as he sat across from me. And again, that was a huge improvement. "Only every once in a while." Oh my God, this was so mortifying. It was almost as bad as telling my mom I was quitting ballet. Well, no, nothing was that bad.

"Were you having one the first time we went for ice cream?" he asked, surprising me. I'd expected questions, but I had expected them to be more about the condition itself, how I was treating it, that sort of thing.

"No." I sent myself back to that day. "I was just...really enjoying that ice cream. But I did have one, or the start of one, in the studio once when you were there."

"You did?" He frowned as if he didn't know what I was talking about, which was probably another good sign. "What do you do when you have them?"

I so did not want to talk about this, but it was a fair question. "It depends on the circumstances. I do this thing called the Emotional Freedom Technique, which is—and I'm aware this sounds a bit odd—a pattern of tapping you do on various parts of your body. The point is to introduce a physical sensation. You focus on that and it helps tip your brain out of the spiral it's in."

"That doesn't sound odd."

"No?"

"When your wife dies tragically and unexpectedly, you do a

lot of therapy. I have my own bag of tricks." I didn't know what to say to that. I didn't have to come up with anything, though, because he asked another question. "What happens if you have a panic attack while you're driving? Has that ever happened?"

I could feel myself flushing. Even though I knew with my rational brain that there was no shame in having these struggles, I still hated that this was something I had to deal with. That I couldn't just...get better. "It hasn't. They tend to happen only when I'm with other people."

"But you'd be with Olivia in the car."

"It's more an issue of people watching me." Which sounded dumb, because what was teaching a dance class but being watched by a bunch of people? "People *judging* me." But maybe they weren't. Maybe they never had been. Maybe that had just been my mother. "It's hard to explain. I'm confident driving Olivia wouldn't be a situation that would trigger one, but if it did happen, I'd pull over and do my interventions."

"You'd be able to pull over?"

"Yes. They don't come on like a ton of bricks. There's...a runway of sorts. I can usually stop them before they become full-fledged."

"You stopped the one in the studio you were talking about. You must have, or I'd have noticed it."

"Yes. And if for some reason I couldn't, I'd call for help."

"All right, then."

I blinked, taken off guard. I'd been half-convinced he would fire me before I even started. "That's it?"

"I trust you."

"But—" Why was I arguing? I'd been delighted not to have to add a car loan to my pile of debt. And beyond that, I really did want to help him. Mike Martin, I was learning, had a kind of inner sadness. Except it wasn't sadness exactly, or it wasn't *only* sadness. It was a...blankness that became apparent when his eyes went flat.

"Gretchen speaks very highly of you," he said. "She says you're disciplined and reliable and that you've only missed four days of teaching in the five years she's employed you and that I should definitely hire you but also try to make you take a vacation." He flashed a little smirk.

"You checked up on me!" That explained why Gretchen hadn't been surprised when I'd told her about the offer.

Click-click-click. Out came the full-meal-deal smile, but it disappeared as he grew serious. "I appreciate your telling me about the panic attacks, but I feel like you are a person I can trust. We all have our demons." He glanced away as if contemplating his.

I blew out a breath.

This would be the obvious moment to ask about the mall. I just thought it would...sound so weird. I wasn't ever going to tell him that he—if it had in fact been him—had been the basis for an entire fictional boyfriend. So that left a pathetic girl who remembered a boy she'd met for five minutes thirteen years ago. What was the point? I would have to live with the mystery.

Mike Martin took a pull of his beer, set it on the table, and said, "Now it's my turn to lay some stuff on you that you'll need to know."

"OK."

"Olivia was a year old when I met her mom. She's never met her biological father. She doesn't know any other father but me. She is my daughter. She's *mine*." His voice had gone a little quivery, and he leaned forward as if to punctuate the declaration, like he had last week at Suz's.

Oof. What would it be like to have someone claim you so vehemently? I cleared my throat. "You've adopted her?"

"That part is in process, but I've been granted guardianship. But there was a dispute over that."

"With her biological father?"

"No. No one can find him, and frankly, I hope it stays that way. He fucked off when Sarah got pregnant and was never heard from again." He sneered, making clear his opinion of the guy. "Sarah's parents tried for guardianship when Sarah died, even though Sarah's wishes had been made clear in her will."

Wow. "You don't get along with them, I take it?"

"I've never been a fan, let's say. It's not some big terrible thing, just that Sarah was never close to them. They're old-money, high-society people. Sarah got pregnant when she was twenty-one and single, and they flipped out and disowned her. She didn't see them for a couple years, not until Olivia was three."

"So *they* bailed on Sarah when she got pregnant, too."

"Yes." There came the sneer again. "They did reconcile, though, and by the time we got married, things were back to 'normal.' I never thought they treated Sarah as well as they should have, but I figured it wasn't my call to make. Olivia was with them in Chicago when Sarah died. Sarah had dropped her with them and flown up to Montreal." He looked out at the lake as he continued. "Ivan and I had a game there and two days off afterward, so Sarah and Lauren were going to join us for a getaway. Sarah rented a car at the airport, but she spun out on some black ice on her way to the hotel."

Oh God. I wanted to say how sorry I was, but I thought of that woman at Suz's. I didn't think Mike Martin would want to hear condolences. He was telling me this for a practical reason.

He cleared his throat and returned his attention to me. "Sarah's parents didn't want to give Olivia back when I flew down to Chicago to get her."

Wow. "Really?"

"Yeah, it was a whole thing. To be fair, they loved—love—Olivia. And they're her grandparents. I was never suggesting they be given no access, but there was *no way*"—he pounded the coffee table—"they were taking her from me."

"And you won?"

"There wasn't a trial, so technically there was no winning or losing. There was a lot of legal wrangling, though, because although I'd been named guardian in Sarah's will, she had never sought to terminate Olivia's sperm donor's rights. So there was a lot of back and forth, including Sarah's parents filing for guardianship. That was dispensed with pretty easily given the will, but then they invoked grandparents' rights. We sorted it all out in court-ordered mediation. They get her for five days starting at noon on Christmas Day, and a week in the summer. I was never suggesting they not see her at all, but the guardianship filing had me spooked as hell. They tried to argue that not only was I not a blood relative, but all my travel made me a less good prospect—they're retired and have nothing but time."

"I have to say, on paper that's not a crazy argument."

"I know. The whole thing about my going back to hockey is..." He blew out a breath. "Complicated. I was never so scared in my life as during those mediation sessions. I half expected them to fail, and that we'd end up in court. Honestly, I was surprised when the mediator said Olivia should stay with me, and even more surprised when Sarah's parents accepted it."

"What do you think swayed everything your way?"

"Olivia."

"Really?" I hadn't expected that answer.

"Yeah. I mean, I threw everything I had at the situation. Money, of course, and an army of lawyers, but I also told the mediator I *would* quit hockey if I had to. We argued that after having lost her mom, the best thing for Olivia was to stay with me, the person she knew as her dad, in Minnesota. Lauren was really close with Sarah, so she was already like a second mom to Olivia, and she agreed to take Olivia while the team's on the road. Olivia's grandparents had raised concerns about a nanny who didn't know Olivia spending so much time with her. Lauren came to a session and helped us quash that argument, painting an idyllic picture of the girls hanging out when the guys were off playing hockey."

"So Lauren saved you?" This Lauren lady sounded pretty amazing. "I thought you said it was Olivia's doing?"

"Lauren did a great job, but ultimately, I think it came down to Olivia. She hadn't been at any of the sessions, but she asked me if she could come to one. In consultation with the mediator, I agreed—kind of against my better judgment; I was trying to keep from her how heated things were getting. We got there, and she asked if she was going to get a say. 'Yes, of course,' the mediator said. 'You can say whatever you want. Do you want to speak to me privately?' Olivia said no. I'm not going to lie; I panicked. Things have not been great between Olivia and me since Sarah died. But she told the mediator she wanted to live with me. The mediator asked her why. She looked right at me and said, 'Because he's my dad. Why would I not want to live with my dad?'"

I had noticed, a few times in the past month, Mike Martin's eyes going flat. Now they were doing the opposite. The gold flecks in them looked like they were about to start sparking.

"Olivia's lucky to have you."

"*I'm* lucky to have *her*." He swallowed hard but then did that little smirk of his. "But I don't want to paint too rosy a picture here. As you might have picked up, she's not doing super well—emotionally or academically."

"She's had a big loss—and she's, what? Eleven? I teach a lot of tweens and young teens, and it's an age of upheaval under the best of circumstances."

"My point is, she's on her best behavior at class. She likes you. But around here, the only creature she's consistently decent to is Earl 9. As she spends more time with you and grows more comfortable, I think it's entirely likely that her inner shithead will come out."

I smiled. "I think I can handle it."

"Anyway, I'm telling you this long, sordid story because I thought you should know what's going on. Sarah's parents FaceTime Olivia a lot, which is fine, but I'd rather they not do that when you're here. They want to talk to Olivia about Sarah *all* the time. I'm not opposed to that, if Olivia is into it, but it only seems to make her sad. Sadder. *Madder*." He blew out a breath. "It's hard to explain."

"No, I get it. Trust me, I get it." He raised his eyebrows inquisitively, and I said, "I have personal experience with toxic mothers."

"Ah. I'm sorry." I shrugged and gestured for him to continue. "I'm making all this sound more dramatic than it is. Basically, it's going to be: Drive Olivia here and encourage her to do her homework until Lauren shows up. Don't answer calls from Sarah's parents. The hardest thing will be trying to get Olivia to do these reading responses she has to do every night."

"Great. Anything else I need to know? House rules, anything like that?"

"I'll get you keys and garage and alarm codes—and the car, of course. Everything else I figure we can muddle through as we go, except…" He tilted his head back and looked at the sky.

"Yes?"

His eyes had gone flat when he righted his head. "I really fucking hate liars, so don't lie to me, OK?"

Whoa. "I…"

His eyes went back to normal, and he shook his head sheepishly. "Sorry. That was…" He waved a hand in the air. "Not about you. That was about me and some of my shit. I just…I want to know if stuff happens, OK? I want to be in the loop."

I looked at him for a long time. I almost told him. But then I didn't. He was talking about Olivia. He'd want to know if Olivia was doing her homework. If she missed him. If she was OK.

Or so I told myself.

———

I hadn't told Gretchen about dinner at Mike Martin's house that evening. And I told Gretchen everything. Which was why it was a bit awkward that when Mike Martin dropped me off, Gretchen was standing outside my building doing something with her phone. I got mine out, realizing I'd unintentionally ignored it all evening. There was a series of texts from Gretchen beginning with one saying she had an idea for the Tap 3s for the holiday recital and a profile of a Tinder guy she wanted me to weigh in on, escalating into demands to know why I was ignoring her, and finishing with I'm done at the studio, and I'm coming over.

Even though it was starting to get dark, Mike Martin and I had made the trip with the convertible top open at my request.

There was something so compelling, so freeing, about cruising along with the top down, as if you were a person who was immune to the elements.

"Hey, Miss Miller!" Mike Martin called, and Gretchen raised her eyebrows in a way that would look benign to not-in-the-know onlookers but I recognized as her the-plot-thickens face.

Gretchen did not speak as we climbed the stairs to my apartment, but I could *feel* the questions emanating from her. When we got inside, she dropped her dance bag and lay down flat on the carpet in my empty living room. "I know I told you earlier to get some furniture as a way to move on after Ian," she said to the ceiling, "but upon further reflection, I am digging this empty space. It's got a Zen vibe."

I sat next to her on the beige carpet. "There's no point in getting new furniture until I know the specs of my new place." I'd been apartment hunting, but not very seriously. I needed to step up the search now that the end of my lease was looming.

Gretchen sat up suddenly and said, with faux innocence, "Did you have a nice evening?"

I smiled. Her question was intrusive and a little bit snarky, and I loved it. Sometimes it blew my mind that Gretchen Miller was my best friend. Sometimes it blew my mind that I had a best friend, period.

I don't mean this to sound like a huge sob story. I hadn't been bullied in high school, not overtly. I just hadn't...had friends. Or fit in. I'd never learned how to. How could I have when I spent every nonschool weekday hour at ballet and my weekends at the mall? And as the school started to make accommodations for me so I could be in professional productions, the idea took hold that I thought I was better than everyone else, and my isolation intensified.

I was friendly with a few girls at ballet, but it wasn't like we were hanging out in the real world. We were more like fellow soldiers. And then in New York, well, I was too busy falling apart.

So falling into best-friendship with Gretchen had been a surprise, but probably the greatest one of my life. I still remember the first day she called me her best friend—like, out loud. She'd said it in passing to a parent at a studio open house—"Miss Rory, my best friend, has an impressive dance résumé." I had only ever seen best friends on TV or read about them in books. The Baby-Sitters Club. Or even, from my lonely only-child vantage point, Laura, Mary, and Carrie Ingalls—sisters but also friends. Girls who braided each other's hair, adopted orphaned racoons, and called each other their rides-or-dies in a Ye Olde Frontier sort of way.

Maybe I should have invented Gretchen when I was in high school instead of Mike Martin.

"Did you have a nice evening?" Gretchen repeated when I didn't answer the first time.

"Cool your jets. He had me over so he could orient me."

I expected her to launch an interrogation, but she just said, "Where was Olivia when he dropped you off?"

"With a neighbor she's going to be staying with when Mike is on the road."

She didn't say anything more, but to make sure we were done with the topic of Mike Martin, I prodded her arm. "So let's see this Tinder profile." Getting Gretchen started on the indignities of modern dating, and the mediocrity of modern men, was a surefire way to distract her from any wildly inaccurate inferences she might be tempted to make about Mike Martin and me.

"Right!" She futzed with her phone, and when she turned it

to me, the screen was filled by a photo of a man in a suit with a caption that read, "Talon, 39."

"Is that...his name?"

"It sure is."

"His real name?"

"Yes! I asked him exactly that when we were messaging, and he sent me a picture of his driver's license."

"That seems..."

"...unwise?" she supplied cheerily.

"I mean, *I* know you're not going to steal his identity and ruin his life, but *he* doesn't know that."

"Talon is a mystery. On the one hand, he's kind of dumb. On the other, he's apparently some kind of high-finance stock trader dude."

"Huh."

"So I have to go out with him, right?"

"I don't see how you can pass up a date with a dumb stock trader named Talon."

"I mean, you're the one always telling me my standards are too high."

"I don't think I've ever said it in exactly those words." But I'd thought it in exactly those words. Gretchen hadn't had a boyfriend in all the time I'd known her. She *dated* all the time—she was on all the apps—but no one ever seemed to stick. "If there was a 'Miss Miller's Morals for Men' list, it would have ten pages of criteria," I teased.

"No, it would just be 'Must love cats. Don't be a dick.'" She paused. "And also 'Have a dick.'" She snorted. "'Must love cats. Have a dick, but don't *be* a dick.'" I laughed as she made a silly, self-deprecating face. "But I'm taking your point. I'm going to give Talon the Trader a chance." She grew serious.

"I think maybe you and I need to meet somewhere in the middle. I can have lower standards—slightly lower—and you can have higher standards."

Gretchen had never been the president of the Ian fan club. She had always been accusing me of being too eager to please, too quick to forgive when we had fights. Too willing to let him leave me with an apartment I couldn't afford when technically both our names were on the lease.

She wasn't wrong.

And weirdly, even though it had been inconvenient to have my best friend openly disapprove of my boyfriend, I'd always found it mind-blowing but strangely refreshing how, in the land of Midwestern passive aggression, Gretchen always said what she meant.

"Anyway," she said, "look at you. Not even two months post-Ian, and a hot, rich hockey player moves in to fill the void."

"Get up and show me your brilliant recital idea for the Tap 3 kids," I said, instead of arguing with her about Mike Martin.

She hopped up. "OK, so my idea is it's an all–Go-Go's recital."

"I don't know that many Go-Go's songs, but I love the idea."

"You were too busy being immersed in Tchaikovsky to know the Go-Go's," she said, executing a purposefully affected series of glissades. "But also I suppose you're too young."

We worked on some of her ideas, laughing and dancing together, and when we ran out of steam, she hit me with her signature "You're the best" on her way out the door.

As I got ready for bed, I thought about what it meant to be "the best" in Gretchen's estimation and to be someone Mike Martin could trust.

It occurred to me that I would be neither of those things if I had stayed in New York.

Dear Mike,

I've been putting off writing this letter, I guess because things don't feel real until I tell them to you. Which is normally a good thing. But this...I would rather this not be real.

But here it is: I had a panic attack yesterday. I was at a costume fitting for the spring ballet. You know how I'm Rosaline but I'm understudying Juliet? Juliet's costume doesn't fit me. I could tell it wouldn't, but they kept saying that I was almost certainly not going to have to step in, so if they didn't have to make me my own costume, it would be so much less hassle. They tried to stuff me in it, and they asked me to do part of "Juliet's Variation," and it was just too tight. My chest felt like it was imploding all of a sudden, and I was crying, except no sound was coming out because I couldn't breathe. They called an ambulance. I thought I was going to die. But no, the doctors ran a bunch of heart tests, and I'm fine. Panic attack. They told me to start doing yoga.

I guess the only good part is that on the way back to the studio, I asked the teacher who'd come with me if we had to tell my mom. She said, "I'm not sure that would do anyone any good." So we didn't.

What I want to know is do you ever feel this way in hockey?

Love you to the moon and back,
Rory

P.S. Thank you for the charm bracelet! I should have opened with that! It's a little lightness in all this junk—I look down at it and it gives me a little lift. Emma asked me, in a snotty way, about it, implying that a Snoopy charm was immature. How much did I love telling her it symbolized my first kiss with my Canadian Boyfriend at the Camp Snoopy amusement park at the Mall of America?!

5 — FAILED BALLERINA

MIKE

I'd been thinking about the concept of panic attacks since Aurora and I spoke about them. I had my share of demons, but I'd never had a panic attack. But a couple weeks later, I came as close as I ever have on the flight to San Jose for our first away game. I was sitting by Ivan, as per usual, and Badger was acting like an idiot in the row ahead of us, telling off-color jokes to his seatmate, also as per usual.

Everything was the same, yet nothing was the same.

Sarah was dead, her parents were on my ass, and I'd been "invited" to a meeting next week with Olivia's teacher to discuss "behavioral barriers to her academic progress."

Also, I really missed my mom.

Sometimes, when I was teetering at the edge of the abyss, I did this thing where I concentrated on a bad feeling in order to distract myself from another, worse feeling. Missing my mom was an entirely different thing from missing Sarah. This trick was my own little invention. I hadn't told Dr. Mursal about it. I didn't want her to pronounce it junk science and make me stop.

My mom ran a home day care, had since I was a kid. She

was sixty-one and hadn't planned on retiring anytime soon. She and my dad had stubbornly refused my attempts to help them out, beyond the Tim Hortons franchise my brother and I bought that my dad ran. That had been a huge, uncharacteristic coup, and we'd only succeeded because we'd framed it as an investment. But when Sarah died, Mom spent two weeks closing down her day care, flew to Minnesota, and settled in to stay with Liv and me. She cooked. She helped me get the homeschooling stuff organized. She made me lift in the garage and go running with Ivan, insisting that I couldn't get so out of shape that I had trouble going back to hockey in the fall—like Dr. Mursal, she seemed to think quitting was out of the question.

In short, she, with her signature mixture of tenderness and tough love, was an enormous help. Until, according to her, she wasn't. "I'm not helping anymore; I've become a crutch." She gave me two weeks' notice as if quitting a job, told me it was time for me to start getting ready for school and hockey and for her to reopen her day care for the coming school year.

She was right. I barely knew how to cook. I didn't know there was a dress code at Miss Miller's—and once I got that figured out, it turned out the outfits weren't the same for tap and ballet.

But damn, I missed Mom. And not only, or even primarily, because she was so helpful. I, a grown-ass thirty-four-year-old man, missed my mom so much it sometimes became a physical ache.

But here's the key: being in that place, aching there, was a lot less bad than what happened when I swapped out "missing Mom" for "missing Sarah." There were still moments, after all these months, when the combined forces of loss and betrayal knocked the wind out of me, emptied my body out, made me aware of those little holes inside me that needed filling with... something. Air, I supposed, to begin with, so I concentrated on taking deep breaths.

I felt a hand grab mine.

Ivan. There he was, same as ever, with his shaggy eyebrows and almost-black eyes. I looked at his hand on mine—he had probably noticed I was freaking out—and he let go. We didn't do stuff like this. I wasn't on social media; I kept my shit locked down. But when Ivan first came to Minnesota, there had been articles about our so-called bromance. That's what the public called it when men on the same sports team were friends and expressed affection or admiration for each other. I was fine with the label. The funny part, though, was that Ivan and I had never had a particularly deep relationship. We'd just clicked, from the moment the surly Russian and I had been assigned to room together on our first away game when we were playing in Chicago. After he came to the Lumberjacks and I lured him to my corner of the Twin Cities, we went running together almost every morning we were home. I taught him to fish, and more days than not in the offseason, we'd be out on the lake.

Ivan and I were a quantity-time duo rather than a quality-time duo, is the point. We hadn't really talked about Sarah's death and its fallout. Hell, Lauren knew more, directly from my mouth, about how I felt than Ivan did. *She* was the one who had rushed up and wrapped me in her arms when the news of the accident had reached us at that hotel in Montreal.

But Ivan was a smart guy. He was observant. That's why he was such a good defenseman—he could read plays and just *know* where a puck was going. His grabbing my hand as we sat on the tarmac waiting to push back from the gate was a lifeline.

It made me think of Aurora and her tapping therapy, a physical sensation being used to interrupt a panic spiral. It startled me enough to turn my attention away from the abyss.

Then good old Badger finished the job.

When Badger joined the team, he'd explained that his nickname referenced his time at the University of Wisconsin, but I quickly discovered it was an apt moniker for the dude in other ways, namely that he did not hesitate to badger the shit out of everyone both on and off the ice. He was always bugging you to switch seats, or rooms, or dinners with him. "Order envy," he'd declare, and he'd try to make me take his risotto inflected with truffle whatever in exchange for my steak salad.

"Hey, Martin." He popped up over the back of the seat in front of me. I wondered if he'd seen the hand-holding thing. That wasn't the kind of thing Badger would let slide.

But I went with it. Badger was a distraction that would pull me even further back from the edge. "Yeah, what?"

"Now that you're free of the old ball and chain, you gotta come out with us. Get yourself some puck bunny action."

I unbuckled my seat belt and retracted my arm in a flash, fully intending to punch him, but Ivan, with his defensive Spidey-sense, intercepted me. Ivan and I were never paired these days, but it was almost like we *were* on the ice together, our bodies working together for the desired outcome. "Yeah, OK, OK," I said once I realized what an idiot I was being.

"Sorry, man," Badger muttered. "That was, uh, not cool of me." The thing was, he *was* sorry. He was young and stupid, but his heart was in the right place. Badger and the rest of the team never made the fake-sorry face, which was something I appreciated the hell out of. That was a big part of why I was back.

Badger was still looking at me, stricken. There was no precedent for me reacting like this. I hated that people felt like they had to walk on eggshells around me, but I also wasn't sure what choice they had, given that I was, objectively, highly breakable.

"*I'm* sorry," I said to Badger as I buckled myself back in. "That was way out of line."

Badger looked like he was going to say something more, but my phone dinged with a text from Aurora that I fumbled to open. I could already tell I was going to treat texts from Aurora—and Lauren—like personal summons letters from the league commissioner.

"We good?" Badger asked.

"Yeah." I waved him off.

Aurora: Hi. One of the headlights burned out in your car today, so I took it to your mechanic. Just wanted you to know. All sorted, but I feel like an idiot that I have incurred a car-related expense on day one.

I smiled at the way she was calling it my car when I had been behind its wheel for all of the fifteen minutes it had taken to deliver it from the dealership to her building.

Had I bought a car for Aurora Evans? Yes I had.

Had I lied about the whole thing to make her think I was lending her a car I already owned? Yes I had. I saw it as an investment in setting Olivia and me up for success. I would have paid any amount for that, so a two-year-old Hyundai Elantra was nothing. (Had I bought a Hyundai Elantra because it had a Top Safety Pick+ rating from the Insurance Institute for Highway Safety? Had I bought a *two-year-old* Elantra because I thought Aurora would be skeptical if I gave her a brand-new one? Yes and yes.)

Mike: No problem. These things happen. You used the card I
gave you, right?

After some arguing, Aurora had agreed to accept a credit
card to use for gas and Olivia-related expenses. I'd encouraged
them to keep up the ice-cream tradition, for example.

Aurora: I didn't. I haven't even had the car for a week!

Mike: But that's what it's for!

Aurora: I know. I should have used the card. I will next time.

I would reimburse her but decided to let it drop for now.

Mike: Hey, can I ask you a favor? Can you text me tomorrow
night after Lauren gets Olivia? Let me know how Olivia
seemed to you? I know I'm being paranoid...

Aurora: Not paranoid. It's a big change for you guys.
Of course I'll text.

————

When we got to the hotel room, I sat down for a remote session
with Dr. Mursal. She and I had agreed to keep to our schedule
as much as possible while I was on the road.

"Hi, Mike. How's it going?"

"I should just quit."

"Let's talk about this again."

I smiled at that "again." That was classic Dr. Mursal. *This
is a settled question, you fool, but sure, let's rehash it; and by the*

way, I cost two hundred bucks an hour. She would never say it that way, but I appreciated the subtext. She was supposed to be Olivia's therapist—and she was—but having sat in on their first few sessions and determined that I liked Dr. Mursal better than the dude I was supposed to be seeing, I'd asked her to take me on, too. She didn't usually see adults in her current practice, but, as I pointed out from my research into her background, she was qualified to do so. If I'd had an image, before all this, of what psychologists were like, I would have said they had plants in their offices and spent a lot of time saying, *Hmm, let's explore that.* Dr. Mursal had snacks in her office, asked me specific questions, gave me bits of actionable homework—*ask someone besides Lauren and Ivan for help*, for example—and sometimes directly *told* me shit I did not want to hear.

Also, she didn't give a crap about hockey. I once asked her why, and she said, "I'm from Somalia." When I'd looked at her like, *So?* she'd added, "It's hot there." And when I'd pointed out that I used to play for Tampa, she'd said, "It's hot, *and* my main focus at the time was not dying in the war." So I'd said, "Touché," and enjoyed the fact that I was just another guy to her.

"My sense," she said, leaning forward and examining me through the camera, "is that you're feeling some emotions associated with your first trip, and that instead of dealing with them, you're jumping to the idea of quitting."

"It would be so much easier. I don't need the money."

"But *would* it be easier?" she pressed. "Logistically, perhaps, but would it be emotionally easier?"

"Probably for Olivia."

"We're talking about you now. We've established that you have a deep, profound love for what you do, that hockey is more than a job. We've established that your team is your community. We've established that it's time for you to start moving on from questions you can't answer."

"Well, I think I've answered the big question."

"You haven't. You can't answer it without a time machine. You can't answer it without Sarah. Therefore, it is unanswerable, and you have to find a way to be OK with that."

"I *have* answered it, though." I was a big fan of Dr. Mursal, but she and I did not see eye to eye on this topic. "Sarah was lying to me."

"It may not be so cut-and-dried."

"How is it not cut-and-dried? I thought we were trying for kids. I thought we were on the same page." That Montreal trip had been timed—pointlessly—for when Sarah was ovulating. Which Dr. Mursal knew. "Why are you always taking her side?"

"I'm not taking her side. There are no sides." She paused. "But if there *were* sides, you know I'd be on yours."

"Yeah. I mean, I'm the one paying you, right?" I was trying to make her laugh, but it didn't work. Dr. Mursal wasn't humorless, but she kept our sessions focused.

"My point is that yes, you know Sarah was lying about being on the pill. You know she had agreed to a course of action she was undermining." I winced. Hearing it said so plainly was painful, but it was an oddly welcome sort of pain. This straight talk was why I liked Dr. Mursal. "What you don't know, what you'll never know, is *why.*

"I don't think having this conversation again is the best use of our time today," she went on. "Can we agree to shelve it and focus on the more immediately relevant point, which is that you're feeling as if you may need to quit hockey?"

"Yeah, OK." Dr. Mursal had encouraged me to go back this season. She'd told me I'd been in survival mode, that I'd been prioritizing Olivia, and that while that strategy had been fine for the short term, it couldn't go on forever—it was as if she and my mom had ganged up on me. She'd said that since I was a veteran who had always embraced the role of looking after the rookies, it would be good for me to return. To be needed. Then she'd asked a question, which had sealed the deal: "If you don't go back, what are you going to do all day when Olivia's in school?"

My answer had been: Stare into the abyss. Fall into the abyss. *Become* the abyss.

When I thought about people dying of a broken heart, it was always really old people. "They were married for sixty years," the neighbor would be quoted as saying in the newspaper. "He didn't know how to live without her." It wasn't that, for me. It was that I was always standing a little too close to the abyss. I *couldn't* fall in. It would mesh with all the little voids inside me so easily. And then where would Olivia be?

That wasn't a rhetorical question. The answer was: with Sarah's parents.

So, motivated by fear, I'd allowed myself to be coached. I'd listened to Dr. Mursal when she said I should go back to work. She'd also said a lot of stuff about it being OK to be mad at Sarah even as I missed her, and OK to want things for myself.

I'd listened to my mom, who was always saying that thing about the only way out being through.

"Let's talk about what's happening that's making you say it would be easier to quit," Dr. Mursal said, back in the reality of a hotel room in San Jose where I was still so far from through that it freaked me out if I faced it head-on.

So I didn't face it. I answered the question in front of me. "Nothing's happening. I just got here." Well, I had almost hit Badger, and I should probably fess up about that, but I decided to wait until next week when my appointment would be in person and I could eat pretzels while confessing my Rocky Balboa moment.

"What's happening in your *mind*?" she asked. "Not as it relates to Sarah, but to your return to hockey."

"I'm worried about Olivia. I can't fall asleep at night, I'm so worried about leaving her."

"But you trust Lauren."

"Yes."

"What words did you use to describe Lauren when we were first talking about Olivia staying with her?"

"I said she was the best thing that ever happened to the best man I know," I recited obediently. Dr. Mursal had often had me repeat that line in the run-up to the season.

"Is it Tuesday you're worried about? Olivia's time with…" She shuffled through her notes. "Aurora?"

"No. I trust her, too."

"Why?"

"She's been Olivia's dance teacher for years, and I don't know, I just like her."

"Why?"

"Well, mostly I like that she doesn't care that I'm a hockey player. But also…" I thought about how to explain it. "I like that she sometimes answers a question with another, totally unrelated question."

"Can you give me an example?"

I cast my mind back. "We were eating ice cream once—in the convertible—and she had an…exaggerated reaction to her first bite." By which I meant she looked like she was having an orgasm, but that was not a clinically relevant detail. "I asked her if everything was OK. Instead of answering, she said, 'Why do you call this the Depression Car?' It was such an out-of-the-blue question."

"But was it really?"

"Well, it was unrelated to what was happening."

"But what if you zoom out and think more generally about what was happening? *Was* the question so misplaced?"

"I guess not?"

"It sounds as if Olivia is in the hands of two women you respect and trust."

"Yes." I could not argue with that.

"Why don't we talk more about this idea of quitting once you've actually played, are home, and can assess how things went, both for you and for Olivia?"

I sighed, and it felt good. Sometimes talking to Dr. Mursal made me sigh in a satisfying way, as if I'd been flitting along over the surface of my life like a kite over the lake on a windy day, but then I'd suddenly fall back into my body. It was a bit painful to land like that, but the relief outweighed the pain. "Dr. Mursal, are you saying I shouldn't make a grand pronouncement about my plan for the future failing when I'm only five minutes into that plan?"

"That is what I'm saying." We'd been at this long enough that I could recognize her I'm-trying-not-to-smile face. I didn't see it often, but it was gratifying when I did.

I glanced at the time—we only had a couple of minutes left. "How's Olivia doing? Did she seem OK today?" She'd had a lunchtime appointment that Lauren had taken her to.

"You know I can't answer that."

That was another thing I liked about Dr. Mursal. She was scrupulous about patient confidentiality. Well, I *didn't* like it, but I did.

"I hope your game goes well," she said. "What do you say in hockey? Break a leg?"

I grinned. "Yeah, maybe not that, but thanks."

―――――

Dr. Mursal couldn't tell me how Olivia was doing, but Aurora could, and she did the next evening. I read her texts in the locker room after the game.

> **Aurora:** All fine here. We went for ice cream. Olivia says she doesn't have homework. I pressed a little on the reading responses you talked about, but she says she did it at school. Now we're watching Fuller House.

The bit about being done with the reading response was almost certainly a lie, but I didn't expect Aurora to be a human lie detector.

> **Aurora:** Also, I'm really sorry, but I broke one of your glasses—one of the short blue ones. Can you let me know where you got them and I'll replace it?

Ah, my no-lying outburst had her confessing this minor-league shit. I felt bad about that.

There was a third and final text time-stamped an hour later:

> **Aurora:** I'm back at my place now. Lauren came to get Olivia, and they were going to pick up pizza. I think our first night together was a success!

I waited until I was back in my hotel room to reply.

> **Mike:** Thanks for the info. Glad all is well. Don't worry about the glasses.

I wanted to ask so many questions. *Did Olivia ask about me? Did she seem like she missed me? Or was blind with rage at me?* But I needed to take *everything's fine* for an answer.

Mike: Sorry to be so late replying, btw. Your texts came in during the game.

Aurora: Which you lost, I see, according to Google. Bummer.

Mike: Eh, it's all right.

Aurora: I hope getting back to it was…okay? Fun? Not terrible?

I paused, considering. I'd been consumed with the question of whether to resume my career, but only in terms of its effect on the grief situation: how Olivia would handle my absence, whether going back would occupy me sufficiently to keep me out of the abyss. I hadn't thought about the game itself today. How it had made me feel.

Mike: You know what? I don't even know how it was.

Mike: That makes no sense, I realize. I've been thinking a lot lately about hockey. Why I play it. What I get from it— besides a salary. But today I kind of zoned out, I guess?

Mike: That sounds dumb. Sorry. It's only a game. No need to get all philosophical about it.

Aurora: You're talking to a failed ballerina, so I get it.

Mike: Really?

I was intensely curious about that. I'd wondered how she'd gone from the Newberg Ballet School to teaching tap in suburban Minnesota.

Aurora: Really. I had to ask myself all those questions about what I was doing and why. I ended up leaving ballet school halfway through.

I wanted to know more, but there was a rap on my door—Ivan picking me up for dinner. I answered it and said, "Almost ready."

Mike: Well, thank you. I appreciate your help more than you know.

Mike: And sorry about Fuller House. It's terrible.

Aurora: It really is.

Mike: I should have warned you. I put up with it because it's one of the few times I get to see Olivia uncomplicatedly happy. But there's no reason for you to. She LIKES you.

Aurora: It's okay. I have a scheme as it relates to Fuller House.

Mike: ??

Aurora: Stay tuned.

6 — HALF PINT

MIKE

I did stay tuned. And to my surprise, over the next month, two things happened. First, Aurora got my daughter into *Little House on the Prairie*. Like, the show from the 1980s. American pioneers. Pa and Half Pint and Walnut Grove and panning for fool's gold and mean Nellie Oleson at the general store. Aurora owned the entire collection on DVD, which struck me as charmingly old school.

Second, Aurora and I became texting buddies.

Which was nice, because when I hatched this whole plan, I hadn't thought through the fact that it would mean the end of my seeing Aurora. And apparently I hadn't realized how much I *liked* seeing Aurora. She had the car now, so on Tuesdays when I was in town, she didn't need a ride home. I only ever saw her at the studio when my days off overlapped with Olivia's classes. I'd taken to studying Aurora's teaching technique. OK, I'd taken to studying *her*. But not like that. Or not *only* like that. I wasn't, to my great surprise, as dead inside in that regard as I had been over the past year. Aurora was a striking woman, with her leotards and her Snoopy bracelet and her long, muscular legs. I had always thought of dancing, ballet in particular, as kind of lightweight. I could not have been more wrong. I'd fallen down a ballet YouTube rabbit hole on a recent trip, and holy cow, did those people have legs.

Sometimes, unbidden, the memory would flash through my mind of the first day I'd met Aurora, when she'd kicked up her leg from behind the reception desk, so high and so suddenly. She'd only been showing me her Band-Aid, and jokingly at that. But I'd been so startled. Shocked to life, even if only for a moment, and being alive had been such a different thing from standing vigil at the abyss.

The texting—aside from our usual Tuesday check-ins—started one Saturday when I was in Nashville. I had to ask for help. Again. It was hard, but a bit less so this time.

Mike: This is a big ask, and don't feel pressured to say yes. But if you're free this afternoon, any chance you could get Olivia from Lauren's and take her to dance and back? Lauren has been hit with a migraine and can't drive. Not a big deal for Olivia to skip class, just thought I'd ask. I'd pay you for your time, obviously.

She had agreed, and after our afternoon game, I had texts waiting for me.

Aurora: Hey, class is underway, and all is well. Olivia wants to spend some time at home afterward. I'm happy to hang out with her there for a while this evening. Is that okay? It would give Lauren a longer break, too.

Mike: You are an angel.

Mike: A well-compensated angel.

Aurora: You don't have to pay me! I'm having a grand time, sitting here gabbing with Gretchen.

I had come to understand that Aurora was prickly about money. After that first trip when she'd broken that glass, I'd come home to find a new package of four on my kitchen counter even though I hadn't answered her question about what store they'd come from. And she had resisted when I'd reimbursed her for the broken headlight she'd paid for.

Back at the hotel, I checked in.

Mike: Are you guys still there? Would it be weird if I FaceTimed? I try to catch Olivia every night when I'm on the road.

Aurora: Still here, and not weird. I'm not sure she'll talk to you, as that would require interrupting Little House, but let's try.

"Hi," Aurora whispered when she picked up, her expressive face filling the screen of my phone. "This is a big episode." She waggled her eyebrows. "She's riveted." She reversed the phone to show Olivia seated cross-legged on the chesterfield, staring at the TV as if hypnotized, then turned the phone back around. "Did you win?"

"Nope."

"Did you...do any important hockey things?" She made a self-deprecating face.

"I got an assist."

"Good for you." She tried to get Olivia to talk to me, but all I got were monosyllabic answers. Eventually I gave up, and we said goodbye.

But Aurora and I kept texting.

Aurora: Sorry that was a bust. You want me to turn off the TV, and we can try again?

Mike: God, no. You've got her onto something other than Fuller House. Little > Fuller when it comes to fictional houses.

Mike: How'd you get into Little House anyway? I remember watching it in rerun format when I was a kid, but aren't you too young for it?

What I really wanted to know was how old she was, but I didn't want to ask outright. I guessed thirty, tops.

Aurora: My mom was into it. She grew up near De Smet, South Dakota, where the real-life Ingalls family went after Walnut Grove. There's a summer pageant there, and my mom played Laura one year. She used to profess to hate the show, but we always watched it in syndication. She harbored show-business dreams at one point.

Mike: What happened to them?

Aurora: She got pregnant accidentally with me.

Wow, OK.

Mike: So what did she do instead? For a job, I mean? Or what does she do? I don't mean to talk about her in the past tense.

Aurora: You mean besides being a retired dance mom? She's a real estate agent.

Aurora: You know what? Let's talk about something else.

I smiled, stupidly pleased she wanted to keep talking to me. I wasn't sure why. It wasn't as if I were lacking social outlets. A bunch of the guys were going to dinner later. But texting with Aurora was...nice. I decided not to interrogate the feeling. Nice, these days, was novel.

Mike: So what's Half Pint up to?

Aurora: This is an Albert episode. He's addicted to morphine!

Mike: I remember this one! He barfs all over the road!

Aurora: Haha, yes! I probably should have run it by you first. I forgot how dark some of these episodes are. Now you're going to have to have a big "don't do drugs" convo.

Mike: It's okay. Unfortunately, Olivia is used to dark.

Aurora: Yeah. I'm sorry.

Mike: It's fine. Well, it's not. But it's life.

Aurora: By the way, I bought Olivia a set of the Little House books, thinking they might help with reading responses. I thought she and I could read them together. I have copies from when I was a kid.

Aurora was so great. Like, super, elementally great.

Mike: Excellent idea. Maybe I'll read them, too.

After that, we kept in touch when I was on the road. But also sometimes when I wasn't. Not-on-the-road texting started when Olivia and I were watching a *Little House* episode— Aurora had left the DVDs at our house—that was so bonkers I spontaneously texted.

Mike: We're watching Little House, and it's the one where Ma almost cuts off her leg.

Aurora: OMG, yes! She gets some kind of infection in a scrape on her leg and takes that bit from the Bible about cutting off thy limb if it offends thee too literally!

Mike: But Reverend Alden rescues her just in time.

Aurora: Yes! She was baking pies for the church fundraiser, and he came to pick them up. Saved by pie.

Mike: Well, if anything can save you, it's pie. What's your favorite kind?

It was pie that first lured me to Sarah's diner—it was famous for its dozens of homemade varieties. It was interesting that I

could think back without the stab of pain that used to accom-
pany those sorts of memories.

Aurora: I don't know. I've only ever had apple. So I guess it's
apple?

Mike: How is that possible?

Aurora: My mom wasn't into pie.

Aurora: Or dessert.

Aurora: Or food in general.

I was starting to get a picture of Aurora's mom, based on a
few comments she'd made. I wanted to ask Aurora why no pie
in the years since she'd lived with her mom, though. She'd called
herself a failed ballerina. Even if she'd been on a strict regimen
back then, why did that translate into no pie in the intervening
years?

Also, why did these all feel like such burning questions?

Aurora: I should go to bed. I open tomorrow at five.

That was one question that *had* been answered. Her second
job was as a barista at a Starbucks near her place.

Mike: Do they have pie at Starbucks? You should treat
yourself tomorrow.

Aurora: They have apple fritters—is that close enough?

Mike: No, that's more like a donut. We need to expand your
pie horizons.

Wait. Was it weird that I'd said *we*?

Aurora: What's your favorite kind?

Mike: I'm partial to the cream pie family, probably because
coconut cream pie is a specialty of my mom's. But
chocolate cream, banana cream. It's all good. Totally
different from the fruit category. Which is also good. Just
maybe not quite as good.

There was a long pause while the dot things that indicated
she was typing appeared, disappeared, and reappeared.

Aurora: I haven't had much pie because I spent the first
twenty years of my life thinking I was going to be a
professional ballet dancer, and ballet dancers can't eat pie.

Wow. I had not been expecting that.

Yet also I had? Or at least I was not surprised. What *did*
surprise me was the realization that I knew Aurora better than
I should, given how little we had interacted in real life.

I had no idea what to say. I was tempted to tell her I understood. Keeping in shape was harder the older I got, and I
couldn't eat as much pie as I had back in my Chicago diner
days. But I sensed this was a different sort of thing from her
avoidance of pie. Still, I wanted to acknowledge that she'd told
me something real. I thought about Dr. Mursal, who always
said that when you don't know what to say, you usually can't

go wrong with the truth, even if it makes you or other people uncomfortable. In this case I was interpreting the truth to be the question that was at the tip of my tongue.

Mike: Does this have something to do with your mother?

Aurora: Yes. And honestly, I don't want to sound like I have an eating disorder. I mean, I think I did, when I was younger. You kind of have to, to be in ballet.

Mike: That's kind of screwed up.

Aurora: Right?

Mike: I get it, though. I think any athlete understands that your sport rewards a certain type of physicality. You can only get so far on discipline and practice, then you're kind of screwed if you don't have the particular kind of build your sport demands. Not all wannabe swimmers have Michael Phelps's wingspan.

That had turned into a bit of a monologue. I worried it sounded preachy. But thinking of young Aurora starving herself—it hurt me.

It was a strange sensation, to have something hurt me that had nothing to do with Sarah's death, those damn birth control pills, the abyss, or Olivia's calling me Mike.

Aurora: To be fair, some people tend more toward the ballet body type naturally, so I can't say everyone has to have an eating disorder to succeed. I don't mean to condemn ballet as a whole. It just wasn't good for me. At that level, anyway.

Aurora: And I'm better now. I've pretty much broken myself of my food issues on the savory side. I'll eat pizza and chips. But I still have this block about sugar. My mother used to call it poison. She used to say you might as well inject arsenic directly into your bloodstream. She never touched the stuff, even though she didn't have a professional reason to avoid it. I know with my rational brain that she was wrong, but...

Aurora: Anyway. Sorry, that was a lot.

Aurora: I should eat some pie. I'm going to eat some pie.

I wasn't responding fast enough. I was thinking about that first time we went for ice cream. I was also thinking about her telling me about her panic attacks.

Mike: Don't take this the wrong way. I'm only saying this because I'm currently undergoing lots of it myself, but have you considered therapy?

Aurora: I did a bit of it. When I first came home from New York, I was still covered on my mom's insurance for a while. It helped.

Mike: But no insurance now?

Aurora: I do have it through Starbucks, which is the main reason I'm working there. But the deductible is big. Too big for normal, nonemergency things. But if I get hit by a bus, I'm covered.

I had gone from living in a country where everyone had health care to working for organizations that provided me with generous medical insurance because they had a vested interest in my health. I was not paying a single cent out of pocket for Dr. Mursal. When I broke my teeth, I could get the fanciest fake ones known to science. I knew I was incredibly lucky, but damn.

Aurora: Speaking of Starbucks, I really should hit the sack.

Mike: Right. Sorry.

Aurora: There you go again!

She found it amusing that I was always apologizing.

Mike: Can't help it. It's a known side effect of being Canadian. Anyway, have a good night.

Aurora: You, too. Don't accidentally cut off any limbs like Ma. There's no such thing as lifesaving pie in the real world.

––––––

The next Tuesday, I was supposed to be back in town, but not until late. Aurora had agreed to stay and put Olivia to bed. But the air travel gods smiled on me. The team got to the airport early, and there was one open seat on a flight leaving imminently. I didn't even have to play the sad single dad card;

my teammates rose as one and insisted I take it. I decided not to tell Aurora I was getting home early. I wanted to surprise Olivia. Which, come to think of it, didn't really explain why I didn't tell *Aurora*. I guess I wanted to surprise both of them.

I heard the music from the garage. It wasn't a song I recognized as one Olivia had in rotation, but it seemed vaguely familiar. I kicked off my shoes and tiptoed from the mudroom into the kitchen, shushing Earl 9, who had rolled over to greet me. Olivia and Aurora were dancing, but not like in class. They were *rocking out*. There was no choreography except whatever was moving them from inside their bodies. And that's what it looked like, like some internal, insistent power source was impelling them to move. And Olivia was singing. I was gobsmacked. My sour, angry girl who'd had so much taken from her was *singing*. She and Aurora were both shout-singing along with the chorus, something about "the beat."

Olivia was rotating as she boinged in place, like Tigger from Winnie-the-Pooh if he'd stopped moving forward and was spinning on his axis. She was looking at the ceiling, so she didn't see me as she spun, but *I* saw *her*. I saw pure, unmitigated joy on my daughter's face. It made me realize how long it had been. It made me realize the sheer, exhausting *effort* we had both been expending—the only way out is through—dragging ourselves through the weeks, the days, the minutes. With so much to carry, too. But all the stuff she carried, my Liv, she had, at that moment, set aside. I wasn't kidding myself that this surrender I was seeing, this liberation, was permanent. But it was happening, and it was amazing. And watching it happen to her sort of…made it happen to me? A little bit? My body felt different all of a sudden, like it wanted to dance, too, even though I was not normally a person who danced.

It made me tear up. I went back to the mudroom and got hold of myself. I had been judging my progress by how often I cried, congratulating myself on the fact that I did so with decreasing frequency. What I had failed to account for was the possibility that tears could be *happy*.

I had not imagined a future in which I would ever cry happy tears again.

But here we were. I swiped them away, though. As much as I was glad—and grateful—to have had this moment, I had to get my shit together and go back in there. I didn't want to miss the dancing.

Dear Mike,

I finally quit the mall in anticipation of senior year. Something had to give, and even though my mom had been saying it was "my choice" whether to quit or not, what else was it going to be? I miss it. I knew I would, but maybe not how much or how intensely. I realized (once it was gone) that the mall was the only place I could be free. I know that sounds dumb. It was just a chain coffee shop—I don't need to be so dramatic. But when I was at work I didn't have my mom breathing down my neck. People only knew about ballet if I told them. And if I did, they generally thought it was cool. Probably because most of the staff were college students, or genuine adults. Anyway, I felt less lonely at the mall for some stupid reason.

But on the plus side, not working at Caribou means no temptation to drink five-hundred-calorie coffees. And my timing was good, as I quit before they started putting out their pumpkin spice stuff, which was always hard to resist. I'm already down three pounds, and I think I might have a shot at Clara this winter. Remember last year when Emma got Clara and I was a mouse? She was the star, and I was a rodent? This year's motto is: Mouse No More!

Love you to the moon and back,

Rory

7 — PIE DEALER

RORY

In a surprising twist, Mike Martin had not responded to my admission about my food problems—I still had no idea what had possessed me to tell him—with alarm. He hadn't been shocked or appalled. He hadn't tried to fix me. He had, however, started putting pie in his fridge. And since he'd previously made it a point to tell me to help myself to whatever I wanted when I was at his house, I ate the pie. Well, I ate a sliver of each one. And holy cow, pie was *amazing*. I never knew what happened to the rest of each pie after I'd had my slice, because I knew Mike Martin had to watch his diet, but next time there would be a whole new kind of pie in there.

It sort of felt like Mike Martin and I were becoming genuine friends. For example, here it was a Thursday night, Mike Martin was in a hotel room in New Jersey, and I was lying on my bed supposedly cruising apartment listings, but really texting with Mike Martin. We were not talking about Olivia. We were ranking pies.

Aurora: It's still pecan as #1 for me, but I might accept
  your argument about cream cheese pecan as #2 in my

rankings, even though I know you're trying to convert me to your cream pie cult.

Mike: I still don't understand how you can like nuts in pie so much. I mean, pecan pie is better than no pie, but...

Aurora: Have you ever heard of butter tarts?

Mike: Yeah, but how have you?

Oh crap. I had discovered the existence of the Canadian pastry known as a butter tart years ago in my research.

Mike: I've never met an American who's heard of butter tarts. I don't know why, because they're amazing. Like pecan pie without the pecans. There are actually a lot of Canadian desserts that for some reason have never crossed the border. Have you ever heard of Nanaimo bars? Iconic Canadian sweet.

That made me think of *The Nutcracker*.

Aurora: One year I was a candy cane in *The Nutcracker*. There are all these dances inspired by sweets from different countries in that ballet. There should have been a Nanaimo bar dance.

Mike: So you could dress like candy but not eat it.

Oof. This was what I liked about Mike Martin. He wasn't making a big deal about my food problems, but he wasn't ignoring them, either. He managed to telegraph this radically nonjudgmental vibe, but sometimes he made really wise—but still nonjudgmental—observations that...invited me to confide in him.

Aurora: You want to know what's even more screwed up? One year, the school had a fundraiser and we were all assigned Nutcracker-themed treats to make. I had marzipan. I went home and made it as assigned, but I didn't taste it. Not even one bite. I was really hoping to get cast as Clara, which is the lead role. Instead, I got cast as a mouse. I should have tried the marzipan.

Mike: It's not too late. Except...I think marzipan is actually kind of disgusting.

Aurora: Haha.

Mike: I'm not kidding. You can do better than marzipan.

I was a little overcome by how kind he was, how he managed to strike exactly the right balance of humor and gravity when we talked about this stuff.

Mike: I'm going to make Nanaimo bars when I get back to town. I'm going to ask my mom for the recipe. Way better than marzipan.

My first instinct was to deflect. To tell him not to go to the trouble. But why? Why would I do that? Did I not think I was worth the trouble?

Aurora: I look forward to it.

———

"I've been thinking about Ian," I said when Gretchen appeared at my door a week after the pie-ranking texting with Mike Martin.

"God. Why?" She dumped her bag and twirled into my empty living room. Her fondness for the space now that Ian—and all the furniture—was gone had grown, and she'd taken to coming over in the evenings to work on recital choreography, which was funny because she had a literal dance studio in which she could have done that.

But I wasn't complaining. I loved having her here. I loved having her here without Ian around. And she was right. There was something oddly pleasing, and freeing, about dancing in my empty living room. It was like I was dancing my way into a new life. That wasn't something I'd ever realized dance, or I, could do.

"Well, not just Ian," I said. "I've been thinking about past boyfriends. About my romantic history in general."

She sprawled on her back on the carpet. She looked like she was lying on the ground staring up at the stars instead of at my ugly popcorn ceiling. "What about it?"

"Well, things with Ian were fine, you know. Or at least I thought they were."

"News flash. They were not."

"What does that mean? You always made your feelings about Ian clear, but you never really said *why* you disdained him so much."

"Let me count the ways."

"OK."

She lifted her head, surprised. "Oh, you're serious."

"I am."

"It's postmortem time, huh?"

I made a bring-it motion with my fingers, and she pushed herself up to sitting cross-legged. I joined her.

"OK," she said with typical Gretchen directness, "here's a representative thing: You remember how before your car fully died, it would sometimes be in the shop and Ian would be lined up to pick you up after class, but he'd forget?"

"Ian had his head in the clouds a lot of the time." Or his head in his video games. "It wasn't personal."

"It was literally personal. You were supposed to be his person, and he forgot about you. More than once. Yet you always went out of your way to do nice things for him."

I sighed. "I always thought breakups were supposed to be traumatic."

"So, what? You're not traumatized but you want to be?"

"No, but I thought I'd miss him more."

"Still not getting it. You're upset that you don't miss him?"

"I'm not explaining myself well. With the advantage of retrospect, I'm seeing how you're right. I *did* always go out of my way to do nice things for him. I did all the cooking. I made his favorite dishes." Even when they were so rich I could only eat a tiny serving. "We got this place because he wanted a two-bedroom so he could have a gaming room, but we split the rent fifty-fifty." I paused. "Why did I do all that?"

"Because, and I say this with love, you're a bit of a doormat. You go out of your way to please people, to keep them happy. You accept life on their terms as long as it means they'll keep you around. I mean, I love you, but not making Ian pay his already-too-small share of the rent for the rest of the term of the lease when his name is on it along with yours, and when *he's* the one who left, is insanity."

I blew out a sharp breath, and tears gathered in my eyes. It was that sucker-punch feeling only the truth can deliver. "That's why I stayed in ballet so long," I said, my voice a meek squeak, "to keep my mom happy."

"Aww." Gretchen patted my leg. "It's only fifty percent you. The other fifty percent is called being a single woman in the modern era. We all do this shit."

"You don't."

"Well"—she preened—"we can't all be as self-evolved as I am."

"The New York boyfriends weren't real boyfriends, you know?" I said, circling back to the original point, which I had yet to make. "When Ian and I moved in together, I thought, *This is what it's like to have a* real *boyfriend, to share a life with someone. You become…co-CEOs.*"

"Except you *weren't* co-CEOs. As you just said yourself, you did everything around the house, you paid half the rent even though he made more than you and was the one that wanted the second bedroom."

"To be fair, that was about not wanting to feel like I'm in debt to someone." After spending my first twenty years exquisitely aware of how much my mother had invested in me and my training, I was done with that.

"Well," she said skeptically, "I think that can be true, *and* you can be a doormat."

I chuckled. Gretchen was so very much herself.

"Maybe. But if a bunch of different things can be true at the same time, I think the problem was also the fact that Ian didn't know what kind of pie I like."

"Huh?"

"No," I said, ignoring Gretchen's confusion as I formed my argument in real time. "It's bigger than that. Ian didn't know that I didn't eat pie. No. He didn't know *why* I didn't eat pie." Furrows appeared in Gretchen's brow. "He dumped me, but now I can see that I'd been settling. That's my point. I don't want to do that anymore. I don't want to settle."

I expected Gretchen to launch into an I-told-you-so speech, but she leaned forward and hugged me. My mind flashed back to when I'd told my mom I was quitting ballet. I'd wanted her to hug me then, so badly, as I'd been standing on her literal doorstep crying. Instead, she told me she wouldn't let me in unless I agreed to go back to New York.

I clung to Gretchen for longer than was seemly, but she didn't seem to mind. She only hugged me harder.

When we pulled away, I tried to return things to normal by asking, "How's Talon?"

"Oh Lord." She rolled her eyes. "Long story, but I am, against my better judgment, going out with him next weekend. When it turns out to be the disaster it is almost certainly destined to be, we shall return to the topic of Talon. Oh, hang on!" She dug around in her bag. "I forgot I have a lead for you on an apartment that Ingrid's boyfriend's brother manages. He said he'd knock a hundred bucks off the rent for someone who came with a reference and was willing to sign a two-year lease. And if you're willing to shovel the walk in the winter, he'll take off two hundred."

Ingrid was Gretchen's sister, but I hadn't realized she had any apartment connections. I took the card she handed me. "This is in St. Louis Park?"

"Yep, so it's a bit farther from the studio—and me—but now you have Mike's car, so that shouldn't be a problem."

She was looking at me kind of funny, so I got up and said, "Great, thanks. So we're gonna work on the 'Vacation' routine?" The all–Go-Go's recital was a go.

She got up and started circling her arms to loosen what I knew was a tight shoulder. "Wait." She paused midcircle and turned her fingers into pointy guns. "Does Mike know what kind of pie you like?"

How did she *do* that?

I almost told her then. Told her that yes, not only did Mike Martin know what kind of pie I liked, but Mike Martin was also the one who had gotten me eating pie in the first place. That Mike Martin had become my pie dealer. But if I told her that, I might not be able to stop telling her things. Like about how I was pretty sure I had met Mike Martin more than a decade ago and had created a whole fictional version of him that turned out to be simultaneously nothing like him and everything like him.

Gretchen stared at me for a few more beats with her finger guns cocked. I expected her to bust my ass over...something. I wasn't even sure what. She must have taken pity on me, though, because she only said, "Guess what? I finally fired Riley."

8 — THE HOSER

MIKE

"Hang on a sec. I have to get this. It's Aurora."

It was a Tuesday, and I was on a walk with Ivan in Denver before our morning skate. Aurora always called, as opposed to texting, when something serious was going down. I got nervous when I saw her name on the display but reminded myself that what Aurora deemed serious—like the time she accidentally drove home with Olivia's school backpack in her car—was generally not the same as what I deemed serious.

"Hi, did I wake you? It's early there, right?"

"No worries—I was up. What's happening?"

"I'm sorry to do this, but I can't take Olivia home this evening. I'm not going to be teaching my last class today. Gretchen is going to cover it." I desperately wanted to know what was happening to pull her from class, given what Gretchen had told me about her stubborn refusal to take any time off. It was none of my business, though, so I kept my mouth shut as she explained that Olivia could hang out at the studio and Gretchen would keep an eye on her. "Then I can come get her later."

As per usual, Aurora's definition of urgent was not setting off any alarm bells. "No problem. I'll ask Lauren to make sure she has her reading response stuff with her, and she can work on it after class." I glanced at Ivan, whose attention had been drawn by the sound of his wife's name.

"Are you sure? I'm so sorry."

"Don't worry about it." I paused. Well, hell, maybe I *could* ask what was happening. Even though we barely saw each other in person, Aurora and I had developed a genuine friendship over text. "I hope everything's OK?"

"Oh yeah, I'm just looking at an apartment. I have a lead on a place I might be able to get for a steal. But I have to commit tonight if I want it because it's getting listed publicly tomorrow."

"I didn't know you were moving." Though it made sense. She had mentioned that she was shouldering all the rent at her place since her breakup.

"I really don't need a two-bedroom, so it's time to downsize."

An idea rose inside me, all at once and all of a sudden. Like the Grinch with his wonderful awful idea, but I was pretty sure this one wasn't awful. I felt a little bit like you do on a breakaway, when you know you're going to score, when adrenaline and confidence mix together to power your legs, creating a sense of inevitability, like you're skating toward your destiny.

The image of Aurora twirling in my kitchen with Olivia, her charm bracelet clinking, rose in my consciousness.

"No worries about tonight." I needed to hang up and think through my idea and decide for sure that it was unawful.

"What was that?"

Right. Ivan. It wasn't that I'd forgotten him. We were still strolling Denver's downtown pedestrian mall after a coffee run.

Except…I *had* sort of forgotten him. "Aurora is moving, and she has to go look at an apartment tonight so she can't take Olivia home."

He nodded, apparently satisfied with this answer.

"She and her boyfriend broke up a couple months ago, and she can't afford the place on her own," I added, waiting for more of a reaction but getting none. I don't know what I was expecting. For him to bust my balls, I guess, but hello, were we twelve? And more to the point, there was no reason for him to bust my balls over Aurora's relationship status.

"I'm thinking of asking her to move into my house."

His head whipped around. "What now?"

Ha. There it was.

———

I called her before the game. I would have preferred to do it after, because of the argument I knew we were going to have to have, but I didn't know what time she was looking at the apartment, and I wanted to get to her before she signed anything.

"Hi," she answered. "Everything OK?"

It cracked me up how when one of us called the other, the callee assumed something was wrong. I launched right into it. "Move in with me." Wait. That sounded wrong. "Move in with me and Liv." Nope, try again. "Move into my house."

"What?"

"There's the bedroom downs—"

"I can't move into your house!"

"Hear me out, OK?" I took her silence as assent. "When I decided to go back to work, my shrink and I talked through how I could pull off this hockey season. On paper, the solution was to hire a live-in nanny, but we decided Olivia was already so volatile that introducing a stranger wasn't a good idea. And to be honest, I wasn't crazy about the idea. You may have noticed how I..." God, it was embarrassing. But she had to have noticed. To my ongoing surprise, she knew me better than anyone did, except maybe my mom. "I have trouble letting people into my life. Trusting them."

"Yes," she said, drawing the single syllable out warily.

"I'm on year one of a two-year contract right now. The plan was always..." Well, I didn't have to tell her all that. "I've been telling myself we'll muddle through this year with Laruen, then we'll see what next year brings. But in the meantime, here's this perfect confluence of factors. You need a place to live, and I need..." What did I need? To call her a nanny seemed wrong. "I need someone to help with Olivia. Lauren's doing so much for us. I never imagined I'd be able to find someone else. Someone who knows us, someone who *gets* us."

"But...what about my jobs? I work three shifts a week at Starbucks, sometimes at night."

I had thought about that. "You said you're at Starbucks for the insurance. This would come with insurance."

"What?"

"One of the perks of my job is that I can offer insurance to household employees," I said, lying through my teeth. "And I'll pay you whatever you want. Then all that's left is the dance studio. Olivia's already at your Tuesday-night class. Lauren can still drop her off there like we do already, so that's sorted. It seems like all your other classes are on weekdays during the school day"— I had looked at the schedule in advance of this conversation— "except I think you teach one on Sunday afternoon?"

"Yes," she said, still wary.

"Maybe Olivia can switch from Saturdays to Sundays. Or

she goes to Lauren's on Sundays when I'm away and you're teaching. As it is, this will be so much less commitment for Lauren."

"I actually just got offered some more classes at the studio because Riley is leaving." Riley was Olivia's Saturday teacher. "Maybe I could…pick up that Saturday class and drop my Sunday one."

She sounded tentative, as if she were trying out a language she wasn't fully proficient in. "I don't want you to change your teaching schedule on our account."

"You've probably noticed that Riley hasn't been the most reliable." I had. I didn't expect anyone else to be as good a teacher as Aurora, but Riley wasn't even there half the time. "Gretchen fired her, but don't tell any of the other parents that. She offered me her classes. They're mostly during the day, because they're for little kids who aren't in school yet, so that wouldn't conflict with anything Oliviawise, and there's that one Saturday class…"

"I sense a *but* here."

"But Riley's classes are ballet."

"And you don't teach ballet," I said, because I somehow knew, even though I hadn't heard the failed-ballerina story yet.

"I don't teach ballet," she confirmed.

"You don't need to, because I'll pay you enough that—"

"I can't just move into your—"

We'd been speaking over each other. Normally I would have let her go first, but I pressed on because I *needed* her. Well, no. *Liv* needed her. Maybe I should have led with that. "I talked to Olivia about this, by the way, she loves the idea." I'd called the school, in fact, and had them pull her from class so I could ask for her thoughts. "There's a spare bedroom upstairs, but I was thinking you might rather be in the basement—which you know isn't really a basement, as it walks out to the lake. You can have the whole level. Forget how it's arranged now. The bones of it are a bedroom, bathroom, living area, and there's that kitchenette. It's not a full kitchen, but there's a minifridge and a microwave. When I'm home, you're off duty. I mean, you'd be welcome to eat with us or use the main house whenever." The image of Aurora at the breakfast table in her pajamas popped into my head. I shoved it away. "The gig is only weekends and evenings when I'm gone, is what I'm trying to say. And when the team isn't on the road, I'm at the training facility most of the time during the day, so I wouldn't be in your way." I rested my case and took a breath. "There is Earl 9, of course," I said, belatedly thinking about dog logistics. "He doesn't need walking. Walking around the house is a lot for his front legs. And he's geriatric. But he does have to be let out, and—"

"*Mike*." The way she said my name with a heaviness, an emphasis, was…interesting. "I really appreciate this, but I don't want to feel like a kept woman. It's too generous. I'm sorry, but—"

Huh? I'd come to understand that Aurora didn't want to feel indebted to anyone. But a kept woman? "That doesn't make any sense. This is a *job*."

"Yeah, but—"

"Do you remember the time I came home unexpectedly and you guys were dancing in the kitchen? To 'We Got the Beat'?" I had since learned the name of that song, and that the studio's upcoming recital was going to be Go-Go's themed. As a result, Olivia had them on constant rotation.

"Yes," Aurora said warily. I'd taken her off guard. I'd taken *myself* off guard.

"I actually came in earlier. Before you saw me. I watched

you." I winced. "I'm aware this makes me sound like a weirdo. I just...I hadn't seen Olivia like that for so long. She was *happy*. I can't ever seem to give that to her." Aww shit, my voice had gone all wavery. Still, I pressed on. "But you can."

I kind of felt like maybe Aurora could make me happy, too. Or at least that being around her bright-thing energy might make me feel less bad. And less bad? I would take it.

There was a long pause. I shouldn't have said the stuff about watching them dance. It was creepy, and now I was all *You're the only person in the world who can bring my daughter joy.*

"All right," she finally said, and it felt like a million pounds of weight slid off my shoulders as easily as a puck sliding down freshly flooded ice. "But you're not paying me. I'll take the extra classes at the studio, and the insurance will allow me to quit Starbucks. And with no housing costs—and no car costs; don't forget you've already given me a car—I'll be way ahead. I might even finally get my student loans paid off."

"Are the loans from ballet school?" The one she'd told me she quit? It would suck to be saddled with debt and to not even have the degree it was supposed to pay for.

"No. My mother paid for my school in New York—my program at the Newberg was academic and ballet combined. But when I quit and came home, she cut me off. I transferred what credits I could to Augsburg College and finished up there, though honestly sometimes I wonder why I bothered. All it got me was a pile of debt."

The more I heard about Aurora's mom, the less I liked her.

"Anyway," she went on, "as to your offer, I'll happily move in and look after Olivia. But it's in exchange for housing, continued use of the car, and medical insurance. I can't accept payment, too. I have this...block about people spending money on me."

"Yeah, what is that about?"

"It's a long story. It ends with me being disowned on my mother's doorstep. I'll tell you later."

I got a little thrill over how casually she'd said that. *I'll tell you later.* Like we were friends who told each other personal stuff as a matter of course. "I reluctantly accept your terms," I said. "But only if you agree that your grocery and household items go on my shopping lists." I figured that if she wouldn't let me pay her, I could take care of her expenses as much as possible.

"Do you actually go grocery shopping? Like, personally?"

She seemed incredulous. I wanted to be able to say that yes, I went grocery shopping, but I wasn't going to lie. "Not very often. I get most stuff delivered. And I have a house cleaner who comes once a week, and I send my laundry out. Anything that doesn't have to do with Olivia, I outsource." I wasn't sure why I was telling her this. Maybe because I was daring her to suddenly turn into the kind of person who was starstruck by me. "Look. I know this is maybe a little awkward, but I'm rich. That's the truth. Let's acknowledge it. But that isn't *me*. If I hadn't made it in the NHL, I would be working at my dad's Tim Hortons. I'm a hoser. I just got lucky. But I'm still the same person I've always been. And I need help. I don't know if I can—" Aww shit. My voice was wavering again.

"I have two questions," she said suddenly, with a decisiveness bordering on brusqueness.

I cleared my throat. "Shoot."

"What is a hoser? And when do I start?"

RORY

When I moved into Mike Martin's house, the first thing we did was get into a fight. After I walked Gretchen, who'd helped me move, out to her car and stood there while she whisper-yelled at me about the amazingness of Mike Martin's house, I decided the first thing I was going to do was call my new insurance company and find myself a therapist.

That didn't go so well.

"You lied to me about the insurance," I said as I came up the stairs into the kitchen. I was pissed.

I didn't do angry—usually. Aside from that confrontation with my mother the day I came back from New York, I couldn't recall a single time I had instigated a conflict. I was a peace-keeper. Or, to use Gretchen's infinitely less flattering term, a doormat.

"Huh?" Mike Martin turned from where he was unloading groceries into his ginormous fridge.

"I called the insurance company and mentioned that I was on the NHL plan—that's what you called it—and apparently there's no such thing. I have a normal-people, one-off plan, but she did make a big speech about how it was a gold-plated one, the best money can buy."

"Right." He closed the fridge even though the counter was still covered with perishables.

"Why would you lie like that? I thought you were Mr. Anti-lying."

He winced but rallied. "I'm not sure what the big deal is. I'm your employer. It's my responsibility to get you health coverage."

That was how my mother used to talk. She knew what was best. She was responsible for me. "I'm not your child."

"I never said you were." He tilted his head and looked at me with confusion. "What is going on here?"

"I don't like being in people's debt."

"I am aware. But are you in Gretchen's debt because she pays you?"

He was so literal. "Of course not."

"Why is this different?"

"Because it's too much!" I shouted, but then I clamped my mouth shut. Yelling at my employer on day one—day one as his roommate, too—wasn't a great idea.

But also, look at me, yelling at someone! I was coming to understand that my peacekeeping had been about my fear of losing people—maybe I wasn't so much a peacekeeper as a people-keeper. I'd always done whatever it took to hold on to the fragile friendships I'd managed to make in ballet school, the guys I spent time with in New York, Ian, and, of course, my mother. As Gretchen had pointed out, I *was* always twisting myself to suit other people, trying to tread lightly so as not to alienate and/or disappoint them.

For some reason I didn't have that fear now. Maybe because now that I'd had my eyes opened to this pattern, I was starting to break it. But I kind of doubted that changing years of deeply rooted habits was that easy. I suspected my newfound comfort with yelling had more to do with the person I was yelling *at*. I had seen the way Mike Martin never let Olivia's anger change how he treated her. Though that was a stupid thing on which to base my confidence. She was his kid. I was…whatever I was.

I waited for him to say something in response to my outburst, maybe one of his reflexive apologies. He stared at me with a dumb, bewildered look on his face. "So, Mr. Canadian who says *I'm sorry* to a chair when he sits on it has nothing to say?"

Look at me, goading now in addition to yelling.

"I'm not going to apologize for getting you health insurance! I'm not even paying you! Unless you want me to apologize for *that*? I *will* do that, because I think it's pretty shitty!"

Wow, OK, he was yelling back. That was actually kind of interesting. Ian and I had never fought, probably on account of my aforementioned doormat tendencies. Not that I was comparing Mike Martin to Ian. Just that this was my first real fight. With anyone—witness all those years I did what my mom wanted even though it was breaking me. Even at the end, when I'd finally made my stand, I'd been weepy instead of defiant. *I'd* ended up apologizing to *her*.

So this two-way yelling was…actually kind of refreshing? Was that insane?

Clearly, because Earl 9 came wheeling over to Mike Martin, whining. He didn't growl at me, but it was clear whose side he was on.

"The amount I'm saving in rent, car payments, and insurance measured against the number of hours I'm actually working means you're paying me a ridiculous hourly wage," I said, lowering my volume. "Like, how dumb do you have to be to—"

He looked away. I'd gone too far. It had not occurred to me, as I'd gotten carried away with the thrill of yelling, that I had the power to hurt the feelings of a man like Mike Martin. Who had to apologize now? I opened my mouth to do exactly that when Lauren came up the stairs from the basement. Earl 9 barked happily and rolled over to her.

Mike Martin blinked. "Lauren, hi."

"I knocked on the door downstairs, but I guess you didn't hear." She looked between us as she stooped to rub Earl 9's head. The implication that we hadn't heard because we'd been too busy yelling at each other went unspoken.

"Now that Aurora is living downstairs, probably best to use the front door when you come and go," Mike Martin said. To me, he added, "They usually boat over here, or walk across the ice in the winter, so they come in through the basement."

I started to object. It was his house. People should be able to come and go via whatever means they normally did. But Mike Martin talked over me. "We're having a fire outside and going skating. You're welcome to join us."

I didn't have any skates, but I went outside after a little cooling-off period. I didn't want to leave things unresolved. Everyone was zipping around on the lake. A portion of it had been cleared of snow, and lights were strung from poles stuck into the snowbanks around the perimeter of the makeshift rink. There was a fire burning in a pit on the shore. The whole thing looked like a commercial for something. For Canada, maybe.

The air was frigid but clean smelling and had an instant calming effect. Mike Martin had taken the dock in before winter hit, but there was a deck-like portion that remained, on land but going right up to the water. I sat on it with my feet hanging over the edge. Mike Martin and Ivan were chasing each other around the ice. They didn't have hockey sticks, but they were flying. I should probably have my Minnesotan citizenship revoked for admitting this, but I had never been to a hockey game, despite my research into the sport in high school. If that was how hockey players skated, I hadn't fully grasped the speed and power of the game. There was grace in it, too, in the footwork required for those sharp, precise turns. It reminded me of ballet, but inverted. Everyone always thought of ballet as light and graceful, but it was actually powered by brute strength. Hockey, if it involved this kind of skating, was strength and force, but it required an underlayer of refinement, of delicacy almost.

Olivia skated up to me, sure and steady. "Come on out!"

"I don't have skates."

Lauren joined us, executing an impressive quick stop on the edges of her blades. "You can just slide around in your boots."

"OK." I lowered myself off the deck, and when my feet hit the ice, I immediately started to slip. There was a flurry of laughter and exclaiming, and Lauren and Olivia arranged themselves on either side of me so they each had one arm.

"Ready?" Lauren asked.

"As I'll ever be."

"And here I thought dancers were graceful," Lauren teased. I liked Lauren, whom I'd gotten to know a little. She had a dry sense of humor that made it easy to be around her.

"Maybe when the floor isn't made of ice," I said as I shuffled forward. It was fun, though. "Olivia, doesn't this seem like something the Ingalls girls would do? Skate together like this?"

"Yes!"

We made a slow circuit, the guys lapping us. At some point, they finished whatever game or race they'd been doing and joined us, Mike Martin skating leisurely backward ahead of us.

"You gonna be OK if I let go?" Lauren asked, and I nodded. "Check me out," she said. "I've been practicing." She skated around to gain speed, then executed a jump-turn, a single axel or something—I didn't know figure skating. It was impressive.

Everyone cheered, including Olivia, and when she let go of me to applaud, I fell.

Mike Martin, whose backward skating had kept going, abruptly reversed and was by my side in a second with a spray of ice, like we *were* in a commercial for Canada…or for stupidly attractive hockey players. He looked down at me, and, apparently satisfied that I was OK, did the three-stage smile that popped out his dimple and said, "We have to stop meeting like this."

He stuck out a hand. I didn't really see myself getting up under my own steam, so I had no choice but to grab it.

"I'm sorry, Miss Rory!" Olivia said.

"No worries," I assured Olivia as Mike Martin stabilized me. "And you should call me Rory here. Save the Miss for class." To Mike Martin, I said, "Thanks. I've got it now— Ah!" I did not have it. He grabbed me again. "As fun as this has been, I and what's left of my dignity are gonna go sit by the fire."

"I'll take you," he said.

"Can I try that jump Lauren did?" Olivia asked.

He hitched his head to indicate that Olivia was dismissed. She swooped off. "I think she's a better skater than she is a dancer," he whispered.

I laughed. "Have you tried to get her into hockey?"

"I have. Like, *really* tried." He shrugged. "She's not interested."

He put one arm all the way around me and held his other out in front of us so I could grab it. It reminded me of an ice-dancing stance. Except I wasn't dancing; I was shuffling.

"I'm sorry I said you were dumb," I said quietly once we had shuffled sufficiently far enough from the group that I wouldn't be overheard.

"It's OK," he said. "You weren't wrong."

"Yes I was!"

"Well, I barely graduated high school."

"Because you were playing hockey!" And more to the point, Mike Martin was smart. Witty. Bantering with him made me feel alive. He reminded me of Gretchen that way. But also kind of not. Gretchen's smile didn't make my insides go squishy.

We had reached the deck. "You want a boost?"

I did not want a boost, but I also did not see how I was going to heave myself onto the deck without being able to get purchase on the ice. "Dignity is overrated," I said.

Mike Martin, even though he was standing on thin metal blades, literally picked me up, swung me around, and sat me on the deck. He hopped up next to me, and I felt like we were Laura and Almanzo, sitting on the banks of Plum Creek. If Almanzo appeared in that book. And if Plum Creek were frozen. And lined with mansions.

"I never answered your question about what a hoser is," he said as he unlaced his skates. "A hoser is..." He stared out at the lake. Lauren was attempting to teach Olivia the jump she'd done, and Ivan was doing slow laps. "It's hard to explain. It's kind of the Canadian version of a redneck, but maybe without such negative connotations. You know Bob and Doug McKenzie, the fictional characters?"

"I don't think so."

"You're probably too young. *I'm* too young, but they're pop culture icons in Canada." He paused. "How old are you, anyway?"

"Twenty-nine." Here was my chance. "How old are you?" I'd been wondering if the Wikipedia article was wrong. He *had* to be the Mike I'd met at the mall. But I couldn't square the timeline.

"Thirty-five this spring."

See? It still didn't make sense.

"Anyway, Bob and Doug McKenzie, who you're too young to remember, were hosers. A hoser is a sort of cheerful loser. Wears a toque like this all the time." He pointed to his winter hat— I could only assume *toque* was Canadian for *hat*—which he *did* wear a lot, even inside. "A hoser is a beer-drinking, hockey-playing, going-nowhere, not-that-smart, small-time *dude*."

Mike Martin was about as far from small time as it was possible to get. "Look at your life." I gestured vaguely around. "You didn't go nowhere."

"Yeah, but I would have, if I hadn't made it in hockey."

"But you *did* make it in hockey. You—"

"We're arguing again." He hopped to his feet. "I'm going to go sit by the fire. You want to come?"

I did want to come, but I ignored his outstretched hand this time and got up on my own.

He pointed at the house. In the sunroom, Earl 9 stood in silhouette, watching over us.

"Does he want to come out?"

"Nope. He hates the snow. He wants us to come in, though."

Earl 9, clearly able to tell that we were talking about him, started shaking his head back and forth, which seemed to be his version of tail wagging.

I laughed. It was hard to stay mad when confronted with Earl 9. "Anyway, I really am sorry. I'm going to chill. It's not a good idea to argue with your boss."

"I'm not your boss."

"Was it not you, less than an hour ago, who was all, *It's my responsibility as your employer to get you health insurance*?" I deepened my voice to imitate him, and he smiled. "If you're not my boss, then who are you?"

He lowered himself onto one of the chairs surrounding the fire. "I'm your friend."

"Who kind of employs me." I sat, too.

"I'm your friend who kind of employs you," he agreed cheerfully, tossing me a fleece blanket that had been draped over a nearby chair. "But..." He made a funny face. "Am I your employer, even kind of, if you won't let me pay you?" He winked.

I sighed. He was so nice. Not superficially nice, but truly, genuinely kind. I thought he was wrong about how he saw himself, but instead of continuing to object, I decided to tell him the truth. Well, not *the* truth, but *a* truth. He had a way of drawing those out of me, with his steadiness and his lack of judgment. "You know how much my mom spent on ballet for me?"

"I don't, but I'm guessing you do."

"Eighty thousand dollars for lessons here in Minnesota over the years. The Newberg Ballet School cost sixty grand a year, and I went for two. That's a total of *two hundred thousand dollars*. And for what? For nothing."

"Is that you or your mom talking?"

That was a fair—and disarmingly astute—point. This was exactly what I meant about him being smart. "A little of both? The point is, it made me sensitive about feeling like I owe people."

I expected him to argue, but he just said, "Was it really

worth nothing? So you're not a professional dancer. Does that negate everything? Why did you start ballet to begin with? Why did you go down a path that required so much work?"

"Why did *you*?"

"I ask myself that a lot."

"How do you answer yourself?"

"I'm pretty sure I did it, and continue to do it even though it's extremely inconvenient right now, because I love it."

"What do you love about it?"

"There's a kind of freedom in it, which I realize makes no sense, because it's not like I'm free skating. I'm playing a game with specific rules."

"I know what you mean. It was the same for me. There's a kind of liberation in being a cog in a larger machine that's doing something remarkable."

"The corps de ballet."

I was tickled that he remembered that. "Yes."

"I'm sorry I lied to you," he said quietly. "I had a hunch you wouldn't accept the insurance otherwise, but lying about it was crappy. Especially given that lying is…very much not cool with me."

"It's OK. I'm sorry, too." Wow. Look at me. Not only had I had my first fight, I'd apologized and it sort of seemed like I was not going to die. "I overreacted." I grinned, trying to lighten the mood. "I blame my mother for my freak-out."

He chuckled. "It almost sounds like you could use some *therapy* to deal with your unresolved feelings toward your mother. I wonder how you would get that? Not totally sure, but that sounds like something you would access with your *medical insurance*." He bumped his shoulder against mine.

"Yeah, yeah." I rolled my eyes, and we fell into an easy

silence, the only sounds the crackling of the fire and the slicing of skate blades on the ice.

"I have to tell you something," he eventually said. "I didn't already own the car you're driving. I bought it for you to drive."

"OK." So I wasn't driving Sarah's car.

"I thought you'd be mad."

I shrugged. I was too tired of fighting to object. "If I got mad, we'd just have the same argument we just had about the insurance."

He smirked. "Well, that's my big confession. I figure I can't insist on honesty and then have this lie hanging between us."

This lie hanging between us. I should tell him. This would be the logical point to tell him.

I did not tell him.

––––––

One thing I hadn't expected about living with Mike Martin and Olivia was that they fought. A lot.

Well, Olivia fought. Mike Martin just took it. He laid down the law on stuff that had to happen, like homework, but other times, she was downright mean to him and he let it slide.

Which was fine, seeing as it was none of my business. But I could see how capable she was of wounding him. The way she called him Mike at home when he was Dad out in the world was so...shitty, really.

I had feared being the third wheel, worried that things would be awkward. They weren't. We'd segued easily into being roommates. They left me alone when I was downstairs, but we all hung out a fair bit when Mike Martin was home. We had fun. We watched *Little House*. We skated, often with Lauren and Ivan. We played fetch with Earl 9, which meant tossing a chew toy shaped like a human mouth. Earl 9 would fetch it and roll back with it in his mouth. And I'm sorry, but there is no mood that can't be improved by the sight of a dog with human teeth rolling toward you radiating joy.

But when Mike Martin and Olivia fought, I didn't know what to do with myself. I tried to stay out of the way, but sometimes I couldn't avoid them. Like now, when we had to leave for class. In a moment of probably misplaced optimism, I had followed through with my schedule shuffle at the studio, and today was my first day doing Olivia's Saturday class.

"I'm *sick* of hockey," Olivia was saying—sneering—as I came upstairs from the basement to the kitchen.

"I thought you liked coming to games."

"Well, you thought *wrong*."

Mike Martin glanced at me and smiled weakly. "Hi."

"Hi," I answered warily.

"Olivia doesn't want to come to the game tomorrow."

Mike Martin had been trying all season to get Olivia to come to a game, which I gathered she used to do all the time, but she'd been refusing. "She can stay with me," I offered, not sure if I was undercutting him. I leaned down to pet Earl 9, who had come over to greet me. He tended to seek me out when Mike Martin and Olivia were fighting, and I was not too proud to accept the love I got when his number one and number two humans were busy.

"Not your job," Mike Martin said. We seemed to have come to an understanding about me not taking a wage, but it had resulted in him being extrascrupulous about not leaning on me when he was home.

"You know, I've never been to a hockey game," I said, trying to change the subject.

"You want to come?" Mike Martin asked at the same time that Olivia said, incredulously, "*Never?*"

"I know, right?" I said to Olivia. "It's strange for a Minnesotan, but nope. Hockey's just…not my thing, historically." I looked at Mike Martin and felt guilty.

He turned his attention to Olivia. "If you don't want to come, we can see if you can spend the evening at Sophia's. Lauren will be at the game, so that's pretty much your only option." Sophia was a friend of Olivia's from school. Her parents were a little annoying—whenever I dropped off or picked up Olivia, they asked personal questions, as if they thought I was Mike Martin's new girlfriend. But I was glad Olivia had friends. Not having friends could mess you up.

"Nope," Olivia said. "I changed my mind. I think I should take Rory to her first hockey game."

Mike Martin blinked, probably taking a moment to adjust to the abrupt change in stance, and shot me a questioning look.

"Sounds like fun." I was excited to see him in action, if his lake skating was indicative of what a game would be like. There was something about that power, the way it was so tightly leashed, then let out in huge yet controlled bursts of speed.

"Can we sit behind the glass?" Olivia asked. "Or do we have to sit with Lauren?" She turned to me. "The WAGs usually sit in a private box."

"WAGs?"

"Wives and girlfriends," she said matter-of-factly.

I laughed. "Did you make that up?"

"No!" Olivia said.

"It's a real thing," Mike Martin confirmed.

I couldn't help thinking of all the opportunities I'd had to use that acronym back in the day. I'd been a WAG and hadn't known it. But not really, of course.

"They're all nice people," said Olivia, suddenly quiet, almost abashed. "I just...don't want to sit there."

"Did you used to sit in the box with your mom?" I asked, as gently as I could. I probably shouldn't have said anything, but I wasn't sure Mike Martin realized this particular conflict had a pretty obvious cause.

He had not, judging by the way his mouth fell open. And by the way his eyes got the empty, green-hole look in them when Olivia said, so quietly it was almost imperceptible, "Yeah."

Sarah Kowalski seemed like she had been a pretty great person. There were pictures of her in a few spots in the house, and she was always smiling broadly in them. She had Olivia's dark hair and wide-set eyes. And though Olivia was usually pretty tight-lipped about her, she'd let slip a few things that made me see the depth of the hole her mom's death had left. One time, we'd decided to try to make a pie, and in going through some cookbooks, we'd found a grocery list in what Olivia informed me was her mom's handwriting. "My mom used to write notes in my lunches," she'd said. "She would make up silly horoscopes, or do a code all week that I wouldn't be able to figure out until Friday when she included the key." I never knew how to respond to these stories, other than by being glad she felt like she could talk to me. And by telling her it sounded like she'd had a great mom.

Mike Martin moved toward Olivia, and she tried to turn away, but he wasn't having it. He got right into her space and hugged her. He caught my eye over her shoulder and mouthed, "Thank you." Olivia, who had started out stiff and unyielding, relaxed in his arms. I went to the mudroom to give them some privacy as he said, "I'm sorry, Liv. I didn't realize. You can sit wherever you want, but if you don't want to come, that's totally fine."

"I want to go with Rory if she wants to."

"I want to!" I called back, and the mood was light as we piled into the car.

Well, *their* mood was light. I should have driven myself to the studio in the Normal Sedan. I should have realized I wouldn't want company.

The closer we got, the harder my heart beat and the more my stomach fluttered. Damn it. I'd been doing so well lately.

I did my tapping. It worked well enough that Mike Martin didn't notice I was starting to freak out. Or maybe that was thanks to Olivia, who was now all sweetness and chatter, going on at length about the year-end semiformal dance, which although it was months away was an increasingly frequent topic of conversation. It was for the middle schoolers at her private school, and this was the first year she was eligible.

Mike Martin kept looking at her in the rearview mirror and smiling like a dope.

By the time we got to the studio, I was sweating, despite the fact that it was freezing out. "Do you mind dropping me at the door before you park?" I croaked.

Mike Martin did as I asked, but he also put the car in park and laid a hand on my arm as I unbuckled my seat belt. "You OK?"

I was not OK. But *not OK* wasn't really an option here, so I squeaked out a "Yep!" and fled.

We were early, which in retrospect hadn't been a great idea. I'd been thinking that since I was taking over this class midsession, I should show up early in case any parents wanted to talk to me.

They did, it turned out, but not about their kids.

"Oh, Miss Rory," said a mother I didn't recognize, "I was just talking to Miss Miller—where has she been hiding you all this time?"

"She's been hiding in plain sight, in tap and jazz, apparently!" said another.

"Who knew we had a former member of the Newberg Ballet under our noses this whole time!"

I wanted to point out that I had been a student, not a member of the company. And that their kids were ten to twelve years old, and that if any of them had been good enough to truly make a go of it in ballet, they wouldn't be studying at Miss Miller's of Minnetonka.

I pushed past them into the studio, ignoring Gretchen at the desk. There had been a time when a dance studio was a place of refuge for me. The scuffed wooden floors, the walls of mirrors, and the smooth barre had, long ago, been soothingly familiar. But not today. A bunch of girls were already in the studio, in their black leotards, white tights, and buns that looked like walnuts affixed to the backs of their heads.

I tapped. I didn't care if I looked weird. I had to calm down. I knew enough by now to trust that I wasn't having a literal heart attack, but damn.

"Miss Rory, are you OK?"

It was Sansa, who I hadn't realized was in this class. Which meant Sansa's mom was nearby, which only made everything worse.

Why did I have to be like this? It made me so *angry* sometimes. In the ramp-up, in the space where I could try to arrest things, there was still room for something else, and right now that something was anger. At my traitorous body, at my stupid brain, at my mother, whom I had given too much power.

At myself, for daring to think that since I hadn't had an episode for months, maybe I was done with them.

"Miss Rory?"

I fled through the viewing area into the lobby, where I heard Gretchen saying something from behind the reception desk but not the actual words she used. On my way to the stairs, I passed the entrance as Mike Martin was coming in. He'd been holding the door for Olivia, but he froze when we made eye contact. Only for a second, but it was enough for me to register that *he* was registering that there was something wrong with me. I wondered if my eyes were giving me away, the way his sometimes did with him.

I broke free and ran downstairs.

I was getting control of things a few minutes later when he appeared in the doorway of the studio I was hiding in—Gretchen had a small downstairs studio she used for private lessons. I was staring at myself in the mirrored wall, doing my tapping and taking deep breaths, when his reflection joined mine.

"I'm sorry," I said, meeting his gaze in the mirror without turning.

He ducked under the lintel—the ceilings were low down here. "No reason to be sorry."

I let my hands fall to my sides. "It's so *embarrassing*."

He took a step closer. "I don't want to tell you how to feel, but I don't think there's any reason to be embarrassed. No one up there saw you, if that's what you're worried about."

"You did."

"Right." *Click.* One side of the smile appeared. "Well, I'm not exactly the poster boy for mental wellness at the moment, am I?" The smile clicked off abruptly, and he took another few steps until he was right next to me. We were shoulder to shoulder, looking at each other in the mirror. "But even if I was, I would never judge you." He was so *good*. It almost brought tears to my eyes. I wanted to look away, to drop my gaze, but he was giving me the green kryptonite stare. "I think if you're feeling embarrassed," he went on, "it's because you've been trained to, by the experiences you've had, or by the people in your life. But there's no reason to be on my watch. Shit happens. Life is hard sometimes."

I hugged him. It was either that or let him see me cry, because the tears that had threatened earlier were *here*. Except no, that was the excuse I gave myself, and I wasn't standing for my own bullshit right now. After that little speech of his, I knew he wasn't going to care about a few tears. I hugged him because I *wanted* to. Because what he'd said was so generous. The vehemence of his words stood in such juxtaposition to the tenderness of the sentiment they contained. And beyond what he'd said, it was also *him*, the rare and particular and wonderful combination of strength and gentleness that had produced this tall, gruff man with such a kind heart. I wanted to surround myself with all of that.

He obliged, wrapping his arms around me. We stood like that for a long time. I would have said we stood like that until embarrassment crept in, but I didn't let it. It tried, but I thought back to him saying "Life is hard sometimes," pulled away, and just said, "Thanks."

"No problem. When I was on my way down here, Gretchen said to tell you she'd take the class if you need her to. Want to bust out and go for ice cream?"

Did I ever. But I couldn't. "Thanks, but no. If I don't do this, it'll turn into a bigger deal. I'm scheduled to take over two more of Riley's old classes this coming week." I looked at my watch. "But I have ten minutes, and I'm going to spend them down here."

I was about to say he was excused, but he said, "OK," and slid down the wall to sit on the floor with his back against the mirror. "So, ballet really did a number on you, eh?"

"Yeah." I slid down, too. "I'll tell you the whole sordid story sometime. I know I said that before, but ten minutes isn't enough."

"Is this related to crying on your mother's doorstep?"

"Yep."

"I look forward to hearing about it."

"Really?"

"Are you kidding me? Someone else's sordid story instead of my own? Hell yes."

I chuckled. "The stupid thing is that those"—I pointed at the ceiling—"are children, and not very talented ones at that." I winced. "Sorry." He waved away my apology. "So what am I so afraid of?"

"Hey, now, children are terrifying. And have you met some of those mothers?" He whistled in an exaggerated way that made me laugh.

I looked at my watch again. "Let's talk about something else. Something not ballet related."

"What's the story behind the name Aurora?"

"I'm actually named after a character in a ballet."

"Oh crap, sorry. Ballet is everywhere, eh? And here I was thinking the northern lights. Aurora borealis."

"I've never seen them. Always wanted to."

"We see them sometimes in the winter at home."

"It would be a cool thing to be named after. Maybe I'll revise my origin story and tell everyone I'm named after the northern lights. Remember when we first met, you said my name sounded like a superhero?" Oh crap. Of course he didn't remember that offhand comment.

"We were trying to think what your superpower was."

He did remember. "You know how movies are always rebooting superhero franchises and pretending the past never happened? Maybe I can do that for myself."

He chuckled, and after a few beats of silence said, "Your mom really named you after a ballet?"

"Yep, Aurora is Sleeping Beauty's actual name, and there's a famous *Sleeping Beauty* ballet. I got to play the role once. It was..."

"What?" he asked gently.

"I was going to say it was fun, but..." I thought of that framed picture of me from that performance, the one I couldn't bear to display. "It was fun for my mom, anyway."

"What if you'd grown up and wanted nothing to do with ballet? What if you'd wanted to become a sumo wrestler? Or an accountant?"

I smiled. "If it had been solely up to my mom, she would have named me Giselle or Odette—Odette is the white swan in *Swan Lake*. The one thing my absent dad did for me was prevent that from happening. He was a hippie, to hear it told, so he was into Aurora. It's the hippie-dippiest of all the famous ballet names."

"To hear it told?"

"Yeah, he split a month before I was born."

"Hmm."

I knew what he was thinking. I wanted to address it instead of turn away from it, because I was feeling braver than usual. Or maybe it was just Mike Martin—maybe he in particular made me brave. "They met at a concert. He was a roadie. He stuck around for a while. Long enough for him to pretend to be into the idea of my mom being pregnant—and to name me. Then one day, she woke up, and he was gone. Never heard from him again."

Mike Martin winced.

"Yeah."

"I'm sorry."

"I used to google him when I was younger, and look for him on social media, but his name is Rob Johnson."

"Ah."

"I confess I have thought of doing 23andMe, seeing if I can find him that way."

"But?"

"Well, *he* left *me*, right? My mom's had the same phone number forever. She has a real estate website. He could find me if he wanted to."

He nodded, and I knew he was thinking of Olivia's biological father. "It's sort of amazing how easily some people—well, some men—can just waltz away from..."

"...from their responsibilities?"

"I was going to say that, but that's not really what I meant."

"What did you mean?"

He snorted and ran a hand through his hair, as if embarrassed. "Well, it sounds cheesy, but I suppose I meant love. Do even a half-decent job, and a kid will love you unconditionally. Well, she will until her mom dies, then things might get a little iffy."

"She loves you. She's just struggling right now."

"I think so. I hope so. Anyway, my point is that when you leave a kid, you leave a lot of potentially great stuff behind. It's a dumb move. Kids aren't responsibilities, or aren't *only* responsibilities. They're opportunities." He shook his head. "What's your middle name?"

"Lake."

"Aurora Lake. Wow. Forget ballet, that is a *total* superhero name. Your sperm donor really was a hippie, eh?"

I smiled. I loved when he peppered his speech with his Canadian *eh*s. "Yeah, they settled on *Aurora*, and my mom was happy with that, so she let him do the middle name, and he chose *Lake*. He apparently thought it was unique." I scoffed. "Which goes to show he wasn't from Minnesota—the Land of Ten Thousand Lakes."

"But only one Aurora Lake."

I wanted to hear more about this business about kids being opportunities and not responsibilities. I wanted to know why Mike Martin and Sarah had never had one together if he felt that way. But I was out of time. "I'd better go face the Go-Go's." The Ballet 3 girls were doing a routine to "Circle in the Sand."

He got up and offered me a hand. This time I took it unhesitatingly, even knowing it would probably do a number on me. "Have you done any ballet since…" He trailed off.

"Since I flamed out? Nope."

"Wow."

"Yeah."

"All right," he said. "You're gonna giv'r."

"I'm gonna what?"

"Sorry, that's a Canadianism." His brow furrowed. "Or maybe it's a hockeyism. Anyway, it means to do a really great job."

I was shaking like a leaf as I introduced myself to the kids, who fell into line in a cute little demonic row, but I held it together. I was gonna giv'r, right? Mike Martin watched me in the mirror as I led them through barre work. Not in a creepy way, just as if he were holding me in his sights. Bolstering me. He usually watched Olivia. A lot of parents, Mike Martin included, only had eyes for their own kids, which I loved as long as they were watching so closely because they were delighted. Like, *Look, that's my genius kid right there!* There were always one or two whose attention seemed critical rather than adoring, and those I was not thrilled about. But what could I do except be extra kind to their kids, which was something that might have helped me when I was in their ballet slippers?

The weird thing was how my body knew what to do. Once we started, it was actually easy to turn off my brain. It was funny: ballet was the thing that had caused me so much damage, the thing that had made me into a person who was afraid of sugar and needed coping mechanisms to stave off panic attacks, but in a way, the actual act of dancing, the familiar port de bras I opened the floor work with, was much more effective than tapping at calming my brain. There was a kind of sentience, an intelligence that went beyond muscle memory, in my body, and, remarkably, it was *still there*, even after lying dormant all these years. I let it lead, and before I knew it, class was over. I looked in the mirror as I led the kids in a *révérence* combination, and there was Mike Martin, steady as ever, beaming his green-eyed surety at me.

When I stepped off the dance floor, *he* hugged *me*. Caught me up in a giant bear hug that lifted me off the ground. When he set me down, he was grinning. I grinned back. He didn't say anything, and neither did I; we didn't have to. I had done it, and he knew what that meant.

———

The next afternoon Lauren picked up Olivia and me for the hockey game.

"I heard you guys aren't sitting in the box," she said as we got on the highway. "But maybe you want to come for a visit? I think some of the families would love to see you, Olivia, if you feel like popping in."

"Mm, maybe." Olivia was being noncommittal, but I could tell she didn't want to.

At the arena, I leaned into the idea of Olivia as my tour guide, both because I wanted her to feel important and because I wanted to keep us busy so there was "no time" to get to the box. I let her lead me to a concession stand that sold edible cookie dough, and with my cup of brownie batter in hand— look at me, this was way more advanced-class than mint chocolate chip ice cream—bought us both foam lumberjack axes. When we found our seats with only minutes to spare, she was looking fussed, glancing around the arena as if she didn't quite recognize it.

"Does this make you miss your mom?" I asked gently.

"I always miss her, but yeah." She looked alarmed. "Are you gonna make me go up to the box?"

"No, no," I said quickly. "We're cool here."

"I don't like talking to people who are going to make a huge deal about my mom," she said, and my heart twisted. "I know they mean well, but I never know what to say. It's better out here anyway. You're right in the middle of things."

She was right. The theater of it all, even before the game started, was exciting. The cold air, the music, and when they introduced the teams—wow. They started with Boston, then there was this overdramatic yet awesome song-video-montage thing on the JumboTron. It included these jerky, artistic close-ups of individual players, and when Mike Martin came on, it was from behind—you could see his jersey with his name and number—and then he turned around and he was all sweaty and intense looking. I couldn't help it: I screamed. Olivia did, too. We grinned at each other and shrieked like we were at a Beatles concert in 1964. After the video, the announcer shouted, "Here are your Minnesota Lumberjacks!" and the team skated out with music blasting and logos being projected everywhere. Olivia and I kept screaming. I didn't even really know why, except that it felt so great to stand there and scream. When Mike Martin whooshed by the glass that was a few rows in front of us and patted his chest and extended his arm in our direction—he must have known where we were sitting— I thought I might die. When Olivia's generalized screaming transformed itself into "Dad! Dad!" I think I did die for a second. But I revived myself. I had brownie batter to eat and hockey to watch.

Dear Mike,

My mom bought me a T-shirt as a going-away present that has that iconic "I heart New York" phrase on it, and I want to take a red Sharpie and draw one of those circles with a diagonal line over the heart—like "I (do not) heart New York." Everyone here is so good and smart and skinny. And, oh my God, the <u>classes</u>. I don't know which is harder, the ballet or the school. You know how my mom and I battled over if I should join a company right away or do a combined academic/ballet program? I hate to say it, but she might have been right.

I have something to tell you, and it's hard. There's this guy here, Luc. He's French. I told everyone about you, of course. Luc stopped by my room the other day. I assumed he was there for Emma, but he was actually there to see me. He asked about you, and I told him we broke up. It just popped out, and all of a sudden, he was kissing me. It wasn't bad. It was kind of exciting, actually, and then he came back the next day, and the next. Things started to heat up, and honestly I didn't want them to go so far so fast... Why didn't I say that?

The weird part is, afterward, I thought, well, it will be nice to have a local boyfriend, one that I actually get to see (ha ha). But then the next day was the Friday before Christmas break and we were all talking about people we'd see at home. Turns out Luc has a girlfriend in France. They met in high school; she's at the University of Paris now studying philosophy. They agreed to open their relationship while they're apart. What? Are they French teenagers or middle-aged swingers?!

The bigger question is: Why didn't he tell me any of this before I slept with him? Was I supposed to ask?

One more question: Why do I feel guilty? ~~It's not like you're going to care.~~ (That was supposed to be a joke, but I'm not laughing.) I guess I feel so bad because at the first inkling that a boy might like me, I just…dumped you. What kind of person does that make me?

I just want to go to the moon and not come back,

Rory

10—EMOTIONAL LABOR

MIKE

When I got home from a mid-December trip to Vancouver, I had to face the fact that it was almost Christmas and that I had done shit-all to get ready for it. Olivia and Aurora weren't home, so after changing into sweats, I went around the side of the house and got to work on some wood.

Splitting wood was my meditation, the thing I did when I wanted to chill out. I had chopped so much wood last winter and spring, it was almost comical. I would push myself relentlessly, heaving the ax up and bringing it down so many times that my muscles gave out and my hand blistered—or I knocked out a tooth.

I felt so much better than I had a year or even six months ago. I wasn't so close to the abyss. The little holes inside me felt like they were letting less air through, like they were starting to seal up.

But man, now that life wasn't just about survival anymore, I could really see where I was screwing up. If you had asked me before, I would have said Sarah and I had a pretty equal relationship. If you looked at our actual division of domestic labor, yes, she did the cooking and the grocery shopping and I did the lawn mowing and took in the dock in the fall, but I'd always thought that wasn't a gender split so much as a logistics split. I wasn't home half the time, so I wasn't going to be the guy who knew we were almost out of milk.

And it turned out you could outsource a lot of that stuff. But wow, I'd had some rude awakenings about what Dr. Mursal called emotional labor. Because some things could *not* be outsourced. Like, the communications from the school were enough to do me in. There's a field trip next month we need to pay for, and would you also like to chaperone? Sarah always did. Don't forget to send some nonperishables for the food drive. And guess what, sucker? It's Dress Like a Pirate Day *today*.

I was perpetually being taken by surprise, and I knew enough to know that didn't reflect well on me. Christmas was an extreme example. Christmas used to just…happen. Of course I realized now that wasn't true. *Sarah* had made Christmas happen. Yeah, I wielded the saw when we cut down the tree, and I carved the turkey. (Had my contribution to Christmas just been cutting stuff?) The point is, I got the slideshow of happy Christmas memories that came with swooping in and doing that kind of photo-op stuff. But everything else, the behind-the-scenes grunt work, had not happened this year. Mistletoe. An Advent calendar. A bunch of little wrapped stocking stuffers for Olivia. Presents for Sarah's parents. Hell, presents for *my* parents. Presents for the teachers—including the dance teachers, ha. So many presents.

I was having to confront a hard truth: Sarah had probably had a point, back when we'd been arguing about kid number two. Or kids number two, three, and four. Then we could field an entire hockey team, I would joke. Except I hadn't been joking. Sarah and I would play defense, Liv would be the goalie, and the new generation would play offense.

I wanted it so badly, I could almost taste it.

I thought I understood when Sarah said she didn't want to talk about more kids until I retired because she didn't want to do the newborn thing alone again. I truly thought I'd gotten it, and so I laid out a comprehensive counterargument involving nannies and night nurses. Oh my God, I was so *happy* when she finally said we could start trying.

I cast my mind back to the shock of finding those pills in her purse. Figuring out how to log onto the pharmacy account from which she'd managed our prescriptions—more emotional labor—and seeing that she'd been on them for six months before she died. The gut punch of doing the math in my head and realizing that lined up with when her IUD had come out. That had been when we started trying. I'd thought.

But as time passed, I was remembering those feelings more than I was actually feeling them. The anger and feeling of betrayal had receded, leaving behind a residue of bewilderment. Why hadn't she just *told* me?

As I contemplated the mountain of stuff that needed to get done for Christmas, as I thought of all the things I probably didn't even know about that had to get done, that bewilderment was overlain with a sort of understanding.

And with that understanding came a hot, sinking feeling. Shame. Had Sarah felt coerced? The fading of my anger at Sarah had been allowing me to remember the good times without their feeling tainted. The problem now was that my memories were tainted by *my* actions. By the idea that I hadn't truly understood what Sarah's life was like. Was it possible she'd felt coerced when it came to the kid issue? Not knowing the answer to that question was going to be the greatest regret of my life.

I was in the middle of heaving the ax up when Aurora appeared in my peripheral vision.

"Am I interrupting?"

She was looking at me kind of funny. Probably because I was in shambles. I'd gotten overheated and had shed my outerwear, so I was wearing a sweat-soaked undershirt and generally looked like a criminal.

She, on the other hand...Well, it wasn't polite to ogle one's sort-of nanny, but she had on a bright-red coat that should have clashed with her auburn hair but somehow did not. She just looked so...bright, even in the dim light being cast by the lantern I had set up.

There was that word again: *bright*.

I grabbed my flannel and shrugged into it even though I was so hot, steam was rising from my skin. "Nope, not interrupting."

"And here I would have thought, given that you have pretty much everything else delivered, that it was possible to buy firewood ready to burn."

"It is. This is..." I waved at the woodpile I had going out here because I couldn't fit any more in the garage. "Therapeutic."

"Ah. I'll leave you to it, then."

"I was out here thinking about how much has to get accomplished before Christmas. And I have to play right up until then." We had a break in the schedule between December twenty-third and New Year's Eve, but that wasn't going to help me now. "I should be inside doing that stuff instead of out here splitting wood we don't need."

"Olivia went to Sophia's for dinner—I'm just back from

dropping her off—and I was thinking I'd rustle up something to eat. You want to join me?"

"That sounds great." I thought about my recent reckoning regarding emotional—and actual—labor. "Except let me do the rustling."

She made a confused face, but I shooed her inside and, once in the kitchen, pointed to the stools at the island. I marveled, as I had pretty much every time I'd seen Aurora at home, out of her dance-teacher guise, that she had *freckles*. Not a lot, a smattering over her nose and cheekbones that you could see when there was enough light. They weren't visible when she went out to teach—or to do anything, really. She must cover them with makeup, which was a shame, because they were so freaking *cute*.

"How was the game?"

"We lost."

"Bummer." I shrugged, and she said, "You really take losses in stride."

"I guess I do." It wasn't that I didn't care. I loved hockey, and I gave it my all whether we were playing a game, doing drills, or in the weight room. But I didn't get as wound up about the outcome as I had when I was younger. "White wine?" I asked.

"Sure, thanks," she said as Earl 9 rolled over and presented his head to her for scratches. She hopped off her stool to oblige. Earl 9 and Aurora were getting on smashingly. I was pretty sure he liked her better than he liked me. I couldn't blame him.

"What kind do you want?" I asked.

"Surprise me."

She always said that. *Surprise me.* She liked white wine, but she never seemed to care beyond that. "Do you really not have a preference?"

"I really do not have a preference. I don't drink much, so I never developed one."

"Sounds like me and beer." I went to the fridge and extracted a Labatt Blue. "Don't get me wrong. If you give me a fancy craft beer made from hops that grew up listening to Bruce Springsteen, I will drink it, but I won't like it any more than this." I set my can on the island. "Sarah was the wine person." I pulled a bottle out of the wine fridge at random. "And she had eclectic taste, so this could be an eight-dollar bottle or a fifty-dollar bottle." It was funny that Sarah had been dead almost a year but this wine fridge was still half-full. It was also funny that I could notice that without it feeling like someone had shoved a spear through my chest. I really had come a long way—well, if you counted guilt replacing grief as my coming a long way.

"White wine roulette. Hit me."

I filled a glass and moved to set it on the counter in front of her, but she thought I was handing it to her. So we did this little dance with our hands.

"Sorry," I said, but we kept doing it. She laughed, and I used my free hand to take her hand. Held it, I guess, but only so I could, once and for all, set the wine down.

Damn, she had soft skin. I already knew that, but touching it now made me feel kinda…sweaty. And not in the way chopping wood did. I dropped her hand and cleared my throat. "At least you like wine."

"Yeah, you're a hoser, right? I still don't think I get it. Is your beer taste related to your hoser status?"

I leaned against the fridge and contemplated the question. "The whole hoser thing is kind of a shorthand. I come from a modest background, and I will freely admit I have a bit of a chip on my shoulder about it. Not that I feel like I don't belong or anything, more like..."

"You don't want to belong among people who wouldn't like you in your hoser guise," she finished.

That was exactly it. "I have the fancy house with the wine fridge." I nodded at her glass of wine. "But I don't *need* the fancy house and the wine fridge, you know?"

"You don't let yourself need it."

I wasn't sure what the difference was, but OK. "Sarah had no idea who I was when we met. I loved that. We were flirting, but she didn't know I was a hockey player. Mind you, back then I was only playing in the AHL, but hockey had been so much a part of how people saw me for so long, at every level. It was refreshing that she didn't give a crap. As far as Sarah was concerned, I was just a guy who kept showing up in her section at the diner she worked at. That was incredibly appealing."

"I can see that. How did you go from sitting in her section to marrying her?"

"Eventually, I asked her out. Which took a lot of nerve, I might add, because I was kind of terrified of her."

Aurora laughed. I loved her laugh. It sounded like music, almost. "Why?"

"For the same reason she shot me down. She was too busy to go out with me, she said. She had a one-year-old, a job that had her on her feet all day. There was no room in her life for a guy. She had her act together in a way that I both admired and found intimidating."

"Something must have broken the logjam."

"She did. I took no for an answer, but I still came to the diner to eat every now and then—they were famous for their pie." I paused, wondering if it was weird to be telling Aurora this. Nah. Why would it be weird? "Then one day, she sat down across from me and propositioned me."

"What!"

"Yeah." I chuckled, remembering. "She said she didn't have room in her life for dating, but she had an hour before her neighbor who took care of Liv expected her home—she was getting off early that night because the place was dead."

"And then what? You wowed her with your mad skills and suddenly she had time for you?"

I grinned. "I kind of wormed my way in. And Olivia liked me, which helped my cause." I took a swig of my beer.

Aurora grew serious. "You must miss her so much."

I tried to think of a way to articulate some of the stuff I'd been thinking at the woodpile. "I do, but it's not as... close of a missing as it used to be. It feels less and less like an emergency the more time passes." I cleared my throat. I didn't mind talking about this, but I also sort of felt like I'd said as much as I wanted to for now, so I pushed off the fridge and opened it, trying to think what I could make us to eat.

Grilled cheese. That was one thing I knew how to make, and we had some good cheese. I might not be into fancy beer, but I did like a nice brie. So maybe I wasn't as much of a hoser as I claimed. "How do you feel about grilled cheese?" Aurora had told me her food issues mostly had to do with sugary stuff, but I wanted to check.

"I feel good about grilled cheese."

"My parents are *great*," I said, returning to the topic of my hoserdom as I got out a pan. "They drilled modesty into us— 'us' being my older brother and me. When we go home, we're doing dishes and sleeping in our childhood bedrooms like we aren't hot-shit NHL dudes. My brother's a coach in Pittsburgh,"

I added, because how would she know that? "Anyway, I try to retain some of that single-bed, doing-dishes energy in my life." Apparently not enough, though, or I wouldn't be so defeated by the prospect of making Christmas happen.

"So it's grilled cheese and Labatt Blue."

Exactly. "But the secret is I actually *like* grilled cheese and Labatt Blue as much as, I don't know, caviar and chardonnay." She laughed and I said, "See? I don't even know what to hold out in contrast."

The conversation turned to Olivia as I made the sandwiches, but when I plated them, I said, "Don't get me wrong. I have developed a taste for the finer things in life." I walked around the island and sat on the stool next to her. "This cheese, for example, is amazing."

She picked up her sandwich, took a bite, threw her head back and went, "Uhhh," in a way that, well...I'm not going to lie. It did something to me.

"But it's just fancy cheese," I went on. "This sandwich"— I picked up my own—"would taste as good with Wonder Bread and Kraft Singles."

"Would it, though?"

I chuckled. "My point is that I would genuinely enjoy the low-rent version." I paused. "And that I appreciate people who understand that about me. I think you're the only person I've met since I joined the NHL who doesn't think of me as a hockey player first." I lifted my drink. "So cheers to you, Aurora Lake, from Olivia's dad."

"Cheers," she echoed, but her voice sounded oddly quiet. She opened her mouth like she was going to say more but then closed it.

I waited a beat, but whatever it was, she'd changed her

mind. I searched for a new topic. Our discussion about my humble roots had gone on long enough that I was starting to feel unhumble. "We gotta get a Christmas tree." But why the "we"? This was not her problem. "*I* gotta get a Christmas tree."

She cleared her throat. "You're gone again tomorrow, right?" Her voice was back to normal.

"Yeah, then back here for two games, then—hallelujah—an eight-day break." The longest in the season.

"When you get home, we'll go get a tree."

"OK."

"Hey," she said, "I want to tell you something, but I feel a little awkward about it."

Oh shit. "OK…"

"It's about your game last week. You know when you were on the JumboTron as part of that whole introductory video?"

I rolled my eyes. That was so embarrassing. The filming for that had been excruciating. When it was my turn for a close-up, they'd spritzed water on me to look like sweat.

"Well," Aurora said, "Olivia was screaming in delight, and when you guys skated out and you gestured toward us, she started shouting, 'Dad, Dad, Dad!'"

Oh my God. I'd been thinking, a bit ago, about how I could confront certain things these days without feeling like someone was shoving a spear through my chest, but the spear was back. I opened my mouth to say something, because that's what was called for in this situation. "Thank you for telling me that," was all I could manage.

"I know you've maybe been hurt by her calling you Mike, but I think she's just trying to protect herself. Same with her not wanting to go to games. We talked a bit, and that was definitely about her not wanting to sit in the box and have to talk about her mother with everyone, not about the games themselves, or you."

Damn. "Aurora, I don't know what Liv and I did to deserve you." She started to get embarrassed, so I moved on. "Hey, what did Olivia give you for Christmas last year? What do other kids get you?"

"Honestly, I can't remember what Olivia gave me. If people give me anything, it's often dance-themed stuff—figurines and crap."

"Well, as I'm learning, it's hard to find meaningful gifts for all the people we're supposed to be giving meaningful gifts to."

"Nobody wants 'meaningful' gifts." She made quotation marks with her fingers. "Just get gift cards."

"To where?"

"Doesn't matter. Amazon, Target, Starbucks—which maybe isn't the jackpot for me it would be for someone else. The point is, we don't want dance figurines; we want a proxy for cold, hard cash. I bet schoolteachers are the same."

"Well, that makes it easier."

It occurred to me that that's what Aurora did for us. For me. She made things easier.

————

I treated the next week like that song "The Twelve Days of Christmas," except every day I tried to get a few more things done than I had the previous day and hoped it would add up to something approximating Christmas. I worked at it even when I was on the road, ordering presents for Olivia, gift cards for teachers, and a cheese tray to bring to Christmas Eve at Lauren and Ivan's. When I got home, we got a tree. I couldn't quite see my way through to tromping out on a cut-your-own outing as we had traditionally done. We went to a church parking lot, and it was fine. I was half expecting Olivia to kick up a fuss because we weren't cutting our own, but she didn't. She led us through every row, methodically assessing trees and talking about how they might "fall" inside the warm house. Eventually she pointed to a huge Fraser fir that was 120 bucks, aka highway robbery, but I said, "Great," and got out my wallet.

And so we had a tree. That was half the battle, or so I told myself. Olivia hadn't noticed there was no mistletoe in our house, and she hadn't said anything about the lack of an Advent calendar, which, without a time machine, wasn't something I could give her. I feared that decorating the tree was going to be a big deal, though, that it might degenerate into conflict. But it was fine. It was more than fine; it was actually pretty great. We did the stuff we used to do, like starting the decorating with the ornaments Olivia had made over the years. She didn't call me Mike. She didn't call me Dad, either. She didn't address me at all, but I was taking it as progress.

When we were all done, I plopped myself on the chesterfield, and to my shock she cuddled in next to me. "You remember that time we finished the tree and we were all sitting here and the whole thing slowly tipped over?" She giggled, the same girlish laugh she'd had since she was a baby, and it made something inside me relax to hear it.

"Yeah," I said. "It was that piece-of-crap stand we had."

"It's funny how sometimes things that seem like they're bad at the time end up making the best memories."

"You're right." That was actually pretty profound. "Remember the time we were camping in Manitoba and we got all the way to the campsite and realized we'd forgotten the tent and had to drive two hours back to Nana and Pop's?"

"Yes! But then we pitched the tent and camped in their yard! Mom didn't want to. She said she couldn't sleep on the ground when there was a bed inside calling to her, and you went and got the mattress from your bed from when you were a kid and *put it in the tent*!"

"Yeah, that was pretty great." Olivia had been astonished by that. Sarah, too. "Does this make you miss Mom?" I asked tentatively as I gestured to the tree, trying to follow Dr. Mursal's advice that when Olivia brought up Sarah and seemed to want to talk about her, I should run with it.

"Yeah, but I knew it would."

"Does knowing ahead of time make a difference?"

"Yeah. I can handle it better if I can prepare myself."

"That makes sense." My girl was a philosopher today.

"Also, I know you get it."

Well. I'd been paid a lot of compliments in my day, most of them to do with my skills on the ice. None had ever hit quite like that one.

"Grandma and Grandpa are going to want to talk about her twenty-four seven when I'm at their house."

They were. I didn't want to poison Olivia's relationship with her grandparents, but they could be such assholes, subtly implying it was my fault Sarah was dead. I could take it, but I didn't want Olivia subjected to any of that.

"You think we should invite Rory up to see the tree?" Olivia asked before I figured out what to say.

I'd thought about inviting Aurora to join us for the decorating but hadn't because I hadn't been sure how it was going to go. "Do you want to?"

"Yeah."

"Me, too."

_____

We did a lot of things differently over the next few days. We skipped the team party. I asked Olivia if she wanted to go, and when she said no, I made our excuses. We spent most of our time bumming around, sometimes the two of us, sometimes with Aurora. We went skating. We watched movies. We made pie, which was something Aurora and Liv had experimented with while I'd been on the road.

It was all actually pretty great. In past years we'd've spent this time running errands, going to parties, dropping off gifts. I was digging the quiet, homebody vibe of this holiday, and I think Olivia was, too, as she stayed in a good mood.

On the afternoon of Christmas Eve, we were planning to walk across the lake to Ivan and Lauren's. "Hey," Olivia said when Aurora came up to the kitchen to see us off. "Am I going to see you before I leave?"

"Good point," I said. Aurora was going to her mother's and staying over, and Sarah's parents were due here to pick up Olivia at noon tomorrow.

"You will," Aurora said. "I'm not going to my mom's tonight after all."

I raised my eyebrows.

"My therapist suggested that since I actually dislike spending Christmas with my mother that I just…not do it." She shook her hands like what she was saying was crazy.

I loved that Aurora had started therapy. I was aware that I had the zeal of a convert when it came to sitting down with a professional and talking about your shit, but damn, it really worked. It wasn't that I thought Aurora was broken or anything, just that we all had our demons and now that I'd had a glimpse of hers, I was glad she was working on taming them.

"Not going at all seemed extreme to me," she went on. "So I decided on Christmas Day only. I'm going over there tomorrow at three for an abbreviated visit. I don't think she minded. Maybe my mom doesn't like spending time with me any more than I like spending time with her." She made a face that was supposed to be goofy but fell short.

I tried to smile back, to play along, but really, there wasn't anything funny about a parent not wanting to spend time with her kid. I couldn't imagine it, though as was well established, I was a kid person. I glanced at Olivia, who was staring at Aurora with her mouth hanging open. She couldn't imagine it, either. At least I was doing something right.

Olivia and I tried to convince Aurora to come with us. It was as if we'd entered into an unspoken agreement to try to ease the shitty-mom situation. Aurora wasn't having it, insisting that she was looking forward to a cozy night watching Christmas movies and would see us when we got home.

Liv and I had fun at Lauren and Ivan's, stuffing ourselves with dinner and exchanging gifts. When we tromped back across the lake, our bellies full and our spirits as high as they'd been in a long time, Aurora was, as promised, still up.

"I have a present for you," Olivia said to Aurora, who raised her eyebrows at me.

"News to me," I said.

We sat on the chesterfield by the tree. Well, Aurora and I sat. Olivia was buzzing with excitement. It must have been rubbing off on Earl 9, who was wheeling in a circle, which was something he only did when he was extra amped. "I saved my allowance, and Lauren helped me get this."

"That was so nice of you!" Aurora opened the small box to reveal…a figurine of a dancer. I had to cough to cover a laugh.

"Oh my gosh!" Aurora exclaimed, glancing at me, then quickly away. The little ballerina had a huge head and big eyeballs, and she was posing with her leg out behind her. A kitten sat at her feet, gazing up at her adoringly. "I love it!" I could hear the laughter in Aurora's tone, but it wasn't mean laughter. "Thank you! I have something for you, too."

Olivia opened a startlingly large present to reveal…a cauldron? It was a big cast-iron pot that hung on a rack. "So Miss Miller's is a cover for a coven, eh?" I asked.

Aurora swatted my arm, and it did something weirdly zingy to me. Goose bumps rose beneath my flannel. "I thought we could do some pioneer cooking over the fire outside, Ingalls style."

"Yes!" Olivia was thrilled. "This is so cool!"

It was a great idea. "And from me, to go with your ballerina figurine." I handed over a Target gift card.

She looked a little crestfallen. "I'm sorry I didn't get you anything!"

"It's OK," I said, and I bit my tongue to stop myself from adding something way too schmaltzy. *You already got me something. You got me everything.*

11—LOW STAKES

MIKE

Whatever progress I'd made with Olivia evaporated the next morning when she was getting ready for her trip. She was huffing around and making everything I suggested into an offense of the highest order.

"Is this making your mom's look like not such a bad option?" I whispered to Aurora after Olivia flounced off, offended by my suggestion that she take her reading journal to Chicago and get a jump on the responses she had to do over the break. For a time, the *Little House* books had broken the logjam, but the reprieve hadn't lasted. "Having to write responses about a book *ruins* it," she would say. "I just want to read them to read them."

Which was a certain kind of progress, I supposed, as normally she never wanted to read for its own sake.

Aurora didn't answer my question, just shot me a concerned look. I'd been trying to make a joke, but it'd come out more pissy than joking. Probably because I *was* pissed. We'd had such a nice few days, and now Olivia was going to leave in a snit.

She clomped down the stairs and reappeared in the kitchen

holding her reading journal. She shoved it roughly into her backpack. "There. Are you happy now, Mike?"

"*Don't* call me that," I snapped.

"What? Mike? Aka your name?"

"Yeah!" I yelled, and I felt terrible when her eyes widened in shock. I tempered my tone but could not get rid of the quaver in my voice as I asked, "Why are you doing that?"

She deflated. Her shoulders rounded forward, and her eyes filled with tears as she said, "I love Grandma and Grandpa, but I don't want to live with them."

Huh? "You don't have to. It's just a visit."

"But how do you know that?"

"Because it's decided. That's why we did that mediation stuff."

"But what if?"

"What if what?" I wasn't following her logic.

"What if you change your mind?"

Oh my God. Was she seriously worried about that? Worse, had she been worried about that all this time? "Liv, love." I had to stop to catch my breath. "That is *never* going to happen."

"But how can you *say* that? How can you *know* that? I'm so mean to you. What if you don't want to pick me up at the end of the trip? What if you like it better here without me?"

I saw then what she had been doing. *Trying* to get me to snap. Poking at the edges of what she feared, like when you can't stop prodding an aching tooth with your tongue. The same way I'd skirted the edge of the abyss in those early months, needing, for some morbid reason, to remind myself of the proximity of this huge, horrible thing.

"Sit." I pointed at the island. "I have to go get something I want to show you." She opened her mouth—to protest, no doubt—but I wasn't having it. We were doing this. "*Sit.*"

She sat, and I turned to Aurora, who was backing away in the direction of the stairs. "You sit, too." She opened her mouth, but I cut her off. "*Sit.* Make sure she doesn't go anywhere."

I visited the safe in my bedroom and came back down and stood at the island like I was a bartender, but instead of a drink, I slid a stack of papers toward Olivia.

"What are these?"

"Adoption papers. Just got them from the lawyer." I'd been planning to show them to her when she got back to town, but no time like the present. "We have a court date in February, then it's done, and you're legally my kid. Not my stepkid. My *kid*. Nobody can take you away from me. *Nobody*. I never needed a piece of paper, and I should have done this years ago, but there it is on paper. We'll get a copy of the court judgment, too, once that's done."

She burst into tears. Wild, hysterical sobs. I ran around the island and grabbed her off the stool. She was trying to apologize, but she was crying so hard it was coming out all garbled. Eventually she calmed down and said, "I'm sorry I've been so mean. I'm sorry I keep calling you Mike. I don't even know why I do that."

"I don't care what you call me." I pulled away and wiped her eyes with my sleeve. "How about you keep calling me Mike, and I'll start calling you Daughter? Great job in class today, *Daughter*. Do you want to go for ice cream, *Daughter*?"

She laughed through her tears, which had been my aim, even though under the surface I wasn't feeling very jokey. "I still don't want to go to Grandma and Grandpa's."

"Why not? Is it because they talk about Mom so much?"

"Yeah. I know that sounds bad, but it's like they're *obsessed* with her."

"Well, she was their kid. They miss her so much." I was

trying to be generous. "What if I talk to them? Ask them to cool it on the constant talking about her?"

"Would you?"

"Of course." I blew out a breath. "Anyway, you're going to have fun. Aren't you going to Disney on Ice? And you know they're going to bury you in presents."

"I know." She was still staring at the papers.

Aurora cleared her throat, and when I looked over at her, she mouthed, "Sorry." I waved away her apology. I didn't mind that she'd witnessed our reckoning. In fact, it would save me having to tell her about it later.

Not that I'd've *had* to tell her about it. But I would have wanted to.

Aurora rested her hand on Olivia's arm. "What if you took a picture of those papers with your iPad? Then you could look at them anytime you want while you're away."

Oh my God. There was the spear to the chest again. The idea of Olivia comforting herself that way. The thoughtfulness of Aurora's having had the idea to begin with.

"That would be good," Olivia said.

I heard the sound of gravel crunching outside. "Sounds like they're here," I said, though I had to clear my throat to dislodge the spear. "Why don't you run upstairs and finish your packing? Maybe Aurora can help you with that?" I raised my eyebrows at Aurora, who nodded. "That will give me some time to talk to your grandparents."

"Let me run downstairs and grab my stuff," Aurora said to Olivia. "I need to change for my mom's. I'll meet you upstairs and we'll get ready together."

"Yeah, OK, thanks, Rory." She turned to me. "And thanks, *Dad*."

———

Talking to my in-laws went about as well as I'd expected, but what could I do but keep trying? "It's not that Olivia doesn't care," I explained. "It's that remembering is a fine line. Sometimes it's good to do, but sometimes talking about Sarah all the time makes her sad."

"Well, it *is* sad, Mike," Renata said. "Losing a daughter is a sad thing."

Normally this was where I would point out that the first time they "lost" Sarah was when they turned their backs on her when she got pregnant with the kid they now loved so much. But what was the point? But I couldn't resist saying, "So is losing a wife."

"I know," Renata said in a placating tone I had learned not to trust. "I think of you sometimes, of how you must be consumed with guilt over the fact that Sarah died on her way to one of your games."

Oddly, I wasn't. Sarah's death had utterly upended my life. It had almost destroyed me. But as to the actual means of it, she'd lost control on a patch of black ice. It could have happened anywhere. It could have happened a mile from our house. I suppose I could have blamed myself, but I just…didn't. They clearly did, though, which I suppose was their prerogative, and it would let them win the grief one-upmanship contest we were apparently having, but I didn't want them spouting that bullshit in front of Olivia.

I swallowed my anger. "Olivia is excited about this visit. She's been talking nonstop about Disney on Ice. I think she views her time with you as a respite. A little bit of mental recharging away from school and stuff." Maybe I could manipulate them into being decent. "All I'm asking is that you let her lead the way when it comes to talking about Sarah. That's what her psychologist advises." If they wouldn't take advice from me, maybe they would from an authority.

They made some noncommittal murmurs of agreement, which was probably as good as it was going to get, so I called Olivia. I didn't want her to go, but since she had to, I wanted to get the show on the road for all our sakes.

She came running down, and Aurora, who'd been taking the stairs at a more sedate pace, appeared a few seconds later, looking stunning in a fancy black dress. Her lips were painted scarlet, she was wearing dark eye makeup, and she had her hair in a severe dance-class bun. Renata's eyes hardened. Shit. No matter what I said, they were going to get the wrong idea. Well, onward. "Renata, Stefan, this is—"

Aurora cut me off and stepped forward with her hand outstretched. "The nanny. Rory Evans."

Olivia's eyebrows shot up, and she looked at me. Yeah, this just went to show that whatever Aurora was, she wasn't a nanny. Unlike Aurora and me, Olivia had never tried to put words to Aurora's presence in our life, but she knew instinctively that *nanny* wasn't right. Still, the lie served our purposes right now.

"It's nice to meet you," Renata said. "Aren't you lovely?"

Aurora smiled in a way I recognized as false. "Now that Olivia's leaving, I'm headed to Christmas at my mother's house, which is a bit of a formal affair."

"Oh, how nice. Everyone today has become so…" Renata's gaze flickered over to me in my sweatpants and flannel shirt. "Casual." She turned to Olivia, who was crouched next to Earl 9 saying her goodbyes. "Shall we go, honey? Are you finished with that…canine?"

Then it was over. Suitcase loaded, hugs exchanged, and they were gone.

"Oh my God," Aurora said through her fake smile as she stood next to me in the driveway waving at the retreating car.

"Right?"

We went back inside, and I leaned against the door and put my head in my hands.

"They're terrible!" she exclaimed, but then gasped as if she hadn't meant to say that out loud, and when I looked up, she'd clamped a hand over her mouth.

I chuckled and heaved myself off the door. My body felt like it was made of concrete. "It's OK. You're right."

"I overheard some of your conversation with them. Olivia said she wanted privacy to pack some stuff in her room"—she shrugged to indicate she had no idea what that had been about—"so I started to come downstairs, but I could hear you arguing, so I was stuck on the stairs. I'm sorry!"

"It's OK." It was more than OK. I found myself thinking again that I was glad she'd heard. Like I *wanted* her all up in my business for some damn reason, even though I was usually an ultraprivate person.

"But that was good, earlier, right?" she asked. "Seems like you and Olivia cleared the air?"

"Yes. Thank you for helping. I wasn't..." I didn't even know what I was trying to say.

"Are you going to be OK when I go to my mom's?" Her mouth fell open abruptly, then formed itself into a smile, as if something had first astonished, then delighted her. "Hey! Do you want to come with me?"

Did I? I scanned my body. I was still buzzing with adrenaline from the breakthrough with Olivia and the confrontation with Renata and Stefan. What I really wanted to do was put my feet up, crack open a beer, and admire the tree. Maybe go for a skate later.

But I kind of wanted to do all that with Aurora. Hmm.

She waved her hands in front of her face. "Forget it. That was a crazy idea. I just thought you might not want to be alone after all that family drama. But clearly the answer isn't to expose you to *my* family drama."

"I'd love to come."

"Really?"

"Well, not *love*, but you know. You had my back earlier. Time to return the favor." I cracked my knuckles. "How bad can Aurora Senior be?"

She laughed. "Oh, pretty bad." She tilted her head and regarded me. "But probably less bad with witnesses."

"Let's do it." I looked down at my raggedy-ass self. "What do you think? Fancy enough?" I fingered my black-and-red flannel. "At home we call this a Kenora dinner jacket."

She assessed me with dancing eyes, but her expression changed as her gaze slid down my body. She'd gone all serious, but it didn't feel like disapproval. It felt...kinda warm? When she finally spoke, her voice was low. "You look great."

So off we went to her mother's, who lived in a town house in Wayzata. The redbrick houses had a generically high-end look about them, and we'd entered the development through a gate. "Fancy. Is this where you grew up?"

"Nope. My mom's real estate career has taken off now that she's not 'putting all her energy into supporting my dreams.'"

I snorted. How nice that her mother was living it up while Aurora worked at Starbucks for the insurance. But to be fair, I suspected Aurora would never take money from her mother.

I still had not heard that whole story, the one she'd twice said she'd tell me later.

"I grew up in a tiny house in Richfield," she said, ringing the doorbell. "She moved here five years ago. It's amazing how quickly you can move up the property ladder when you're not paying for the Newberg Ballet School."

OK, now I was spoiling for a fight. These Minnesotans with their passive-aggressive bullshit. And directed at someone as... bright as Aurora. The day was bright, too. It was one of those sunny, blue-sky Minnesota winter afternoons. I could see Aurora's freckles peeking through her makeup.

The door swung open to reveal a thin woman with a severe gray bob cut in one of those slanted styles that was longer in the front than in the back. "Did you remember to—" The sight of me gave her pause.

"Merry Christmas. I brought a guest. Mom, this is Mike Martin. He's my...landlord."

I choked back a laugh. Our relationship was probably more nuanced than she wanted to get into with her mother. We'd joked about my being her "friend who kind of employed" her, and of course we'd stumbled over the word *nanny*. But to hear her call me her landlord was so absurd, especially given the day we'd had so far, it made me want to cackle.

"Mike, this is my mom, Heather Evans."

I stuck out my hand. "Nice to meet you, Ms. Evans. I found myself at loose ends this afternoon, and Aurora was nice enough to invite me to join you. I hope you don't mind."

Heather waited a beat before saying, "Of course not," and that beat, that silence, said more than her words did.

Inside, I was directed to the living room while the women held a confab in the kitchen. They'd said they were going to check on the turkey, but I could hear them talking about me, so I eavesdropped.

"I wish you'd called ahead," Heather whispered aggressively. "I'm not sure we'll have enough food."

"You're always eating turkey for days after Christmas."

"I like to have leftovers. And you know I like to make you a big pot of turkey-veggie chili. Turkey is one of the leanest sources of protein out there, if you stick to the white meat." There was a pause, and when Heather spoke again, she sounded cheered. "Do you think your landlord will eat the dark meat?"

"I'm sure he will."

"He *is* very handsome," Heather said, as if my looks made up for some other unnamed but undesirable trait. "In a...rugged sort of way." I stifled a snort. She should see me—and smell me—post–wood chopping. "Is he single?"

Aurora paused before saying, "He is," and I sent her a silent thanks for not mentioning my widowerhood.

"You'd better run upstairs and use some of my concealer. Your freckles are coming through. It will be a little too dark for you, but it's better than nothing. It's in the top left drawer in my bathroom."

Oh, for fuck's sake. That was not happening. I grabbed the champagne I'd brought and headed for the kitchen. "Hi. Sorry, I forgot to give you this." Both women's eyes widened. Yeah. It was a bottle of Veuve Clicquot, which even I knew was some fancy shit. We had a couple bottles left over from an end-of-season party Sarah and I had hosted a few years ago when the Lumberjacks had had a good run in the playoffs. I'd stashed one in my backpack at the last minute in case we needed some ammo against Aurora's mom. What was a fraught family Christmas with the evil mother of my friend I sort of employed if not a special occasion?

"How thoughtful of you, Mr. Martin. Shall we open it now?" Heather looked me up and down, probably trying to reconcile my sloppy appearance with my bringing champagne.

"Call me Mike. And sure."

"What is it you do, Mike?" She had no idea who I was, which was usually something that thrilled me. In this case, not so much. I found myself oddly willing—*wanting*—to use whatever bullshit status I had to bolster Aurora in her mom's eyes.

"I play hockey for the Lumberjacks."

She'd been working the cork out of the bottle, but she stopped and eyed me. "Do you now?"

"Sure do."

She filled and distributed champagne flutes and led us to the living room, whereupon I was interrogated about how I'd met Aurora.

"Aurora's my daughter's dance teacher."

"Is she now?"

What was the deal with this woman? *Do you now? Is she now?* Who talked like that, questioning every statement a person made? She sounded like a Disney villain. "We're big fans of Miss Rory."

"How lovely. Miss Miller's is such a..." She performed the smallest of sniffs. "Special little place."

And here I'd thought Renata was the reigning champion of saying words but having them mean the opposite of what they were supposed to mean. "Sure is."

As we continued to talk, mostly about Aurora having moved into an "apartment" in my house, which I made sound like a legit separate unit, I realized two things. First, Aurora had been silent this whole time, a spectator while her mother and I talked, mostly about her. Second, I was starving. I hadn't had lunch, what with the drama earlier, and it was going on four o'clock. I looked around for a bowl of nuts or something. There was nothing. I was no Martha Stewart, but even I knew to put out a bag of chips when people came over.

Since I couldn't fix the second problem, I tried to tackle the first. "My daughter really loves Aurora's classes. When her mother died"—I saw Heather's eyebrows shoot up, but I pressed on, not wanting to get into it with her—"her psychologist asked her to name the two things that made her happiest, and one of them was Aurora's class."

"Did she now?" Heather said at the same time that Aurora exclaimed, "She *did*?"

I chose to answer Aurora. Looked at her and smiled. "Yep. Her two favorite things were the convertible and your class."

"That's so nice!" She was blinking rapidly.

"Well, you *do* have a dance pedigree," Heather said.

"I don't think it's that," I said, trying to keep my tone even, when really I wanted to call this woman some unflattering names. "It's more that she's a great teacher. Funny, patient, kind."

"I've been encouraging her to seek employment at the Minnesota Ballet Center, where she trained before she gave up on her career. I'm sure they'd take her in a heartbeat, and it would be much more gratifying than that...suburban place."

"'Encouraging,'" I echoed. "Hmm. Yes, it's wonderful to have a parent who can encourage you."

Aurora started coughing, and I was pretty sure she was trying to cover laughter. So I kept going. "I personally am always encouraging my daughter." The coughing amped up.

"I'm sure you are." Heather beamed at me. "To what end?"

"Mostly I encourage her to be less of a jerk, but you know, also to do her homework and stuff."

Aurora lost her battle and started audibly laughing. Heather looked startled, though I wasn't sure if it was because of my answer or her daughter's mirth. "Most former ballet dancers find a career in teaching," she said weakly.

Aurora cleared her throat. "I'm sure the turkey must be done by now. Shall we eat?"

Dinner was turkey.

That's it. That's the end of the sentence. Christmas dinner was turkey.

To be fair, as Heather was carving the turkey, Aurora microwaved a package of frozen green beans.

We didn't stay long after dinner, fending off Heather's suggestion that we should go for a walk to "burn off the big dinner." I behaved myself as we said our goodbyes and waved as Aurora backed out of the driveway—we'd come in her car. My car that was hers. Whatever.

Once we'd put enough distance between ourselves and Heather, I turned in my seat and said, "What the hell?"

She laughed. "I know, right? I'm sorry."

"*I'm* sorry. I don't know why you haven't cut her off."

"I don't know why I haven't cut her off, either."

Actually, I knew, or I thought I did. "Is it because she supposedly invested so much energy and money in your ballet career? Do you feel indebted to her?"

"Ding, ding, ding. I think we have a winner."

"Well, I'm sorry, but that's not right. You don't owe her. She owes you. She owes you what every parent owes their kid: love, support, cheerleading. But mostly love."

"I think my mother probably does love me."

"Probably?"

"That's kind of screwed up, isn't it?" She scrunched her nose. "You want to hear something embarrassing? I wear makeup when I see my mother because she doesn't like my freckles."

"Your freckles are cute!" I protested.

She glanced at me, then back at the road. Shit. Should I not have said that?

"You know what's even more embarrassing? I wear makeup all kinds of places I otherwise might not, like to teach. It's a reflexive habit. Like I have to do what my mother wants me to even when she's not there. I...bend myself to please her."

I wasn't sure what to say, so I went with, "Well, I'm glad you didn't go over there yesterday and spend twenty-four hours bending yourself."

"Yeah, the shorter duration was better."

"So maybe you *don't* bend yourself. Or at least not as much as you used to?"

"Maybe," she said thoughtfully.

"I have one more question."

"Shoot."

"Can we find a McDonald's or something that's open and get some actual food?"

———

Back at home, we decided to eat our burgers by the tree. "Too bad we didn't take some of that Veuve to go," Aurora called as I headed to the kitchen for napkins. "Champagne and McDonald's would be a fitting end to this epic day."

"Ah, but your wish is my command," I said, making my way back with another bottle and turning off lights as I went until the only illumination came from the tree. "We had a bunch of this for a party a couple years ago, and there were two bottles left."

"We can't open the other bottle! Save it for when you have something to celebrate."

I plunked it down on the coffee table along with a pair of squat juice glasses—champagne flutes were too fiddly for me, and I'd done my time with one earlier. "One, we can do whatever we want. Two, if surviving your mother and Sarah's parents—and my daughter, God bless her—isn't something to celebrate, what is?"

"Good point."

I popped the cork and poured, and we clinked our glasses. I took a gulp—this stuff was not bad at all—heaved a sigh, and slumped against the back of the chesterfield. What an exhausting day. I felt like I'd played an entire game short a man.

Aurora had not leaned back along with me. She was still perched on the edge of her seat. "Thanks for all that, at my mom's."

"Thanks for all that here, earlier." I picked up my Big Mac and took a bite. "Unnhh." My stomach rumbled its appreciation.

She unwrapped her cheeseburger and finally sat back, but she twisted to face me. "Yeah, sorry about the starvation. The all-turkey dinner really is something, huh?"

I turned to face her, too, and we ate in silence, looking at each other as we chewed. Olivia had been playing with the settings on the tree lights, and they were blinking in a complex pattern that was reflected on Aurora's face. She looked like... I didn't even know, but I was suddenly suffused with gratitude that she'd come into my life. I felt like Scrooge being visited by a ghost who had turned his life around.

When I finished my Big Mac, I leaned forward to grab some

fries. Olivia's present to Aurora was on the table, and I gestured toward it and snickered. "Sorry about the figurine."

"I will treasure it always," she said, deadpan.

"Ha."

"I actually will. It will remind me of you guys and the time we spent together."

That pulled me up short, and I froze with a fry halfway to my mouth. It was strange to imagine my life without Aurora in it, and not good strange. All those ghosts left Scrooge once they'd done their thing, right?

She yawned. I didn't want the evening to be over. "So what's the deal with you and ballet and your mother? You've said it was a long story, and now..." I picked up my champagne. "We've got nothing but time." We could stay up all night talking if we wanted to, and I kind of did. "I gather your mother was not pleased when you quit ballet?"

"She was not. But I could see the writing on the wall. I had to face the fact that I wasn't good enough. I was good, but not good enough. And before you say anything—"

"I wasn't going to say anything."

"Usually this is the part of the story where people go, 'Oh, no, I'm sure you were great.'"

"It sucks, but sometimes in elite sports, people just aren't good enough." I thought about some of the great players I'd shared the ice with over the years. "You don't get to the NHL without seeing most of your colleagues at every level fall away. I guess the thing is to remember that while it might be true that you weren't good enough, it's not a moral statement."

She cocked her head. "What does that mean?"

"You weren't good enough to make it at the highest levels,

fine, but that doesn't mean *you* aren't good. It's not a personal moral failing."

She raised her eyebrows like what I'd said surprised her—but pleased her, too? "The thing was, I might have been good enough. I had a few physical things to overcome, but I couldn't hack it emotionally."

"Well, I stand by what I said. It's still not a moral failure. And honestly, if the people in New York were anything like your mother, I'm not surprised."

"They were worse," she said with a mirthless laugh. "Well, that's not fair. Some of them, individually, were good, but the system..." She blew out a breath. "It wasn't good for *me*, anyway."

"What physical things did you have to overcome?" Maybe I was getting too nosy, but I was pleasantly surprised by how easily she was telling this story, and I didn't want her to stop.

"Weight. I couldn't stay thin enough. I could get there, but I couldn't maintain it."

"What was 'there'?"

"A hundred and five is what they wanted my so-called ceiling to be."

Holy shit. "I don't think it's physiologically possible for a grown woman of your height to maintain that weight. That's not an emotional failure."

"I also kept fracturing my toe. It's a common thing, so common that that particular break is sometimes called a dancer's fracture. I think I did it four times in two years. We had a doctor on staff, but he was on vacation that last time, so I went to a walk-in clinic. The doctor there treated me, but she asked all these questions. She told me I was malnourished and said that's why I kept breaking my toe. She said I was going to keep reinjuring myself if I didn't eat more."

Jeez. I understood training regimens, but who were these people?

"I had stopped getting my period. Actually, the really screwed-up part is that when I started school, I *was* getting it, and I *wanted* it to stop because I viewed its absence as a badge of my dedication—lots of the other girls weren't getting theirs. But when this doctor asked about it, she treated it like a big deal. It freaked me out. *Malnourished.* That's quite a word." She sighed and stopped talking. I wanted to keep prompting her, but I didn't know if I should. She pulled her legs up and kind of curled in on herself, but she resumed talking. "The next day after class, I was cleaning up my feet—pointe shoes are hard on feet—and I was so hungry I was dizzy. I asked my roommate, 'Why do we do this to ourselves?' She said, 'Because we love it.' I roomed with this girl I'd gone through training with here in Minnesota. She was kind of mean. Well, not kind of. She *was* mean. So then I asked someone else, a girl I was friendly with and who was a decent human being, and she said a variation on the same thing. And then I thought…" She trailed off.

"You didn't love it like they did," I said gently, wanting to spare her the telling.

"I didn't," she confirmed, her tone infused with sadness. "I loved some parts of it. I still love dancing. I just…didn't love ballet enough to keep hurting myself. And it *hurt*. And not only physically."

"I know," I whispered. It hurt *me* to hear this. It made me want to rage when I thought of all that had been done to Aurora, not just back then with the weight stuff and the broken bones, but today, when she was so clearly still dealing with the fallout. "I'm sorry."

"I quit about a week later, came home, and had a fight with

my mom. She made this big speech about all the time and money I was wasting by quitting. This all went down on the doorstep of the house I grew up in. She said she was done 'investing' in me. She always used that word—like I was a mutual fund or something. She called me a coward."

"Are you fucking kidding me?" I wanted to go back to Heather Evans's house and give her a piece of my mind. "It's the opposite. Turning your back on all that, having the foresight to recognize that what was happening to you was unsustainable, defying your mother...that was *brave*."

She smiled, a really big one that took my breath away.

We were silent as she finished her burger. I slowed down on my fries so I could offer her some. She waved them away. "Do you think I should try to get a different job, like my mom says? I'm not talking about this job." She gestured between us. "But Miss Miller's. In some ways, my mom is right. I'm not exactly killing it on the career achievement front."

I was both flattered and stressed that she was asking me. Flattered that she thought highly enough of me to ask for my opinion, but stressed because I had no idea how to answer. "Do you like teaching at Miss Miller's?"

"I do. You probably don't know this, but it's much more chill than your average dance studio. I never imagined teaching again. I really owe Gretchen for helping me find my way back to dance. I just don't know if working for Gretchen the rest of my life is...enough."

"What would you do if you could do anything?"

"I don't know," she said quickly, so quickly it seemed like she was deflecting.

"Don't overthink it. First answer that comes to mind."

She answered right away, which made me think I'd been

right about the deflecting. "Well, this is new, but since I started teaching ballet, once I got over my fear of it, I realized I've missed it. Lately, I've started thinking, you know what would be cool? Teaching ballet to adults. Not because they want to become ballerinas, just because they want to dance. If you get away from the quest for perfection, there are a lot of things ballet can offer."

I could see this. She was such a good teacher. "What are those things?"

Again, she had answers at the ready. "Balance. Concentration. Strength. Endurance. Plus it's fun. Well, it hasn't been fun for me, not historically. But I think it could be?"

"Is that a question?"

She laughed. "No. It could be fun." She screwed up her face. "I think."

"Is there a way you can teach ballet that focuses on the things you like and leaves the rest behind?"

"The problem is, I'm not sure how marketable it would be. Isn't the whole point of ballet—at least nonprofessional ballet—that it's for little girls who want to do it because of the tutus?"

"Does that have to be bad, though? Olivia always gets excited when it's time to shop for dance clothes for the next level."

"Dance clothes are so often tied into all the other garbage, though—body-shaming and, you know, the creation of an army of disordered eaters. Not at Gretchen's, but you know what I mean. Anyway, it's a moot point. Who wants to do ballet with no recitals, no thing you're working toward?"

"You might be surprised. No-contact hockey leagues are cropping up everywhere. A lot of people would have said there's no point in hockey without checking and fighting, but a lot of people feel differently. Anyway, there has to be something inherently of worth in all these sports or pastimes, doesn't there? Otherwise why would they have been invented in the first place? Strip away all the context, and what do you have?"

"What do you have in hockey?" She leaned forward, studying my face.

"You have a kid skating on a bumpy pond, the air cold and sharp in his lungs, the thrill of speed and precision. Sometimes, you get this sense of...I don't know how to say it. Rightness, I guess. Not to sound too woo-woo, but like you're where you're supposed to be, in sync with the universe. You have—" Whoa. She'd kept leaning forward as I talked, and now her face was only a couple inches from mine, and she was staring at my lips. "Are we about to kiss?"

Shit. I should have kept that question in my head. Because if we *were* about to kiss, which I suddenly very much wanted us to be, doing a play-by-play was a surefire way to scare her off.

It didn't, though. It made her smile. "It seems like a pleasant and low-stakes thing to do."

"'Low-stakes'?" I couldn't stop looking at her lips. They were pink and plump and a little bit chapped. *I* felt chapped, too, like my whole self was raggedy and in need of soothing. Like she, with her soft hands and her chapped lips, was the only person in the world who could do that soothing. I almost rolled my eyes at myself. Overdramatic much? I needed to get out of my own head.

Which didn't help. All it did was remind me that I was incredibly turned on—and all she was doing was talking really close to my face. It had been a long time. And she was a bright thing.

I wasn't sure I agreed about the "low-stakes" thing, though.

"Well," she said, "you're a hockey star, and I'm a glorified nanny. That seems pretty low-stakes."

"I'm not a star, and you're not a nanny." I tried to surreptitiously rearrange myself so she wouldn't notice the effect she was having on me and forced my gaze up from her lips to her eyes. I needed to think of a better comparison than mud for their color, but to be fair, I didn't mean it as a bad thing. They were a gorgeous gray-brown. Maybe there was some kind of horse comparison for her eyes. Bay? Chestnut? I didn't know anything about horses. I leaned in a little more to try to get a closer look.

"Right. You're a...What did you call it? Reliable stay-at-home defenseman? And I'm the person who drives your kid around and lives in your basement."

"Sorry, what?" I snapped myself out of my eye-color trance.

She grinned. The mud eyes went all twinkly. "I'm just saying, the stakes are what we make them. If we kissed, which I kind of can't believe I'm even suggesting, it would not have to be a big deal."

"What would it be?" I was pretty sure my eyes were twinkling, too. I could feel them doing it. Which I knew was impossible, but it was happening. Being this turned on but also this lighthearted made for an interesting combination. Maybe she *was* right about the low stakes. I hadn't had any low-stakes intimacy for a very long time. Maybe I *never* had, since even when I'd been having supposedly casual sex, before Sarah, I'd always get myself tied up in knots wondering if the woman would be sleeping with me if I weren't a hockey player.

Not that we were talking about sex. She'd said kissing, which, honestly, was about all I could handle right now.

Aurora repeated my question. "What *would* it be?" She got even closer, so close I could feel her breath. She was almost talking against my lips as she suggested an answer for her own question: "A nice way to end a shitty day?"

I licked my lips, and I tried to be not-subtle about it. Part of me still thought this was a mistake, but a larger part of me didn't care. "Yeah. It would be."

"Not a big deal," she repeated. "It can just be a little deal. A blip. Temporary Christmas insanity."

I chuckled.

"So are we doing this, then?" she asked.

"Yeah," I said, "we're doing this," and I closed the rest of the distance between us.

12 — SAVE THE CHIHUAHUAS

RORY

The morning of Boxing Day, Mike Martin drove Lauren and Ivan to the airport because they were going to Florida to see Lauren's parents, and I drifted around the house freaking out about last night's kiss. *What* had possessed me? Yes, Mike Martin was stupidly attractive, but being aware of that fact was one thing; acting on it was something else entirely. All I could come up with to explain my out-of-character and possibly-fatal-to-my-ongoing-employment behavior was that at that moment, in the cocoon of Christmas lights and confession, it *had* felt low-stakes. Safe. Inevitable, almost.

Either that, or I actually *had* been rendered temporarily insane by too much Christmas spirit. And/or too much Veuve.

I was driving myself crazy with worry when the man himself arrived home—with Lauren's skates. "I thought we could skate later," he said like it was any other day. "Lauren said you could borrow these. What's your shoe size?"

"Seven, but I don't know how to skate," *I* said like it was any other day.

"Seven. Jackpot."

"Still can't skate, though." My outings to the lake thus far had only been on my boots.

"I thought you two might be the same size."

"Um, hello? Are you not hearing the part where I can't skate?" *Are you not concerned about the part where I kissed you last night?*

He looked up and *click-click-click*, out popped the dimple. "I'll teach you."

When I recovered from my smile-induced stupefaction, my instinct was to argue. I didn't like the idea of being bad at skating. Who was I kidding? I didn't like the idea of being bad at anything. But it occurred to me that I hadn't tried something new since…ever. I'd come back from New York and gotten jobs teaching dance and making coffee, both of which I already knew how to do. I hadn't picked up any hobbies or really extended myself in any way.

As much as I didn't like the idea of being bad at something, I liked even less the idea of myself as frozen in time, unable or unwilling to evolve.

All right. Maybe Mike Martin had taken my low-stakes disclaimer to heart and there was nothing to worry about. And maybe it was time to put myself out there—literally, on the lake.

"I suppose having an NHL star teach you to skate is a big deal," I said a few minutes later. I was sitting with my feet dangling over the edge of the deck, and Mike Martin was kneeling in front of me lacing up my skates. It was a gorgeous, sunny afternoon.

"Still not a star."

"I suppose having an NHL reliable stay-at-home defenseman"— I made a silly face—"teach you to skate is a big deal. This is the kind of stuff that gets auctioned off for charity. 'Thirty-minute skating lesson with Mike Martin. Bidding starts at a thousand dollars, all proceeds to the teacup Chihuahua rescue.'"

"All proceeds to the English bulldog rescue."

Well, here went nothing. "I need one of those walker things kids push around when they're learning," I said as I shuffled out onto the lake, arms extended as if warding off an attack.

"Nah, you'll find your feet. You have balance and grace and strong legs. You just have to get used to being on blades." He offered an arm, and I clung to it.

I squinted at him through my sunglasses, which weren't up to the task of defending against the blinding white of the snow beyond the makeshift rink—or against the radiance that was Mike Martin. The sadness I sometimes saw in him, the heaviness, wasn't evident today. I could see my reflection in his *Top Gun* sunglasses. I looked happy, too. "How do you know I have grace and balance and strong legs?"

"I've watched you." There was a pause. "Did that sound creepy?"

I laughed and shook my head. It was actually kind of flattering to think that he'd looked closely at me and come away with positive impressions. "But now I have to live up to my reputation." I started shuffling forward again, and he accompanied me, except without the shuffling. He was all grace and easy agility.

"It'll probably be easier if you let go of me," he said eventually. "You'll be able to balance better."

I could sense that he was right, so I let go. "Stay by me, though."

"Always."

I was a little startled at the vehement tone that *always* was delivered in, but too focused on not falling to parse it.

"Eventually," he said, shadowing me like a fighter jet escorting a poorly piloted drone, "you can try to start picking up your back foot on each stroke. Use that foot to push off, then lift it up and glide on the other."

I did what he said and laughed in delight when it worked. I did it again. "I'm skating!" I exclaimed.

"You sure are." There was something about the difference between the power and speed I knew he was capable of and the way he had both qualities leashed, coiled up tightly inside him as he glided next to me with his hands clasped behind his back. Eventually, sensing that I was getting more comfortable, he stopped hovering and let the distance between us expand.

I had a few bobbles, and he swooped in close to me with each of them, but I never fell, and once I got the hang of things, I picked up some speed. I did have all that stuff he said—grace and balance and strong legs. And although this was mechanically different from dancing, some of the skills were transferable. Eventually, I stopped having to think about it consciously, and once my mind was free to wander, I started to see what he meant about the kid on the bumpy pond breathing the sharp, cold air. Unlike in a dance studio, the air my lungs sucked in felt like it was capable of scouring them clean, like maybe whatever was stale and dingy inside me could be purged.

"One thing you forgot to tell me," I called after several minutes of losing myself in the rhythmic scraping of my blades, "is how to stop."

He vroomed over to me. "Easiest stop is called a snowplow. You push your feet sharply out to the side, and the forward momentum turns your toes in and your heels out." He demonstrated, skating into the center of the rink. "Your blades scrape against the ice like a snowplow." He did it again, creating a little spray of ice.

"Why do I feel like you're making that look easier than it is?" I asked as I continued my laps.

He whooshed over to the deck and did a stop I was pretty sure was not a snowplow but some kind of advanced-class move. "Try it in my direction, and I'll grab you if you run into trouble."

"OK, here goes nothing!" I was on the far end of the plowed area, and I shifted my weight to tip myself out of the lapping circle I'd been in and cut across the rink.

"Now push your blades out!" he called.

I'd been trying to slow on the approach, so it was an anticlimactic landing. Less fighter-pilot-lands-on-aircraft-carrier—speaking of *Top Gun*—and more toy-train-runs-out-of-batteries. I crashed into him, but it was a slo-mo crash. He fell back onto the dock and took me with him.

Except, as we sputtered and laughed, I realized we weren't actually falling. Mike Martin was a man in possession of an almost annoying combination of brute strength and graceful precision. There was no way my little paper-airplane landing was knocking him over. If we were falling, it was because he wanted us to.

He ended up on his back with me on top of him. We were both laughing like we had no cares in the world, which for two people with an objective shit ton of cares was pretty remarkable. I was panting, too, and for a minute we just laughed and stared at each other. My heavy breathing sent little puffs of steam into the air, and I fogged up his glasses. He took them off, and then he came for mine. I had to squint under the spotlight of the cold yellow sun.

"This is still low-stakes, right?" I whispered.

"Yes," he said. "It...has to be."

"Yes." I was far from an expert on relationships, but I knew enough to know this couldn't be one.

With that out of the way, we were suddenly kissing each other like it was no big thing.

Making out with Mike Martin was like being a teenager again. Well, it was like being what my idea of a teenager was. I'd never been a proper teenager. The point was that I could kiss him forever. He seemed to concur. Last night we'd made out on the couch—*chesterfield*—for a long time before finishing our drinks and saying good night. We seemed to be settling in again for the long haul.

I'd had the two "boyfriends" in New York—fellow dancers I slept with, one because I wanted to and one because I didn't know how to say I didn't want to. And there had been Ian, of course. Which I realized was not a huge sample, but with all those guys, kissing had been a prelude. Depending on the scenario, kissing was either an appetizer, a pleasant but minor experience to whet the appetite, or an item on a preflight checklist meant to be moved through as quickly as possible. *Ladies and gentlemen, please secure your tray tables and pucker up to prepare for takeoff.*

For the record, I'm not blaming the guys here, or at least not entirely. Spending a ton of time kissing was not going to happen when there was something else lurking that you were either excited to get on with or anxious to get over with.

But with Mike Martin, kissing felt like the whole point.

It probably didn't hurt that he was really good at it. He would hold my face and look at me like I was a delightful gourmet snack and then...snack. It *was* like snacking, long stretches of deep kissing interspersed with little nibbles and moments of backing off for sighing and smiling. But then something would flash in his eyes, and his mouth would come down on mine again.

Don't get me wrong. There were *sensations*, sensations in areas of my body far from my lips, and those sensations ramped up, became more urgent. But we both knew we weren't going there, so we just kept kissing.

Eventually things started to wind down. Like we'd run out of steam. Or maybe we'd generated *too much* steam, and we instinctively agreed to head for the off-ramp. Like last night, the process of disengagement was remarkably not-awkward. We kissed for a while, and then we stopped kissing and went back to what we'd been doing, and it all seemed totally organic. Last night it had been sipping champagne by the Christmas tree, and now it was me being de-skated by Mike Martin.

"This is like being a kid at a shoe store," I said as he undid my laces.

"This is a full-service experience." He grabbed my boots and started putting them on.

"Well, I would expect nothing less. I did pay for the 'learn to skate with an NHL star' package, after all."

"Anything for the Chihuahuas," he said as he pulled on his own boots, hopped to his feet, and extended a hand.

"Ah yes, the Chihuahuas. I do it all for them."

I had the sudden, crazy thought that maybe he wouldn't drop my hand after I found my feet, but of course he did.

"I want another dog," Mike said as he held the basement door for me. "I *really* want another dog. Maybe not a Chihuahua, though."

"Why don't you get one?"

We de-geared ourselves, and he motioned for me to follow

him upstairs to the kitchen, where I sat on one of the stools at the island and he flipped on the kettle.

"Sarah wasn't into the idea of more animals," he said as he grabbed the milk from the refrigerator. "She didn't have a choice about Earl 9, because he and I came as a package deal, but Earl 9 is low maintenance. I made the mistake of floating the idea of a second dog in front of Olivia, and . . ." He winced.

"You and Sarah had a fight?" I wasn't sure if I should be asking that, but I wanted to know. Mike Martin seemed to have no problem talking about Sarah in front of me—not that there was any reason he should—so I was following his lead.

"No. She was right. Who was going to walk the dog when I was on the road?"

He was staring at me intensely. Was I meant to actually answer the question? "Sarah?"

He pointed at me. "Yep. And I got that. I mean, I'm a hoser, but I have a grasp on reality. If you're not home, you can't walk the dog. So, no, no fight."

He gave me another weirdly intense look, and I had the overwhelming urge to apologize. Maybe I was becoming an honorary Canadian. But I didn't want him to think I was fixated on sources of conflict in his marriage. I didn't want him to think I thought about his marriage at all. Mike Martin and I were friends who kissed sometimes. Or sort-of-employer and sort-of-employee who kissed sometimes. I understood that, and I needed him to know I understood that. "You made such a face, it looked like you were remembering something unpleasant. I thought maybe you'd had a battle over the dog. Also, for the record, I'm still not buying this hoser thing."

"Nope, no battle. She was right. If I was making a face, it was only because I've come to realize . . ."

"What?"

He waved a hand dismissively and went back to the fridge. "Sorry. You don't need to hear my Things I Realized Too Late About My Marriage sob story."

Uh, yes I did. I totally did. "No, it's OK, hit me."

"Yeah, OK, but let's figure out something for lunch." He rummaged around in the fridge. "More grilled cheese? Sorry. I'm a one-trick pony."

"Will you stop apologizing and tell me your Things I Realized Too Late About My Marriage sob story?"

He chuckled as he pulled out some cheese. "OK, well, it's not like I don't know that it takes a certain amount of work to keep a household running. Cleaning. Cooking." He reached up to a pot rack hanging above the island. He was wearing a heather-gray Henley, and a slice of his stomach peeked out as he reached for a pan. A slice of *my* stomach did a little floppy thing, and not of the usual panicky variety. "I made a conscious decision to outsource as much of that as I could after the accident."

"Right." Groceries and pies and clean laundry magically appeared at the house, and I continued to be simultaneously delighted and appalled by how often and thoroughly his cleaner polished my basement bathroom to sparkling perfection.

He set the skillet he'd grabbed on his fancy-person six-burner gas stove. "I'm lucky enough to have the resources to do that, and I told myself I needed to focus on Olivia, on making sure she was OK. On making sure *I* was OK." He met my eyes. "Which, for the record, I was not for a long time."

"Yeah," I said, trying to infuse that single word with understanding. Not that I was agreeing he had been a basket case, but that it made sense a person in that situation would be not OK.

"I mean, I was functional on a day-to-day basis. Mostly. But also very much not OK."

"Oh, I know what it's like to be functional yet not OK. Believe me, I know."

"Yeah." He looked at me for a few beats before plopping into the pan a knob of butter the size of which would have alarmed me if I hadn't been so riveted by what he was saying. "I've learned, though," he went on as he moved the sizzling butter around with a spatula, "that there's so much more to keeping a household afloat than cooking and cleaning. My psychologist calls it emotional labor."

I wasn't sure I got it, and my confusion must have been visible, because he said, "Here's an example. Olivia's school is always having these theme days. They're supposed to be fun. Dress Like a Pirate Day. Pajama Day. Who doesn't love Pajama Day? You get up, and you don't have to change."

"This feels like a trick question."

He laid two slices of bread in the pan. "It turns out parenting is basically a series of trick questions. In order to prepare for Pajama Day, first you have to know it's happening, which means you have to read the school newsletters. Which I do." He held up a finger and stopped talking while he sliced the cheese, which wasn't brie this time but some kind of hard cheese veined with green. I wanted to ask him what kind it was and also if a hoser would be in possession of that kind of cheese, but I did not.

He closed the sandwiches with a top layer of bread and resumed talking. "I do now. I didn't before. These days, I read the newsletter and put everything in the calendar and feel very smug about how on top of things I am. But then, in the run-up to theme days, I forget. Because I don't look at my calendar. Other than my hockey calendar. Which isn't merged with the household calendar.

Because apparently I can't be bothered to take this single step that would solve half my problems. You know why? Because I can't figure out how to do it on my phone, and I can never remember to sit down at a computer and google how to do it."

Oh, Mike Martin. He was such a good person. He leaned over and rested his chin on his hands on the far side of the island, his body angled so he could talk to me but keep an eye on the sandwiches. "Anyway. Pajama Day. Which should be easy. But it turns out you can't wear actual pajamas to Pajama Day. Last year, Sarah and Olivia went shopping for special pajamas. Which, in regrouping from the news that Olivia couldn't wear the pajamas she'd slept in, I made the mistake of suggesting she wear again. But she can't do *that*, because someone might remember what she wore last year."

"And you can't be seen repeating pajamas," I said, like I knew. Like I'd ever hit any of the right notes with my clothes or my hair or my entire self on any days at my school, themed or otherwise.

So maybe I *did* know.

"Exactly. They probably wouldn't have fit anyway, after a year. So we had a huge scramble that morning. She wasn't even mad at me. She was telling me the facts as she knew them, about reality as she perceived it. She ended up wearing leggings and one of my T-shirts, but it was clear she was settling."

"Damn. How did you handle Dress Like a Pirate Day?"

He smirked. "I had a football jersey from my time in Florida—someone gave me a welcome package with all the major-league jerseys in it—so I gave her that and printed out an online thesaurus entry that listed *buccaneer* as a synonym for *pirate* and told her to show it to any naysayers."

I cracked up. "Brilliant."

"I thought so, but she decided to sit out Dress Like a Pirate

Day." He sighed. "The point is not dress-up days. It's all this shit you have to keep in your head. I always thought I 'did my part'"—he pushed up from his elbows and made air quotes with his fingers—"but I have come to realize that though I did a lot of individual tasks, I never had the to-do list in my head, and having the to-do list in your head is like..." He pressed his palms to his head and then extended his fingers to mime his head exploding.

I felt like he was telling me something real. It was about the mundane details of everyday life, but that made it feel all the more authentic, somehow.

"Anyway," Mike Martin said, shaking his head and making a face as if he thought the proceedings had grown too serious. "The dog idea came from the old me. We had two dogs when I was a kid. But Sarah was right. My mom was the one walking them while my dad was at work and my brother and I were at school. Though that's not emotional labor so much as actual labor. I think the two are tied up together."

I sensed that he wanted to move on from the heavy conversation, though I was still not even close to done processing it. "What about a cat?"

"Yeah, maybe. I like big broods, though. Noise and mayhem. That's how I grew up, and how I always imagined my life. Cats are cool, but they're pretty chill, you know?"

I wanted to ask him why he and Sarah had never had another kid if he liked big broods and noise and mayhem, but I didn't want to disturb the air of confession between us. This whole Christmas thing, now that we were past the fraught family parts, was beginning to feel like a vacation from reality. Like I'd always imagined slumber parties.

But with kissing.

He changed the subject as he poured his tea, signaling an

end to *True Confessions*. "I can't believe you grew up in Minnesota and you never went skating." He gestured toward me with the kettle, asking if I wanted a cup.

I shook my head no. "You've met my mother. I've never done a lot of things."

"Like what else?"

"What do you mean?"

"What else did you want to do when you were a kid but never got to?"

"I always wanted to go to one of those play places—you know, like that chain Tomfoolery?—and go in the ball pit." The answer was right there, even though it wasn't like I'd spent any time actively mourning my ball pit–less childhood. "Oh, and do Skee-Ball! You know where you bowl the little ball into those rings and you get prizes?"

"You dream big, eh?"

"No, I dream small," I said with a smirk. "I'm saving the Chihuahuas, remember?"

I'd been going for humor, but he paused with a sandwich perched on his spatula while he regarded me. "I don't know if you dream big or small. I don't know if you realize that you can have dreams that are yours and not your mother's."

Oof. There was another little truth bomb.

"Food's done," he said almost breezily, probably because he could sense that I didn't know what to say. He finished plating the sandwich and slid it across the island to me. "Sage Derby grilled cheese. Let's eat by the tree again, possibly followed by some more low-stakes making out, should you find yourself amenable to the idea."

———

"I've been kissing Mike."

You might think I was talking to Gretchen, but no, I was talking to my therapist, Mary-Margaret Madigan, who, despite her name, was not, in fact, a recently fallen nun.

I had not told Gretchen I was kissing Mike Martin. I wasn't sure why. She would probably figure it out soon enough anyway. If Gretchen ever decided she was done running a body-positive suburban dance studio, she could make an effortless transition into the world of espionage.

"Well, that's a plot twist," Mary-Margaret said drolly. I liked Mary-Margaret. My first and last spin through therapy had been really helpful. That therapist, Nancy, had taught me the EFT tapping technique and had told me to listen to my inner voice. Nancy's inner voice, however, had in the intervening years suggested that she retire to Boca Raton. I don't think I really got the inner voice thing back then, but after I experienced my breakup with Ian more as a relief than as a heartbreak, I started to get it. If I'd listened to my inner voice, we probably would have broken up earlier—and both been happier. So when Mike Martin's gold-plated insurance plan kicked in, I'd poked around and found a listing for Mary-Margaret, who was a psychotherapist *and* certified as an intuitive eating counselor. I hadn't known what that was, but her website mentioned making peace with food, and even though I'd never thought of myself as at war with food, something inside me said yes.

"Do you think it's bad that I've been kissing Mike?" I asked.

"Do *you* think it's bad?"

"I..." I had no idea.

"How does kissing him make you feel?" she prompted. "In the moment, I mean."

"Well, he's a really good kisser." I grinned. "And I like kiss-ing. Like, *just* kissing. There's so much less pressure that way."

"It sounds like you're having fun."

"Yeah. It's only afterward that I start having second thoughts."

"What are those second thoughts?"

"He's sort of my employer. He's recently widowed."

"It's been what? A year?"

"It'll be a year next week, first week of January." That didn't seem like that long to me, when you were mourning a marriage. I wouldn't have thought there were timetables for grief, but then again there was that stages-of-grief notion you sometimes heard about, and that seemed like an official, psychological thing, so what did I know? "My point is, we're never going to be a thing. We're just having fun, and that's been in short supply."

"For both of you, I think?"

"Yes." That was *definitely* true.

"The reason I asked about second thoughts is I wanted to find out if you were having any that were intrinsic to you. If you were feeling uncomfortable. But it sounds like your second thoughts are about external things—societal ideas about what's proper and such. Or about what you think other people in your life would think, or say."

"You mean my mother." We had, unsurprisingly, talked about her a lot.

"Maybe. My point is that when you're having doubts, or negative thoughts about behaviors or desires, sometimes it can be useful to ask what the source of those feelings is. Is it *you*, or is it an idea you have about how society, or people in your life, are going to react?"

"So you're telling me to keep making out with him?"

She smiled. "I'm not telling you anything. I will remind you that you told me one of your goals was to stop trying so hard to please other people, to start listening more to your inner voice."

"My inner voice is telling me to keep making out with him."

She laughed. "OK. You want to talk about this some more, or do you want to move on? I have in my notes from last week that you wanted to turn our sessions more toward food?"

I did. We'd spent our first several sessions talking about my past. Then we'd talked a fair bit about my scaling back the usual Christmas plans. We hadn't delved into my food issues yet. "I've gained two pounds this month. I've now put on a total of eleven pounds since the summer."

"And I would say to you that that's OK."

"It doesn't feel OK." My inner voice was loud and clear on that topic.

"I know. And *that's* OK. Let's start by thinking about food as morally neutral."

"What do you mean?"

"There's no such thing as good food or bad food, and you aren't good or bad because you did or did not eat certain food."

I blew out a breath.

"It can be hard to wrap your brain around that if you've been at war with food your whole life," she said gently.

"I was thinking of this time Mike told me that failing at ballet wasn't a moral failure."

"That's a great insight."

"When he said it, I believed it. All of a sudden, it shifted my thinking. But that's not happening here, even though I hear what you're saying. I get that I'm not supposed to be dieting. And I truly want to get over my issues with sugar. But I still want to stay in shape. Is that so bad?"

"Of course not, but I want you to interrogate what you mean by staying in shape. Is that just a less overt way of saying thin?"

"I...don't know." It was, but saying so would make me feel shallow.

"I hear you saying that you want to be OK with not being thin. But I *also* hear you saying that you want to be thin because being thin is better than not being thin."

I started crying.

Holy cow, therapy was a lot of work. It sometimes felt like my brain was simmering away, and then suddenly, with no warning, it would boil over. I guess that meant it was working. We talked some more, and by the time I left I felt lighter—metaphorically speaking.

When I got back to the house, Mike Martin was splitting wood. Drawn by the sound of the ax, I walked around the side of the house. And there he was in his T-shirt, doing his lumberjack thing.

He stopped when he saw me. *Click-click-click.* "Hey. What are you doing tonight after teaching?"

It was December 27, and it was a Tuesday, so I had my usual run of afternoon classes, though they were liable to be poorly attended. Lots of kids, like Olivia, were out of town.

"Nothing." Well, I was going to try to eat a full-size slice of pie and truly believe it was a morally neutral activity, but that was all I had on my agenda.

"Are you up for an adventure?"

I so was. "Yes!"

"OK, I'll pick you up after class."

"Where are we going?"

"It's a surprise."

"Should I just meet you back here? If you pick me up, we'll have to leave my car at the studio."

"That's all right. We'll pick it up later." I made a confused face, and he said, "Come on. My kid's gone, and I'm on vacation. What else am I going to do? Throw a guy a bone."

I grinned. "OK."

I did not want Gretchen to witness me getting the Mike Martin chauffeur service and thus had told him I'd meet him in the parking lot, but halfway through my last class he strolled in and took a seat in the viewing area, damn him.

I had no choice but to carry on, teaching my reduced cohort with a smile on my face and a click in my heels. I could feel his attention. He was watching with the same intensity he usually applied to spectating at Olivia's classes, but Olivia wasn't here.

I knew his attention would not go unnoticed by Gretchen and the Minnetonka Moms™.

I smiled vaguely at the parents in the lobby as I went to the computer to enter attendance.

"So sweet of you to come by even though Olivia's away," Kylie's mom said to Mike Martin.

"Miss Rory and I are going out," he said, and I could see the moment he realized his mistake. His eyes darted around like he was trapped. He *was* trapped. The question was whether he would try to backpedal, thereby making things worse, or let it lie.

He chose curtain number one. "Not going out–going out. With Olivia at her grandparents, and no games the last few days, it's just me and…"

Argh! While some of the parents knew I drove Olivia home on Tuesdays, no one besides Gretchen—I assumed—knew I was living at Mike Martin's house. "Ready?" I said brightly, stepping out from behind the desk. I fake-smiled at him and tried to ESP him a message to cut his losses and stop talking.

"Sorry about that," he said in the car. "I kind of forget how this"—he nodded in my direction—"looks."

"It's OK," I said, though there was no way I was getting out of having a chat with Gretchen later. "Where are we going?"

He grinned. "You'll see."

"Oh my God!" I exclaimed when we pulled into the parking lot of a Tomfoolery. My surprise was replaced, though, all at once, with a weird, squishy feeling, as if I might cry. I sucked in a shaky inhalation.

"Are you OK?" he asked urgently as he cut the engine and turned to me.

I nodded, opening my eyes really wide to try to beat back the tears that were threatening. "I'm not having a panic attack. I'm just…"

"What?" he said quietly.

"I'm a bit overwhelmed, to be honest. I don't know if anyone has ever done something this nice for me."

He frowned for a moment before reversing his lips into a smile. "Well, don't get too excited. It's entirely probable that the reality of this place is going to fall short of your childhood imaginings."

It wasn't Tomfoolery per se, though. It was that he had listened to what I said, taken in a stupid little detail, and gone out of his way to take me here. The fact that Tomfoolery probably actually sucked only made me *more* emotional.

"Also, you know you're too tall for the ball pit, right?" He bumped his shoulder against mine as we crossed the parking lot.

I stopped walking. "What do you mean?"

It took him a minute to register that I was no longer by his side. He turned and said, "There's a height limit." He was wearing a quizzical expression. "It's like four feet or something. The ball pit's only for kids. Or parents who have to go in after their kids."

"Are you serious?"

"You didn't know that?"

"Why would I know that?"

"I guess you wouldn't."

"Well, damn. I knew I was likely to be the only grown-up in the ball pit, but I thought that would be more a function of the size of my dignity, which apparently is very small, than my literal size." I was trying to keep my tone light, but I was actually disappointed. "There is Skee-Ball, though, right?"

"There is Skee-Ball," he confirmed. "And if it makes you feel any better, ball pits are disgusting."

"What do you mean?"

"Think about it. All those snotty-nosed kids. They're cesspools. And what do they do when someone barfs in there?"

"Eww."

"Exactly."

I forgot my disappointment as we were assailed by a wall of happy sound. The *bloop-bloop* of arcade games, the gleeful, sugar-jacked shouting of kids. The whole carnivalesque atmosphere of the place made me want to literally skip.

Mike Martin tried to buy us tickets, but I objected. It was one thing for him to pay for my ice cream after class when we had Olivia with us, but this was different. As he had just informed the Minnetonka Moms™, we were *not* dating. We were kissing but not dating. It should have been confusing, but somehow it wasn't.

"Come on," he said. "This was my idea. *I'm* taking *you* here. That's the whole point."

"Yeah, but you know I'm weird about money." Also weird?

That he *did* know about that hang-up. That I could reference the fact that he knew, casually in conversation.

"I know, but it's not a childhood dream fulfilled if you have to pay." I opened my mouth to issue a rebuttal, but before I could get it out, he said, "Humor a guy, Aurora Lake."

The way he said my whole name gave me pause. Long enough for him to buy two passes. No one ever called me by my whole first name—I was *Rory* pretty much everywhere. Except Mike Martin always called me *Aurora*. But this first-*and*-middle business was new. It made me feel warm. Cared for.

Was that...an OK way to feel around someone you were just kissing?

"All right," he said, as we walked deeper into the space. "We have two hours of play." He handed me a card. "Apparently we can pause the time, though, so what do you say we do some games, then take a time-out for dinner in a bit?"

"Sounds great."

He surveyed the space and, seeming to find what he was looking for, pointed. "Your Skee-Ball awaits, milady."

It turned out that while Skee-Ball was as fun as I'd always imagined, I was really not good at it. "I'm glad you're not paying by the game because apparently Skee-Ball is not my calling."

"The key is to keep your arm and wrist straight." He demonstrated from his own lane. "It's like bowling but with a slope."

"What makes you think I know how to bowl?"

"Surely you've been bowling?"

"Nope."

"Oh, wow. We gotta fix that. But we'll wait for Olivia. She loves bowling."

After a break for food, we played some arcade games. I sucked at all of them until we found a dancing game.

"Ah!" I had heard about these games, where you have to hit marks on the floor, but I'd never had a chance to try one. "You might be the Skee-Ball champion, but what do you want to bet I kick your ass here?"

"I would never take that bet," he said, swiping his card with a smile. It wasn't lost on me that we'd both spent the last hour grinning like kids yet were not kids. Our adulthood stood out here; we were the only grown-ups playing games without kids in tow.

The dancing game was harder than I'd anticipated, but I got the hang of it, and, as predicted, I cleaned Mike Martin's clock. You could choose your level, but even on the easiest one, he struggled to keep up. Eventually he gave up and I played solo. It was ridiculously fun, like should-be-illegal levels of fun.

When I had to give up because I couldn't breathe anymore, I stepped off the platform and Mike Martin kissed me.

"Oof." I hadn't been expecting it—I hadn't thought kissing in public was a thing we did—so our teeth clacked together and, startled, I recoiled a bit. He planted his hands on my cheeks, which I was starting to recognize as a signature move of his, but this was a more urgent version of it, as if he were trying to calm my startlement and get me to stay still so he could kiss me senseless.

It didn't last, though. He stepped back with his eyes wide. "Oh shit. Sorry."

Yeah, see? Kissing in public *wasn't* a thing we did.

I didn't want any awkwardness, so I said, "Let's turn in our tickets for prizes."

"How many've you got?" he asked as we stood at a prize counter that looked like a tsunami made of cheap, brightly colored plastic crap had struck it and receded.

"Enough for…" I looked around. "A rainbow Slinky? Or…" I laughed and picked up a fuchsia plastic…item. "Whatever this is."

"Take mine, too." Mike Martin had a fistful of tickets thanks to his Skee-Ball domination.

"Get something for Olivia. We shouldn't even be here without her. She loves arcade games, doesn't she?"

"Yeah, about that." He turned serious. "Maybe don't tell her we came here without her?"

"Of course. I'm sorry. We should have waited."

"No, we shouldn't have. And don't be sorry. I'm not, not even fake Canadian sorry. This was about you getting to do something you never got to. Olivia wasn't invited."

Well. I was in danger of getting a little verklempt.

"Take these. I'm going to hit the washroom." *Washroom*, I had learned, was Canadian for *restroom*. "Get something better than a plastic Slinky."

"What if I *want* a plastic Slinky?"

"Then get"—he bent over to look at how many tickets a Slinky went for—"two plastic Slinkys. Wow, this is a huge rip-off, isn't it?"

I checked out a stuffed frog that cost three thousand tickets. "Yep."

"I'll meet you out front in a few?"

"Thanks," I said. "For these." I lifted the tickets. "But also for…" I used my other hand to wave vaguely around. "This." I hoped he knew that I meant *Thank you for taking me here, but also thank you for being the kind of person I can confide in about my childhood disappointments.*

And the kind of person who would try to right them.

Click-click-click. "You're welcome."

13 — PUBLIC DISPLAYS OF AFFECTION

MIKE

I took too long in the washroom. I was trying to figure out what in God's name had possessed me to kiss Aurora out there.

Well, I knew the answer in a literal sense. She was doing that thing she did sometimes where she looked so wild and free, it felt like she was a giant magnet. Like if you let her draw you in with her pink cheeks and her wide smile and the clinking of her charm bracelet, you might catch her beat, be enfolded into a secret rhythm that would pulse through you and make you believe, for a second, that life was good and that everything was happening the way it was supposed to.

She'd been doing a lesser version of it earlier, in class. It didn't always happen when she taught, but occasionally the class would be working on a long combination and she'd stop cuing them verbally and they'd go through it silently. It usually didn't work. Someone was always out of step or forgetting what came next. But on the rare occasion when everything aligned, it seemed like she and the students were part of a larger whole, strands in an invisible web, as woo-woo as that sounded.

It was why I'd gone into the studio, even though Olivia

wasn't there. I'd been waiting in the car—I'd arrived early because I was embarrassingly excited for our outing—and I'd thought, *What if it happens and I miss it?*

But yeah, kissing in public: not a good idea. I hadn't been recognized at the arcade. I had met the gaze of one guy and seen a spark of recognition and done the Minnesota finger-lift wave and moved on, willing the spark not to catch fire. So I don't think anyone noticed anything. It was more the idea that I had lost control of myself. Like I thought I was someone else. Someone with a different life. A life where I was on perpetual vacation, no kid to worry about, just a date with a pretty girl in that limbo time between Christmas and New Year's where nothing seems real.

But it was real. My life was real. I was a widower getting an F in work-life balance.

The larger question was whether kissing was a good idea at all, even at home. The answer, of course, was no. Aurora was our not-nanny, and we needed her. It wasn't even about Aurora. I couldn't date *anyone*, not for a long time—probably not till Olivia was out of the house. Dating led to breaking up, and I couldn't risk Olivia getting attached and getting left. Again.

I'd been drawn in by Aurora's low-stakes claim. It had *felt* low-stakes. Initially. But an impromptu *public* kiss? One I hadn't known was happening until it was *happening*? That had poured a metaphorical bucket of water over the proceedings. The stakes were not low. They never had been, not really.

She was waiting near the entrance, staring at a group of boys putting on coats after a birthday party. They looked to be about six or seven. She was looking at them almost hungrily. With anyone else, I would have said she was staring at them with a ticking biological clock. *I* looked at them that way. But I told myself to knock it off. That ship had sailed for me.

Aurora, though, was looking at the childhood she'd never had. I could bring her here and play Skee-Ball with her, but I couldn't actually give her the other stuff, the intangible things she'd missed out on that had to do with being a kid among other kids. Those long summer afternoons with nothing to do but drive with my buddies, blasting the radio and measuring, by the height of the corn in the fields, how many days left until the start of the hockey season. She didn't have those kinds of memories, and it about broke my heart.

"Hey," I said, "sorry to keep you waiting."

She turned, and maybe I needed to chill on the whole she's-mourning-her-lost-childhood front, because she shot me an exaggerated grin, and she was wearing fake vampire teeth.

I barked a surprised laugh.

"I thought I'd get some teeth and wear them to play fetch with Earl 9. I got this, too." She held up a multicolored Slinky. "You ready to go?"

As we got into the car, the boys from before spilled out into the parking lot, and she said, "I always wanted to have my birthday party here. Or be invited to *someone else's* birthday party here." Once situated in the passenger seat, she said, "Thank you. This was the most amazing evening. I mean, vampire teeth *and* a rainbow Slinky."

I started to say that the bar was low if an evening at a Tomfoolery rated so high, but I checked myself.

Anything I would have said was preempted anyway because she stuck the vampire teeth back in and said, "Best. Day. Ever" while she waved her hands around and wiggle-danced in her seat.

I started to understand that I might have a problem here.

But not really, because I was going to shut down the kissing. No harm, no foul.

"Everything OK?" she asked.

I was taking too long, staring out the windshield. I shifted to face her. She was leaning over, retying her boot, and her torso was twisted in such a way that her shirt rode up and exposed the bare skin of her belly. Something twisted low in *my* belly. All the kissing had awakened my long-slumbering libido. In a way, my entire acquaintance with Aurora had been a slow process of the revival of parts of me I'd thought dead. Starting from that time at the studio when she'd kicked her leg up high to show me her Band-Aid. That had been like a slap to the face.

And there was another slap. Just the sight of her bare skin delivered one.

"Yeah, yeah. Everything's fine. I just think we need to cool it on the, uh…"

She froze, looking startled. "We need to stop making out like teenagers?" she said, recovering quickly, and though the words themselves suggested she was teasing, her tone was serious. Almost solemn.

She sat up, fixed her shirt, and buckled her seat belt. Her tone adjusted itself as she said, breezily, "I keep thinking of it like that—making out like teenagers. I don't know why. I never made out with anyone as a teenager." She tilted her head. "Well, I guess that's not true. I did some making out in New York, and I moved there when I was eighteen. But you know what I mean. No making out in high school."

My first thought was that that was hard to believe. It was impossible to imagine teenage Aurora not being an object of admiration and/or lust of every boy in a ten-mile radius. But it was *not* impossible to imagine Aurora, daughter of Heather, who had never been to an arcade or a bowling alley, going through her teen years solo. "I guess that's another one we have to thank your mother for."

"Mm, I don't know. I might have to take some of the blame for that one."

"What do you mean?"

"I was...not popular."

"Yeah?" I prompted, wanting to know more even though I was supposed to be putting some distance between us.

"I wasn't stuffed into lockers or anything. I just didn't have friends. An idea took hold at my school that I thought I was too good for everyone. I wasn't around that much by the end, so it was...Well, I was going to say it was OK, but really it wasn't."

"Good for you." I smiled. "Your therapy must be working."

"Therapy is"—she blew out a breath—"bracing but effective. Anyway, no friends in high school, so certainly no boyfriends. But enough about my teenage loserdom. We're supposed to be discussing modern-day making out. You want to call a halt to it."

"I don't *want* to, but..."

"I know. Olivia's going to be home. Back to reality."

"I don't want things to get...leaky." What if spontaneous PDA happened again? What if it happened in front of Olivia? I *couldn't* risk bringing someone into Olivia's life who might leave. I didn't know how to say any of that, though, so I said, "I just think we have to stop."

"I get it. It's a bummer, but I get it."

That—the "bummer" part—was incredibly flattering. In keeping with the teenage theme, I felt like a kid who'd found out his crush liked him back.

"Your virtue is safe with me," she said, and even though I kind of wanted to take it all back—call off the calling off— what could I do but start the car and drive us home?

———

Reuniting with Olivia was great. She ran right into my arms like she used to when she was little. The handoff went remarkably well. Stefan and Renata didn't invite me in; we chatted for a few minutes in their driveway, and when Renata hugged Olivia, they both held on tight. When they parted, Renata said, "Email me that picture and I'll get it ready for your next visit," and Olivia enthusiastically agreed.

"That picture" turned out to be of Olivia herself, one we had framed on a table in the living room, and "getting it ready" meant having it printed onto fabric they were going to embroider.

"It's so cool!" Olivia enthused on the way home. "We did counted cross-stitch, which Mom used to do when she was young and is also basically math. Grandma says I'm good enough to start embroidering, which is different from cross-stitch, and she found this service where they'll print *any picture* on the fabric. So we're going to try to do a picture of me and see if it looks weird."

"Great," I said warily. "And everything else was...cool?" We had FaceTimed a few times, and Olivia had seemed fine, but I hadn't been sure if she'd been performing for the benefit of her grandparents. As I had recently learned, she could put up a good front.

"Everything was cool. We only talked about Mom a little. And they're going to ask you if I can go down there for spring break, which I know isn't in the plan, but the embroidery pattern will be ready, and..."

She was trailing off because she thought she was hurting my feelings. She thought me versus her grandparents was a zero-sum game. I regretted my part in making her think that way. "Sure," I said, even though it about killed me. I wasn't as resilient and nimble and forgiving as Olivia. "I'll talk to them."

The closer we got to home, the more the past few days began to feel like a dream from another life. That time Aurora kissed me by the Christmas tree. That other time she smiled at me with vampire teeth. Did all that happen to me or to some shadow, alternate-universe version of me?

"Is Rory home?" Olivia asked after she reunited with Earl 9.

"I think she's downstairs." I could tell by Olivia's puppy-dog face that she wanted to see Aurora. I'd been expecting Aurora to emerge to welcome Olivia, but perhaps she was taking some of that distance I'd been thinking we needed. "Sorry, kiddo. We have to respect her privacy. You'll see her soon enough."

Liv performed an exaggeratedly resigned sigh.

I understood.

———

Dr. Mursal told me, early on, that some people have trouble with "firsts" after the death of a loved one. First time the departed's birthday rolls around, first Christmas, and so on. Historically we had spent Christmas at our place but with Sarah's parents visiting, then we'd fly to Manitoba on Boxing Day for a quick visit. It was always a whirlwind as we attempted to cram all the visiting into the few days I had off. Stefan and Renata obviously weren't with us this year, and I'd told my parents that Liv and I would take a pass on the Canada visit. I wanted her to have some downtime at home after her Chicago trip, which I hadn't expected to go as well as it had. So all in all, it had been a low-key Christmas.

New Year's Eve, by contrast, Liv and Sarah had always

spent at home, and I would join them when I didn't have an away game. The vibe was always relaxed. We were glad to be together, glad to be done with the bustle of the holiday. Though of course I, newly acquainted with the work involved in pulling off Christmas, now knew how much gladder Sarah had probably been.

This year, armed with Dr. Mursal's warning, I'd thought New Year's might be hard. Christmas hadn't been, at least after Olivia and I had our little breakthrough—though I was aware the ease of Christmas for me might have been directly proportional to the amount of kissing that had occurred after Olivia left town.

So maybe my grief reprieve was about to be over? I was braced for melancholy, is the point.

There wasn't really time to be sad, though. Mostly because we had an afternoon game, and by the time I got home, I had to get right into party prep mode because Ivan and Lauren were coming over for a late dinner and skating.

"I'm going to change, but can I help you with anything before I do?" Aurora asked, wandering into the kitchen.

"I'm good, thanks," I said as I plopped some spinach dip into a bowl. "You're bringing Gretchen back here later, right?" Aurora and Gretchen apparently had a tradition of going out to an early dinner on New Year's Eve, then having a sleepover. I'd encouraged them to do part two of the tradition here. I wanted Aurora to feel like this was her home, too.

Also, I just wanted her around.

Even if we weren't kissing anymore.

It was confusing.

"Yeah, if that's still OK," Aurora said.

"Of course. We're going skating later even though it's freezing. Tell Gretchen to bring her skates."

"Great. And actually..." She lowered her voice. "I wanted to talk to you about something."

"Yeah?"

"Gretchen doesn't know about the making out," she whispered.

Ah. "Noted." It made sense that Aurora didn't want our "temporary Christmas insanity," to use her phrase, to bleed into her life any more than I wanted it to bleed into mine.

"No offense, I just..."

"None taken. I get it," I said.

Because I did.

Right?

A bit later, Olivia called me into the den, where she was watching TV with Aurora. It was novel to see Aurora so dressed up. Well, she'd been dressed up for Christmas with her mother, but that had been a formal sort of dressed up. Which I realize makes no sense, as *formal* and *dressed up* mean the same thing. But today she was wild-fancy instead of formal-fancy. She had on a flowy dress printed with little flowers. It only came to her knees, and she was wearing purple tights that matched the flowers. The ballet bun had been replaced by some kind of updo consisting of pinned-up braids, but they were loose braids that looked like they might fall apart at any moment. And even though I'd appreciated the scarlet lips of Christmas, I *also* appreciated their current glossy pink incarnation.

She looked like her hippie name. Aurora Lake going out for New Year's Eve.

Realizing I'd been staring at her, I turned my attention to the TV. "*Full House*? What happened to *Little House*?"

"This is the *Full House* New Year's episode," Aurora said, her amused gaze meeting mine.

Lauren and Ivan arrived a few minutes later, and we all

watched the Tanners ring in the New Year with kisses. One of the little Olsen twins even got to kiss the dog. "There's a lot of kissing in this episode," I said. I didn't mean anything by it, but as soon as it was out, I had to laugh at myself. I'd called an end to kissing, but now everyone on TV was smooshing their faces together.

Aurora met my gaze with twinkling eyes. "Except Stephanie," she pointed out. "She's eating an onion to prevent it."

"Just wait," Olivia said, and sure enough, soon Stephanie was tackle-kissing the boy she'd supposedly been trying to avoid.

"So much for not kissing," Aurora said, and I had to physically look away from both her and the TV so as not to laugh.

It did occur to me that for a guy who was done kissing, I sure spent a lot of time thinking about not kissing.

When the doorbell rang, I went to get it. "Can I interest you ladies in a predinner cocktail?" I asked as Aurora appeared in the entryway.

"If you can make it mocktail—I'm driving—absolutely," Gretchen said, shrugging out of her coat.

After I performed introductions, Olivia latched on to Gretchen and started telling her about Disney on Ice. Gretchen enjoyed near-celebrity status among her students. Olivia was tickled by the extra exposure to Gretchen that came with Aurora's being part of our lives.

Everyone walked the ladies to the door after drinks—the rest of us were headed to the kitchen to heat up the meals I'd ordered from our local lakeside place.

"You sure you don't want to take a cab?" I asked, aware that I was hovering over Aurora and Gretchen like a dad.

"We're good," Aurora said.

"Well, call me if you get into any trouble. Or if you decide you want to have some drinks, Gretchen, I can come pick you up. I'll lay off until you get home."

Gretchen made a strange face—like she was trying not to laugh at me, but not in a mean way. I liked Gretchen. Another big realization since Sarah died was that she had been the social gatekeeper of our family. I had my block about feeling like I could never trust people. That, combined with how busy my life was—the season was long—had meant Sarah took the lead on that front. I trusted the people she trusted. I literally could not remember the last time I—on my own—had made a non-hockey friend.

After they left, we ate and played board games for a couple hours before heading outside. Ivan and I were tired from the game, which felt like it had been a thousand years ago, so we sat by the fire while the girls hit the ice. When Aurora and Gretchen got back, they joined Lauren and Olivia—Aurora and I had gone skate shopping after her first lesson in the borrowed pair.

Gretchen professed not to have skated for years, but like Aurora, she had a dancer's grace and strength. Soon the four of them were laughingly making up a synchronized routine. I pulled my chair closer to the fire, cracked a Labatt now that I knew no one needed chauffeuring, and lifted the can to tap it against Ivan's bottle.

The stars were out in force, the stripe of the Milky Way slashed across the center of the sky. I thought back to that skating party last year, before Christmas. I'd watched everyone skate and thought about how good life was. And not a weak, superficial kind of good. Not like, *I'm rich and happy.* More like…I don't even know. When I was little, we used to go to church—just a run-of-the-mill United Church like you find in every Canadian town. Church had fallen by the wayside when hockey began to swallow our weekends, and I wouldn't call myself religious today, but the one thing that had stuck with me from those days was this saying that was probably from the Bible. I wasn't even sure, but it had been stitched on this giant quilted tapestry on the wall in the sanctuary. I, usually zoning out during the service, used to stare at it. It said, "Our mouths were filled with laughter, our tongues with songs of joy."

I'd thought of that phrase that night. That's what it had felt like.

I didn't believe in fate, so I didn't think I was being punished or hit with karma when Sarah died. But if you'd asked me last summer, when Olivia was lashing out and I was standing so close to the abyss, if I would ever get to have that feeling again, that sense of *rightness*, I would have said no. And I would have been OK with that, in a weird sort of way. I'd had it once. That was probably as much as anyone deserved.

But here I was having a version of it again. I felt that same sense of marvel sitting by the fire on the edge of the lake and the edge of the stars, listening to the happy chatter of my daughter against the background noise of scraping skate blades. Was there any better sound?

There was a hole in the feeling, of course. In the scene. How could there not be? But it felt like a normal sort of hole. The kind of hole you were *supposed* to have when you lost someone. It was a world apart from my pinpricks of doom. The abyss was in the distance now. It was a place I had once visited.

It changed things, that hole, but maybe not entirely, or not only, in the ways you would expect. There was a sense of loss, a person missing. But the proximity of that loss to *this*, to skating and a fire and friends who felt like family, made the evening all the sweeter somehow. It meant I had survived.

It was a frigid night, so the girls didn't last long on the ice. After a bit, they joined us at the fire and shortly after went inside.

"Do you think it's smart to get involved with Rory?" Ivan asked after a few minutes of silently staring at the fire.

I was shocked. We didn't really talk about this kind of shit.

"I'm not involved with Rory," I said quietly, aware that to object too indignantly would only make me look guilty. Which I wasn't. But he wouldn't understand that.

"OK."

He didn't believe me, which irritated me. "Look. If you think—"

"I don't think anything."

"I'm not—"

He held up a hand. "Will you just let me talk?" I rolled my eyes but gestured for him to continue. He huffed a breath, and the steam it made was illuminated by the light from the fire. "I want you to know that if you want to start dating again, Lauren and I are with you. I don't think there's any right or wrong timeline." He sounded like a robot, like he was reading a rehearsed speech. Maybe he was. "And God knows, Rory is great. But that's the problem. You need her."

"I know." Aurora was irreplaceable. "Which is why it's handy that there's nothing going on with us—other than, you know, school lunches and dance classes and stuff."

He shot me a look that suggested he didn't believe me. While I wasn't in the business of hiding things from Ivan, I didn't think it was worth explaining everything. Aurora and I were on the same page. We'd agreed to put our surreal few days of making out behind us. So I doubled down. "Look. I like Rory." It felt strange to call her *Rory*. From the moment I'd met her,

she'd been *Aurora* to me, and more recently, I'd started thinking of her with her whole hippie name. *Aurora Lake.* The skies
of my original home and the lake of my adopted home. *Rory*
didn't seem big enough, or beautiful enough, for her. "She's
great, and she really gets Olivia. So we've become friends. But
I'm not dumb enough to get involved with her."

Wait. Did "I'm not dumb enough to get involved with her"
suggest I *wanted* to get involved with her? Damn. I was confusing myself.

I eyed Ivan. Did I need to say more to get him off the scent?
"Regardless, it's too soon." Wasn't it? "I can't do that to Olivia.
Even if it's not too soon for me, it's too soon for her. I can't date
anyone. It's not like I'm going to marry the next person I date.
So when it inevitably ends, Olivia will lose another important
person in her life. That can't happen." There. Even if I was
confused about some stuff, I was sure about that.

Ivan nodded and turned his attention to the fire. I allowed
myself to relax, and a companionable silence settled. This was
familiar. How many hours had I spent sitting next to Ivan
while we either zoned out or paid attention to something
else? Airplanes, team meetings, fishing on the lake, watching
TV in hotel rooms. That's what I meant about us being more
quantity-time than quality-time friends. Obviously, there was
an underlying compatibility, but we didn't talk about our feelings and shit.

"Lauren's pregnant," he said, "and I'm afraid you're going to
be mad at me."

I would have laughed at the timing of that bomb, given how
utterly it flew in the face of everything I'd just been thinking
about how Ivan and I rolled. But of course when your best
friend told you he was going to have a baby, you didn't laugh.

"Of course I'm not going to be mad at you." I sounded mad, though, and I hated that. I also hated that I hadn't started with what I recognized objectively was the most important thing. I started over. "Congratulations. I'm happy for you guys. When is Lauren due?"

"May twelfth." He paused. "I know we talked about..."

Yeah. We used to joke about how it would be great if our wives got pregnant around the same time. The kids would be honorary siblings. Except for me, it hadn't been a joke. I'd had it all planned out in my mind.

I had learned the hard way that nothing is guaranteed.

I told myself there and then to try to remember that.

———

Inside, we found the girls watching the Times Square broadcast. Watching and dancing. A band I didn't know was playing a peppy, drum-heavy tune, and they were bopping around formlessly. But when the chorus came on, they got into formation and, laughing their heads off, did a dance version of the synchronized choreography they'd been doing on the lake.

Normally I loved watching Olivia and Aurora dance, and sometimes I even let them drag me into it, but as Lauren grinned at Ivan, I mumbled something about refilling drinks and headed for the kitchen.

Ivan's news had thrown me for a loop. Set me back from my kumbaya, everything-in-the-universe-is-as-it-should-be moment outside. I couldn't help but wonder what my life would be like now if Sarah and I actually *had* been trying. I wasn't angry at her anymore, but I was overcome with a kind of wistful sadness, nostalgia for the life I could have had.

I could have been standing here right now, everything the same, except with *two* kids.

I wanted that missing kid. I wanted that missing kid so badly it made my throat hurt and my eyes prickle.

Eventually I told myself I was going to miss New Year's if I didn't get over my bullshit. So I grabbed a bottle of sparkling wine, a bottle of sparkling cider, and beers for Ivan and me and headed back to the den.

The dancing was done, and Lauren and Ivan were all cuddly on the love seat. I wondered if, when Ivan told me I needed Aurora, he'd really meant *they* needed her. I wondered if he and Lauren felt they'd bitten off more than they could chew with all they'd been doing for Olivia and me. Regardless, they weren't going to be as accessible when the baby came.

I handed out drinks and sat next to Olivia on the chesterfield. She snuggled into my side, which had an immediate calming effect. "You remember last year?" she said, her voice muffled by my arm. "Mom wouldn't let me stay up?"

"Yeah." There hadn't been a game on New Year's Eve day last year. Sarah, who had always been big on the importance of sleep, had done an early countdown at nine. It wasn't that I disagreed about the sleep thing, but I also didn't think one night was going to do any harm.

"This is better," Olivia whispered, pulling away enough to meet my gaze. She had Cheetos residue on her face. Gretchen, apparently a big Cheetos fan, had brought an astonishing number of bags.

"This is pretty great," I agreed.

"Do you think that's bad?" she whispered. "To say that something's better without her?"

"Not at all. Your mom and I didn't always agree on everything, you know."

"Really? Like what?"

If she only knew. "My point is it's OK to enjoy yourself without her. It's even OK to notice times you're enjoying yourself *because* she's not here."

"I would go to bed early if it brought her back, though. I'd go to bed early every night for the rest of my life."

Oh God. This night. "I know, kiddo, but it doesn't work like that."

"I know," she said, in a voice that sounded too world-weary for an eleven-year-old.

She perked up as midnight drew near. We counted down and cheered when midnight struck. Well, most people cheered. I hugged Olivia, and my eyes automatically sought out Aurora, who was already looking at me.

~

Dear Mike,

I'm writing this from a bench in Washington Square Park because Emma locked me out of our room. She has a new boyfriend. He's a "filmmaker"—quotes because as far as I know he has never actually made a film. Anyway, I'm not slut-shaming her, but she never gives me any notice, and I have my meal-prepped food in our room. (Though I guess skipping a meal or two isn't the worst thing in the world, as we have our end-of-term performances coming up.) She puts a hair scrunchie on the doorknob when I'm not supposed to come in. She said I could use the same system, but she said it in a smirking way, like she knew I wouldn't need to.

I was drifting around this evening in exile when I ran into this guy Piotr who's in his last year. He's tall and quiet and gorgeous and, we all thought, gay. We started talking. He's serious by nature, and we sort of skipped small talk and went right to baring our souls. It was such a <u>relief</u>, honestly, to talk to someone like that. Turns out he's bi. Turns out he just got dumped. He told me about his broken heart, and I told him about Luc, who didn't exactly dump me since we weren't actually together—you know, on account of his French philosopher girlfriend. I can't even say Luc broke my heart, but as I told Piotr, he definitely broke something. Maybe just my naivete. Maybe that's a good thing.

Piotr wrinkled his nose and insulted Luc's turnout. We walked to Washington Square Park and looked at the budding trees and sipped from a flask filled with Polish fruit brandy from his hometown. When we got back, he walked

me up to my room, but the scrunchie was still on the doorknob, so he said, "I think this means you're meant to come
back to my room." He looked at me intensely and said, "I
have a single," and I knew what he meant by that.

I have to tell you, he was good at it. Much better than
Luc. He actually seemed to care that I was enjoying myself.

Which is why it was a surprise to discover that after he fell
asleep, I felt more lonely than ever. And now, since the stupid
scrunchie is still on the doorknob, I'm back in the park. It's
full of people. The whole city is full of people, but I'm alone.

I'm almost halfway done with year two, and nothing
about being here has grown on me. I want to go home. I
know I can't. But it helps just to say it. Thanks for still being
here.

Your friend to the moon and back,
Rory

14—HOW TO HAVE A DANCER'S BODY

RORY

It was a warm April day, and I was doing well on all fronts. I mean, first of all, look at me teaching ballet like it's no big deal. I even subbed in Gretchen's senior class when she was sick. They were an interesting bunch because although they weren't bound for ballet greatness, they had more mastery than my younger classes. Older teens tended to fall away from the studio because they joined their high school dance teams. The prestige—and, I assumed, the social aspect—of dance at school was generally a stronger draw than Miss Miller's for that age group. So I concluded that these senior girls were here because they wanted to be.

After class they came up all smiles and breathlessness. I had come to accept that I was low-level famous at the studio. Once I started teaching the Saturday ballet class, for example, enrollment went through the roof. Gretchen even had people from the next level trying to drop their kids down so they could be in mine. It was amusing. And flattering, I guess, though I wasn't sure what part of "ballet school dropout" was so appealing to them.

Anyway, my reputation must have preceded me, because these girls were full of questions about my time in New York.

I decided to go with the truth. "Honestly, it was pretty awful." That shocked them, and they exploded into a frenzy of follow-up questions. I tried to answer honestly as I entered attendance and shut down the computer—this was the last class of the evening. "I'm sure for some people it would have been different," I summarized. "But I came away with an anxiety disorder and an eating disorder. I'm not sure it was worth it."

That stunned them into silence. I low-key stunned myself, too. That was the first time I'd uttered the words *eating disorder* out loud, in casual conversation. Mary-Margaret was having a slyly profound impact on me, teaching me new ways of thinking and guiding me to look back at my past with those new ways.

The girls followed me outside like a line of ducklings, and when I finished locking up, there they were staring at me, my little flock. It was an unseasonably warm April evening. "Do you guys want to…go for ice cream? Is it too cold for ice cream?"

A few of them couldn't because their parents were waiting, but some of the older ones drove themselves to class, and I ended up at Suz's with two of them.

"So, eating disorder," said Taylor, the one who had started the interrogation. "I guess that's gone now?" She nodded at my scoop of mint chocolate chip. Wow, Taylor didn't beat around the bush.

"Pretty much." That was a lie. I guess my willingness to be honest with these girls only went so far. I was certainly improving. I ate all kinds of things now, even sugary ones. But I still cared about the number on the scale, even if I didn't think about it as much.

The anxiety part was better, though, objectively speaking. Not gone, but dramatically improved, in a way that felt real. I think a lot of it had to do with the ballet classes. After that initial freak-out at my first class, everything had been... fine. More than fine. I looked forward to ballet now, more than my other classes. I remembered what I liked about it. Not only with my mind, but with my body. "It feels like waking up after a nightmare and recognizing the surroundings of your comfy bedroom," I'd said to Mary-Margaret. "You've been far away, but now you're back, and you know this place. You *missed* this place. You forgot how much you appreciated it."

"Let me ask you girls a question." Time to turn the tables. "Why do you do ballet?"

"To be honest, just to keep my skills up," Taylor said. "I'm on the dance team at school, but that's mostly jazz and hip-hop. I'm going to major in dance at the U of M. I want to be a choreographer in the music industry—for music videos and tours and stuff. So ballet is never going to be my bread and butter, and it's not my fave—no offense—but I feel like I need to stay literate in it."

I smiled. Taylor had her act together in a way I never had. She reminded me of Gretchen and her no-nonsense approach to her career path. "No offense taken. What about you, Abby?"

"I don't know. I like ballet."

"What do you like about it?" I asked.

"It's hard to explain. Ballet is hard, but it's so great when you master something."

It was interesting that each of them had a different reason for being here—Abby for the love of it and Taylor for more practical, strategic reasons—but both felt legit. I didn't sense the ghostly presence of any dance moms here.

"I mean, I know I don't have a dancer's body or whatever," Abby went on, glancing at Taylor. Taylor was tall and thin, whereas Abby was a foot shorter and had curves. "But it's not like I'm going to do it for my career like you, Taylor. I just like it."

"You know that saying about the way to get a beach body is to have a body and go to the beach?" Taylor asked. I had not heard that saying, but it was delightful. I filed it away to tell Mary-Margaret. "I think the way to have a dancer's body is to have a body and to use it to dance."

Suddenly I was blinking back tears. In some ways, I felt like I'd learned more about ballet from Taylor and Abby and the senior ballet girls in one day than I had in years of study.

So yeah, things were good on the work front. The other work front, too. Since the breakthrough at Christmas, Olivia and Mike Martin seemed to be doing better, both individually and as a unit. Olivia was still a brat sometimes, but it seemed more like normal tween bratdom. Homework was less of a battle, and we had fun when Mike Martin was away. And when he wasn't, we went to some of his games, always sitting near the glass. Lauren joined us sometimes, and it was fun hearing about her ultrasounds and nursery decor plans. Olivia was excited to meet the baby and had declared herself honorary big sister.

And Mike Martin. Oh, Mike Martin. He was just so . . . him. The dude was the full package. He was funny and sweet and handsome, and I could not stop staring at his lips, even though it had been months since they had touched mine. It was as if that period of making out had ignited a strange lip-awareness in me. It used to be his eyes. And his dimple-igniting smile. Now it was his lips, too. So basically his whole face.

Despite my face ogling, nothing was awkward between us.

In fact, I'd say we were true, genuine friends. More than that. It sort of felt like we were partners. Not in a life-partner way, but in that we were united in managing Olivia, both logistically and emotionally. We had joked a few times about how to label our relationship. We remained difficult to categorize, but it didn't feel like it mattered. We trucked along well, we liked each other, and I was making a huge dent in my debt since I had zero life expenses.

I did miss the kissing part, but a girl can't have everything.

Sometimes, though, and increasingly, I was starting to get the sense that he might miss the kissing, too, even though he was the one who'd put a stop to it. It wasn't anything overt, just a sense of…awareness in the air around us. But then I'd tell myself I was imagining things, that wishful thinking was clouding my perception.

"Hey," Mike Martin said when I let myself in after my confab with Taylor and Abby. He was cleaning the kitchen, and I could hear the sounds of Olivia's favorite iPad game coming from the sunroom. "How was it?" His brow knit slightly. He knew I'd been subbing for a new ballet class tonight, and he was worried about me.

"It was good." I thought about my after-class chat. "It was great, actually."

He did the smile. The dimple did not appear, though—because he had a beard.

The Lumberjacks were in the playoffs. They'd advanced through the first round, but were down 0–3 against St. Louis in the second. The team had a tradition of growing postseason beards.

But yeah, the beard did cover up the dimple.

"You want some food?" he asked. "There's leftover pasta in the fridge."

"Thanks." I got myself a bowl, and we did a little dance. I'd headed for the microwave and, in so doing, blocked his reach into the cabinet he was aiming for as he unloaded the dishwasher. We did the side-to-side thing, each moving to try to make room for the other.

This was what I meant about the tension. That wasn't really the right word, but lately, the air between us felt charged, clumsy-making.

He laughed and pointed with a fork. "You go that way." As we successfully executed our pass, I noticed he had something stuck in his beard.

"You have some food in your beard, and judging from the look of that pasta"—I pointed at the microwave—"I think it's highly likely that it's Alfredo sauce."

"Damn it." He grabbed a paper towel but only managed to smear it around.

"Nope, it's more over here." I pointed at the corresponding spot on my cheek, and he smeared some more. I tried not to laugh as I shook my head.

"I hate this damn beard. Not only does it itch, it's disgusting."

"Here." I tore off some paper towels, dampened them, and approached. "May I?"

He held his hands up as if surrendering. "Please."

I used one hand to hold his face in place, and honestly, it caused a stupid little spike of desire in me. I hadn't physically touched him since Christmas. I wondered if he was experiencing something similar, because he took a sharp inhalation I would have said was a gasp except I don't know if you're allowed to call it that when it's a big beefy hockey dude doing it.

I kept my cool—on the surface; there was a lot of secret roiling going on underneath—and got the gunk off his beard. I was about to pull away when his hand clamped down on mine, keeping it there. He was beaming those green lasers at me. My stomach lurched. Was he going to *kiss* me?

The microwave started beeping, and we jumped away from each other.

I wanted to flee, to take my pasta downstairs to eat, but I also didn't want him to *think* I was fleeing.

How had I just been thinking how easy and not-awkward our relationship was? I searched for something to say as I sat at the island. "I always thought men liked growing beards because it was the path of least resistance. I thought you welcomed the break from shaving."

He blinked rapidly, and as I was about to repeat myself—or to actually flee; the jury was out—he unfroze and resumed unloading the dishwasher. "I don't get that. If you shave every day, it's fast, and beards are the worst."

"Well, you'd better hurry up and lose, then."

"Or, I've been thinking, I could just tell the guys that the presence or absence of facial hair has no actual impact on the outcome of a game, and shave." He smirked. We were back to normal.

"No, no. You can't do that."

When he was done with the dishwasher, he leaned against the island and...contemplated me. OK, maybe we weren't back to normal.

I worked hard to keep things light. "So you only grow the beard when you're in a team setting where everyone else is doing it for junk-science reasons."

He barked a laugh. "Yep."

"When was the first time you grew one?" This was so stupid. It was him that day at the mall. I knew it. If I wanted or needed it confirmed, I should have asked him. But the thing was, I should have asked him when I first met him, or at the very least when I moved into his house.

"Probably in the WHL. Beards were always kind of funny there, because some of the guys were so young they couldn't really grow them. They wanted to, but what came in was patchy and pathetic."

"You were pretty young then, too, right?"

"Yeah, but I was cursed with this"—he stroked his chin—"from pretty much the moment puberty hit." He stared into space like he was remembering something. "Nope, the first time I was forced to grow a beard for team superstition reasons, I was in Chicago. I remember now because I'd gone out of town to watch a high school tournament, and I was going crazy with the itching. I had to get some dental work done, and I was considering shaving and telling the team the dentist required it."

He chuckled. I tried to join him, but my heart started hammering like it was wearing its own little tap shoes.

"In fact, it was here!"

Well, *shit*.

"Well, at a rink in Bloomington," he qualified. "My old high school was part of it—my high school at home, I mean, where I played the one year. My buddy's little brother was on the team, so I drove up from Chicago to see a couple of their games."

And there it was. I'd known it all along, though, hadn't I? That there was some explanation for the age math that didn't add up? My tap-dancing heart was going for an encore. I took a deep breath and tried to tell myself it didn't matter.

"What was his name?" I asked. "Your friend's little brother?"

"Erik," he said thoughtfully. He had resumed looking into

space. His eyes narrowed. Oh my God. Was he going to *remember*? After all this time?

"I was just trying to think if I know what he's up to these days. I'm in touch with his brother, but only sporadically, and I've kind of lost track of Erik."

My heart calmed, but I was still feeling gross in a way I couldn't articulate when Olivia came clattering in and turned her iPad toward Mike Martin. She had lately been cruising online stores for dresses for the year-end dance. He leaned toward it eagerly—he was always so genuinely into whatever she wanted to show him—but then pulled away. "Two hundred dollars for a dress? For a middle schooler?"

She made a noise of frustration, and I picked up my plate and started backing away. Mike Martin met my gaze, and I expected him to tell me not to go, but he just sent me a little eye roll as he listened to Olivia talk about sequins.

I took the opportunity to flee.

———

Mike: Sorry about that.

The text came a bit later as I was sitting in my bedroom thinking about Mall Mike and trying to decide if I believed in fate.

I wasn't sure what he meant. Sorry because he thought I'd been chased out of the kitchen by Olivia's dress demands, or sorry because we'd almost kissed? *Had* we almost kissed? And if so, did I *want* him to be sorry? Well, whatever the answer to all those questions, it wasn't like it was going to affect my response.

Aurora: No problem.

I could hardly be like, *I am not sorry we almost kissed, if that is in fact what you are sorry about.*

Mike: I'm not spending two hundred bucks on a dress for an eleven-year-old.

Mike: That's crazy, right? On principle?

He did this sometimes—he was, on the surface of things, making conversation, but I had come to understand that he was seeking confirmation that he was a good parent. I was happy to give that.

Aurora: It does seem outrageous.

There was a long wait for his reply. He was typing, but then those bubble things disappeared. Then reappeared.

Mike: Olivia's grandparents want her over spring break, and she wants to go.

Yes. I'd heard them talking about this.

Mike: It's the week after next, and I have to stop waffling and make a decision.

Aurora: You don't want her to?

Mike: I do want her to go—I mean as long as she wants to. Is that terrible?

Aurora: Not terrible. We sometimes need breaks from
people, even people we love.

Mike: It's not that so much as…

The bubble things came and went approximately a million times, and I started to get jumpy. I felt crappy in a way I couldn't parse after listening to him talk about his trip to the Twin Cities all those years ago. I was irrationally afraid that he was suddenly going to remember me. I stared at the bubbles as if they were the means of my execution.

Mike: If Olivia is gone for a week, maybe we can make out
again.

Well. Holy shit with a grand plié. My mouth fell open, but that was the only body part I was capable of moving. I was paralyzed for long enough that he started showering me with a series of backpedaling texts.

Mike: If you want to.

Mike: You probably don't want to.

Mike: I'm sorry, that was out of line. I'm the one who called
a stop to it last time, so why am I talking nonsense now?
There are so many reasons this is a bad idea.

I wanted to ask him what those reasons were. He hadn't really articulated them back in the Tomfoolery parking lot beyond his aversion to "leaks."

I wanted to ask him what his intentions were, but that sounded kind of medieval.

I reminded myself that I was learning how to do things differently. Looking at my life with the new knowledge and skills I was getting from therapy. I was not the girl who bent herself to please men anymore. I was the girl who listened to her inner voice.

I closed my eyes and asked my inner voice what it wanted. I used Mary-Margaret's trick, thinking about what *I* wanted, what I truly, intrinsically wanted, versus what I felt like I *should* want.

The answer was clear: I wanted to resume kissing Mike Martin.

Mike: The biggest of those reasons being that I'm your employer.

I had to get with the program. I shoved back my vague feelings of guilt.

Aurora: No, you're my friend I kiss sometimes, remember?

There was a long pause, and more bubbles. I held my breath.

Mike: Am I your friend you want to kiss the week after next?

I answered before I could do any more overthinking.

Aurora: Yep.

Mike: With any luck we'll lose next week and I'll be able to shave this damn beard.

Aurora: Are you wishing for your team to lose?

Mike: I wouldn't say that. I'm just saying if we did, there
would be a silver lining.

———

I had thought earlier that *tension* was not quite the right word
to describe the vibe between Mike Martin and me. Except now
it absolutely was. Pretty much every interaction we had in the
week following was tension filled. We were constantly getting
in each other's way or trying to get *out* of each other's way. We
were clumsy, as if our reflexes were broken. Olivia was our over-
seer, stepping unwittingly into the crackling air around us, as
if the rules of chaperonage were reversed and we were awkward
under the scrutiny of a twelve-year-old.

And oh, the anticipation. If the air crackled around us, the
anticipation *roared* inside me. I passed the time between the
announcement of the kissing to come and the day it would
actually commence in a mixture of frustrated lust and jittery
unease. I thought Mike Martin must be on edge, too. Gone was
his usual breezy façade. When he went to St. Louis for what
turned out to be the last game of the season for the Lumberjacks, we didn't text about anything other than Olivia-related
essentials. When he got back, he didn't wink at me or flash me
any ChapStick-tube smiles. He just…got in my way. He was
always *there*, mumbling apologies when we bumped into each
other in the entryway, joining me with a newspaper when I
was reading in the living room, sitting too close to me at the
kitchen island.

It did occur to me how strange it was that all this emotional
drama was being expended on kissing. Just kissing. Like, sure,

pretty passionate kissing. "Making out," we had called it. But that was it. It made me think about all the stuff I had done in the past that *wasn't* just kissing, and whether I had always wanted to do that stuff. I thought about it so much I made Gretchen come over to talk about it after Mike Martin and Olivia left for Chicago. He was staying the night and would be back the next day. Renata and Stefan had invited him to brunch at their country club, and in the name of trying to get along better, he'd accepted.

"I need some advice," I said all of five seconds after she'd sat at the kitchen island.

"Ah yes, come closer, young Jedi." Gretchen said in a funny Yoda voice. She was eight years older than I was, but it sometimes felt like she was eighty years older when it came to life experience.

"Were you ever sexually attracted to someone but didn't have sex with them?" I asked.

"Uh, all the time? Michael B. Jordan? Mikhail Baryshnikov? Hello?"

I laughed as I set a glass of wine in front of her. "No, I mean someone you know. Someone you *could* conceivably be having sex with. Someone you're attracted to and who finds you attractive in return."

"Oh my God! Are you having sex with Mike?"

"No!" I hadn't even told her about the kissing, even when she'd pressed pretty hard after he picked me up at the studio for the arcade date and told the Minnetonka Moms™ that we were going out but "not going out–going out." But I was prepared to. I knew I couldn't open with a question like that and not fess up.

She raised her eyebrows. "Then you're going to have to stop speaking in code."

"OK," I said, muscling through a thicket of half-formed thoughts. "What about the reverse?" That was really what I was asking, right? That's what all the anticipation of kissing to come had me thinking about. "Have you ever done something physical with someone when you didn't necessarily want to? I'm not talking about sexual assault or anything. I'm talking about when you consented, but somehow, you still didn't really want to be doing it." That sounded dumb. Gretchen was the opposite of a pushover.

"Of course I have. I think that's called being a single woman. No, I think that's called being a woman, period."

Hmm. That was a relief, even though I was sorry that she, not to mention all of womankind, apparently, had shared my sense of ambivalence after—or during—sexual encounters.

"Hon, what is going on?"

"What's going on is I'm realizing that pretty much every sexual encounter I've had has been...complicated. There were two guys in New York, one I liked a lot, and sex with him was good."

"This is Piotr, right? You've always spoken well of him."

"Yeah. He was a good guy, but if I'd been honest with myself about what I wanted, I might not have slept with him. We met when we were both kind of heartbroken, and he propositioned me in this silly, romantic way. I thought, 'Well, this is how this movie goes. Now we have sex.' We had fun, but I wanted a boyfriend and I knew he was only going to be around for a few months because he was going to graduate. He joined the Dutch National Ballet, and that was it for us." I paused, thinking of my other example. "The other guy was a jerk."

"Luc," she said, making a face.

"Yep. I don't know, I guess I was flattered that he wanted

me?" I rolled my eyes. "In a way, that one is easier to parse, because he was my first, so I kind of didn't know any better."

I expected her to ask why I was thinking about this stuff, for it to lead to an interrogation about Mike Martin, and I was mentally preparing my confession. But she just grabbed my hand and squeezed. "What about Ian?"

I sighed. Ian felt like someone I had known a lifetime ago. "Ian and I were a mismatch. But not, like, a spectacular one. And I would say that went for all aspects of our relationship. I mean, sex was fine. It was fun. Sometimes, I'd come out of it thinking, *He is really seeing me.* But then..." I shrugged. "Anyway, here's what I've been thinking about: Say you were attracted to someone but you knew you *weren't* going to have sex." Gretchen scrunched up her face. "Hypothetically. Run with me here. What if you knew nothing was going to happen, beyond, say, kissing? Even if you would be into more, it's not on the table. How would that make you feel?"

"How would that make *you* feel?"

"It would be oddly freeing. Maybe a little frustrating, what with all the pent-up lust, but you'd feel safe. I don't mean safe from assault; I'm not talking about that, but, like..."

"Emotionally safe."

"Exactly."

"Well, that sounds lovely. *Hypothetically.*"

I eyed her. She should be able to figure out why I was suddenly interested in a philosophical discussion about sex, but she was being oddly chill.

"Can I add something?" she asked.

"OK." I braced myself.

She surprised me, though. "As lovely as this kissing-only scenario would be, sometimes, sex is the greatest thing ever.

Sometimes, you want it, your partner wants it, and you're in sync about both the sex and the emotional context—or lack of it—around the sex, and everything is great. We're making it sound like the woman always wants a lifetime commitment, and the man doesn't. You asked me earlier if I'd ever had sex when I didn't really want to. Sure, but I've also had my share of hot, no-strings sex that I enjoyed the hell out of." She smirked. "It doesn't have to be complicated. Sometimes great sex is just great sex."

I smiled. "That is good to hear." Not that I was going to be having any sex, great or otherwise.

15—HAT TRICK

RORY

We had sex.

Ha.

But not right away. Let me back up.

Gretchen and I shook off the philosophical chat and ate dinner and watched a movie while I tried—and failed—to stop thinking about Mike Martin. I still didn't know why Gretchen wasn't busting me about him, but whatever. She left, I went to bed, and I awoke at seven the next morning to texts from him.

Mike: Hi.

Mike: I'm leaving now.

Aurora: I thought you were staying for fancy brunch.

Mike: Changed my mind.

Hmm. Dare I entertain the extremely flattering thought that his early departure had something to do with me? While I was trying to decide how to respond, more texts came in that settled the matter in a way that made me blush.

Mike: I'm going to lead-foot, so I should be there in about five-and-a-half hours.

Mike: Get ready.

He arrived in five hours and twenty-seven minutes. I heard his car pulling up the graveled drive and about jumped out of my skin. Should I go out to meet him? I was frozen in the mudroom, indecisive, when the door banged open.

He didn't speak, just stalked toward me, dropping everything he was holding in quick succession—keys, phone, backpack. Plop, plop, plop, they hit the floor one after the other like little bombs being detonated.

The beard was gone since the Lumberjacks had ended their postseason run, but the dimple was not in sight. Because he was not smiling. He was looking at me like I was a vexing problem he was intent on solving. No, actually, he was looking at me like I was a sworn enemy he planned to wipe off the face of the Earth. In the best possible way.

He planted his hands on my cheeks and, with neither word nor ceremony, lowered his head and covered my mouth with his. He started walking, even as we kissed, which had the effect of walking me backward. We stopped when my back hit the wall near the staircase. As we had last winter, we kissed like feral teenagers, and it was *glorious*.

But unlike last winter, I didn't have that I-could-kiss-Mike-Martin-forever feeling. In fact, kissing him, as great as it was, was kind of agitating. Possibly that was due to the fact that our bodies were plastered against each other, which was a new twist. The winter kissing had been an upper-body-only activity; this was...not that.

Something happened then that I couldn't really explain, except by saying that we started communicating without words. I rubbed myself against him, he picked me up, I wrapped my legs around his waist, and he started up the stairs. We both knew what was happening.

But of course, Mike Martin, being Mike Martin, as he sat on his bed with me on his lap, did use words to double-check, after emitting a tortured groan when I rewrapped my legs around him in this new seated position. "It sort of seems like we're moving beyond kissing. Is that OK?"

Was it? On the one hand: yes, it was very OK. I wanted this.

On the other...What? I had the tiniest niggle, like something was holding me back, but I couldn't put thoughts to it, much less words.

So I decided not to overthink it. To run with the Mary-Margaret idea that it was OK to have fun, that letting in any outside notions of what I should or should not be doing wasn't useful.

"Yes," I said, and from there, it felt like the most natural thing in the world to tilt my head up so Mike Martin could scrape his teeth gently against my neck. And when his hands slid up under my T-shirt, tracing a line of sparks up my back, it wasn't at all awkward to move things along by pulling away long enough to take the shirt off.

He made another of those almost dismayed-sounding groans. I laughed, partly from pure delight and partly because I was objectively amused. I was wearing the world's ugliest bra. I'd assumed we were only going to be kissing, so I hadn't given it any thought. I didn't have a lot going on in the boob department, so I tended to wear bralettes. Most of them were cute, but this was a ratty old beige one I wore to teach in. It had a permanent sweat stain near one armpit. Leave it to me to wear my ugliest bra. Leave it to Mike Martin to admire it.

I decided to give him something more to admire and took off the bra. He closed his eyes as if pained, but his hands floated up and cupped my breasts.

I laughed again. I was a little bit high on the power I seemed to have, and laughing was begetting more laughing. I hadn't ever laughed while having sex.

He cracked one eye open. "What's so funny?"

"I don't know. This. Everything. That ugly bra."

The other eye opened.

"You do know I'm laughing with you, not at you, right?" I said.

"I'm not laughing." But he was grinning, and his eyes were doing the green-sparking thing. "You thought that bra was ugly?"

I started again, I couldn't help it. It was bubbling out of me. He joined me this time and, in a repeat of that day out on the dock, fell slowly back on the bed, taking me with him. "You have the *best* laugh," he said.

Then we were kissing again, but our entire bodies were involved. He was wearing his usual sweatpants, and I was wearing leggings, so I could feel his erection. It made me bold. I ground myself against him, and he responded by tweaking my nipples, which made me stop laughing and gasp as sensation shot through me.

"Sensitive?" he asked, tweaking a little harder, and all I could do was nod frantically. He grabbed my hips and scooched me up his body, which on the one hand I objected to because it broke the contact between our hips, but on the other...

"Oh my God," I gasped as he fastened his mouth on one nipple. He hummed his approval as he worked it over, and yes, I had always been sensitive there. There was an invisible cord between that stiff little peak and the growing heat between my legs.

It was all happening too fast. I didn't want it to be over yet. I had a split second where I thought, *How can I communicate to him that I don't want this to be over yet?* but then I opened my mouth and said, "I don't want this to be over yet, and I'm getting too close. So you should take your clothes off."

The laughter burbled up again—both over how easy that had been and at how quickly he responded to my suggestion, flipping me onto my back and shucking his shirt, followed by his sweats and underwear. When he was done, he crawled on top of me, but he stayed on his hands and knees—one hand on each side of my torso and one knee on each side of my hips—and contemplated me.

I contemplated him, too: Mike Martin, naked. He was all athletic and muscly, which was not a surprise. But he had a big tattoo of a bird of prey of some sort on his chest. He was so earnest and clean-cut outwardly that the ink *was* a surprise.

"How far exactly are we moving beyond kissing?" he asked.

"I'm not on birth control. Do you have any condoms?"

"I...don't." If I'd thought for a second that something dark had passed over his eyes, I must have been mistaken, because they started sparking again as he said, "So I guess we're not moving *that* far beyond kissing."

"There are a lot of other things we can do," I said.

"You got that right." He heaved himself onto the bed so he

was lying on his side next to me and reached a hand down my leggings.

It took very little time. He had the other end of that imaginary string now, and I was helpless to resist. The tension ratcheted up as he rubbed, circling my clit but not quite touching it. I had the vague sense that I should be paying some attention to him, but when I reached for him, he used his free hand to bat me away. "You first," he said in a growly whisper. "I want to watch."

Oh God. I lurched toward the cliff, shamelessly humping his hand, and it only took a minute or two until I fell. I watched him the whole time, and he watched me. It was intense, but also...fond. We smiled at each other, and this time when I reached for him, he only groaned. He was hard and hot and smooth in my hand. I hadn't done this for so long. Well, maybe I had never done this. I had never stared into a man's eyes while I gave him a hand job. I had never let a man stare into mine while he gave me one. Both things were easy, the staring and the orgasms. His arrived as rapidly as mine had, and with a self-deprecating snort—I assumed over how quickly he'd come, but I didn't mind at all—he flopped onto his back. I rolled over to face him. "That was—"

Oh shit.

"Are you OK?" I whispered, even as I realized what a dumb question that was. He was clearly *not* OK. He was crying. Even though he had his head turned away from me, I could tell.

"Yeah," he said, rolling his head back and swiping at a few tears. "Shit. I'm sorry."

"*I'm* sorry," I breathed, crashing back into reality. "This was a mistake. We got carried away. It won't happen again." I should have listened to that niggle I'd had before we started.

I'd been so focused on whether this was the right thing for *me*. Maybe that niggle had actually been an intuition about this being a bad idea for *him*.

He rolled to face me and flashed a smile that was almost a smirk. "Oh, it will happen again. Preferably with a condom. Which I intend to go out and get ASAP."

My face must have telegraphed the confusion I felt. He grabbed my hand and laced his fingers through mine. With his other hand he gestured at his now-tear-free face. "That was... some kind of reflex. I should probably be embarrassed, but I'm pretty sure you're not the kind of person who cares about shit like that."

I didn't know how to say that I didn't care that he had cried, but I did care about *why* he had cried.

"I would really, really like to do this again," he said, grinning. But then the grin faded. "If you do," he added.

Did I? I mean, yes, I did. But there was still the mystery niggle. "I do want to do this again, but I think we should talk about this"—I copied the gesture he had used earlier—"reflex."

He sighed and looked past me, staring off into space over my shoulder. I waited. He transferred his attention back to me, his eyes boring into mine. "I realize it's extremely shitty to talk about her when I'm in bed with you."

"No, it isn't. She was your wife." I'd assumed his reaction had something to do with Sarah. I was pretty sure this was the first time he'd had sex since she died. I didn't know what Mike Martin got up to on the road, but I had a hard time seeing him entertaining puck bunnies. "Are you feeling guilty?" I asked, as gently as I could. I hated that I'd experienced our coming together as so amazing, and he was feeling guilty.

"No, it's more that I never imagined myself having sex with

anyone else. Marriage vows, you know..." He rolled his eyes, making fun of himself, but of course Mike Martin was the type to take marriage vows seriously. "One of the things I've learned about grief is that there are these milestones you're supposed to care about, like birthdays and holidays. I find myself passing them without fanfare. But then there are milestones you *don't* know are going to be a thing until they rise up and slap you in the face."

I laid my palm gently on his newly smooth cheek. I didn't know if that kind of thing was allowed. Was it too tender a gesture? It must have been OK, because he quickly put his on top of mine to keep it there. "There's also—"

"What?"

"There's also some other junk going on in my mind that I don't really want to talk about, if you don't mind. I promise it has nothing to do with you."

"Of course I don't mind." I mean, I desperately wanted to know what this "junk" was, but I was in no position to push.

He lifted his hand, so, taking that as my cue, I started to retract mine. He stopped me, grabbing my wrist and fingering my bracelet. "What's the story with this?"

"Just a charm bracelet." I started to get hot. I didn't know why.

Well, I did know why. Because I'd lied to everyone I'd known and told them my Canadian Boyfriend had bought it, and all the charms on it, for me.

"It's awfully cute."

"Thanks." I tugged against his grip, but he didn't let go.

"Ballet shoe, state of Minnesota, apple—is that the Big Apple as in New York?" I didn't give an answer, but he didn't seem to need one. He moved on. "Those all make sense, but what's the deal with the Snoopy? Oh, and look—is that a maple leaf? What are you, some kind of closet Canadian?" He grinned.

I used his own words. "I don't really want to talk about it, if you don't mind."

"Of course I don't mind," he said, using my words as the smile slid off his face, replaced with something that looked dangerously tender.

What I could not do was use his other words: *I promise it has nothing to do with you.*

———

We had a lot of sex that week. Seeing Mike Martin naked became normalized. (Seeing Mike Martin naked became normalized!) The niggle was gone, and we had a blast. For the first time in my life, I got myself into that space Gretchen had talked about, where I was having great sex with a man and we were both in sync about the context of said sex. I knew we weren't going to become boyfriend and girlfriend. We didn't sleep in the same bed. We jumped each other wherever and whenever was convenient, and sometimes we'd nap a bit after sex, but we seemed to have an unspoken agreement to eventually retreat to our own bedrooms. I knew what this was, and what it wasn't.

The morning of the day Olivia was due to be dropped off, I seized what I assumed would be my last opportunity to ask Mike Martin about his tattoo.

He looked at me very seriously for a long time, and I feared I had unwittingly opened a Pandora's box of some sort. Until he grinned and said, "I was eighteen, away from home, and I thought it looked badass."

"There's no big, deep meaning?"

"There's no big deep meaning."

We both cracked up.

"I think I better examine this eagle a little closer," I teased, leaning over to lick his chest.

"Hey now, this is a falcon. Would a good Canadian boy get an *eagle* tattoo?"

"Oh, excuse me, my mistake."

We cracked up. Laughing in bed had remained a thing—after those initial tears, anyway. Great sex could be fun. Funny. Who knew? Great sex could also, it turned out, make everything else better—like some kind of orgasmic Mrs. Dash sprinkled over your entire life.

After our second go-round, we went back to the laughy stuff when he said, "Do you know that your orgasm face is the same face you made the first time we went for ice cream?"

"It *is*?"

"I thought maybe you didn't like the ice cream, but now I know that wasn't the case."

"Yeah, that was the first time I'd had ice cream in eleven years."

"Really?"

"My mom never let me have it—I've told you about her and sugar." He nodded. "I tried to have some in New York—a little act of rebellion, I suppose. I only got a couple bites down before I freaked out."

"Panic attack?"

"No, those were always about being the center of attention. Being tested or fitted for a costume, stuff like that. With the ice cream, I don't know, I guess I'd internalized the whole sugar-equals-poison thing so much that I couldn't enjoy it."

He got quiet, staring at me while he played with my hair. "I didn't know any of this when I started buying pies for you."

"No," I agreed.

"Maybe I shouldn't have?"

I shook my head. "No. You couldn't have known. And it helped. You didn't foist anything on me—you weren't even here. It was...a safe way to experiment." I made a face. "Listen to me. I sound like I'm talking about drugs. Anyway, I'm making a lot of progress with the therapist." I was finally starting to *believe* her about food being morally neutral. It was making it so I could choose to eat or not to eat something without it feeling like such a big deal.

He smiled at me with what looked an awful lot like tenderness, but then he grabbed my boob and said, "Hat trick?"

"What trick?"

He chuckled. "It's when a player scores three times in a game."

OK, this was it. The hard part. "I can't. I'm going out with Gretchen."

He lay back in the bed and clutched his chest like he'd been slain.

Yeah, same. But I'd made the plans specifically to avoid awkwardness at the end of our week. I knew he was going to call a halt to things again, like he had with the kissing over Christmas. Somehow, it felt easier to be the one who initiated the disentanglement.

"You going to be out late?" he asked, though we both knew what he was really asking.

"Yeah, probably," and we both knew what I was really saying.

"Right." He sat up, all traces of humor gone from his demeanor. "Should we talk about this?"

"I'm not sure what there is to say. You can't be having a fling with the nanny once the kid is home." I understood that, though it didn't mean it was going to be easy to go cold turkey after such a spectacular week.

"You're not the nanny."

Right. The longstanding joke about what we were to each other. It was starting to feel less funny. "But this is a fling, right? *Was* a fling," I added, emphasizing the past tense to telegraph that I understood. That I was not the kind of girl who was going to press him for more than he could reasonably give.

He looked at me for a long time. "It can't be anything else."

My first instinct was to ask why, but I knew why. His fear of "leaks." Even if I still didn't know exactly what that meant, I understood that it was shorthand for a lot of bigger stuff. Not being ready for anything serious, maybe. Or not wanting to upset his hard-won balance with Olivia.

"Of course. It was…" I cleared my throat. "Fun while it lasted." That was true, so I wasn't sure why the words felt so clunky in my mouth. I got out of bed. "I'll see you tomorrow. Say hi to Olivia for me."

Getting ready to meet Gretchen, I thought again about her theory that the best sex happened when you and your partner were in sync with the sex stuff *and* with the emotional context surrounding the sex. Mike Martin and I had been in sync all week. So what was my problem now? I had to get myself back in sync, or someone was going to get hurt, and I very much feared that someone was going to be me.

16 — TRICK QUESTIONS

MIKE

"Lauren and Ivan had their baby," I said to Dr. Mursal the moment I sat down the third week in May.

"And?"

"Her name is Annika and she's tiny and perfect." She looked exactly like Ivan, and even though his features should have looked weird on a baby, the big dark eyes and wide mouth just kind of worked.

"And?"

"They invited us over a few days after they got home from the hospital. It sounds like it was a long delivery, and she's colicky, but she calms right down when Ivan sticks his tongue out at her and makes this stupid squeaking noise. They let Olivia hold her with a pillow in her lap, and she was beside herself with excitement. She kept talking about how old she would be when Annika hit certain ages, and how she was going to babysit."

"And?"

I rolled my eyes. Dr. Mursal did this sometimes, kept pressing me to answer her questions in a different way. "I'm a thirty-five-year-old man with baby fever and a dead wife, and I'm consumed with jealousy."

Dr. Mursal sat back and stopped with the "And?"s. I guess I'd finally hit on the correct answer.

"You're sleeping with Aurora," she said after a few beats of silence.

"Not anymore. That was only while Olivia was out of town in April." And I'd thought of it every day since. "Anyway, what are you saying?" I wasn't sure how we'd gone from my being jealous of Ivan's baby to my having slept with Aurora. "You want me to knock up the nanny?"

"That is not what I'm saying. As an aside, I would like to point out that Aurora is the nanny when it's convenient and not the nanny when it's not."

"What does *that* mean?" I was peevish today. The nice thing about talking to a shrink as opposed to a friend was that you were allowed to be peevish without anyone taking it personally.

"Part of your rationale for sleeping with Aurora was that she wasn't the nanny; she was your friend. Yet when I challenged you just now, she was the nanny."

"Point taken, but I still don't know why you're pointing to my sleeping with Aurora like it's relevant. You're going to need to dumb it down."

"I merely meant that you found intimacy with someone else. Your dream of a baby isn't an impossible one."

"Yeah, OK, we had sex, but I'm not *emotionally* intimate with Aurora."

But was that true? The image of her having that panic attack in the studio popped into my head. Of my looking at her reflection in the mirror and knowing what was happening without her having to say anything. That had been so long ago. Before we slept together. Before we even kissed.

"You told me you trusted Aurora to take care of Olivia. You told me she didn't care about your job or your money, that she cared about you. You told me—"

"OK, OK. But we're not emotionally intimate in a *coupley* way. We're friends. We're emotionally intimate friends...who also used to be physically intimate."

Wait.

"I'm not trying to trick you. I'm not saying have a baby with Aurora, or date her. I'm merely holding up your relationship with her as an example of how life goes on. You thought you and Sarah were going to have a baby. That turned out not to be true. Then you thought you'd never have another child. Perhaps *that* will turn out not to be true. Life is long. That's all I'm saying."

"OK," I said, though in my heart I knew she was wrong. I got what she was saying, hypothetically. Like, if I was some other guy, maybe. But I was me. I knew somehow that I was only going to get one shot at the whole marriage-and-kids thing. I couldn't even *date* anyone until Olivia was much older. I appreciated Dr. Mursal's optimism, but that ship had sailed.

———

"Well, don't you clean up nicely?" Aurora came down the stairs, stuck her hands on her hips, and eyed me as I stood in the entryway on a Friday night in early June waiting for Olivia. It was finally time for the big dance. Olivia was going with Sophia and some other friends after pizza at Sophia's, and I— God help me—was chaperoning.

"Thanks." We had to wear suits coming into and out of

games, so Aurora had seen me dressed up plenty of times, but her compliment in this context was making my face heat. "Olivia almost ready?"

"Yep. I finished with her hair, but she's having second thoughts about the tights, so she's switching them up." Her eyes danced.

Thank God for Aurora, who knew how to do the French braids Olivia wanted to wear to the dance.

"She's sulky about your chaperoning, though," she added.

"I don't know why. Sarah chaperoned all kinds of stuff—though I guess nothing like this dance." It was weird to think that Olivia was aging into doing things that Sarah had never experienced.

My attendance at the dance was another of those "Sarah always did it" situations. A PTA mother who somehow didn't realize Sarah had died had called asking for her, wanting to know if she'd chaperone. Awkwardness had ensued when I'd informed her that Sarah was, in fact, dead—and for some reason I'd decided to smooth over that awkwardness by volunteering myself? I was not looking forward to it, but now that Sarah was gone and I was having to confront how much I had not been around—mentally, I mean, in addition to my more obvious physical absences—I had to man up and do my job.

Olivia came down the stairs, and she looked so old all of a sudden, in her swingy purple dress. It came to her knees in the front and was longer in back and was studded with sparkles. It was very her—and it had not cost two hundred dollars. "You look great."

"I decided not to wear tights at all. I was already getting hot in them, and I think the gym will probably be stuffy." She glanced at Aurora like she was looking for reassurance.

"Good move."

"I like your shoes," I said. She was wearing her runners, which were also purple—a perfect match for the dress.

"*Dad*," she said, and although the word was laden with annoyance, I was pretty sure it was fond annoyance. I'd take it regardless since it wasn't Mike. "I'm only wearing these till I get there. I have my real shoes in my bag. I'm going to change at the last minute since they hurt my feet."

"Or you could wear shoes that don't hurt your feet?"

She rolled her eyes. I glanced at Aurora, who was trying not to laugh. I had the sudden, absurd wish that she were coming with me.

At the dance, I helped set up tables around the edge of the gym, then went to mind my drinks station.

"Dad!"

"Hey, Liv!" I was pleasantly surprised she was even acknowledging me, much less trotting up to my side.

"I forgot my shoes!"

I looked at her feet, and sure enough, she was wearing the purple runners.

"I thought they were in my bag, but I went to change into them, and I don't *have* them! I remember now I took them out to try them on with and without the tights, and I *left* them in my *room*! I tried to chase down Sophia's mom when I realized, but she was already pulling away and didn't see me."

Her emphasis on so many words was amusing me, but I schooled my face. "At least your runners are a perfect match for your dress."

"I can't wear *these*!"

"Well, there's nothing I can do about it. I've got a job here."

"Can you call Rory and ask her to bring them?"

"No, but you can." I handed her my phone.

Twenty minutes later, my phone dinged.

Aurora: I'm here with Olivia's shoes. She said she'd meet me out front, but she wasn't there, so I've parked and am making my way inside.

I eyed the lineup of kids at my station.

Mike: Sorry about that. I'm at the drinks table in the back right corner of the gym, and I can't leave. You mind coming here and leaving them with me?

She appeared a few minutes later. "Wow, peak school dance."

"You went to a lot of them?" That surprised me, given what she'd told me about her school years, but maybe being a dancer made school dances more fun?

"I went to none of them. But this looks exactly like my image of a school dance based on movies." She pointed at the two-liter bottles of pop and jugs of juice on my table. "Except I think this is supposed to be a punch bowl."

I chuckled. "Yeah, but I think I'm here for the same reasons the punch-bowl guard would've been in the movies." The kids were serving themselves, but I'd been told to keep an eye out for flasks and had even confiscated one from a kid who looked like this was maybe not his first crack at grade eight. I surveyed the room. "This does sort of look like a school-dance set, doesn't it?"

"Yeah. Did your school dances look like this?"

"I didn't go to them, either. My middle school didn't do dances that I can remember."

"What about high school? Prom?"

"No prom for me. I was barely part of the high school I went to."

"Still, I would have thought you'd've been a hot commodity for prom—the hotshot hockey player." She wasn't wrong, but I didn't know how to explain my aversion to socializing in high school. I didn't have to, because she quickly added, "But I suppose that's exactly why you *didn't* go. You don't like people seeing only the hockey player."

"That's..." So spot-on, it was disconcerting. "Why didn't you go to your prom?" I asked, wanting to deflect attention from me and my hang-ups.

She looked at me for a long time, long enough that I had to break eye contact so as not to be neglecting my beverage-policing duties. She finally said, "I didn't have a date."

I'd been expecting a more involved, possibly more fraught, story, given how intently she'd been looking at me.

"I secretly wanted to go, though," she said with a touch of wistfulness.

Aww shit. Every time I thought of Aurora alone, outcast, it made my stomach feel funny. I understood intellectually that kids were dumb and cruel, but at the same time, I *didn't* understand how anyone could hurt someone as...bright as Aurora.

"I know that's stupid," she added dismissively.

"It's not stupid." Wanting to lighten the mood, I grabbed two cups from the stack in front of us and filled them with room-temperature ginger ale. "Here's to the prom losers."

She took the cup I gave her and tapped it against mine. "To the prom losers."

"Hi there." Two women approached. One of them was holding a clipboard. "You're Mike Martin, right?"

Crap. Here we went. "That's me." I could sense Aurora
stiffen beside me.

The woman looked at her clipboard. "OK, great. I just went
up to another guy and asked him if he was Mike Martin. I
thought Leslie had you down for coat check."

I almost laughed. Apparently she wasn't looking for Mike
Martin, hockey player, but Mike Martin, coat check guy. "Oh
yeah, she did, but then she told me to come here instead."

"Well, you're off duty. Sharon"—she gestured at the woman
with her—"is taking over."

"You sure? I thought I was on till nine."

"We have more parent volunteers than we know what to
do with, so you're off the hook." She made eye contact with
me for the first time, made a funny face, and said, "Run! Save
yourselves!"

I felt kind of bad for having assumed the worst about this
woman. "Thanks."

"I need to find Olivia," Aurora said.

Right. I'd forgotten that Aurora was not in fact here to chat
about our high school experiences but to deliver a pair of shoes
to my child. "Come on, we'll find her, then get out of here."
My beverage station was tucked into a corner that was semi-
obscured by the gym's retracted bleachers, and when we rounded
it, we spotted Olivia standing at the edge of the dance floor
near the DJ, who was playing a peppy song I didn't know at
near deafening levels.

"Hi!" she said as we approached. She was smiling and…
barefoot? I opened my mouth to scold her, to tell her going
barefoot in here was unsanitary and dangerous. But then I
closed it. Decided to leave it alone as she thanked Aurora for
the shoes and ran off.

The music ramped down to a ballad. This *was* a teen movie, with a disco ball throwing off bursts of light and the kids transitioning from dancing in groups to either awkwardly slow dancing in pairs or standing at the sidelines. A ridiculous idea rose in my brain, and I let it out before I could overthink it. "Dance with me."

"What?"

I held out my hand. "Come on. Let's dance. It's not the prom, but sometimes you gotta make do with what you have."

"I'm wearing sweatpants!"

She was. They were an awfully cute pink tie-dye pattern, and though technically they were sweatpants, they weren't the baggy type I favored. They weren't baggy *at all*. "So?" I challenged.

She hesitated, and she was probably right. Everything she was about to say—this was a silly idea, we'd look like idiots—was true. And oh shit, I hadn't thought about the possibility of a panic attack. She'd told me they tended to happen when she felt like people were watching and judging her.

I was about to start backpedaling when she shocked me by laughing—that high, melodious laugh of hers I liked so much—putting her hand in mine, and saying, "OK, you weirdo, let's dance."

It was a little awkward to start, as I pulled her close. She looked up at me, then quickly over my shoulder. I could feel my pulse kicking up. It was almost like the nervous energy being thrown off by the adolescent crowd was contagious. We settled, though, as we started to sway. I remembered that time we'd talked about dancing, and hockey, and what we got from our respective pursuits. I'd stumbled through saying that, sometimes, hockey made me feel like I was in sync with the universe.

Somehow, having Aurora Lake in my arms on a dance floor in a school gym full of tweens made me feel that way, too.

"Do you know what song this is?" I asked.

"No."

I tried to remember the lyrics so I could look it up later. Why did I want to look it up later? Because I wanted to remember this moment, to create enough of a sense memory that I could revisit it. Because I was happy.

———

The last week of school, I called a dinner meeting regarding the summer schedule. I invited Aurora since one of the items on the agenda was whether Olivia wanted to do a summer dance camp at Miss Miller's. She hadn't last year, in the wake of the accident, but she had previously.

"What's for dinner?" Olivia asked as she clattered into the kitchen followed by Aurora.

I picked up the recipe card that had come with the meal kit I'd just cooked. Since the season ended, I'd vowed we would eat less takeout and more real food, but so far my skills had only expanded as far as kits that came with everything prechopped. "Barramundi tacos with pico de gallo."

"Barrawhat?"

"Fish tacos," Aurora said to Olivia, and to me: "Do you need any help?"

"Nope, all done. Let's eat here." I patted the island, where I had a calendar laid out. I explained my summer philosophy as I handed out waters and cutlery. "As far as I'm concerned, this is the summer of fun. I have to stay in shape, but I can fit in workouts with whatever else we're doing." I slid a plate to Olivia. "Let's pencil in any camps you want to do, then we'll figure out when we're going to Manitoba. Do you want to do dance camp at Miss Miller's?"

Olivia said, "Yes!" at the same time that Aurora said, "Registration for dance camp opened in March."

Shit. "Really?" Yet another ball I had dropped. "Is it full?"

"It is, but luckily you have an in."

Damn. "Thank you."

"I was thinking we'd go to see Nana and Pop at the very end of the summer," I said to Olivia. "School starts later this year since Labor Day is so late."

"But will the pioneer museum still be open in September?"

"Should be, but I'll double-check." I turned to Aurora. "There's an old fur-trading fort near where I grew up." I aimed a thumb at Olivia. "She's been before, but now that you've introduced her to *Little House*, she's keen to go back. It has preserved frontier buildings and a replica pioneer village."

"My mom and I go to the Laura Ingalls Wilder Pageant in De Smet, South Dakota, every summer, so I'm quite familiar with the pioneer village genre." I shot Aurora a quizzical look as Olivia squealed over the idea of a Laura Ingalls pageant. From what I had seen and heard of Heather Evans, spending a day with her on the frontier seemed like no fun at all. Aurora, apparently hearing my unspoken question, said, "It's a tradition. One I should probably take my leave of, but..." She shrugged.

"I want to go to the pageant!" Olivia exclaimed. "Can we do that too this summer?"

"I don't see why not." I glanced at Aurora. "As long as we aren't cramping your style. Will it be weird if we run into you there?"

"Not at all. Anyway, it runs for a bunch of weekends, so I'm sure we won't overlap."

I kind of wanted to overlap. But maybe I needed to let my not-nanny do her own thing.

"Let's all go together!" Olivia nearly shouted—apparently I wasn't the only one who wanted to overlap with Aurora. "We've never met your mom."

Aurora met my eyes over Olivia's head. I wasn't sure what message she was trying to send. But since she hadn't embraced the idea of a group trip to De Smet, I needed to shut down the idea. "Don't forget you're also going to your grandparents' in Chicago this week," I said to Olivia.

Aurora whipped her gaze to mine, and because Olivia was looking at the calendar—my redirection had worked—I shot her a quick wink. I was pretty sure we were both remembering what had gone down last time Olivia was with her grandparents.

I wondered if there was any way it could happen again.

After dinner, it sort of seemed like Aurora was hanging back. I'd made Olivia load the dishwasher, and we quite clearly didn't need her help, but she just kind of…stayed.

"OK, you're excused, Liv," I said, eyeing Aurora. After Liv had run off, I said, "Everything OK?"

"I have a crazy idea."

"Hit me."

"Maybe we *should* all go to De Smet together."

"Wow, yes, that is insane," I teased, even as the notion of spending the day in *Little House* land with Aurora and Liv made something warm happen in my chest.

She laughed. "You know how I've been working on boundaries with my mother?" I nodded. "If we went to De Smet together, I could drive up with you guys. We could meet my mom and spend the day. You and Olivia might want to check out the covered-wagon camping they have and spend the night—it's a long round trip for one day—and I'll drive back with my mom. Only going one way with her will shave hours off the time I have to spend with her. It'll be kind of like Christmas—a planned reduction in exposure time."

"Sounds like a very mature approach."

"I must be maturing. I guess I'm a late bloomer. I mean I *just* went to my first school dance last week. Can you believe it?"

I winked. "Must be all that therapy."

"I have to say, the NHL plan is really working for me." Her eyes danced, but she quickly sobered. "But also, I think it's you."

"What? No."

"I'm serious. Watching you and Olivia...get better. I don't know, it's been inspiring. I mean, yes, I've been through some shit. But it's nothing compared to you guys."

"My shrink says that your suffering is your suffering and there's no point in comparing it to anyone else's."

"I know. I just mean that I've felt sort of...stuck in recent years. But I don't anymore. Or at least I feel less stuck. I have you to thank for that."

"I think you have yourself to thank for that."

"Will you shut up and take a compliment?"

"Yeah, yeah, OK." I grabbed the calendar and pointed at the weekend I thought we were talking about. "De Smet here?"

"Yes, if you're OK with it. I didn't want to say anything in front of Olivia in case you weren't. You've met my mom. She's kind of horrible."

"Eh, she's no match for us." We were a team, Aurora and I. In sync. Heather would need to watch herself.

"There is one more thing," Aurora said, "while we're talking about the summer."

"Hmm?" I said I as wrote "De Smet" on the calendar.

"I can't sleep with you anymore."

It was as if she'd slapped me—so much for being in sync—but I got my shit together enough to say, "OK."

"I mean, if that was the plan for the week this summer when Olivia is in Chicago. Not that I'm assuming that was the plan," she added quickly.

That hadn't been the plan per se, but it had definitely been the wish.

"I just…I didn't want you to think my big speech there about how you'd made me brave was…" She looked at her hands quickly. "It's been really fun. Like, *really* fun." She opened her mouth, closed it, then said, "And it's not like I was looking for anything serious."

I wanted to know what she meant by "was." Was she using that word because our…entanglement was in the past? Or was she saying she'd started out not looking for anything serious but had changed her mind? I cleared my throat. "Low-stakes, right?"

"Yeah." She smiled a little wistfully. "I completely understand that you want to keep this part of your life limited to when Olivia's away, but I can't…switch things on and off like a faucet, you know?"

I did not know. It was hard, the switching on and off, but in my opinion worth it.

Well, shit. If I'd known the last time I'd touched her, tasted her, was going to be it, I might have…What? Lit some candles and said a prayer? I needed to get over myself.

"I thought I could," she went on. "And, I mean, I *could*. I *did*. But I don't think the toggling back and forth is something I want to do anymore. I'm not in any hurry to meet a guy and settle down, but I do want to do that someday, and I don't think this…" She trailed off and waved her hand back and forth between us.

OK, so my not-nanny didn't want to have casual sex with me anymore. It wasn't the end of the world.

"No problem," I said, hoping my words sounded less strangled than they felt in my throat.

17—GETAWAY CAR

RORY

I had started the summer with the idea that I needed to put some distance between Mike Martin and me. When we had that planning session and he gave me the wink-wink and implied things might be getting hot and heavy again when Olivia went to her grandparents', instead of feeling excited, as I had when he'd made the same proposal in advance of spring break, I'd started to fret. I couldn't do the casual thing anymore. It wasn't like I was in love with him. But I was in pretty severe like with him. The idea of slipping back into that easy, laughing intimacy was *so* tempting. But at the same time, the prospect of it didn't feel...fun. Well, no, it *would* be fun. But it was starting to feel serious, too. Dangerous in a way that would outweigh the fun. Intrinsically—to use Mary-Margaret's yardstick—no longer a great idea if I wanted to keep going on this track where my life was getting unstuck. I'd meant what I said: he deserved a lot of credit for the progress I'd made. I'd learned a lot from him, and from the therapy he was paying for. He was a good person, and he was my friend. But at this point, if I kept swimming in these muddied waters, I was going to end up hurt.

I was proud of myself for coming to this conclusion, and for communicating it to him. For not doing things his way because it was the path of least resistance.

So the week Olivia spent with her grandparents in July was uneventful. We swam and hung out and generally had a good time. The only physical contact between us was incidental. It was hard to resist his charms—part of me wanted to say screw it and jump him—but it was for the best. That sense was ratified by how seemingly easy it had been for *him* to let go of the physical aspect of our relationship. He didn't seem bothered at all. Back at the calendar session, when I'd told him I couldn't sleep with him anymore, he'd just said, "No problem." After that, when we accidently brushed up against each other, it wasn't charged in the way it used to be. It was as if he'd flipped a switch and whatever attraction he'd felt in the past had just evaporated.

When our De Smet day rolled around, I was a little worried about how everything was going to go, but Mom was on her good behavior. And Olivia could have been a paid lobbyist for the Rory Evans cause, the way she talked about how much she liked my classes and what a good teacher I was.

"I'm not surprised," my mother said. "She's always been so talented. I only wish she'd stuck it out in her ballet career."

OK, my mom was on her good behavior *initially*.

"Well, *I* don't," Olivia said before I could jump in. She spoke with an air of defiance. "Then we wouldn't have her." She looked at her dad, and I wondered if "we" meant Olivia and the other students at Miss Miller's or Olivia and Mike Martin.

"My daughter and I"—my mom gestured to me when the lunch server came to take our orders—"will be on the same bill, and we'll both have the Greek salad with chicken, dressing on the side, hold the feta."

To my chagrin, I usually let my mother order for me. This annual trip was the only time we ever ate out together, and letting her have her way was easier than fighting. Or so I used to think.

"Actually," I said, "I'll have the BLT wrap."

I was purposefully not looking at my mother, hoping my lack of attention would prevent her from saying anything, but I was not so lucky. "Are you sure that's wise?" She was making the lemon-drop face.

The server paused in writing down my order and glanced between us. I smiled at her and said brightly, "BLT, thanks."

"Did you want fries or Tots with that?"

"I'm sure they'd do a side salad for you," my mother said.

Had she always been this bad? I supposed the answer was yes, but I hadn't felt it so keenly because we didn't usually have an audience.

I was embarrassed, but there was something else in there, too, something that felt a lot closer to...anger? Yeah. I was pissed. At my mother. For embarrassing me in front of Mike Martin and Olivia, but also for screwing me up. For making it so I was almost thirty years old and ordering a BLT was a triumph.

As I sat with my anger, I found I kind of enjoyed it, as unfamiliar as it was. Like that time Mike Martin and I had that argument and I'd felt a heady rush of power. So, not caring if it was petty, I leaned into that feeling, looked at my mother instead of the server, and said, "I will have the Tater Tots, thanks." Though as soon as it was out of my mouth, I had some kind of adrenaline crash. I was shaky and, honestly, starting to panic—and I could *not* do that here. My mom didn't know about the panic attacks; I'd managed to hide them from her after they started my last year of high school. I knew she'd be embarrassed. Genuinely confused as to why I couldn't just get over it.

And more than that, I hadn't had an attack for ages, and I didn't want to give my mother the honor of breaking my streak.

Mike Martin coughed, drawing my attention, and when I made eye contact with him, he winked.

It was just a little wink that no one else saw, but it contained worlds, that wink.

It said he knew what a big freaking deal it was for me to take a stand against my mother. It said he understood, that he supported me.

It said he saw me.

I heaved a shaky breath. I was going to be OK.

And I was going to eat some Tater Tots, motherfuckers.

————

After lunch we went to the pageant. As usual, my mother drew some unkind conclusions before the show even started. I felt bad exposing Olivia to this constant, passive-aggressive parade of negativity, but she didn't seem to notice, and once the show started, she was all wide eyes and exclamations. "She's so pretty!" she'd whisper about Laura, or "I wonder if they're going to use real horses!" My mother was the opposite, narrow-eyed and snippy.

Afterward, I turned into a chipper camp counselor shepherding us through the rest of our itinerary. We went to the cemetery and found some familiar names among the tombstones. We bought a tiny prairie dress for Ivan and Lauren's daughter. I tried to keep my mom from talking to Olivia by keeping up my own steady stream of chatter. Seeing their opposite reactions to the pageant had stirred up something protective in me. It also made me sad for myself. Not in a self-pitying way, more that I'd found a new well of compassion for the girl I'd been.

"Our last stop," I announced, as the end was in sight, "the Ingalls' homestead!" The visit went pretty well, but as we were coming off our covered-wagon ride, the talk turned to dinner. As soon as my mom started telling Olivia that since we'd had "indulgent" lunches we should "compensate" by "thinking carefully" about our dinner choices, I sprang into action. Mary-Margaret had helped me see how incredibly toxic this shit was, and over my dead body was any of it getting directed at Olivia.

They'd gotten a little ahead of Mike Martin and me—we'd been lagging as we discussed whether Pa's obsession with moving was a sign of his optimism or a sign that he was in denial—but I'd been keeping one ear open. Mike Martin must not have been, because when I cut him off midsentence and said, "Oh no you don't," his eyes widened.

I jogged up to them, my adrenaline frothing. "*Mother.*" She turned, her eyes wide. She knew something was up, but she didn't know what to do or say, because there was no precedent for this. No script. Which, on my end, was liberating. It meant I could say whatever I wanted. "There will be no 'compensating.' You will stop talking to her right now. I will not let you fill her head with that garbage."

I had snapped. Except instead of it being like in the movies where someone "snaps" and starts shouting, I was awash in a preternatural calm. I was righteous in my certainty.

"It's important to get started early with good habits," said my mother. "I was just trying—"

"No. We will be eating a normal dinner, at a normal restaurant. Everyone will order what they want, and you will refrain from commenting. If you're not able to do that, maybe it's best if you head home now."

"Well." She paused. "Maybe it *is* better if we go now. We can stop somewhere on the way to eat." Did her face soften a bit, or was that my imagination? "We can discuss our options in the car."

"I'm not going to drive back with you."

I sent myself back to that wink from lunch. Mike Martin would have my back. He would drop me off at a car rental place, no question. In fact, since he was physically behind me, I tried to tune into his presence, to feel him there as I geared up to push my way through the rest of this conversation. Because I was pretty sure Mom would have more to say.

"What do you mean you're not driving back with me?"

There it was. OK, we were doing this. "I don't want to spend four hours in a car with you. I don't want to spend any time with you, actually, not the way things are." She opened her mouth, blinked rapidly, and closed her mouth. Was I going to keep going?

Yep, I was. "You have not been good to me. You make me feel bad about myself. So I'm done spending time with you until that changes."

She gasped but recovered quickly. My mother did not like to think of herself as the kind of person it was possible to shock into gasping. "I'm not sure what more you wanted from me, Aurora."

"I wanted a mother. I wanted you to see *me*, and not the ballerina you wanted me to be. And when I came back from New York, I wanted—"

"When you quit, you mean," she interrupted, and it was hard to fathom that she could be so cruel, *still*.

"Yes. When I quit." I paused for a moment to let my easy agreement sink in. I suspected she thought I saw it differently. I didn't. I just didn't see quitting the same way she did. For her it had been failure; for me it had been an act of self-preservation. I hadn't thought of it in those terms at the time, but I did now, and I was grateful to my younger self for making such a hard choice. "And when I came home after I quit, I needed help. I needed kindness."

"You have no idea what I've sacrificed for you. What I've given you." Her voice was shaking, and normally I would have backed down at this point—long before this point, actually.

"I do, though," I said calmly. "You've given me a lot. You've invested money, and time, and emotional energy in me. Not lately, but when I was younger. I understand that. I see it. And while I can appreciate that there was a cost for you, there was also a cost for me. Whatever it was you thought you were doing, the cost was too high for me. I'm still untangling myself from that cost." But I *was* untangling myself, that was the important part, and it was such a relief to be on my way out of this web I'd been caught in for so long. "I'm not a dancer anymore, or at least not the kind you wanted me to be. I think it would be great if you could try to be OK with that, if not for my sake, then for yours. Because what you are right now is a dance mom without a dancer, and I don't think that's good for anyone."

Shaky, I turned and met Mike Martin's kind eyes. He was looking at me the way he looked at Olivia in class, busting with pride. "Can you drop me at a car rental place?"

"Sure can." He held his hand out, not in a romantic way, more in a *Come along; you're with us now* way. So I took it, and I walked away from my mother, maybe for the last time.

It felt amazing.

As we were pulling up to the restaurant we'd settled on for dinner, I started feeling a bit sheepish. "I should have driven the Normal Sedan. I should have known I wouldn't want to drive back with my mother even if we hadn't had that confrontation."

"I like the way we name our cars," Olivia said from the back seat, and something in my chest squeezed at her use of the word *we*. At that pronoun that wasn't really correct but sounded nice all the same. "We never named this one, though," she went on. "What should it be?"

"The Getaway Car," Mike Martin said as he cut the engine and turned to me, his smile and his eye twinkle both calibrated to maximum stun.

I cracked up. "Perfect." I turned to encompass both of them. "And sorry again about..." I waved vaguely. I'd known exactly what to say to confront my mother, but apparently I'd used up my allotment of the right words for the day.

"Don't be," Mike Martin said. Over dinner, I told Olivia a simplified version of what my beef was with my mother, and Mike Martin turned it into a lesson about boundaries and how some families had more problems than others, but I was still embarrassed now that I'd transformed from Hulk Rory back into my usual unassuming self.

"Hey!" Olivia exclaimed as she tucked into her chicken fingers. "I have a great idea! You should camp with us!"

I smiled and shook my head affectionately at her. When I looked to Mike Martin, he was striking an exaggerated *Why not?* sort of pose.

"I can't camp with you! You won't have enough space."

"Not true," Olivia said. "We have a bed and then these two mat thingies."

And so, a few hours later, I found myself sacked out on a

"mat thingy." It was atop a wooden bunk and decently comfy. Olivia had the proper bed, which was tucked into the foot of the wagon, and Mike Martin was on another bunk parallel to mine.

I was having trouble falling asleep, despite the cozy setup and the lulling sound of crickets outside. I wasn't agitated, though. I listened to Olivia's breathing lengthen as she fell asleep, and I felt calm—and free.

I rolled over to find Mike Martin looking at me from the other bunk. I'd thought he'd fallen asleep, but nope. He was lying there all tousle-haired, and he shot me a lazy smile by the glow of Olivia's bear night-light perched on the foot of her mattress.

"Did I just fire my mom?" I whispered incredulously.

He reached his hand across the few feet between our bunks. I followed suit. He grabbed my hand and squeezed. "You did, and you were glorious."

———

A month later, Gretchen came for a swim, and Olivia regaled her with tales of our pioneer adventure. "It was great!" she said in summation as we floated on inner tubes.

Mike Martin, sipping a Labatt Blue from his own tube, said, "Also great was that Aurora told off her mother."

"I heard."

"I wish you had *actually* heard. It was epic."

"Ding-dong, the Wicked Witch of Wayzata is dead!" Gretchen trilled.

"There's a pioneer village near where my grandparents live in Manitoba, too," Olivia, apparently determined to keep the conversation focused on her favorite subject, said to Gretchen. "But it's just a generic one."

I was about to object that it was probably more authentic than Laura Ingalls land, but Olivia shrieked and said, "Hey! Rory, you should come with us and we can compare and contrast!"

This girl could be so sweet, with her big heart. "I can't come to Canada with you!"

"Why not?" Olivia said.

"Well, I have a job, for one."

"I happen to know that your boss wishes you would take a vacation already," Mike Martin called from his inner tube, which had drifted pretty far from us, but clearly he was still tuned into the conversation.

"Yes!" Gretchen said. "Go!"

"You should talk," I said to Gretchen. She was always on me to take time off, but she definitely didn't practice what she preached.

"I'm the boss," she said. "It's hard for me to take off. But it's not hard for you."

"But they're leaving tomorrow!"

"I will cover your classes. When are you back?"

"September fourth!" Mike Martin called.

These people were crazy. "I can't just—"

"We're going camping," Mike Martin interrupted. "It's not unheard of to see the northern lights in late August and early September."

"I don't have the right gear for camping." For some reason, I was still looking for an out, even though I really, really wanted to see the northern lights. "I would have needed time to buy some stuff, like…hiking boots."

"We have stores in Canada. They're in igloos, but they do sell a full range of items. Anything you need, we can buy there."

I couldn't think how to rebut. He was doing some kind of psychological trick on me. "Northern lights, you say?"

He could tell he'd hooked me. "Yes, really, but... it's rare. I can't promise it."

I smiled. That was so him, to suddenly fret that he was luring me under false pretenses.

"*Dad*," Olivia said. "You're supposed to be convincing her."

"It's her birthday August twenty-ninth," Gretchen said.

"Your thirtieth, right?" Mike Martin asked. "Now you *have* to come."

"I was going to go out with Gretchen!" We both had late August birthdays, and we generally spent them together.

"And now you're going to go to Canada for your birthday," Gretchen said. "Upgrade!"

"Well..." I was going to give in. Because I wanted to. "OK."

Everybody cheered, and the next day I was back in the Getaway Car, and we were headed north.

Mike Martin and Olivia were great road trip companions. We played I spy, and Olivia kept a running list of the different states and provinces we saw on license plates. At the border, Mike Martin rolled down the window, and the guard said, tersely, "Citizenship?"

"Two Americans and one Canadian."

"How are you all related?" the agent asked as he paged through the passports.

"Olivia is my daughter. Aurora is my... friend."

The pause was short. Not noticeable unless you were listening with careful attention to see how he would answer. How many ways had we jokingly defined our relationship? It was harder to do when it wasn't a joke.

When the guard got to Mike Martin's passport, his previous no-nonsense façade cracked, and he looked up and grinned. "Mike Martin! For real?"

"Yep," he said, and I could feel him bristle as the guard started narrating the ending of a game from two years ago.

After we were waved through, Mike Martin shook his head as if he were literally shaking off the encounter and said, "Next stop, Dominion City and the world's largest sturgeon."

Mike Martin and Olivia had an affinity for cheesy roadside attractions. We had already seen the world's largest catfish in North Dakota, a forty-foot fiberglass monstrosity. The sturgeon was much smaller than the catfish, clocking in at a measly fifteen feet, and when I asked Mike Martin if that scale was true to life, I was treated to a lecture on the topic. "We could have seen a fourteen-foot statue of a pink bra in Grand Forks, but I decided to skip that one."

"Yeah, if I'm going to go out of my way, it had better be for oversize aquatic wildlife, not oversize lingerie," I joked.

Two hours later, we turned into a neighborhood of modest, one-story homes that looked like they were from the 1950s. It was a world away from Lake Minnetonka. I eyed the street sign as he turned a corner. "You grew up on a street called *Maple*-wood? Could you be any more Canadian? Well, maybe if you'd grown up on Maple Syrup Lane."

"Maple syrup is not that big a thing here. The season is too short."

"What do you mean the season is too short? Do maple trees have seasons?"

"They do for when the sap runs. You need a certain temperature differential between day and night. It's not a long season anywhere, but Quebec is the major spot. Maybe Ontario, too."

"How do you know so much about maple syrup if it's mostly from other provinces?"

"Maple syrup is part of the elementary school curriculum. It's nationally mandated."

I was about to say, "Really?" when he added, "Your parents can write a note to get you out of it, but if they do that, you run the risk of having your Canadian citizenship revoked."

"Ha ha." It was funny, though. Mike Martin seemed extra jokey today. Maybe coming home made him feel lighter. I wondered what that was like.

I was a little nervous to meet Mike Martin's parents, though I didn't know why. They'd clearly raised a great human. I guess because I wanted them to like me? Or maybe it was more that I didn't know how to act around happy, functional families who enjoyed spending time together.

His mom was waiting on the porch when we pulled into the driveway of a white bungalow. Initially she only had eyes for Olivia, and Olivia for her as she busted it out of the car and into her grandma's arms. "Nana!"

Mike Martin's mother smiled at him tearily from her embrace with Olivia. When she moved on to hugging her son, she peeked around his shoulder at me, smiled, and said, "You must be Aurora. Welcome."

The plan had been to drop off Olivia and get me checked into a hotel. That had been a condition of my coming along. I knew their small house got crowded, and I felt like an interloper to begin with. But once the five-foot hurricane that was Diane Martin blew through, that was the end of my plan.

"Ed!" she hollered from the entryway, where we all took off our shoes. "They're here!" A potbellied, grinning, white-haired man appeared.

"Pop!" Olivia scampered over and hugged him.

I barely had a chance to shake his hand before Diane was off down a hallway, beckoning us. "Olivia, I assume you want your Uncle Chris's room as usual."

"Yes!"

"She likes Chris's room because it has a waterbed," Mike Martin explained to me.

"Waterbed!" I exclaimed.

"Chris got a bee in his bonnet in high school and mowed about a thousand lawns and bought himself a literal waterbed," Diane said with exasperated affection.

Mike Martin dropped Olivia's bag and told her to unpack. The rest of us went on to the next room. "Aurora, you're here," Diane said.

"Oh no, I'm—"

"Mike, the sofa bed is made up in the basement. But I need it put back together before seven in the mornings when the kids start arriving."

"No!" I whispered to Mike Martin as Diane left the room.

Diane popped her head back in. "Unless..." She looked between us impishly. I could see where Mike Martin got the spark in his eye. "You both want to sleep on the sofa bed?"

"That's not...what's happening," I said.

"We'll work it out," Mike Martin said after his mom left again.

We did not work it out. We had a late dinner. Everyone talked a mile a minute. Except me, but I was content to listen to them talk about neighbors, reminisce about the backyard rink Ed used to build every winter, and make plans for the week ahead.

Eventually Diane started yawning. "I'm going to excuse myself. I have kiddos coming early tomorrow. Olivia is going to help me while she's here. We settled on five bucks an hour. Is that OK with you?" she asked Mike Martin.

"You're the boss."

"Let me clean up," I said, rising from the table when Diane did.

"Oh no, Aurora, hon. Boys do the cleaning in my house." She shot a look at Mike Martin. "Right?"

"Yes, ma'am." Mike Martin popped up and started stacking dishes.

She smirked and turned back to me. "I cook, but I don't clean." When I made to help Mike Martin, she said, "Ah, ah, ah! *Only* boys clean in my house!"

"She's serious," Olivia said. "I never have to do anything here."

"When you're the only woman in a house of men, you have to draw some lines in the sand," Diane said, blowing a kiss to the table. "Nighty night."

"Liv, go get ready for bed," Mike Martin said over his shoulder as he headed for the kitchen. "I'll come tuck you in when I'm done here."

"I'm going to take your presence here as permission to take a night off cleanup duty," Ed said, and, after wishing us a good sleep, he disappeared down the hallway.

Which left me alone in the dining room. I tiptoed into the kitchen as if Diane had invisible booby traps set to catch any feminine cleaning infractions.

"Hey," Mike said with a yawn.

"Am I even allowed to be in here?"

He clicked on the smile. "Yes, but she's serious about the not-cleaning thing."

"She *never* cleans?"

"She'll clean in the day-care setting—picking up toys,

clearing up the kids' lunches—but other than that, nope. She does all the cooking. And she *cooks*. She makes full breakfasts, she used to pack our lunches every day, and somehow we always had home-cooked dinners even though half the time we were eating them out of Tupperware because we were driving all over the place for hockey. She's always said there were three of us and one of her and all of the cooking versus one-third of the cleaning was a more than fair trade-off. So my brother and I got schooled from a young age in the domestic arts—well, the noncooking domestic arts. You can see now why I can't cook for shit."

"I *have* always thought you had mad dishwasher-loading skills, though."

"I tried to hire a house cleaner for them once, but she wasn't having it."

I was starting to see what Mike Martin meant about his parents instilling humility in him.

He closed the dishwasher, pressed his hands against his lower back, and sighed.

"You OK?"

"Just tired." He stretched. "And creaky from driving." As he extended his arms toward the ceiling, his shirt rode up and exposed his hockey-player abs. *I* sighed.

"Hey," he said, yawning again as he finished his porno stretch and opened the fridge. "How much would you mind if you crashed here tonight and I took you to the hotel tomorrow? I really want to crack a beer, power through this cleaning, and crash."

"I wouldn't mind." The hotel had been about me not wanting to impose, but if staying here was the lesser imposition, I was happy to do so.

So I went to bed in Mike Martin's childhood room. He hadn't been kidding about the single bed, though I was plenty cozy. The walls were plastered with pictures of hockey players I didn't recognize other than Wayne Gretzky. And just to prove how cool Mike Martin was, he had some pictures of women players in and among the dudes. I read the unfamiliar names: Hayley Wickenheiser, Cassie Campbell.

"Olympians," he'd explained when I remarked on it. "Salt Lake City, 2002. *Epic* game. I had a massive crush on Cassie Campbell when I was a kid." He smirked. "Still kinda do. She's on ESPN now."

I drifted off to sleep under an impossibly soft quilt Mike Martin's mom had no doubt made, next to a poster of his childhood crush, marveling over the fact that I was here.

18 — DOUBLE-DOUBLE

RORY

I awoke to the sounds of happy kid babbling. I got dressed and went to the dining room, where I found Diane hanging out with a baby in a high chair and a toddler in a booster seat.

"Good morning!" she said, pausing in feeding the baby.

"Goo mornin'!" the toddler shouted.

"Mike went for a run, but he should be back soon," Diane said.

"Mike is back." Mike Martin strolled in all sweaty, and I was suddenly thrust back to the mall when I'd thought he was talking about himself in the third person. Could I ever have imagined then that I'd be in his house? In *Canada*? Guilt fired inside me.

He made a silly face at the baby and to me said, "I'll shower, then we'll go shopping for hiking boots?"

I shoved the guilt away. "Sure."

"There's scrambled eggs and bacon on the stove and bagels on the counter by the toaster," Diane said. "Coffeepot is full. Help yourself to anything."

I poured a coffee—I hadn't gotten over my long-standing

habit of skipping breakfast, but it turned out that intuitive eating said you didn't have to eat breakfast if you didn't want to. Diane introduced me to the kids. The toddler was singing "Let It Go" in between shoving Cheerios in her mouth. "Never a dull moment around here, eh?" Look at me, adding that Canadian *eh* onto the end of my sentence. When in Manitoba, I guess.

"There'll be three more kids here in a bit, so this is as calm as things will be all day." She made a silly face at the baby. "I thrive on it, though." If this was how Mike Martin had grown up, I could see why he wanted, to use his word, a brood. "You're going shopping?" Diane asked.

"Yes. I'm not properly outfitted for this trip—I'm not sure if Mike told you, but my joining him and Olivia on this trip was a last-minute thing."

"Oh yes, he's told me all about you."

Hmm.

She put down the spoon and grabbed my hand that wasn't holding the coffee cup. "I don't know what he and Olivia would have done without you this past year. Thank you." I blinked, hit with a wave of unexpected emotion. Both the sentiment and the ease with which she expressed it startled me. "I'd been wondering if I'd made a mistake leaving them and had been thinking of closing down the day care again and going back, but you saved the day, Aurora."

"I just did what anyone would do."

"No, you did what *you* would do."

Mike Martin and I went to a shoe store in a mall, which was a funny place to be with him—it made the guilt come back. The window had long since closed on telling him about our long-ago encounter, though, so I told myself to stop worrying about it. So I made up a boyfriend when I was a kid. Mike Martin was a completely different person from that fictional boy—he was better.

Even more surreal was when he said an old friend was going to join us for lunch and I found myself being introduced to a dark-haired man named John in the parking lot of the mythical Tim Hortons. John looked an awful lot like my memory of Erik from the mall, except aged a couple of decades.

"This is your dad's place?" I asked.

"No, this is a different one."

"Mike doesn't like to go to his dad's location because people fuss over him," John said.

"Ah. That tracks. I've never met a famous person so allergic to fame before."

"Right?"

Mike Martin snorted. "I'm not famous, you guys."

"To be fair, it's probably extra bad around here, because everyone recognizes him," John said. "Local son made good, you know?"

"Yeah, yeah." Mike Martin waved dismissively at us.

"Let me ask you a question, John. Is Mike a hoser? He keeps saying he is, but I'm not buying it."

"Oh yeah, he is. Total hoser."

"See?" Mike Martin smirked at me. "Let's go in."

For lunch I ordered a bowl of chili and a coffee—or tried to. "I'll have a small coffee," I said.

"Small regular?"

"No, just a small."

"With?"

"I'm sorry?"

Mike Martin and John had been chatting behind me, but

Mike Martin clued into my confusion, leaned over, and said, "Double milk."

"Why am I so confused?" I said when we sat down a few minutes later. "Why do I feel like I failed Tim Hortons?"

"You tell them what you want in your coffee when you order. *Regular* isn't a size; it means one unit of cream and one unit of sugar. You go up from there. A double-double is two creams and two sugars."

"My order's a medium double-triple," said John, "which is a medium coffee with two creams and three sugars. I have a sweet tooth."

It must run in the family.

"The whole country is kind of low-key obsessed with Tim Hortons," John said. "Which I admit is a bit weird. The coffee is fine, but I'm not sure, objectively, that it lives up to the hype." He glanced at Mike Martin. "No offense."

"None taken."

"This guy"—he jabbed his thumb in Mike Martin's direction—"bought his dad a Tim Hortons franchise."

"I heard."

"OK, first of all, Chris and I bought it together. Second, we only did it because my parents wouldn't accept any other help, and my dad was going to keep working for twenty bucks an hour until he keeled over and died. This way at least he's in charge." He turned to me. "My dad was the manager at a different location when Chris and I made the purchase."

"So how do you two know each other?" I asked as a way to change the subject, because I knew Mike Martin didn't like us talking, even jokingly, about his largesse. I suspected I already knew the answer, though: this was the high school friend he'd referenced, the older brother of Erik.

Probably.

"We played high school hockey together before Mike started in the WHL," John said. "Actually, we've been playing hockey together since we could walk—from U7 on up—Mike and Chris and my brother Erik and me."

Erik. There it was.

"Erik was hugely talented at hockey," Mike said.

Yep. I had known that. I shouldn't have been shocked by any of this, and really, I wasn't. Or my rational brain wasn't. My body, which was suddenly sweating, didn't quite get the memo. Hearing it confirmed was freaking me out.

"John's grandfather was a farmer, and he made a rink at the farm one winter that we all played on," Mike Martin said. "That's what gave my dad the inspiration to do one in our yard."

"And the rest is history." John smirked. "Basically my family is responsible for spawning the NHL star you see before you today."

"Not a star," Mike Martin said.

"What became of Erik?" I asked, praying my voice sounded normal. "Did he go on to play hockey?"

"Nope. He was really good, but it wasn't his calling. He went into politics. He's on the Winnipeg City Council, and he was previously on the Long Plain band council. His big interest is housing issues—on reserves and in the city." John practically radiated pride.

"I used to fly back and do a workshop every year at my old high school," Mike Martin said. "I was in Chicago by the time Erik was in high school, but I'd try to see as many of his games as I could." He snorted. "But clearly Erik was on to more important things." He grew serious. "He used to present like the class clown, but he had brains—and a big heart. I always knew Erik was going places."

———

The next three days were great, once I shook off the discomfort of meeting John. I somehow never got taken to the hotel. The second night, Diane surprised me with a birthday coconut cream pie, Olivia and the day-care kids made me a card, and Mike Martin took me to a store called Canadian Tire and bought me a headlamp he said I would need for camping. I never would have imagined spending my thirtieth birthday like that, but once I had, I couldn't think of anything better.

That night, Mike Martin repeated his question about whether I would mind putting off the hotel. The third night, he said, "Look, unless you really need an escape hatch, we're all set up here, aren't we? Honestly, the pullout in the basement is a queen, and I'd probably stay on it even after you left."

I didn't even put up a perfunctory objection. I was having a grand time, and I was sleeping like a log in Mike Martin's childhood bed. We spent the days taking walks and bumming around town. We went to the pioneer museum. Olivia declared it not as good as De Smet, but I think that was because it was more about looking at stuff and learning, which I quite enjoyed.

Diane was great, full of backbone and wisecracks but also actual wisdom. Ed was great, too, though quieter and therefore harder to parse. I got the sense that both Mike Martin's parents were proud. Inherently—hence their refusal to let him help them financially—but also proud *of* him. But I knew they would have been proud of him whatever job he ended up with. Their pride wasn't conditional on his status as a pro hockey player.

Which in turn made me see why he was always insisting that he wasn't a star, why he bristled under the attention of fans.

His parents had made him that way, and it was a good thing. Mostly. I did wonder if his extreme aversion to the profile that came with his job was holding him back emotionally. If it made him keep people at arm's length, which didn't seem like the best way to live.

Olivia was in her element, basking in the affection of her grandparents and making some cash helping Diane at the day care. I suspected that, Mike Martin's beef with them aside, she had similar experiences at her other grandparents' place. It was good for her to be around other people who loved her, and to be away from the daily grind of school and camp and life at home.

I felt that way, too, about the daily grind. Vacations: Who knew?

My rose-colored glasses were shattered, though, when he tried to get me to go for drinks to meet Erik.

"I didn't know you got migraines," he said in response to my bald-faced lie. His face was all smushed up, and I wasn't sure if it was from concern or from skepticism. Maybe I should have gone with food poisoning. I had been living with the dude for nine months, and I'd never had a migraine or even said a word about them, including that time Lauren had one.

"They're…rare." My weak tone must have convinced him, when really it was a reflection of my feeling like shit for lying to him—about the headache, but also about…everything.

For my penance, I had to go lie in his bedroom all afternoon while Diane knocked every couple of hours with cold compresses, ice water, and heartfelt expressions of concern.

I must have fallen asleep at some point, because I awakened to the feeling of a presence in the room.

"Hey, sorry." He was standing in the doorway, and he was backlit by the hall light. "Just checking on you before I hit the hay," he whispered.

So now my choices were to lie some more...or to lie some more. "I'm feeling better, thanks." I pushed myself up on my elbows and reached for my phone on the nightstand. "What time is it?"

"Late. After midnight. I ended up having a little too much fun with Erik. I think it will be my turn for a headache tomorrow." He stepped into the room and closed the door behind him. He came over and sat on the edge of my bed. "I was worried about you."

Ha! He was drunk—he was slurring a little. "You didn't drive home, did you?"

"Noooo. I took a cab. I'll have to go get the Getaway Car tomorrow." He snorted. "The Getaway Car got away from me."

"I'm glad you had fun."

"I'm sorry I had fun while you were here suffering."

"Are you kidding me? You're apologizing for having fun? Stop that."

"Yeah, yeah, OK."

"I'm glad you let loose. You never do that. If I'd been with you, you would have felt like you had to drive."

"Mmm." Suddenly his hand was in my hair. "You have pretty hair."

I intended to laugh, but it came out more like a purr as his big, strong fingers found my scalp. "You're drunk."

"Yeah, but I don't see what one has to do with the other. I'm drunk. You have pretty hair. Both things are true." He started massaging my scalp. "Does this help your head?"

"Yes," I said, and I was going to hell. But then I told myself it wasn't technically a lie. My head felt better when he was massaging it than when he wasn't.

I only let it go on a few minutes. He started listing to one side, leaning against the headboard.

"Go to bed," I said.

"OK." He sighed contentedly and curled up next to me.

"Not here!"

"Right." He made the world's least graceful dismount from the bed and stumbled toward the door. I prayed he wouldn't wake his parents even as I chuckled at the prospect of fully grown Mike Martin being busted by his mother sneaking out of a girl's room.

He paused in the doorway, the yellow light from the hallway glinting off his stupid dimple as he smiled. "I'm so glad you're OK now."

"Thanks."

"I'm so glad you're here."

Wow. Mike Martin was a schmaltzy drunk. "Thanks," I said again.

He smiled goofily. "Good night, Aurora Lake."

19—HIGH STAKES

MIKE

I was not feeling great the next day, so my defenses were down when my mom found the box of shoes.

"Honey, are these Aurora's shoes?" she asked, coming up from the basement to join me in the dining room. "I'm going to put them by her door."

Shit. I had gotten them out last night after I'd checked on Aurora. I didn't even know why. Well, I did know why. In my drunken state, I think I wanted to test myself. To see how I felt when I looked at them. To see if I felt *guilty* when I looked at them, after my little cuddle with Aurora.

Which was ridiculous because nothing was happening with Aurora. She'd said we had to knock off the fling stuff, so we'd knocked off the fling stuff. Now we were friends. End of story.

"Those are Sarah's shoes."

Mom's eyebrows flew up, and she reversed course and sat with me.

I wasn't going to get out of this without coming clean—I never could get anything past my mother. "I got rid of most of Sarah's stuff last summer. You remember—you helped with some of it."

"Of course."

I sighed. How to explain when I could hardly make sense of it myself? "The shoes in that box were in the entryway for a long time. I didn't want to move them, but I also hated looking at them." I left out the stuff about the void—the big one and the little pinprick ones I used to have inside me. "Eventually, I moved them to the closet in our—my—bedroom." I paused. "I don't want them in the house anymore, but I also don't want to throw them away or give them away, which I realize makes no sense." They were just shoes. But also, they weren't. For better or worse, I'd assigned symbolic value to them. "So I brought them here." I'd stashed the box behind the sofa I was sleeping on, but apparently Mom had found them. "I was going to…leave them in the closet in my room." I just hadn't done it yet. I hadn't wanted to intrude on Aurora's space. *Excuse me, I just need to stick my dead wife's shoes in the closet, then I'll be out of your way.*

"I think that sounds like a fine idea."

"You do?" And here I thought it sounded like a nonsensical idea.

"You have to move on. It doesn't mean you forget, but you have to move on."

"I know. I am."

She smiled. "She's lovely."

Huh? "Who's lovely?"

"Aurora."

"Oh, no, we're just friends."

"Don't play dumb with me, mister. I saw you coming out of her room last night."

Oh shit. "I was just checking on her." *And stroking her hair like a deranged creeper.* "I…wanted to make sure she was OK before I went to bed."

She stood as Olivia came strolling in in her pajamas. "That, my love, makes my point even more forcefully."

"Morning, Liv." I was glad for the interruption so I didn't have to defend myself against my mother and her confusing logic anymore.

"I don't want to go camping," Olivia said.

Oh, for God's sake. "What? Why?"

"I want to stay here and help Nana with the day care."

My mind flashed back to last winter, when she hadn't wanted to come to any of my home games. She'd been doing so much better on the grief front, but as I well knew, navigating grief was not a linear process. "Is this about your mom?" Last time we'd gone camping had been with Sarah.

"No, I just think camping is stupid and boring, and I don't want to go," she said matter-of-factly.

I closed my eyes. I'd been prepared to rally, to fight off my hangover, if Olivia was suffering, but not if she was just being a brat.

"Why don't you and Aurora go, and we'll keep Olivia—lucky us," my mom said.

I opened my eyes, and when my mom put her hand on my shoulder and whispered, "It's OK," I knew she was talking about more than keeping Olivia while I went camping.

Of course, Aurora chose that moment to appear, completing my destabilization. I decided to finish off with Olivia first. "Yeah, OK, Liv. Fine."

"Yay!" she cheered. My mom took her hand off my shoulder. I wished she wouldn't. Everything felt easier with it there.

"It's just as well, because I changed our reservation to Spruce Woods, figuring we'd have a better shot at the northern lights at a more southern park. I got us a backcountry site, so we have to hike in. It's on a creek. It should be nice." Liv wrinkled her nose. I turned to Aurora to explain. "Liv is bailing on camping."

"I *hate* backcountry camping," Liv said.

"I don't know what backcountry camping is," Aurora said, "or why you would want to go south to see the northern lights."

"Backcountry camping means you don't drive your car to your site. You have to hike or canoe in—hike in this case. Though this won't be serious backcountry camping," I assured her. "There are firepits and tables at the sites. We just gotta lug our stuff in."

My mother was watching me closely, with an uncharacteristically serious expression.

I kept talking. "For the northern lights this time of year, you actually don't want to go too far north. The farther north you get, the longer the days are—Land of the Midnight Sun territory. You need darkness for the northern lights. There are forecasts you can look at. There's this thing called the Kp index that's a measure of geomagnetic activity. So we'll keep an eye on that, but…"

OK, I needed to get a grip. Aurora had only been awake a little while and had walked into a confusing conversation, and no one had asked her how she was feeling.

"How's your head?" I pushed out a chair for her.

"How's *your* head?" She sat, and my mom snickered.

"My head…has been better."

She smiled. "Mine is fine."

"Fine enough for coffee?" my mom asked. "You hear about how sometimes caffeine helps migraines."

The smile slid off her face. Maybe she wasn't better. Maybe she was putting on a front. "I'd love coffee, thanks. I'll help myself."

"Good morning!" It was one of the day-care parents—they let themselves in the front door in the mornings.

"Hi, Amy!" my mom called. "Hi, Lucy! I'll meet you in the basement!" She and Olivia headed down to meet them, leaving me alone with Aurora.

"I guess it's just you and me camping." I lifted my tea for a joking toast to cover how unsettled that made me feel. I told myself this was Aurora. I knew her. She was easy to be with.

So why did everything feel so different all of a sudden?

———

"Bye!" Olivia trilled the next morning. "Enjoy sleeping on the ground while I lounge on my waterbed!"

"Yeah, yeah." I hugged her tight. "You be good, OK?"

"Am I not always good?"

I smacked an extraloud, exaggerated kiss on her cheek. "No, you are not."

She dropped her attitude suddenly and wound her arms around my neck. "Be careful, OK? Maybe I *should* come."

"Nah, you don't want to come," I said, but I let her keep hugging me—I let *myself* keep hugging *her*. She was panicking at the idea that a bear might eat me, or I might drown, and she'd be left parentless. She'd had fears like that early on, in the initial weeks after the accident. She hadn't wanted me to go anywhere without her. Dr. Mursal had said it was normal, and it had faded. I'd thought. "I'll be careful. I promise."

"I'll keep my eye on him," Aurora said, and Olivia surprised me—and Aurora, too, I think—by throwing her arms around her and giving her a long, hard hug.

"Want to stop for coffee?" I asked as we pulled out of the driveway.

"Yes, and now I know how to order mine."

As we drove by my dad's Tim Hortons a few minutes later, which I'd pointed out to Aurora on a previous outing, she said, "I thought we were getting coffee?"

"We are, but…"

"…we're not going to this one because it's your dad's."

"Is that dumb?" I always skipped this location, but hearing John mock me for it the other day had made it seem stupid.

"No," she said, but there had been a pause before she spoke.

"Say it like you mean it."

"You want some friendly advice?"

How much of a dick would I be if I said no? "Sure."

"You *are* famous." I wanted to object so badly, and she must have been able to tell, because she held up a palm. "OK, yes, you're not a household name, but you are a certain level of famous in certain circles. You made some choices in life, in your career, that created that outcome. It's not *why* you made those choices, but it comes along with them. If there was a way you could…"

"What?"

"I should stop talking. Like I'm in any position to give advice."

"You're in a position to give me advice. You know me better than anyone." Which continued to be a little surprising, but why should it be? I literally lived with her.

"I wish there was a way for you to be more comfortable with the way people treat you. I get that it can be awkward, but most people mean well. Most people like you, or the idea of you—"

"That's the problem, though. The *idea* of me. That's not the same as *me*."

"I know. But isn't that true of everyone to some degree? My dance kids don't really know me. They know a version of me—an idea of me. The key is, most of them *like* that idea of me. It means something to them. I think that's even more true for you. So even if people's idea of you isn't *you*, it might still be a positive thing in their lives. Is that such a bad thing? And who knows, you might be missing out on some really great people who happen to be fans of yours."

Hmm. It was hard to argue when she put it like that.

"Now that I've seen where you come from, I get the desire to shirk the spotlight. Your parents did a good job keeping you humble. But I don't think they'd want you to hold yourself apart from people the way you do. To have to drive past one Tim Hortons to go to another one. Doesn't it get tiring?"

My impulse was to be defensive, but I reminded myself that Aurora *did* know me like no one else. And my skin was getting hot in the way that sometimes happens when your body recognizes a truth your brain doesn't want to acknowledge. So I flipped on the turn signal and prepared to make a U-turn. What have I always said? I'm very coachable.

I'd only been planning on going through the drive-through at the other place, but now I had something to prove, so I parked.

She ordered her coffee like a pro, and I said, "Look at you. You're an honorary Canadian now." As predicted, when it was my turn and the woman at the cash register realized who I was, she had a minor freak-out. She called for my dad, and soon I had a small crowd of employees and customers around me.

A kid asked for an autograph, and I tried to keep in the front of my mind what Aurora had said. I always got all tied up in knots because I didn't want people to only see the hockey player, but maybe it *was* OK that all this kid saw was the hockey player.

"Ed's so proud of you, you know," said Dorrie, my dad's longtime assistant manager. "He talks about you all the time."

It was hard to imagine Dad talking "all the time" about anything, but I appreciated the sentiment. It also occurred to me that here, to the staff at least, I *wasn't* just the pro hockey player; I was the boss's kid. I found that oddly comforting. Neither of those personae was *me*, but thinking about both of them coexisting made me realize Aurora was onto something. We showed different people different parts of ourselves all the time.

"I don't think I'm wrong, though," I said when we were back on the road.

"What?"

"I take your point about being more graceful in public, but I don't think it's wrong to prefer having people in my life—like, actually in my life—who don't care that I play hockey."

She looked at me for a long moment, like she was trying to figure something out. She finally said, "I don't disagree. But you also have to live your life. Maybe there's a balance where you don't have to skip over the closest Tim Hortons, you know?"

Maybe there was.

———

"This is not at all what I thought Manitoba would be like," Aurora said as we hiked in to our site. "That's a cactus!"

"Yeah, this park is a bit weird. Lots of different types of landscapes, including this desert stuff. Something to do with the remnants of the glaciers. I've never been here, but it's a dark sky preserve, so I thought we'd give it a shot."

We chatted easily on the hike in, and at the site, I strung a hammock between two trees and installed Aurora in it. "You chill out, and I'll put up the tent."

She talked as I worked, asking questions and wanting me to narrate everything as I pitched the tent and unfurled sleeping bags. It was awfully cute. "I thought you were supposed to be communing with nature over there," I teased.

"Sorry, sorry. I'm talking too much."

"Nah, you're talking exactly the right amount. I like it when you talk." I also liked it when she swam, when she danced, when she skated. When she kissed me, when she let me into her body. I really liked that, and would remember it fondly always. I even liked it when she busted my ass in her thoughtful, quiet way, like about my aversion to my dad's Tim Hortons.

I liked when she sat at a stool at my kitchen island and talked to me while I tried to cook. Which was basically what she was doing here, except with a hammock and a tent instead of a stool and a stove.

I just…liked having her around.

Of course, my telling her that I liked it when she talked shut her right up. But she was smiling at me, this really big, delighted, guileless smile.

"What?" I asked, smiling back automatically.

"I think that might be the nicest thing anyone has ever said to me."

I wasn't sure how I felt about that. I understood that Aurora had been shortchanged by life, but it wasn't right that an off-hand compliment received at age thirty qualified as the nicest thing anyone had said to her. We knew her mother was useless, but what about the ex-boyfriend? Had he *never* said anything kind? Although…while part of me wanted everyone to see and recognize how amazing Aurora was, part of me didn't. I was protective. Or selfish. I wanted to be the one who said things that made her smile like that.

"You want some wine?" I didn't want to examine my feelings any further.

"You brought wine?"

I grabbed a can from my kitchen stash.

"In a can!" She sat up in the hammock, and I tossed her the wine. "You brought me wine in a can!"

"It'll be warm, I'm afraid. I wasn't sure if you'd rather have red or warm white."

"Mmm, warm white." She popped the can. "I love this."

"You're easy to please today."

She shrugged, and I built a fire to heat up some cans of stew.

"This is so *good*!" she exclaimed when we tucked into it, continuing to be delighted by my crossing a very low bar. She grew serious. "Why have I never had beef stew before?"

"I don't know."

"I'm glad I can have it now."

"I'm glad you can, too."

She looked up at the sky. "What time is this all going to go down?"

"Late," I said. "We'll have to set an alarm."

"Can we bring our sleeping bags out here and stare at the sky even if the lights aren't going?"

"We sure can."

———

I tried to tell myself it was a long shot. I was disappointed, though, when we got up at midnight and emerged from the tent and there were no lights. At least the stars were out in force. Aurora looked up and exclaimed, "Are you kidding me?"

"It's pretty amazing, isn't it?" I ducked back into the tent and grabbed our sleeping bags. We laid them on the ground a little ways away from the tent. I reached into my backpack and handed her some bug spray, then produced a flashlight, water, some chocolate bars, and another can of wine.

"You're like Mary Poppins with that bag!" she exclaimed. "You came prepared!"

"I *was* in Scouts as a kid." After we got everything organized, I turned off the lantern, and we lay back.

"Wow," she whispered.

"It's something, eh?"

"What is it going to be like if we see the lights?" she asked. "Will I know them when I see them?"

"Yeah, it's not like a shooting star where it's there and gone. When they're out, they're out. People call it dancing, actually. The dance of the auroras." My heart squeezed. "Maybe your mom wasn't so far off with your name after all."

"You want to hear something lame?"

"Yes," I said immediately. I wanted to hear whatever she had to tell me.

"I decided I *am* going to rename myself if we see the lights. Well, not rename myself as in change my name. But change the story behind it. You remember we talked about that in the studio?" She snorted. "It sounds stupid when I say it out loud."

"No, it doesn't. You were Ballet Aurora, now you can christen yourself Northern Lights Aurora."

"That's exactly it—a christening. I thought if I saw the lights on this trip, it could be a self-christening. It's perfect timing. After all, I fired my mother, right?"

She was making light, but I heard the seriousness of her intent. Damn, I would have paid any amount of money to guarantee those lights for her. "It would be better if there was no moon." I was trying to temper her expectations, even as my brain was firing up, trying to figure out how I could take her somewhere this coming winter that would be a slam dunk. Maybe over the holiday break. Maybe I could send Olivia to—

Aurora interrupted my inner travel agent. "You know that saying, *I love you to the moon and back?*"

"Yeah. I used to read that book to Olivia all the time when she was little."

"It's from a book?"

"Yep. It's about parent and kid polar bears."

"*Really?* I thought it was just an expression."

She seemed oddly interested in the origins of the phrase. "Why do you ask?"

"Lying out here looking at all this, I was thinking it's kind of a funny sentiment. It's supposed to be an expression of the most you can possibly love someone. But the moon is the closest thing to us in the sky."

"Maybe we should say, 'I love you to Alpha Centauri and back'...except I think Alpha Centauri is pretty close, too, cosmically speaking."

"But it still sounds good. 'I love you to Star 82673'—or whatever's really far away—'and back' isn't very poetic."

We lapsed into silence and stared at the sky while my heart felt like it was undergoing a slow-motion cracking. The thought of Aurora renaming herself was slaying me. It was amazing how people could remake themselves. I'd thought so much about Aurora's being a witness to my doing it as she moved in and helped stabilize my little family. But she'd been doing the same in parallel, just in a way that was less public than the guy with the dead wife. "The thing about the northern lights is that they're there whether you see them or not." My voice cut through the cozy darkness with an urgency I should have been embarrassed by but was not.

"What do you mean?"

"They're solar flares hitting the Earth's magnetic field. They're happening all the time. They're all around us. Seeing them is a matter of the right conditions, but just because you can't see them doesn't mean they're not there. So you could…" *Still christen yourself.* I was going to sound way too invested in this. I made myself stop talking.

"Yeah," she said quietly. "Maybe I could." We lapsed into silence, and after a while, she started yawning. Eventually, her breathing lengthened. I told myself to stay awake, to watch for the lights.

Hours later, when I woke up shivering, Aurora and her sleeping bag had migrated so she was cuddled against me in mine, and the lights were streaming across the sky. Otherworldly green whorls were tinged with violet wisps around the edges. I'd seen the northern lights a dozen times in my life, but they never failed to take my breath away. It was strange to think about how much upheaval there had been in my life since I last saw them—and strangely comforting how immune they were to the travails of humanity. They just did their thing, displaying their cold beauty regardless of our suffering. I shifted, intending to wake Aurora, but froze, leveled by the image of Aurora under the auroras.

I could see the truth, suddenly and clearly, as if it weren't the northern lights above me but a cosmic spotlight shining relentlessly into the dark corners of my heart.

Like the aurora borealis, that truth was there, in the background, whether I chose to see it or not. It probably had been for a long time.

I was in love with Aurora Lake.

My mom had been right. Ivan had been right.

God damn it. *Fuck.*

I wanted to tip my head back and howl over the sheer fucking unfairness of it all. Because whether I loved Aurora or not was completely irrelevant. It didn't *change* anything—except for the fact that it was going to make everything harder. I *couldn't* take up with Aurora right now. I had to finish rebuilding things, getting Olivia and me back on our feet. I couldn't risk Olivia's happiness. And dating Aurora would eventually lead to not dating Aurora. You don't marry the first girlfriend you get after your wife dies.

I took a moment to let myself feel the injustice of it, to integrate this new and unwelcome information. Another fucking *thing* I would have to carry around.

But I didn't let myself wallow too long, because none of this was Aurora's fault, and she couldn't miss this show. I laid my palm on her cheek, which only had the effect of making her murmur and snuggle in closer. I shifted until I got an arm around her, shamelessly encouraging the cuddle. "Aurora," I whispered.

"Mmm."

"Wake up."

She opened her eyes slowly. She was confused, initially, but when she realized what was happening, she sat up abruptly, like a caricature of someone waking from a nightmare, except wonder was written all over her face, which was illuminated by the dancing lights.

Then she burst into tears.

"Oh, sweetheart." The endearment slipped out, but she either didn't notice or didn't mind, because she rushed to assure me she was crying happy tears.

"At least I think so," she added.

She was christening herself. I was honored to witness it. "Look over there." I pointed in the opposite direction from where she was looking, where there was an especially eerie violet pulsation. She twisted around, and I tugged her arm gently to get her to lie back down. She'd have a view of the full sky that way.

She came easily, and to my shock she snuggled back in against me. "It's so beautiful," she whispered, "but also kind of…melancholy?" She shook her head. "Not melancholy, exactly, but too powerful to be just straightforwardly beautiful." Another head shake. "That doesn't make any sense."

"No, I know what you mean." She transferred her gaze from the sky to my face—there was enough ambient light, and we were close enough, that I could just see her features. "Don't you think those two things are kind of intertwined?" I asked. "It's beautiful *because* it's melancholy. It's a complicated kind of beauty."

"It feels like you have to earn it."

Exactly. "And you have, haven't you?"

"So have you."

"Maybe so."

I smiled at her, and she kissed me. I was in love with Aurora Lake, she was kissing me under the northern lights, and it was about as far from low-stakes as it was possible to get.

20 — CHRISTENING

RORY

Why had I ever thought that ending the physical stuff with Mike Martin was going to protect me? I'd put a stop to it in order to prevent myself from getting too attached. Yet here I was—in love with him anyway.

Which was its own problem, and one that would need to be dealt with, but in the meantime I was undergoing some kind of catharsis under the northern lights in freaking Canada, and I was kissing Mike Martin because he had played a big role in getting me here. Not just physically here, meaning freaking Canada, but to the point where I was a person who ate ice cream and drew boundaries with my mother and hadn't had a panic attack since that first ballet class.

I mean, I took his earlier point: I had done the work, with a big assist from Mary-Margaret. But all that time, he had been *there*, paying the insurance bill, making me grilled cheese, teaching me to skate, showing me, via his interactions with Olivia, what love was supposed to be like.

I'd stopped having sex with Mike Martin because I hadn't wanted my heart to get broken. But now I could see that it was going to happen regardless of what I did or didn't do. This dude was 100 percent going to break my heart. No, he already had. He'd cracked it open, and what did Leonard Cohen say? That's how the light gets in?

The great—the new—thing was that I knew I could survive it. That the light the cracks let in would be worth the pain.

And if it was going to happen regardless, why not give in, now, and take what I wanted? Be happy with what I had in this moment, under this sky, and not think about tomorrow or the next day or the next?

The moment my lips hit his, his arms banded around me, and he rolled me, sleeping bag and all, so I was lying on top of him. Being Mike Martin, he checked in with me, whispering a concerned, "I thought we weren't doing this anymore."

"I know. But can we just...do it anyway?"

He cracked a huge, delighted grin. "We sure can."

We kissed like in the old days when that was all we did. Except not, because it was clear we were going to do more. It was clear to me, anyway. Mike Martin was not going to push it. I was going to have to make the move. I peeled my face off his. He must have thought I was calling a halt to the proceedings, because he groaned in a way that did wonders for my ego.

"You got any condoms in your Mary Poppins bag?" I asked as I shimmied out of my sleeping bag.

The question startled him so much he bonked his head back against the ground. "Why would I have condoms?"

"Because we might have sex? Because you're a Boy Scout? Aren't Boy Scouts supposed to always be prepared?"

"Totally different organization from the American Boy Scouts, actually. It's just Scouts—we let girls in. And I don't know about mottoes, but our oath—at least in Cubs, which was as far as I went because hockey got too time-consuming—was *Do a Good Turn Daily*."

It figured. I snorted.

"Anyway, why would I have condoms when you told me you didn't want to have sex anymore?" His voice was rising, taking on an indignant quality that reminded me of Olivia. It was endearing. "Would you prefer me to be the kind of guy who doesn't listen?"

I lay back down. "I would prefer you to be the kind of guy who didn't listen in just this one instance."

That punctured his indignance. He chuckled and turned onto his side to face me, propping his head on one hand like we were lounging on the beach.

Being back in a position where I could see the sky was a shock. It wasn't that I'd forgotten the lights, but they were, inherently, shocking. And it wasn't the kind of shock that hit you once—bam!—then receded. They were perpetually shocking. I had never seen anything so powerful, and I was pretty sure they were responsible for *my* shocking behavior. Not directly, not in that they'd beamed *Seduce Mike Martin* into my head, but in that they'd put my entire life into perspective, suddenly—almost violently. Like their very existence was shoving me toward a new way of being.

"So you want to get it on," Mike Martin said, having recovered his equilibrium.

"I do."

I could see him pause. He was going to want to talk about it. I held up my hands. "I know what I said before, but let's just...be on vacation, OK? Take advantage of Olivia's absence like we used to?"

He looked at me for a long time, so long I was sure he was

going to refuse, but then he smiled, cracked his knuckles, and started tugging on the waistband of my leggings.

"What are you doing? We need a condom!"

"We don't, though, if we limit ourselves to things that don't require them. We've been in this spot before. Therefore, what I am doing is attempting to remove your pants."

"But…" Wait. Why was I trying to talk him out of this plan?

"OK, forget it, then." He popped up to sitting with a snicker.

"No, no. I mean, you *are* supposed to do a good turn every day, right?"

"Exactly." He smacked his lips. "You lie back and watch the show while I do my thing."

And I did.

———

The next morning we woke up tangled together in the tent. We'd stayed out watching the lights until after three. Well, watching the lights and fooling around. When we'd finally dragged ourselves back to the tent, he, to my shock, unzipped both sleeping bags, reassembled them into one giant one, and climbed in and held out his arms. It took me all of thirty seconds to fall asleep. I was emotionally and physically wrung out.

Christening yourself was exhausting.

I felt a bit sheepish by the light of day, as if last night had been a fever dream. I also dreaded the Talk that surely would have to happen now. Last night had felt like we were out of time, as if we had sidestepped reality, existing only in a dim, liminal space where two things could be true at the same time: I loved Mike Martin, and I was going to let him break my heart.

I tried to hold on to that duality in the bright light of day.

I tried not to let myself hope, to wonder if there was a way I could tell him the truth. Truths, plural: I loved him. And I'd been lying to him all this time.

And a third truth: I wanted us to be together, for real.

I rolled over, attempting to extricate myself without waking him, but nope, he was already awake, all bright-eyed and handsome and sporting some stubble he no doubt hated. "I'm going to hike out to the camp store and see if they have condoms."

I laughed. "Right now?"

"No time like the present?" he said cheerily.

"OK." I waited for the Talk. It didn't come.

He scrambled out of the sleeping bag, built a fire, and set a tiny kettle over it. I had coffee, he had tea, we both had granola bars, and he was off. "I'll be back in three hours."

I crawled back into the tent and dozed until I heard him whistling as he approached. When I first met Mike Martin, that day his eyes had turned into flat, green holes, would I ever have imagined him carefree and whistling?

I made my way out of the tent. He threw a box of condoms on the picnic table like he was anteing up at a poker game and sat on the bench opposite me.

"Well," I said as my nether regions grew warm, "You want some lunch first?"

"I do not."

———

In the tent, we did have the Talk, but not the one I was expecting. So I guess it was more like *a* Talk.

The clothing was coming off and we were kissing when I rolled over on something sharp and yelped. It was the box of condoms. The corner had gotten me in the side boob.

Mike Martin rubbed the spot as if to soothe it and, as we caught our breath, shocked me by saying, "The reason I haven't had any condoms when we've needed them is that Sarah had an IUD."

"OK…" He was acting like this was some big revelation, but for a married couple to settle on a low-effort form of birth control seemed unremarkable to me.

"I just didn't want you to think I was the kind of guy who was a jerk about condoms."

"I never thought that." He had used them uncomplainingly that week in the spring.

"Sarah and I had one major, ongoing conflict," he said, transferring his attention to the ceiling of the tent.

OK, shit was getting real here. I rolled to face him. He glanced over as if acknowledging my attention, then returned to studying the ceiling. I knew immediately that this was why he'd cried that first time. This was the thing he'd been thinking about that he'd said had nothing to do with me.

"I wanted more kids, and she…" He rolled over suddenly and looked at me all earnestly. "I'm sorry. I shouldn't be saying all this."

"Why not?" He had something he wanted to get off his chest, which meant I wanted to hear it.

"We were about to have sex, and now I'm launching into a monologue about my dead wife?"

"She was a huge part of your life. You can't pretend she never existed."

He smiled. "You're the best, Aurora Lake."

"Well, I mean, also, she's your *dead* wife. It's not like you were sleeping with her yesterday." He chuckled, and then he kept looking at me with that big, dopey smile. "So it sounds like you have something to say about wanting more kids? Can I suggest you get on with it? Otherwise I think we should put one of those condoms to use in the prevention of that thing you want." I fretted, belatedly, about making light of such a topic.

He smirked, putting me at ease. "Right. So, I wanted a bunch of kids."

"Define a bunch."

"I don't know. Take it one at a time, I guess. But I wanted to start as soon as possible. She wanted to wait until I was retired."

"Ah."

"She said she'd already been the single parent to a newborn, and that because of my job, that's effectively what she'd be doing again."

"Same as with the dog." He nodded. "As with the dog, I have to say that logic is hard to argue with."

"I *did* argue, though, which is something I very much regret. I suggested we try to time it so the baby was born as the season ended. Then it would be several months old by the time things geared up again. She didn't go for it."

"I'm sorry."

"I used to have these crazy fantasies that I'd succeed, and then she'd get pregnant with twins, and..."

"Instant brood?"

"Yeah. Isn't that stupid?"

"No."

"I didn't understand, back then, what her daily life was like. I mean, I understood with my brain, but really, elementally, I had *no idea* what adding more kids would have actually meant for her."

"This is that emotional labor stuff."

"Yeah." He heaved a sigh. "I didn't understand, and I pushed.

I pushed my wife to have another kid when she didn't want to. I'm going to go to my grave feeling the weight of that regret."

"I'm sorry."

He shook his head. "But here's the thing: I thought we were trying. When her IUD was due to come out, she told me we could start trying. I was so happy, but..." He blew out a breath. "I found out, after she died, that she'd been taking birth control pills. We *weren't* trying."

"She was lying to you," I said, suddenly understanding where his fixation on honesty came from.

"Was she *lying*, though? I used to think so. But was she maybe just telling me what I wanted to hear so I would lay the fuck off? Anyway, you can't be mad at a dead person."

"Can't you?"

He made a vaguely frustrated noise. "I don't know. I *was* mad, but now that some time has passed, I'm mad at *myself*, for pushing. For not *getting* it. And the dumbest part of all, the part that's hard to live with, is that there was an obvious solution if I really wanted more kids that badly: quit hockey. If I'd done that, I'd probably have two kids today."

"But you didn't want to quit hockey."

"I didn't want to quit hockey," he confirmed. "I mean, that's my thing, isn't it? I never want to quit, even when it's the obvious thing to do, even when quitting would make other areas of my life, shit I care about more than hockey—or at least things I *should* care about more than hockey—easier."

"I think you care about hockey in a different way. I'm not sure it's worth setting it up in your mind as hockey versus family. They're apples and oranges."

"Elaborate."

"Well, of course you love your family. You *would* quit hockey if it came to it. You told me that when I first met you. You told a mediator that." He nodded. "But I feel like hockey...gives you life, not to sound too dramatic. It's what makes you you. So of course you don't want to give it up. It's like the saying about securing your own oxygen mask first."

"Hockey's my oxygen."

"Yes."

He chuckled wistfully. "I think you're right, but I also think I'm in trouble, then. Because I don't have much time left, realistically. I have one more year on my current contract, and that's probably it. If I do get another one, it will only be because I'm a defenseman and we're in shorter supply, and then *that* will almost certainly be it. I know you object when I say I'm old, but for hockey, I'm old."

"OK, your days in the NHL are numbered. But that's not all hockey is. You talked about the feeling of being a kid skating on a bumpy pond. That feeling doesn't go away because the NHL does, right?"

"Right." He paused. "You could say the same about ballet, though I recognize your particular ballet context was extremely traumatic."

"You're right. I'm coming around to that notion." I'd gotten to the point where my ballet classes were my favorites. Gretchen had asked me if I wanted to take over her class of older kids—the one with Taylor and Abby—when the session turned over, and I was pretty sure I was going to do it.

"Anyway," Mike Martin said, "my point about the kid stuff, and the condoms, is...you know, I don't even know what my point is. I'm not even sure why I told you all this. I haven't told anyone except my shrink."

I was flattered. But once again, I was holding two truths in my heart at the same time. One was that I was flattered that Mike Martin trusted me enough to share these complicated feelings with me. The other was that I was deceiving him, too.

Not for too much longer, though. I was going to tell him everything when we got home, I resolved. After our vacation. There was no point in hitting him with it here, in the middle of nowhere where neither of us had an escape hatch.

But I *was* going to do it. I'd been anointed by the lights, and shit was going to change now. It had to.

"Is it really OK to talk about her"—he waved his hand back and forth between us—"here?"

"It's really OK." Not only did I not mind talking about Sarah, I relished it. She seemed like a cool woman, and I wanted to know her. I wanted to know what kind of person Mike Martin had chosen.

"Well, first," he said, "you are supercool. Second, I think I do know what my point was meant to be with all my rambling: Remember when I cried the first time?" He rolled his eyes, and I nodded. "I'm still embarrassed about that, but yeah, I've found the process of grieving to be not linear. So while I am thrilled to be here with you, in a position where we need condoms, it's a weird milestone that I *am* the kind of guy who needs condoms." He pointed at the box. "And if I let myself think about it too much, which probably isn't a good idea, I'll start down the path of *Do I even know how to have sex with anyone else?*" He looked at me and made a self-deprecating face. "You know how you sort of get into a habit with someone, you figure out what works and—"

"OK, stop." I hated to interrupt, but I could not let this go on any longer. "One: There's nothing to be embarrassed about. I myself have cried after sex."

"Really?"

"Not in front of the guy, generally, but, like, afterward."

"But—"

I held up a hand. It was still my turn. I was willing to elaborate, and even to take questions, but I wasn't done with my thesis statement yet. "Two: At the risk of giving you a big ego—which I actually think is impossible—you definitely know how to do it. I can honestly tell you that I have never enjoyed myself so...reliably as I did that week in the spring." I could feel a blush starting. "And last night." Last night when Mike Martin had gone down on me while I watched the lights. Was this really my life? Even if only for a moment?

He grinned.

"Not that I have a huge sample size," I added. You're only the fourth person I've had sex with." Since we were apparently chatting about our sexual hang-ups, I felt comfortable telling him that.

"Really?"

"Yeah. There was Ian, obviously, and two guys in New York."

"Well, I'm not that far ahead of you. My number is only seven."

I probably should have been surprised: "Hot NHL Player's Number Is Only 7" was quite the headline. But I wasn't. I only said, "Really?" because I was nosy and wanted him to elaborate.

"Well, I'd only been in Chicago a year when I met Sarah. And we got together young. I had some fun before I met her, but probably not as much as you'd expect, because...I'm going to sound paranoid if I say any more."

"You're going to say that you don't like sleeping with people who are starstruck by you."

"Am I that transparent?"

"You don't even like having passing conversations with people who are starstruck by you, forget swapping bodily fluids."

He chuckled. "Yeah."

I draped myself over his chest. "So. What do you say we stop *talking* about sex and actually, I don't know, have some?"

21—SUPERPOWERS

MIKE

I wondered if it would be different, having sex with Aurora, now that I understood I was in love with her. I considered that prior to now, Sarah was the only person I'd been with where sex and love—real, true love—had coexisted.

All it took was Aurora shoving down my pants and taking me into her mouth for me to abandon these high-minded topics. To abandon all thought. "Oh my God," I bit out.

She smiled even as she swallowed me down. We had the tent windows unzipped, and the sunlight illuminated her freckles. I let myself surrender to the wet heat of her mouth, fighting warring impulses to close my eyes and go limp and to stay at attention, watching her as she worked me over. I watched. Heat built, and pressure, and after a minute, I had to interrupt her. I laid a hand on her cheek and guided her off me. She made a gratifying mew of protest.

"We're supposed to be doing condom things," I said. "You know, things that require the prevention of all those kids I want?" I adored that we could joke about that. I adored that I could tell her my heavy shit and not scare her off. I adored *her*. I couldn't *do* anything about it, but I adored her all the same.

She grabbed a condom and had me sheathed in an instant. Then she lay back on the sleeping bag, and my God, she looked like…I don't even know. Like a painting. Like something I could look at but not have, but somehow the universe had turned itself inside out, and I *could* have her, at least for now.

I didn't waste any time. I settled myself over her and grabbed her legs, encouraging her to wrap them around me. That was another thing I adored: Aurora's legs. They were long, muscular, *perfect*. They'd taken her through so much life, and I ran my hands up and down them as I pushed into her body.

She sighed and gave me a lazy smile. I kept one hand on her thigh but let the other float down to her clit and pressed down on it with my thumb. That erased her smile. We began moving together. She started breathing shallowly, panting, and when she whispered, "I'm so close," I let myself go. I snapped my hips back and forth, keeping the pressure steady on her clit with my thumb, and soon I was shouting my release. She followed a moment later.

Damn. How was I allowed to feel this *good*?

We lay there for a while, and my thoughts drifted to what life was going to be like at home this fall—how hard it was going to be to put the brakes on again. It had to be done, though. But maybe, since she seemed to have come around on sleeping with each other when Olivia wasn't around, we had Christmas to look forward to. That got me thinking about her role in our lives, and about my increasing dissatisfaction with her refusal to take any actual money for her not-nannying.

"I wish you'd let me pay you."

"That's not a great thing to say to a woman you've just had sex with."

I cracked up. "You know what I mean. I feel like I'm taking advantage of you."

"Also not great." She smirked. "You could just as well say I took advantage of you. I'm the one who took leave of my senses and jumped you last night."

I was so glad she had. I didn't feel taken advantage of at all. It *was* going to suck to call a halt to things when we got home, but for now, I felt *great*. Unburdened. "Remember the day we first met, we talked about what your superpower is?"

"Are you going to tell me my superpower is sex?"

"No, I'm going to tell you your superpower is being a really good listener. Your superpower is listening to people and really *getting* them."

Her eyes lit up, but then they did something else. Something that looked like shuttering. But I must have been wrong about that because suddenly she kissed me again, putting an end to all our talking.

———

"Oh, my poor back," I said two days later as I levered myself into the Getaway Car. All this talk of retirement looming had not been a joke. "Sleeping on the ground is not as easy as it used to be." Though I wasn't sure it was sleeping on the ground that had me achy. It might have been the other activities that took place on the ground.

We never saw the northern lights again after that first night, because the clouds rolled in. But the one night had been enough. Enough for Aurora to rename herself.

"You should switch beds with Olivia and recover on the waterbed." She laughed. "I wouldn't have thought a waterbed that old would still be functional."

"It isn't. My parents bought a new one when Olivia was a toddler, because she loved it so much. Funny how they were cheapskates as parents but they can't jump fast enough to open their wallets when it comes to her."

"That's the way of the world, though, isn't it?" She made a contemplative *hmm*.

"What are you thinking?"

"Just wondering what kind of grandmother my mom will be. But as things stand, she wouldn't get to see any kid of mine anyway. That's what finally made me snap, you know, the idea of her spewing all her BS at Olivia. I would never subject a child of mine to the kind of abuse she inflicted on me." She blew out a shaky breath that had me glancing over in concern. "I've never called it that, even in my own head—abuse. And of course, that made me think if I wouldn't subject someone else to it, why would I subject *myself* to it?"

I didn't know what to say to that, and honestly I was a little overcome. Aurora was so brave. And beautiful and funny and smart.

I thought about Aurora telling me, this summer, that she couldn't switch the physical stuff on and off like a faucet. I knew what she meant now. Turns out when you fell in love with someone and smooshed not only your bodies but your souls together under the northern lights, the faucet was really fucking leaky.

But I needed to get my shit together, because this wasn't happening. I was just going to have to find myself a pair of metaphorical pliers and fix the leak.

We had another day and night at my parents', which I welcomed. It wasn't like we were going to sleep together there, so it could function as a kind of step-down, a decompression chamber between camping and reality.

Things got back to normal. Sort of. I caught Aurora watching me a few times, but she always looked away quickly, her expression unreadable. It made me realize I wasn't used to not being able to interpret her expression. And there was a moment when Liv and I were joking about something at the pioneer museum and I looked to Aurora, expecting her to join in, but she just shot us a silent smile that looked kind of…weak.

We passed the first few hours of the drive home mostly in silence. We were all tired. We'd had fun, but I thought everyone was ready to be home. The closer we got, though, the more I felt the pressure of the impending…What? I couldn't call it a breakup because we weren't together. I tried to tell myself it was the same as after spring break, when I'd called a halt to things. At least we had Christmas to look forward to.

When Olivia fell asleep in the back seat, I tried to initiate a conversation, partially just to break up the silence, and partially to make sure we were on the same page. Aurora was the one who'd called our northern lights interlude a "vacation," but I wanted to double-check.

"So," I whispered. "That was a fun trip."

She'd been looking out the window, and we hadn't talked for miles. "It was," she said, but she kept staring out the window.

"Especially camping," I said, infusing my tone with a jokily exaggerated drama, which finally caused her to swivel to face me. She didn't smile as I'd intended, or even say anything, so I kept talking. "I was thinking, maybe when Olivia goes to her grandparents' at Christmas, we could head south for a little break. A resort, maybe? Unless you want to *really* see the northern lights. There's a train from Winnipeg to Churchill, Manitoba, that has a glass roof, and when you get to Churchill—"

"What happens between now and Christmas?" she interrupted. I glanced over. "With us," she added. Unnecessarily, because I got that. I might be a hoser, but I'd been able to tell that things had been off since camping. I'd been telling myself we were tired, trying to sweep this feeling of unease under the rug, but here we were. If I'd learned anything from therapy, it was that you can't do that with feelings. If you try, they only come back to bite you.

"Nothing happens with us," I said, because I'd also learned that honesty really was the best policy.

She nodded and returned to studying the passing landscape. "Right."

"You used the word *vacation*," I tried to explain, "and I—"

"I did." She smiled sadly, but she was still looking out the window. "Don't worry. You haven't made any promises. Your honor is intact."

What the hell did *that* mean? "I'm sorry, I—"

"*Don't* apologize," she said sharply, almost peevishly. When I glanced over, though, her gaze had gone oddly fond, and her tone softened when she said, "When we get home, I have something I want to give you."

"OK." I was wary. Hell, I was scared. But what could I say? We spent the rest of the drive enveloped in more awkward silence, a kind of rift opening up between us. I didn't know how to bridge it. I was both relieved and on edge when I turned up the gravel drive. I opened the back door of the car to rouse Olivia. "Hey, kiddo, we're home."

"Uhhh." Olivia reached her arms out like she wanted me to carry her—like she had when she was little—which made my heart twinge.

"You're so big now, you at least have to get out of the car on your own." She did, but she looked like a rag doll, so screw my camping-induced aches and pains. I hoisted her up, and she went limp in my arms. This was probably the last time I would ever do this. "Let me get Liv to bed," I said to Aurora. "Then I'll come downstairs, and you can give me...your thing."

I got Liv tucked in, but when I kissed her forehead, she said, "You OK, Dad?"

"Yeah. Just thinking about stuff." Like what Aurora could possibly have to give me. Like where the hell that rift, that feeling of alienation, had come from. I'd thought of Aurora and me as teammates for so long, united in our cause of supporting Olivia. It was strange and unsettling to feel we were out of sync.

"I'll sit with you till you fall asleep," I said to Liv. It was a procrastination technique—but not a very effective one, because it took her all of two minutes to conk out.

There was nothing left but to head downstairs, though it felt a bit like walking to my doom.

OK, I needed to take things down several notches. Aurora had something to give me. Big deal. Maybe it was a hockey figurine.

I knocked softly and pushed her bedroom door open. She was sitting cross-legged on the bed. She looked up and smiled as she closed a red three-ring binder she'd been reading. She got up and came to me where I was hovering and said, "Read this, then we need to talk." She handed me the binder, pressed her palm against my chest, and said, "If this was a movie, this would be the part where I'd say, 'I loved you before I knew you.' And that's true. But what I hope you'll see is that it wasn't actually you. It was an idea of you. I know how much you don't like people reacting to an idea of you. Please understand that now I love the actual you. And you—*you*—are so much better than the idea of you."

And then she pushed me out the door.

Dear Mike,

I'm going home. I'm quitting. I can't do this anymore. Dancing. New York. Trying to be what people want. The whole thing.

I haven't told my mother. I'm going to throw myself on her mercy and hope it's enough.

But I don't think I should write to you anymore, either. If I'm going to stop deluding myself about what's possible, I think I should stop on all fronts, you know? And us? We're not possible. I wish we were. I wish it so hard.

Goodbye. Thanks for listening for so many years.

I'll miss you to the moon and back,

Rory

22 — MOMENTS

MIKE

There are certain indelible moments in a person's life when everything changes. When it seems like the world starts moving in slow motion. Sometimes they're good, like getting drafted.

Sometimes they're devastating, like when we got the news that Sarah's car had spun out, that she'd been taken to Montreal General and pronounced dead on arrival.

Or like the time Aurora Evans told me she loved me and handed me a red binder that showed me that everything I believed about her—about us—was a lie.

It was full of handwritten pages—old-school, three-ring-punched lined paper, mostly, though some of the pages were bits of scrap paper that had been jammed onto the metal rings. The crinkly noise of the pages turning as I sat on my bed and flipped through them sounded like thunder to my adrenaline-sharpened hearing.

The handwriting was Aurora's. I recognized it from grocery lists. There was no title, or anything I could use to make sense of what this *was*. So I flipped back to the first page and started reading. There was a date from fourteen years ago, and then: "Dear Mike."

As I read, the past year rearranged itself like a game of Tetris in my wake. Lies interlocking to form a horrible truth: Aurora had been deceiving me.

I'd let her into my home, my life, my heart, under false pretenses.

It made me want to throw up. I had to take a break halfway through the letters. Stagger to the sink in the en suite. Two lines from the letters wound their way through my consciousness and snagged in a corner of my brain as I splashed cold water on my face.

"Dear Mike...I love you to the moon and back."

How could she *say* that?

"If this was a movie," she'd said before she shoved me out of her bedroom, "this would be the part where I'd say, 'I loved you before I knew you.'"

But this wasn't a movie, and that was impossible. It wasn't even me she was writing to.

It wasn't even me she was writing to.

I whipped my head up and looked at myself in the mirror, water dripping down my face.

I tried to keep that thought in mind as I went back to the bedroom and read the rest of the letters. And yeah, one part of my brain got that. One part of my brain understood that she was a teenager writing what was essentially a diary.

The other, bigger part of my brain was utterly devastated. Betrayed. Angry. Because it didn't matter who the Mike of the letters was. The fact remained that she'd been playing me this whole time. My heart was broken.

Again.

At least Sarah hadn't done it on purpose.

Eventually I went downstairs and filled the kettle. She

appeared in the kitchen, looked me right in the eye, and said, "I should have told you when I figured out who you were."

"You think?" I was startled by the timbre of my own voice. It was hard. Merciless. I couldn't make myself care. To think I had *wept* in front of this woman. I had shown her *everything*. "And when was that?"

"I knew for sure when you were growing out your beard during postseason. We talked about your having come to the Twin Cities for Erik's game." She was speaking quietly and her voice was shaking, but she was looking me straight in the eye. "But to be honest, that only confirmed it. I had my suspicions from the start."

I had to make a conscious effort not to double over. The lie revealed by the letters was a deep cut, but hearing that Aurora, who I'd always thought was so immune to my hockey fame, had known who I was from day one was a knife turning in the wound.

Suddenly I was running a lot of things through this filter. Her resistance to talking about the charm bracelet when I asked her about it. Her sudden migraine when I'd wanted her to meet Erik. "There were *so many* times you could have brought this up."

She maintained eye contact, but at least she had the decency to look ashamed.

"I liked you because I thought you *didn't* care about hockey." That's how she'd slipped through. "Because you *didn't* know who I was." I crossed my arms over my chest. I felt like I was having a heart attack.

"I *don't* care about hockey," she said quietly. "Yes, I invented a hockey player. But really I invented a loving, attentive boyfriend. The hockey was incidental. But somehow, you don't, or can't, believe that anyone could care about you the person versus you the hockey player. Sarah slipped through because she didn't know who you were when you met. I slipped through, too."

I was a little taken aback by her choice of words. *Slipped through.* That was the phrase I'd just used in my head.

"I slipped through, until I didn't—until you read those letters. Until you found out I've been lying to you."

I was further taken aback by how easily she said that. *Until you found out I've been lying to you.* I'd come out swinging, planning to accuse her of just that. But here she was, easily admitting to it like it was no big deal.

"I did a shitty thing by not telling you," she went on. "But it was because I was afraid of losing you. I'm not trying to gloss over the 'lying,' but—"

"Why am I hearing air quotes there?" I said, not caring that I was interrupting. "Are you trying to tell me there hasn't been any lying?" Because I might be a bit befuddled, set back on my heels, but I hadn't entirely lost my grip on reality.

"No, I'm trying to tell you that we're muddling two issues here. We're getting tripped up on the first one, when really what we need to do is consider them together."

"So what's the 'second issue'?" I made my own air quotes, and I couldn't hide the derision in my tone. I didn't *want* to hide it.

"The second issue is that I love you. Not some hockey player I met in passing as a teenager. Not an NHL player. *You.*"

Oh my God. My head was going to explode. I couldn't process all this.

"I've come to realize this year that I've always been afraid of losing people," she said, and I suddenly wished she would stop talking. Actively not wanting to hear Aurora talk was not a state I'd ever imagined myself being in, but here we were. "Instead of being honest with people, I've spent my life twisting myself into what I thought they wanted me to be. And where did that get me? Sick. It got me sick."

I couldn't argue with that, but I didn't see how that changed anything to do with us.

"So we've had these three interludes," she continued. "Christmas, spring break, camping. Each time we've...fallen deeper. Then we stop. We pretend it isn't happening. But it *is* happening. It's happening in parallel to so-called regular life. I feel like you think that if whatever's between us stays on that parallel track, it's OK. But the parallel track is an illusion. I mean, look at us. We have sex. We date. I know you're going to object and say we don't date, but we *do*. We go to dances and arcades together. We go camping. We have fun. Over here." She gestured to one side of her body. "And we have sex. Over here." She gestured to the other side. "I was OK with that initially—hell, I was OK with it until very recently, like until a couple days ago. And I know you're going to say that I'm the one who started things while we were camping, which is fair, but—"

"Will you stop saying you know what I'm going to say?" I said, belatedly realizing that I sounded exactly like Olivia when she was being a brat. Who said blood was thicker than water?

She held her hands up, stopped talking as if ceding me the floor. This was what I wanted, right? For her to stop talking? So why couldn't I make my mouth work?

"Something happened to me under those lights," she went on when it became clear I wasn't going to take my turn to speak. "I don't know how to explain it other than that it felt like I suddenly became the person I wanted to be. I realized I could have everything I wanted as long as it was what *I* wanted. Not what my mom, or a boyfriend, or a ballet teacher wanted. Like Dorothy and her ruby slippers finding out she's had the power to get home all along. I've spent my whole life straining toward something without being able to really articulate what it is, only that I can never quite get there. But that night, I realized that it wasn't a thing I was straining toward, it was a person. The person I've been straining toward is me.

"But then reality kicked in on the way home. That didn't make my realization any less powerful, but it did mean it was going to take work to make my life the way I want it to be. Work, and honesty.

"I understood that we were going to come home and you were going to make a speech and push me away. I'm sorry to the extent that I've muddled things by jumping you at the campsite, but this back-and-forth, on-and-off is not going to work for me anymore. What has been my big lesson of the past year? That it's OK to want things. It's OK to ask for what I want. And I want you, for real."

What the hell? She thought I was going to be fine with this big betrayal and now we were moving on to the let's-be-boyfriend-girlfriend stage of the conversation?

"When you said, that one time, that you didn't want things to get leaky, what did that mean exactly?" she asked when I remained mute.

"It meant I didn't want Olivia to see us kissing." I could speak, it turned out, when all I had to do was answer a factual question.

"Why didn't you want Olivia to see us kissing?"

"Because I can't bring someone into Olivia's life so soon." She knew this. This was Life After Widowhood 101.

"I'm already in Olivia's life."

Was she being willfully obtuse? "You know what I mean. Someone who might leave her."

"Are you sure you're talking about Olivia and not yourself?"

I tried to issue a rebuttal. I even moved my mouth. No sound came out. Because there was no air in my body.

"Life is full of risks," she said, oblivious to the fact that I was silently suffocating before her very eyes. "People leave. You should know that better than most. You're afraid someone is going to leave you because without all the hockey trappings, you're not enough. So you try to prevent that from happening by curating the people who get to be around you, making sure they don't care about hockey, which, ironically, is the thing you love most, after your family."

The air whooshed back into my body, so fast and so violently it felt like my lungs had been sliced in half. I didn't understand how someone I had trusted for so long, and so elementally, could say these things to me.

"I mean, maybe," she went on. "That's my take. But who am I? I'm just your friend you used to sleep with sometimes."

Used to.

"Are you leaving?" I wasn't sure exactly what I was asking. Was she leaving me? Us? The house right now?

"I know you have training camp in a few weeks. If you can't find someone for Olivia before then, I'll stay on until you do, but only when you're not here." She picked up her overnight bag, which I hadn't noticed she'd brought upstairs with her. "So yes, I'm leaving."

23 — CANADIAN BOYFRIEND

RORY

I called an Uber as I stumbled out of Mike Martin's house, and I had a full-on panic attack en route to Gretchen's. Hello, darkness, my old friend.

When I got to her house, I sat on the porch and did my tapping until the storm passed.

The panic eventually receded, and I discovered something unfamiliar underneath the regret and heartbreak: peace.

When Gretchen answered my knock and got over her shock to find me at her door in the middle of the night, I told her everything. How I'd met Mike Martin at the mall and spun him into my Canadian Boyfriend. How when I'd remet him all those years later, I hadn't told him about it. How I'd slept with him under the northern lights after I'd remade myself.

"Didn't people from high school notice that you never went to visit your 'boyfriend'?" she asked after installing me on her sofa with a cup of tea.

I smiled through my pain at Gretchen's question. I'd dropped this emotional bomb and her first question was logistical. "I think you're overestimating how much people noticed me to begin with. But there were trips over the years that I may have…embellished. Like to the Youth America Grand Prix."

She cozied up next to me and threw a blanket over our legs. "You mean you'd go to New York for ballet competitions and tell people you were making a stop in Canada on the way home?"

I nodded.

"But if people didn't notice you, why did you need him to begin with?"

"I don't want you to pity me, and I'm not excusing it, but people were crappy to me. They thought I was a snob because of ballet." I'd explained all that to her before. "I was out of school so much, I didn't really know people. And when I was there, I probably seemed aloof when really I was…"

"Racked with as-yet-undiagnosed clinical anxiety that manifested itself as shyness your peers mistook for snobbishness?"

"Exactly." As painful as the memories were, I could smile at her spot-on assessment.

"So, what? You made him up one day? Just like that?"

"Just like that. I still remember the moment I invented him." I sent myself back to that handshake. *I'm Mike Martin*, he'd said, slaying me with that smile. I told Gretchen about everything: about dissecting frogs and not having a date for homecoming. "And then I met Mike. And I thought, *Well, if I can't go to the dance…*"

"At least here's a good reason," Gretchen supplied.

"Exactly."

"And everybody bought the lie?"

"There were enough details that rang true, I guess. Hockey teams really did stay in the hotel at the mall. And people didn't know me, not really. So maybe it didn't seem that implausible?"

"And they probably *did* mistake your shyness for maturity.

You were leaving school all the time for ballet, clearly headed for a professional career. Why couldn't you have an older boyfriend?" She paused, studying my face. "Let me ask you another question." I nodded, preparing for her to want more details about the mechanics of my lie, but she bowled me over with "Are you in love with him?"

I told the truth, as hard as it was. That's what I was doing from now on. "Yes. And I told him that." Her eyes widened. "And then I dumped him."

"What!" she exclaimed, nearly choking on her tea.

"Remember how you said I was settling with Ian?" She nodded. "I realized I was doing it again. Mike is not Ian. Obviously. And I did a shitty thing to Mike. I've apologized, but there's no getting around the fact that I made a huge error of judgment and that it hurt him terribly. That's all true. But it's *also* true that I got to the point where I couldn't accept the terms of our relationship anymore. I realized I loved him too much to keep doing the casual-sex thing."

"Because it wasn't casual."

"Exactly. Because I loved him—love him—too much. But here's the thing: you can love a person, and that person can be, fundamentally, a good person, but you can still enforce standards for what you will and will not accept."

Gretchen made a noise that was a cross between a wail and shriek and hugged me—hard. "Well, damn, my little Rory is all growed up."

"I don't know. Those northern lights. It was like they… changed me."

"I don't think that's exactly right. You know how when you get a gel manicure, there's the nail polish, but then it cures under a UV light in a few seconds?"

"Yeah?"

"I think you did the work this past year or so, with all the therapy, confronting your mom, all that stuff. The northern lights just sealed it."

That was such a generous way of thinking about it, it made me cry. But they were happy tears. Well, no, they were happy-sad tears. But close enough.

"So the lights in this metaphor...are lights," I teased through my tears.

"I might need to work on that." Gretchen grinned and got up. "I'm going to get you some bedding for the sofa, then we should both try to get some sleep. You can stay with me as long as you need to."

I spent the next day mostly staring into space. I tried to turn on the TV to distract myself, but nothing stuck. Around dinnertime, a text arrived that extinguished any hope I might have been harboring. I hadn't *thought* I'd been harboring any, but...hope is a tricky thing.

Mike: I've extended your insurance through the end of the calendar year. Thanks for all your help with Olivia. I'm going to block you now.

And wasn't that just like Mike Martin, to take the time to do such a kind thing for me before casting me out of his life forever? I wanted to howl. I was heartbroken, which wasn't a new state of being for me.

But the difference was, I knew I would survive this.

24—DEAR AURORA

MIKE

The next few days were brutal. It almost felt like the time right after Sarah's death. Like the ground was shifting beneath me and I might fall at any moment. I was gutted to feel that I had backslid so badly. Had all the progress I'd thought I'd made been an illusion?

It was possible. Everything I'd believed about Aurora had been an illusion.

Then something strange started to happen. Everyone began suggesting that I was wrong.

It started with Olivia. I'd told her that Aurora and I had had a disagreement, and that she wasn't going to live with us or babysit her anymore, but that it had nothing to do with Olivia. The next day she had a dance class, and I let her out at the studio and told her I'd meet her in the parking lot when she was done. I would have liked to have been cool enough that I could handle seeing Aurora in a professional setting, but I felt too...I wasn't even sure what. Angry, betrayed, scared? All of the above.

But on the first day of school, as I was scrambling to get Olivia's lunch made and her backpack sorted, she let her spoon clatter into her cereal bowl and said, "Dad, will you tell me what Aurora did that was so bad that you had to send her away?"

I said I couldn't, that it was grown-up stuff. It was a cop-out. It should have been possible to distill it into something a kid would understand. But when I tried to do that in my head, I got all confused.

Next up was Ivan. We were fishing, and I was telling him about the nannies I was going to interview. "This time I'm doing it the right way. One hundred percent official. They're from an agency, so there will be Social Security numbers, contracts, all that." And if a promising candidate turned out to be a fan, I would have zero reaction. Because as upset at Aurora as I was, I recognized that everything she had said to me about our Tim Hortons trip had been true.

It was an uncomfortable feeling, to realize that while Aurora had been lying to me this whole time, she had also been right about me.

"So Aurora's out and some agency nanny is in," Ivan said as he cast his rod.

"Yep." Ivan glanced over at me, and there was something in his look that made me go, "What?"

"Look, I don't know what happened between you—"

"Right. You don't." I'd told him only that we'd had a falling-out. When he'd pressed for details, I'd told him to trust me. Apparently that had been too big an ask.

"I just think if you made a mistake, or she did, can it really be that bad? Can it be unforgivable?"

"Some things are."

"Yeah, like…I don't know, murder."

I snorted. "Dramatic much?"

"Things people do with bad intentions, I mean. It's hard

for me to imagine that happening with you two. If somebody fucked up, you gotta leave room for them to unfuck it up."

"You need to dial it down a notch. It's not like this is a breakup. She was my nanny."

The word felt like so much of a lie in my mouth that a muscle in my jaw twitched.

Ivan's line came back empty, with the bait still on the hook. He cast again. "If you say so."

Next up in the parade of naysayers was Dr. Mursal. Unlike with Ivan or Olivia, I told Dr. Mursal everything—about the trip, the realization that I'd fallen in love with Aurora, the binder of letters.

Dr. Mursal knew me in ways other people didn't. So when she said, "Is it possible you overreacted?" it rankled.

"I don't think I overreacted."

"OK," she said evenly.

When she didn't say anything else, I said, "But clearly you do."

"Remember when we talked about emotional intelligence?"

"Yes," I said warily. "So what? I suppose you want me to put myself in Aurora's shoes."

"No. I want you to put yourself in *teenage* Aurora's shoes."

That gave me pause. "What do you mean?"

I knew what she meant, though. I was jolted back to when I'd been freaking out when I first read the letters. A rogue thought had entered my head, almost like it had come from somewhere outside of me.

It wasn't even me she was writing to.

I'd had the thought, but then I'd lost it. It had gotten buried in all the confusion and pain that followed it.

"Am I doing it again?" I suddenly said.

"Are you doing what again?"

"Is it possible that even though I'm always insisting I'm this modest hoser dude, that I'm actually making everything about myself, even when it's not about me?" She raised her eyebrows. "I should read those letters again, shouldn't I? Now that some time has passed?"

"Probably."

"I'm afraid to, though. Why am I afraid to?"

"You're afraid you'll read them and you'll have to face that whatever lies Aurora told you are nothing compared to the truth she's told you. To the truth that's inside you."

"Yeah," I said quietly, "yeah."

My appointment had been in the morning, and it was a weekday, so when I got home I had the house to myself. I went outside and sat on the deck and reread the letters. When I took myself, and my pain, out of the equation, it was so easy to see that she'd been a *child* when she wrote them. A child with no one. Having seen her mother be such a bitch—I hated to use that word, but it was accurate—to Aurora the adult was different from reading about what Heather Evans had done to Aurora the child. When Aurora started writing these letters, she had been only four years older than Olivia was now.

When I thought about it like that, I started to see the letters differently. I saw them as self-protective. I saw a child struggling, doing what she could to soothe herself in an unkind world. It wasn't even remotely about me. Or her pretend boyfriend, or whoever.

But if it *wasn't* about me, did that mean I needed to apologize? I was still *pissed* she hadn't told me at the outset. Or when we started getting close. Or for God's sake, at least when we started sleeping together.

But what would I have done if she had?

I would have fired her. I couldn't even pretend otherwise. The whole thing would have hit way too close to my insecurities about people only seeing me as the hockey player, and it would have reopened the wound of Sarah's big lie.

I thought of Aurora saying, *You might be missing out on some really great people who happen to be fans of yours* before we went to my dad's Tim Hortons.

In continuing my thought experiment, I wondered if I could apply the same logic to the current situation. *You might be missing out on some really great people who happen to have invented a version of you to be their pretend boyfriend when they were kids.*

Well, shit.

As with Sarah and the birth control pills, I needed to look beneath the surface of events, get over my butt-hurtness, and see what was really going on. With Sarah, it had taken me the better part of a year.

I didn't have that much time here.

Something had happened to Aurora under the northern lights, she'd said. Something had happened to me, too. I'd just decided it didn't matter, or that I couldn't allow it to matter.

But it mattered. It mattered more than anything.

A fire lit under my ass, I called Gretchen.

"Well, Mike Martin, as I live and breathe." Her voice was dripping with disdain.

"Where is Aurora staying right now?"

There was a pause, a long enough one that I feared she wasn't going to answer, that the force of nature that was Miss Miller had turned against me. But she finally said, "With me."

"Any chance you would give me your address?"

"Why would I do that?"

"So I can send her a letter."

25 — SHARP EDGES

AURORA

Dear Aurora,

I'm not good at writing, but I wanted to say a few things, so I'm just going to say them.

1. I really miss you.
2. I'm proud of you for drawing your line in the sand.
3. I'm sorry I was so cold to you last time we spoke.
4. I'm still hurt, though. I'd like not to be, but, even though I understand, with my brain, that you weren't trying to hurt me—that those letters weren't even about me, really—I can't seem to help it.

I don't know how to square all these things. How do I square them?

—Mike

Dear Mike,

I really miss you, too. And Olivia.

I don't know if you <u>can</u> square all those things. But maybe you don't have to, at least not right now. Lately I've been thinking about how sometimes two things that should cancel each other out can be true at the same time. For example: I hate ballet, but I also love it. I love you, but I hurt you. You care about me in some fashion, right? But you hurt me, too. Lately, I feel like once you open your eyes to the possibility, life is full of conflicting truths.

I wonder, though, if time sands down the square edges that seem so painfully sharp now. I honestly don't know. I hope so, for my sake as well as yours.

Thanks for writing. I loved getting your letter.

—Aurora

Dear Aurora,

I do care about you. And I did hurt you. All this time, I've been expecting everything to be on my terms, on my schedule. I'm sorry.

I think you're right, that my brain is having trouble holding contradictory truths. How'd you get so wise?

—Mike

Dear Mike,

I don't know that I'm that wise! In a lot of ways, I'm still that girl who's never been to a school dance. I'm just trying to learn, to get better. You are, too. I know this about you. I've seen you doing it.

So if I'm wise, you are, too. Or maybe it's not that complicated; maybe we're just trying our best to get smarter, to be better. It's hard work, isn't it?

—Aurora

Dear Aurora,

I wouldn't say you've never been to a school dance.

—Mike

Dear Mike,

Touché. I should have said I never went to a school dance WHEN I WAS IN SCHOOL. You were my first and only date to a school dance.

—Aurora

Dear Aurora,

I wouldn't say only. You never know. Olivia's got a lot of years ahead of her in school, and I'm still on the chaperone list.

Yours,
Mike

Dear Mike,

Name the date. Name the school. I will be there.

Love,
Aurora

Dear Aurora,

So, I don't know what to say now, except that I wish I had a school dance I could invite you to. Waiting until next spring for Olivia's seems too long. Because I think the sharp edges have worn down—kind of alarmingly fast, actually.

I love you to Alpha Centauri and back,
Mike

———

That last letter did not arrive via the mail, as the others had. It had been put through Gretchen's mail slot, but at a time— a Wednesday morning at nine—much too early for the mail. And it didn't have a stamp on it, or an address—just my name scrawled in Mike Martin's familiar angular handwriting. And inside, oh, that sign-off: "I love you to Alpha Centauri and back."

I nearly collapsed right there, from a mixture of relief and hope and fear and who even knew what else. But I rallied and yanked the door open, hoping that he hadn't driven away yet, that maybe I could run after him like in the final scene of a rom-com. But I didn't have to run, because there he was on Gretchen's porch, my Canadian Boyfriend. The real one.

"Hi," he said.

"Hi," I said.

He opened his arms, and I stepped into them.

We stood like that for a long time. I was physically shaking, and he held me tight. Eventually he said, his lips against my hair, "You want to go for ice cream?"

"I sure do." The Depression Car was parked in the driveway. "Maybe we should put up the top, though, so we can talk?"

"Nah." He came to a halt in front of the car that matched his eyes. "We can talk later. For now, let's start over, OK?"

"Yes."

He smiled. *Click-click-click.* "Hey, Aurora, can I give you a lift?"

I nodded, a little too overcome to speak, and let him hold the door for me. Then he ran around to the driver's side, and we vroomed away.

EPILOGUE
AND THEY LIVED

MIKE

This is the part where I'm supposed to say that we got married and had kids. We did not. We didn't even end up living together right away. I did take Aurora for ice cream that morning, but then I took her back to Gretchen's.

I went through with my plan to hire a nanny. An actual nanny who was not Aurora. Because Aurora was my girlfriend, and it's weird to employ your girlfriend? There's a question mark at the end of that sentence because I tried to argue that our relationship had already spanned lots of strange categories, but she wasn't having it. She said if we were starting over, we were starting over.

So we dated, though it seemed funny to call it that since I knew in my bones that Aurora Lake was a foregone conclusion. But I took her out to public places and worked on not being a dick when people recognized me. She came over for fires and skating that winter. She spent Christmas with us, and even stayed over a few nights—like, openly, in my bedroom. She did not make up with her mother. She said she might someday, but not now. I got to meet Mary-Margaret, and Aurora came with me to Dr. Mursal for a few sessions. By the summer, we were in full boyfriend-girlfriend territory, and we all went to visit my parents.

She was killing it on the ballet front. She'd started her own business called Ballet for Every Body, doing exactly what she'd talked about that first Christmas: teaching ballet, on her terms, to adults. Word of mouth had been good, and she was teaching five classes a week out of a church basement. She still taught at Gretchen's, but she was in the process of drawing up a business plan to open her own studio, except she wasn't going to call it a studio. She was looking for the right word. I was so proud of her, I could bust.

By some miracle, I'd gotten a one-year contract with the Lumberjacks. It would certainly be my last. I'd started mulling a future in which my retirement had me doing a hockey version of what Aurora was doing with ballet—bringing it, or some version of what it offered, to people who weren't likely to go pro. Maybe I'd start my own skills training and leadership camp for teens. Or maybe I'd volunteer with the teams at Olivia's school. She would never deign to be on one, but that was OK.

I was coming around to the idea that I could have a life full of kids even if they weren't my own. I did get another dog, though. A five-year-old mutt from the Humane Society who came with the name Tinkerbell. The girls had insisted on her, Olivia because of her name and Aurora because she was part Chihuahua. How could I resist? So although I'd always imagined Earl 9's sibling would be a big badass dog named Gretzky—my childhood dogs Bobby and Gordie had been named after Canadian hockey greats—what Earl 9 and I actually got was tiny, fluffy, hyper Tinkerbell. She was a very good girl, and I considered her an example of the old Rolling Stones adage about how you can't always get what you want, but sometimes you end up getting what you need. Another example would be how I kept asking Aurora to move back in, but she kept resisting. She would say that there was no hurry, and insist that everything was great as it was. I couldn't argue with that, but I was greedy.

I took Aurora to Tomfoolery for her birthday that summer before my final season. Olivia and Gretchen joined us, and so did Ivan and Lauren and Annika, who was now fifteen months old. We had a proper party with pizza and cake and games.

"I'm sorry you can't go in the ball pit for your birthday," I said to Aurora at one point when we found ourselves with a moment alone. "For the record, I did ask them if they'd make an exception, and I even, for the first time ever in recorded history, played the do-you-know-who-I-am? card."

She laughed. "That's OK. I have accepted that the ball pit dream has to die."

"So you're thirty-one now. We've been 'dating'"—I made air quotes—"for almost a year. You want to move in with me yet?"

"Yeah. OK."

I choked on my Diet Coke.

She smirked. "I mean, we'll have to work it out with Sabrina"—Sabrina was the nanny—"but yeah, at this point I think I'm just being stubborn, and that seems...dumb."

Well, eff me. My whole body flushed with pleasure. Not sexual pleasure, or not only sexual pleasure, but goofy, teenage-boy, she-chose-me pleasure. "Yes!" I did a little fist pump that made her laugh even though it had been entirely in earnest.

"Let's get married," I said, and immediately regretted it. In my mind that was the endgame. Like I said, Aurora Lake was a foregone conclusion. But I hadn't meant to blurt it out like that. I didn't want to scare her away.

"Let's not get ahead of ourselves," she said, predictably.

I pretended to be slain by her rejection.

"Tell you what, I'll let you renew my health insurance when it comes due."

"Stop. You're too generous."

I leaned over and planted a quick kiss on her lips. I wanted to do more, but you know, we were in a Tomfoolery with our friends.

She was smiling from ear to ear when I pulled away. "As the Magic 8 Ball says, 'Ask again later.'"

"JumboTron at the last game of the season?" I joked, knowing she would hate the idea.

"Oh my God, no. No big public displays." She smirked. "But end of the season sounds about right."

———

AURORA

Spring came late the next year, and we could skate on the lake later in the season than usual, though every time we went out, we wondered if it was going to be the last. One sunny Saturday afternoon in March, the Lumberjacks didn't have a game, and Mike Martin invited the Zadorovs and Gretchen over. Mike Martin and Ivan had gotten back the night before from a road trip, and Olivia and I were happy to have him back.

I was happy, period. It felt like it had been a long time coming, and I savored it all the more for it. I had just signed a two-year lease on a dedicated space for Ballet for Every Body. It was in the back room at a brewery, of all places—it occupied an old grain mill that came with some old office space they were renting to community and arts organizations. I loved the unlikely combination of ballet and beer, and I told Mike Martin he was going to have to develop a taste for fancy microbrews so he could meet me for a drink after class.

Mike Martin was looking at the final month of the regular season, and it looked like the Lumberjacks would contend in the playoffs. I could tell he was a bit melancholy, but he was also brimming with ideas for the next phase of life. He was going to take the summer to recharge—his first summer ever without worrying about staying in shape, which he said was going to be weird but awesome. He was threatening to grow a dad bod.

We didn't have a fire going because it was afternoon, but we had mulled wine, and I was sipping some while holding Annika so her parents could have some ice time together. I watched all my people zipping around the ice and it kind of reminded me of those scenes from *A Charlie Brown Christmas* where everyone's tooling around the rink, snow is falling, and happy piano music is playing. We even had our own Snoopy, in the form of Tinkerbell, who loved the snow and ice. I twisted around to wave at Earl 9, who, sure enough, was standing sentry inside. He wagged his head at me.

Mike Martin swooshed over and did one of his fancy stops, spraying ice and making Annika laugh. He was holding his phone. "The firewood guys are here." He was no longer obsessively chopping his own wood. Look at all of us—happy and well adjusted.

He sat and switched from skates to boots. "I'm gonna go open the garage for them." He didn't come back, but after ten minutes, he called down. "Aurora! There's more wood than I thought, and I need you to move your car."

I didn't know why he couldn't do it himself—or why he'd ordered more firewood to begin with since spring was just around the corner—but OK. Ivan came over to pick up Annika—she had a tiny helmet she wore while he held her and skated.

I went in through the house, grabbed my car keys, and stepped out into the garage...which was not filled with wood.

"Surprise!"

Half the space was taken up with a giant inflatable structure filled with tons of balls. "Did you get me a *ball pit*?"

"I *rented* you a ball pit. Don't get too excited. We have to give it back. But…" He walked over to a hand-drawn sign that read "Height limit: Whatever."

I was speechless.

"But before you get in, come over here."

I had been so dazzled by the ball pit that I hadn't noticed there was also a freaking Skee-Ball machine in the garage. "Are you *kidding* me?"

"You should play this first," he said, pulling a lever that caused the machine to start blooping and playing music as the balls rolled into a slot near the front.

"You know I'm no good at this," I said.

"That's why I set it up so you can't lose," he said. "Or I should say I set it up so *I* can't lose." He pointed. Skee-Ball rings were normally labeled with numerical values, the widest with lower values, going on up to the smallest one, which at Tomfoolery was worth fifty points. Here, though, the numbers had been replaced by little signs. All the rings read "Yes" except for the smallest, which read "No."

"You said to ask again later," Mike Martin said. "It's later. The season is winding down. We're both on to new things professionally." He dropped to one knee and handed me a Skee-Ball. "So, Aurora Lake: Will you marry me?"

"I told you not to do a big thing!"

"No, you told me not to do a *public* thing. So I transplanted my killer idea here to this very not-public setting." He popped up to standing. "Just don't suddenly get good at this, OK?"

"I don't think there's much risk of that." I stepped up to the base of the machine, swallowed a happy throat lump, and tossed the ball. It sank into the lowest "Yes" ring.

Mike Martin jumped up and down like the Lumberjacks had won a game in overtime.

He helped me do the rest of the balls, and the machine spit out a ticket.

"You wanna turn in your ticket for a prize?" he asked, his dimple blazing as he pulled a small box out of his pocket.

"Oh my God. Is this ticket going to get me an engagement ring?"

"We will get a ring, but..." He took my ticket and handed me the box. Inside was a charm. It was a clear charm with swirls of green and violet in it that looked just like..."The northern lights," I breathed.

"Well, I figured one of those things should actually be from me. Like, really me."

He swept me up and twirled me around. Then we called everyone else in and told them the news, which made it feel official—we were engaged. After hugs and kisses and congratulations, I went in the ball pit with my Canadian fiancé.

**Don't miss Gretchen's story,
coming Spring 2025!**

READING GROUP GUIDE

A NOTE FROM THE AUTHOR

One day I was minding my own business and I suddenly thought, *What if a woman created an imaginary boyfriend to get her out of sticky social situations, but then she actually met him in real life?* And then I thought, *What if I wrote a book about that?* Now, since I have no idea how to write sci-fi or fantasy, I couldn't write about it literally—poof, you've conjured a person out of thin air, fairy-tale style, because a dude in a lamp granted you some wishes. Thus was born my Canadian Boyfriend, whom I wanted to be all things stereotypically Canadian (which is why this is the one and only sports-themed romance you will ever get from me) yet also his own unique, wonderful self. I wanted him to be a stereotype at the same time that he transcended that stereotype, which, not to get too deep about it, we all are and do in some ways.

Sometimes people ask if my books are autobiographical, and because I spent my childhood in Minnesota and my adulthood in Canada, I'm expecting to get that question a lot with this book. The answer is always no. Well, 99 percent no. Sometimes little snippets of me slip through, usually irrationally intense opinions about things that don't matter—for example, Jane from *One and Only* and her stance on high heels. In this book, the thing was my yearning to go in a ball pit. I attained my full adult height in fourth grade, so I aged out of ball pits way before my peers did.

So when I was asked to write some discussion questions for this book, the first thing that came to mind was that I would really like to know about the last time you went in a ball pit, and whether you agree that it's a shame they don't make them for grown-ups, as gross as they are. (The ball pits, not the grown-ups. I would never call you gross.)

But the same way that my silly imaginary-boyfriend idea became a book that grapples with some heavy themes, I suppose I ought to ask you some serious questions. Here they are!

QUESTIONS FOR DISCUSSION

1. Mike and Aurora spend time talking about what they love and don't love about their respective pursuits—hockey for Mike and ballet for Aurora. Do you think these pursuits were a net force for good in their lives? Have you ever done a sport or activity that you had mixed feelings about, or about which your feelings changed over time?

2. The term "Minnesota Nice" is used in this book, and Canadians are also known for being pretty nice. Do you think anyone in this book is "too nice"? Do you think a person *can* be too nice?

3. One of the things Mike has to reckon with after the death of his wife is the realization that although he thought they had an egalitarian relationship, she did a lot more of what he learns is called emotional labor. How did you feel about this aspect of his character arc? Is this something you grapple with in your relationships?

4. If you had a charm bracelet like Aurora's with charms that were meant to represent significant places, experiences, or milestones in your life, what would three of your charms be?

5. The book is interspersed with letters the teenage Aurora wrote to her imaginary boyfriend; they functioned as a

diary of sorts for her. Did the letters give you any insights into modern-day Aurora? If so, what were they?

6. Aurora's mother puts a lot of pressure on her, and she always has. Did you have any sympathy for Aurora's mom? Do you think she and Aurora will ever reconcile?

7. Grief is a major theme in this book. Mike is sometimes surprised at how his experience of grief doesn't match what he was expecting. Did this ring true for you?

8. Mike freaks out when he first reads the letters from teenage Aurora. How did you feel about that response?

9. Aurora and Mike experience their camping trip, with its display of the northern lights, as a departure from reality where it feels like normal time has stopped. Have you ever had an experience like this? Did it involve nature?

10. OK, I'm gonna ask it: What is your opinion on ball pits?

ACKNOWLEDGMENTS

I needed a lot of help with this book when it came to making sure Mike's hockey life and Aurora's ballet life rang true—factually, but also in terms of more slippery stuff like culture and norms. I am indebted to Melanie Ting for hockey help and to Chloe Angyal on the ballet side of things. Thank you so much, Mel and Chloe. Of course, any errors are my own.

Kelly Bowen helped me with central Canadian slang, eh? (And also with maintaining my sanity while I was writing this book through the pandemic. Thanks for reading my anxiety-ridden DMs.)

Christine D'Abo was also on the sanity-saving beat, not to mention the butt-in-chair beat. Thanks for the sprints.

I am, as always, indebted to my trusted early readers and true friends Sandra Owens, Erika Olbricht, and Emma Barry. It's so comforting to know I can always rely on you—thank you.

My Facebook reader group, Northern Heat, helped me come up with a fictional name for my Minnesota NHL team. (Also on the list, and oh, was I tempted: the Hotdishes.)

Courtney Miller-Callihan made this book happen in a lot of ways. I'm not just talking about the usual agent stuff, which she is very good at, but it feels like she willed this book into being along with me.

I want to thank Elle Keck for her excitement over this book. It meant a lot.

And last but never least: my Forever friends! Leah Hulten-schmidt for her enthusiasm for this project. Junessa Villoria for embracing it and really making it shine. Estelle Hallick: reunited and it feels so good! Mari Okuda for making sure everything happens when and how it's supposed to happen. S. B. Kleinman for the excellent (as always) copyedit.

ABOUT THE AUTHOR

Jenny Holiday is a *USA Today* bestselling author whose books have been featured by the *New York Times*, *Entertainment Weekly*, the *Washington Post*, and NPR. She grew up in Minnesota and started writing when her fourth-grade teacher gave her a notebook to fill with stories. When she's not working on her next book, she likes to hike, throw theme parties, and watch other people sing karaoke. Jenny lives in London, Ontario, Canada.

You can learn more at:

JennyHoliday.com
Facebook.com/groups/NorthernHeat
Instagram @HolyMolyJennyHoli

YOUR
BOOK
CLUB
RESOURCE

VISIT
GCPClubCar.com

to sign up for the **GCP Club Car** newsletter, featuring exclusive promotions, info on other **Club Car** titles, and more.

 @grandcentralpub

 @grandcentralpub

 @grandcentralpub